THE ALL NEW!
BATMAN
THE BRAVE AND THE BOLD
SMALL MIRACLES

SHOLLY FISCH Writer

RICK BURCHETT DAN DAVIS ROBERT POPE
SCOTT McRAE STEWART McKENNY Artists

GUY MAJOR HEROIC AGE Colorists

DEZI SIENTY CARLOS M. MANGUAL ROB CLARK JR. TRAVIS LANHAM letterers

ROBERT POPE SCOTT McRAE Cover Artists

BATMAN created by BOB KANE

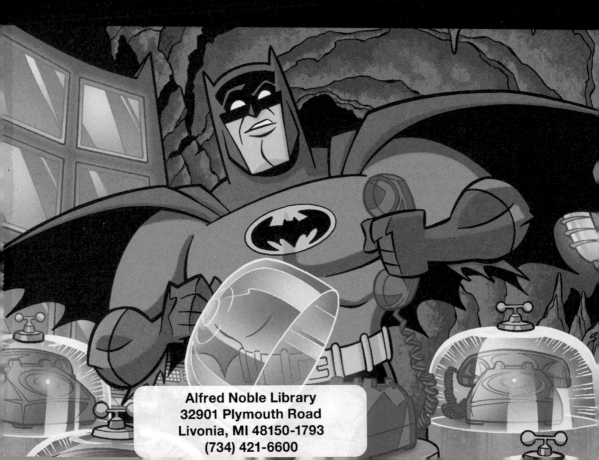

Jim Chadwick Michael Siglain Editors – Original Series
Sarah Gaydos Harvey Richards Assistant Editors – Original Series
Robin Wildman Editor
Robbin Brosterman Design Director – Books

Bob Harras VP – Editor-in-Chief

Diane Nelson President
Dan DiDio and **Jim Lee** Co-Publishers
Geoff Johns Chief Creative Officer
John Rood Executive VP – Sales, Marketing and Business Development
Amy Genkins Senior VP – Business and Legal Affairs
Nairi Gardiner Senior VP – Finance
Jeff Boison VP – Publishing Operations
Mark Chiarello VP – Art Direction and Design
John Cunningham VP – Marketing
Terri Cunningham VP – Talent Relations and Services
Alison Gill Senior VP – Manufacturing and Operations
Hank Kanalz Senior VP – Digital
Jay Kogan VP – Business and Legal Affairs, Publishing
Jack Mahan VP – Business Affairs, Talent
Nick Napolitano VP – Manufacturing Administration
Sue Pohja VP – Book Sales
Courtney Simmons Senior VP – Publicity
Bob Wayne Senior VP – Sales

THE ALL-NEW BATMAN – THE BRAVE AND THE BOLD: SMALL MIRACLES

DC Comics, 1700 Broadway, New York, NY 10019
A Warner Bros. Entertainment Company.
Printed by RR Donnelley, Salem, VA, USA. 2/8/13. First Printing.
ISBN: 978-1-4012-3852-0

SUSTAINABLE FORESTRY INITIATIVE
Certified Chain of Custody
Promoting Sustainable Forestry
www.sfiprogram.org
SFI-01042
APPLIES TO TEXT STOCK ONLY

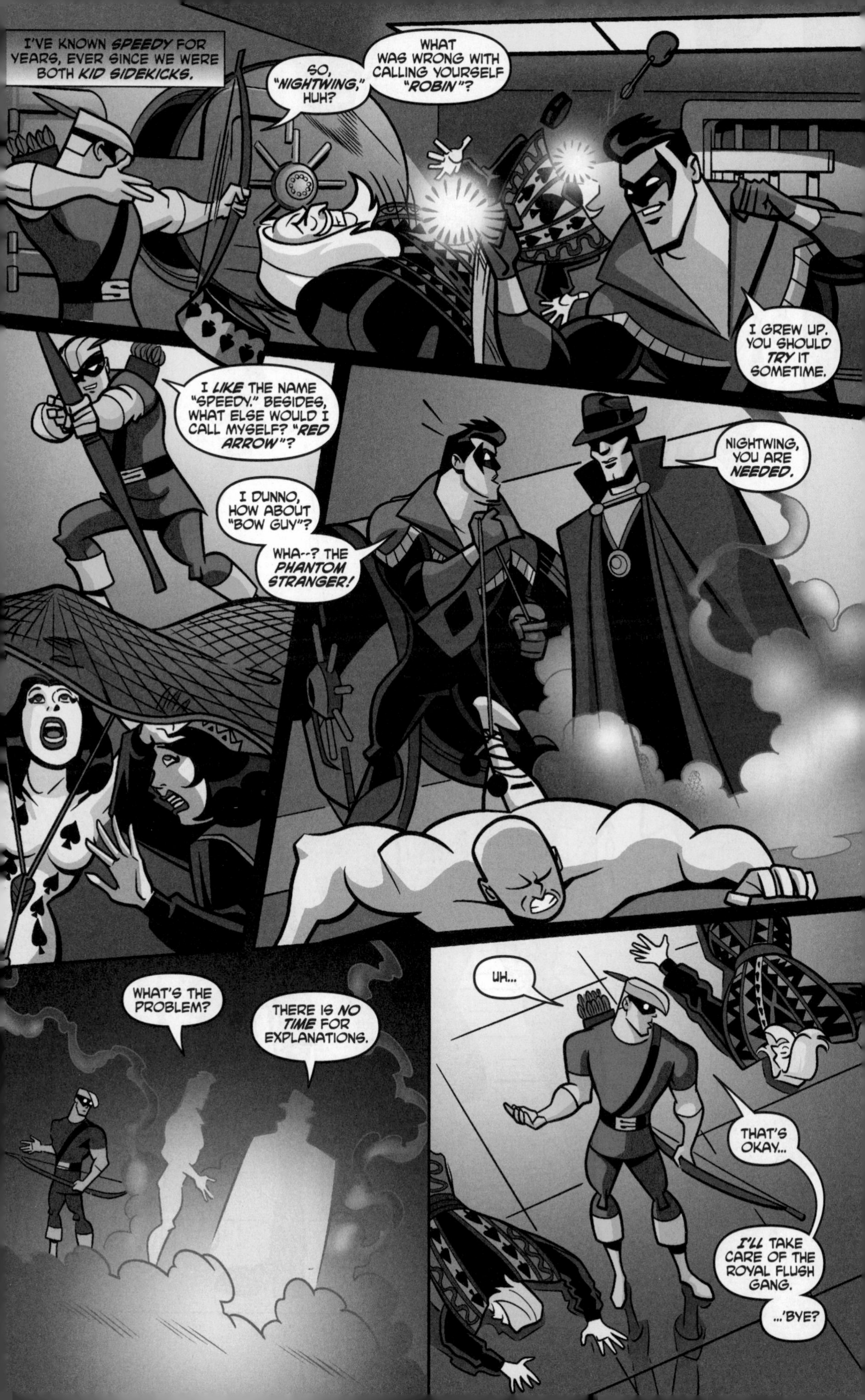
I'VE KNOWN SPEEDY FOR YEARS, EVER SINCE WE WERE BOTH KID SIDEKICKS.
SO, "NIGHTWING," HUH?
WHAT WAS WRONG WITH CALLING YOURSELF "ROBIN"?
I GREW UP. YOU SHOULD TRY IT SOMETIME.
I LIKE THE NAME "SPEEDY." BESIDES, WHAT ELSE WOULD I CALL MYSELF? "RED ARROW"?
I DUNNO, HOW ABOUT "BOW GUY"?
NIGHTWING, YOU ARE NEEDED.
WHA--? THE PHANTOM STRANGER!
WHAT'S THE PROBLEM?
THERE IS NO TIME FOR EXPLANATIONS.
UH...
THAT'S OKAY...
I'LL TAKE CARE OF THE ROYAL FLUSH GANG.
...'BYE?

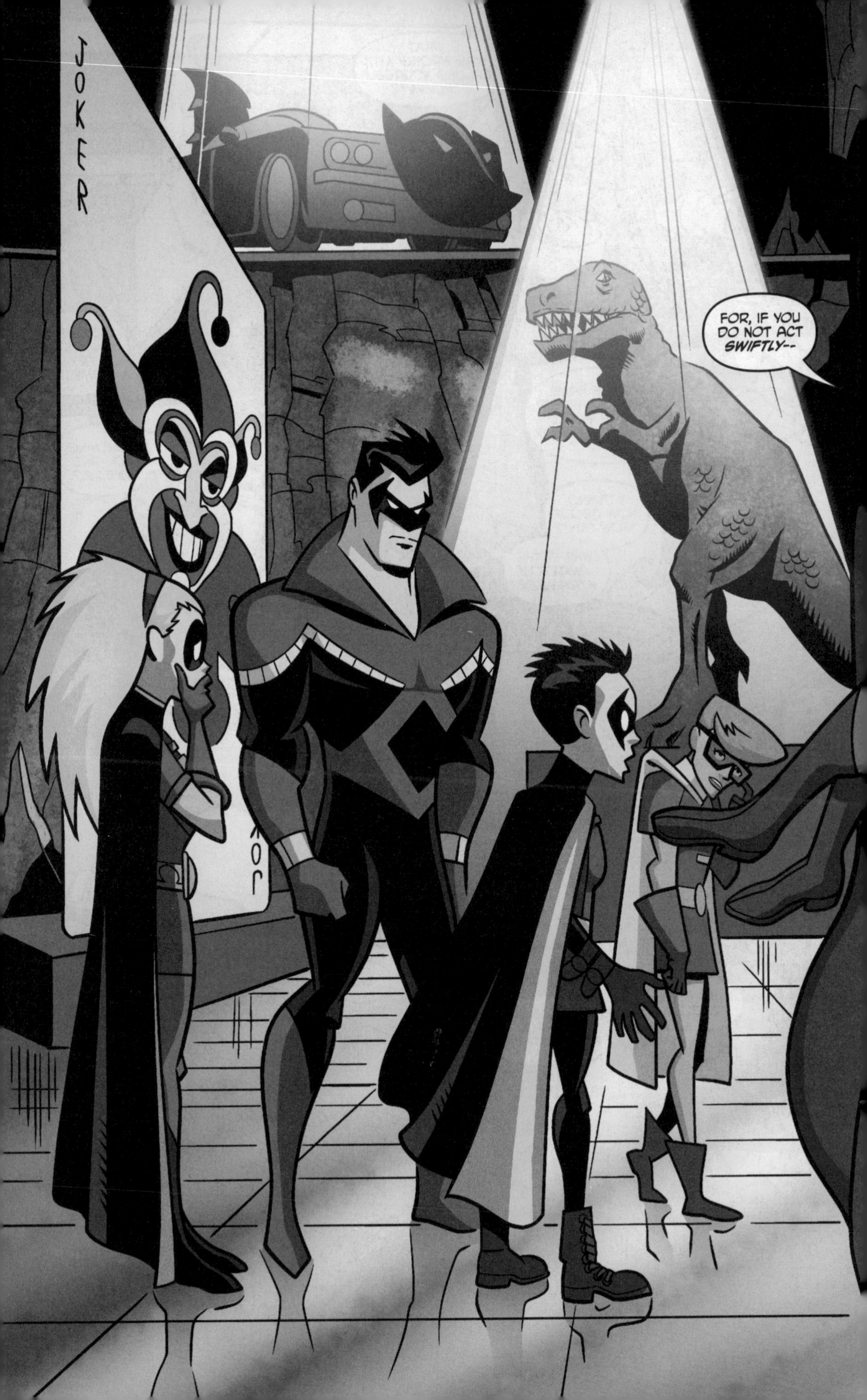
JOKER
FOR, IF YOU DO NOT ACT *SWIFTLY*--

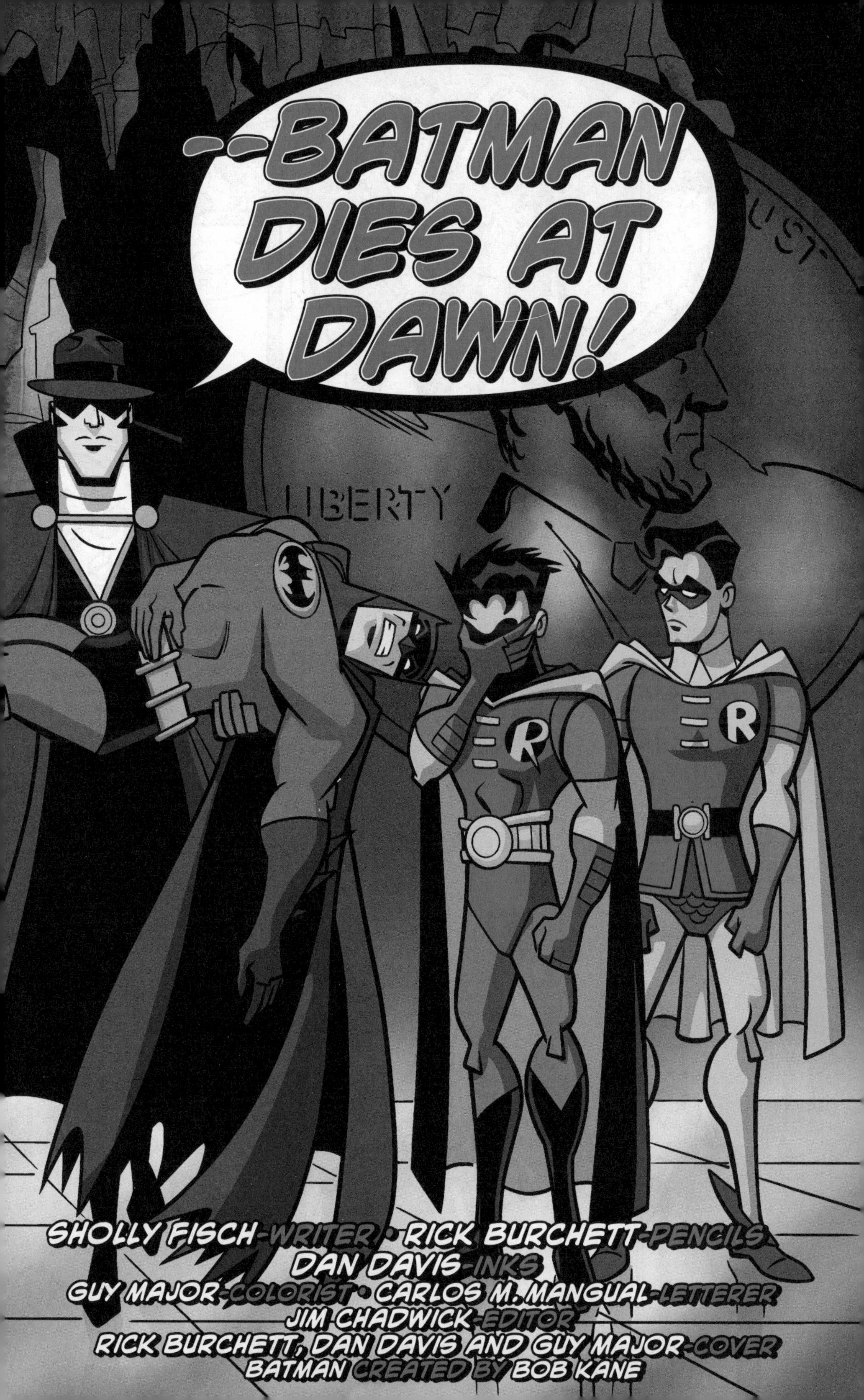
--BATMAN DIES AT DAWN!
LIBERTY
SHOLLY FISCH-WRITER • RICK BURCHETT-PENCILS
DAN DAVIS-INKS
GUY MAJOR-COLORIST • CARLOS M. MANGUAL-LETTERER
JIM CHADWICK-EDITOR
RICK BURCHETT, DAN DAVIS AND GUY MAJOR-COVER
BATMAN CREATED BY BOB KANE

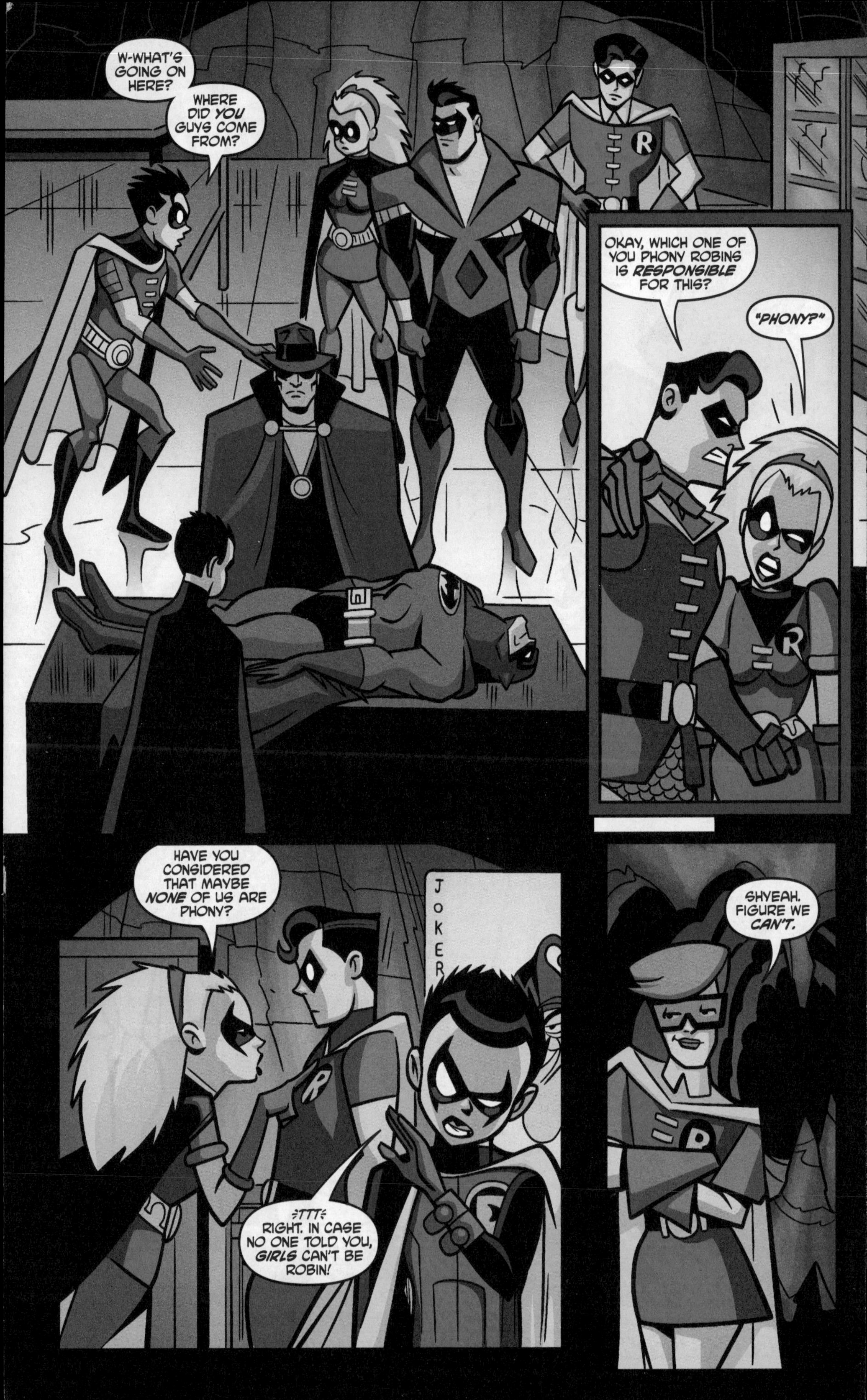
W-WHAT'S GOING ON HERE?
WHERE DID *YOU* GUYS COME FROM?
OKAY, WHICH ONE OF YOU PHONY ROBINS IS *RESPONSIBLE* FOR THIS?
"PHONY?"
HAVE YOU CONSIDERED THAT MAYBE *NONE* OF US ARE PHONY?
JOKER
TTT
RIGHT. IN CASE NO ONE TOLD YOU, *GIRLS* CAN'T BE ROBIN!
SHYEAH. FIGURE WE *CAN'T.*

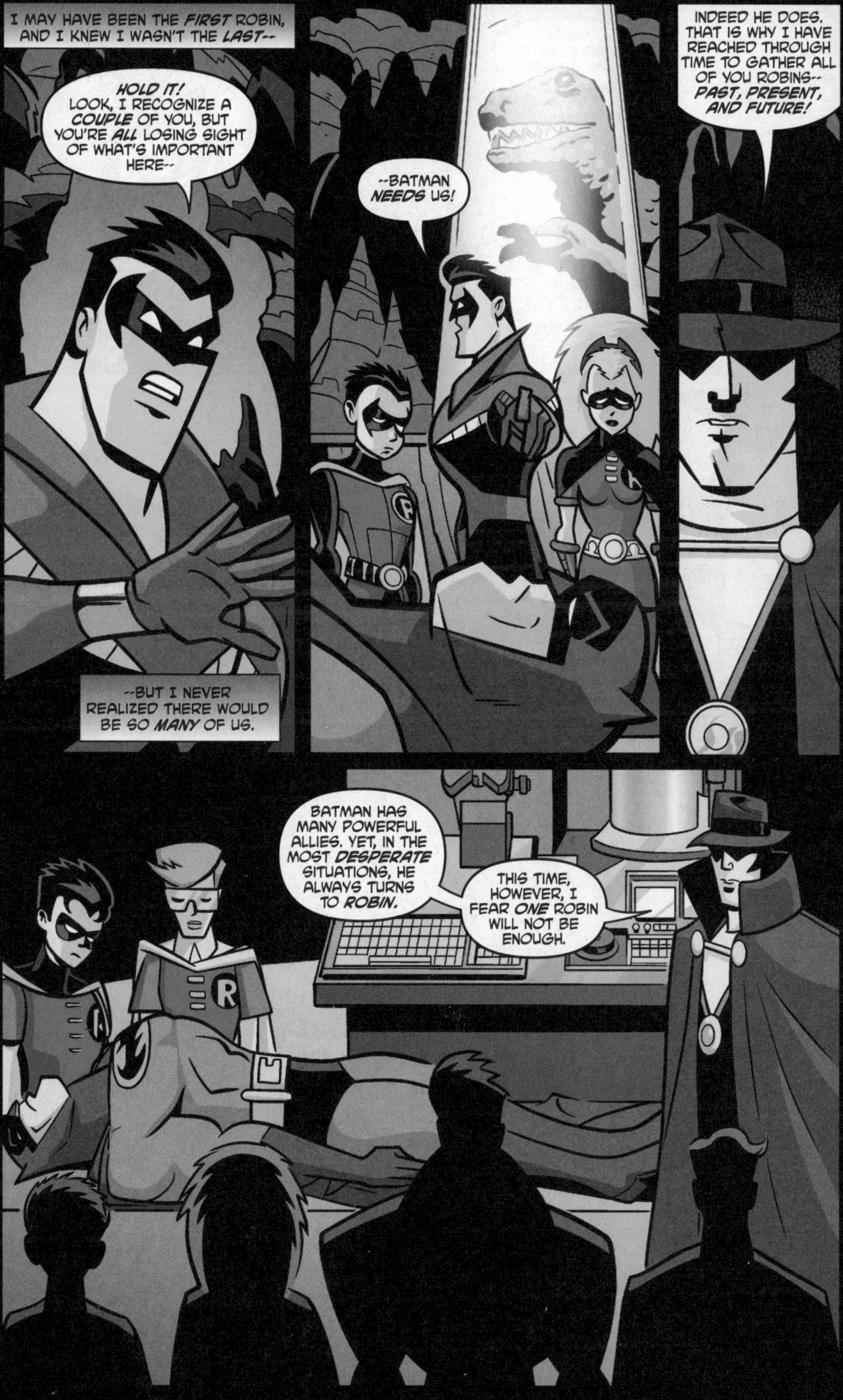
I MAY HAVE BEEN THE *FIRST* ROBIN, AND I KNEW I WASN'T THE *LAST*--
HOLD IT! LOOK, I RECOGNIZE A *COUPLE* OF YOU, BUT YOU'RE *ALL* LOSING SIGHT OF WHAT'S IMPORTANT HERE--
--BUT I NEVER REALIZED THERE WOULD BE SO *MANY* OF US.
--BATMAN *NEEDS* US!
INDEED HE DOES. THAT IS WHY I HAVE REACHED THROUGH TIME TO GATHER ALL OF YOU ROBINS-- *PAST, PRESENT, AND FUTURE!*
BATMAN HAS MANY POWERFUL ALLIES. YET, IN THE MOST *DESPERATE* SITUATIONS, HE ALWAYS TURNS TO *ROBIN.*
THIS TIME, HOWEVER, I FEAR *ONE* ROBIN WILL NOT BE ENOUGH.

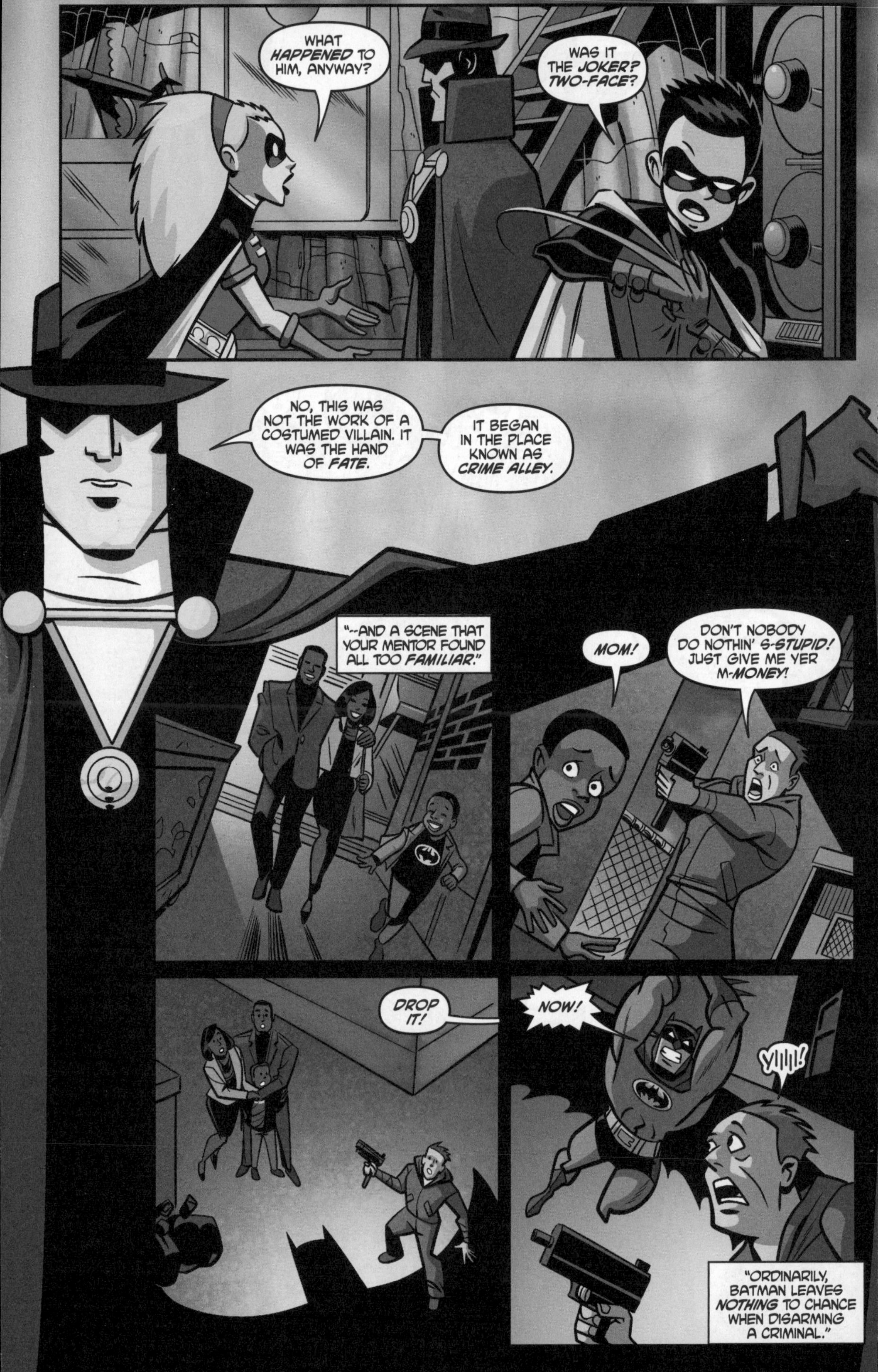
WHAT HAPPENED TO HIM, ANYWAY?
WAS IT THE JOKER? TWO-FACE?
NO, THIS WAS NOT THE WORK OF A COSTUMED VILLAIN. IT WAS THE HAND OF FATE.
IT BEGAN IN THE PLACE KNOWN AS CRIME ALLEY.
"--AND A SCENE THAT YOUR MENTOR FOUND ALL TOO FAMILIAR."
MOM!
DON'T NOBODY DO NOTHIN' S-STUPID! JUST GIVE ME YER M-MONEY!
DROP IT!
NOW!
YIII!
"ORDINARILY, BATMAN LEAVES NOTHING TO CHANCE WHEN DISARMING A CRIMINAL."

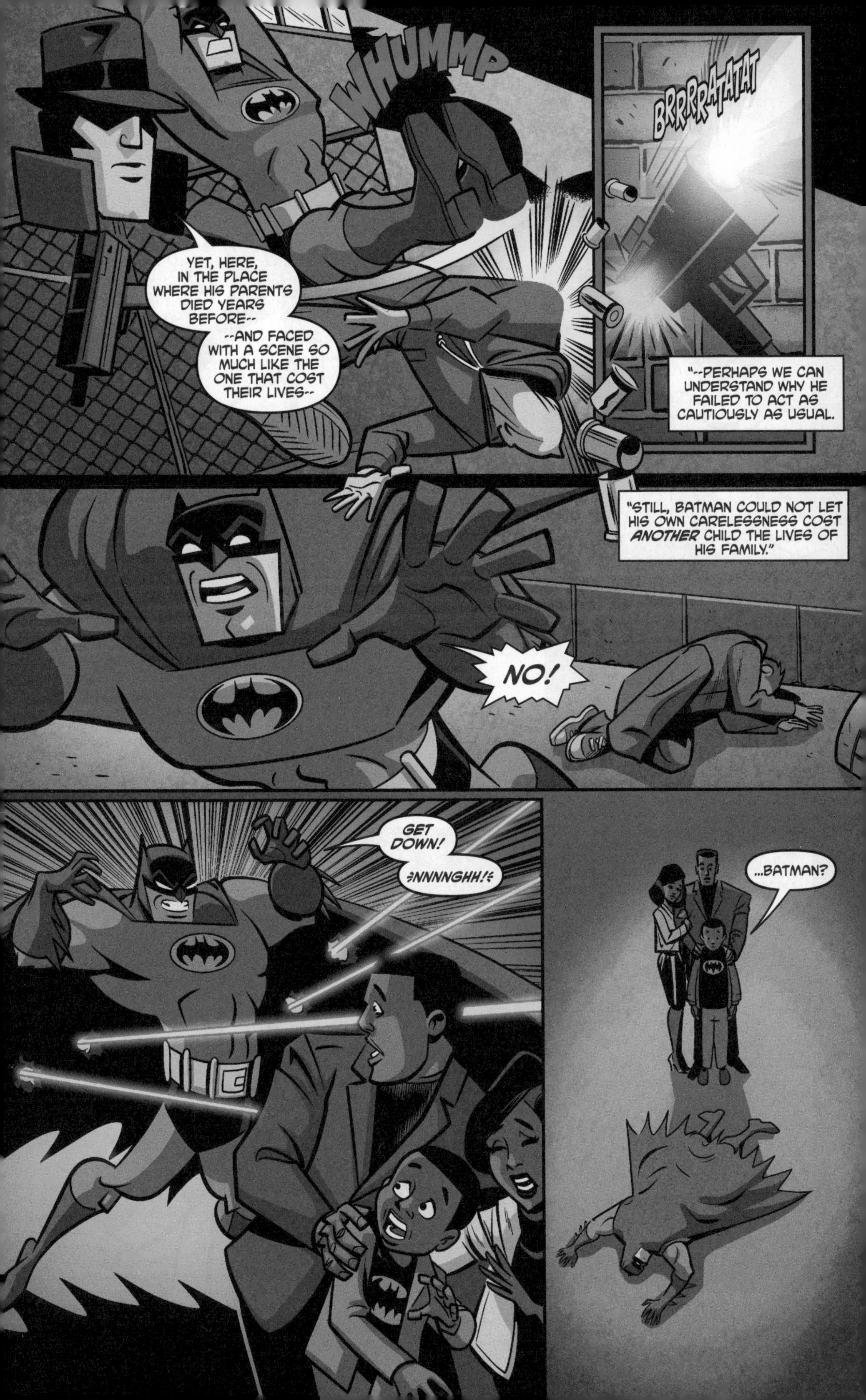
WHUMMP
BRRRRATATAT
YET, HERE, IN THE PLACE WHERE HIS PARENTS DIED YEARS BEFORE--
--AND FACED WITH A SCENE SO MUCH LIKE THE ONE THAT COST THEIR LIVES--
"--PERHAPS WE CAN UNDERSTAND WHY HE FAILED TO ACT AS CAUTIOUSLY AS USUAL.
"STILL, BATMAN COULD NOT LET HIS OWN CARELESSNESS COST ANOTHER CHILD THE LIVES OF HIS FAMILY."
NO!
GET DOWN!
NNNNGHH!
...BATMAN?

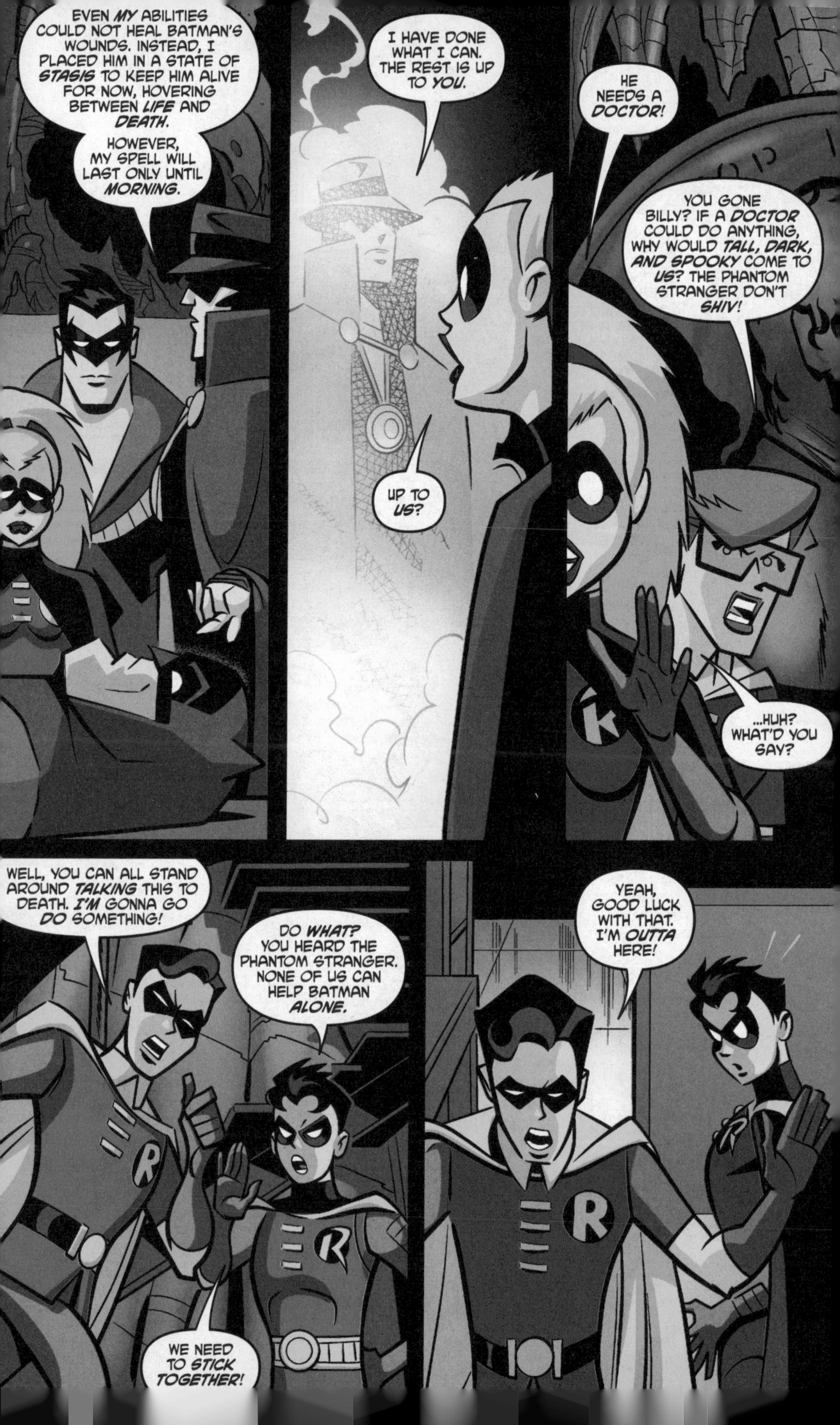
EVEN MY ABILITIES COULD NOT HEAL BATMAN'S WOUNDS. INSTEAD, I PLACED HIM IN A STATE OF STASIS TO KEEP HIM ALIVE FOR NOW, HOVERING BETWEEN LIFE AND DEATH.
HOWEVER, MY SPELL WILL LAST ONLY UNTIL MORNING.
I HAVE DONE WHAT I CAN. THE REST IS UP TO YOU.
UP TO US?
HE NEEDS A DOCTOR!
YOU GONE BILLY? IF A DOCTOR COULD DO ANYTHING, WHY WOULD TALL, DARK, AND SPOOKY COME TO US? THE PHANTOM STRANGER DON'T SHIV!
...HUH? WHAT'D YOU SAY?
WELL, YOU CAN ALL STAND AROUND TALKING THIS TO DEATH. I'M GONNA GO DO SOMETHING!
DO WHAT? YOU HEARD THE PHANTOM STRANGER. NONE OF US CAN HELP BATMAN ALONE.
WE NEED TO STICK TOGETHER!
YEAH, GOOD LUCK WITH THAT. I'M OUTTA HERE!

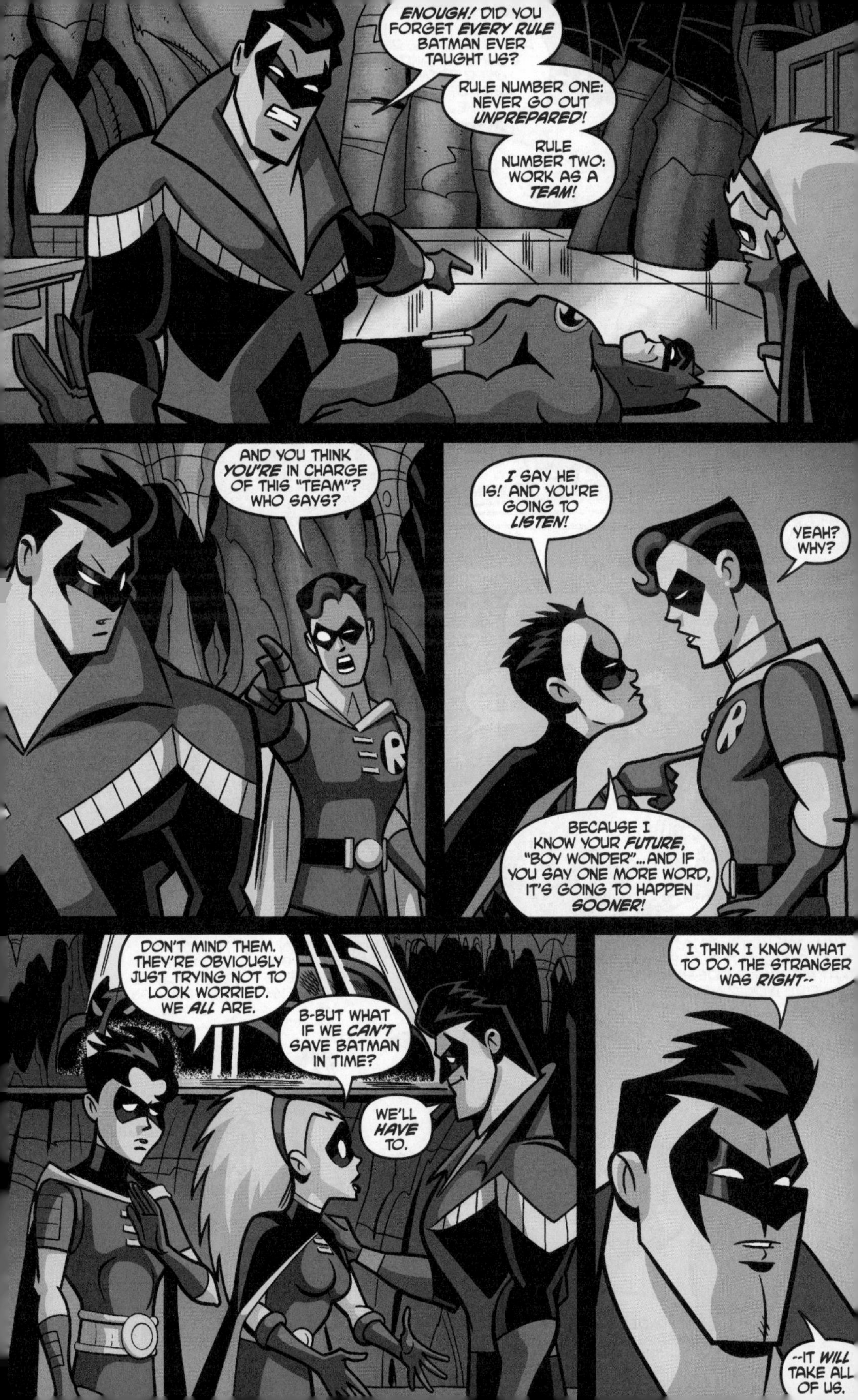

ENOUGH! DID YOU FORGET EVERY RULE BATMAN EVER TAUGHT US?
RULE NUMBER ONE: NEVER GO OUT UNPREPARED!
RULE NUMBER TWO: WORK AS A TEAM!
AND YOU THINK YOU'RE IN CHARGE OF THIS "TEAM"? WHO SAYS?
I SAY HE IS! AND YOU'RE GOING TO LISTEN!
YEAH? WHY?
BECAUSE I KNOW YOUR FUTURE, "BOY WONDER"...AND IF YOU SAY ONE MORE WORD, IT'S GOING TO HAPPEN SOONER!
DON'T MIND THEM. THEY'RE OBVIOUSLY JUST TRYING NOT TO LOOK WORRIED. WE ALL ARE.
B-BUT WHAT IF WE CAN'T SAVE BATMAN IN TIME?
WE'LL HAVE TO.
I THINK I KNOW WHAT TO DO. THE STRANGER WAS RIGHT--
--IT WILL TAKE ALL OF US.

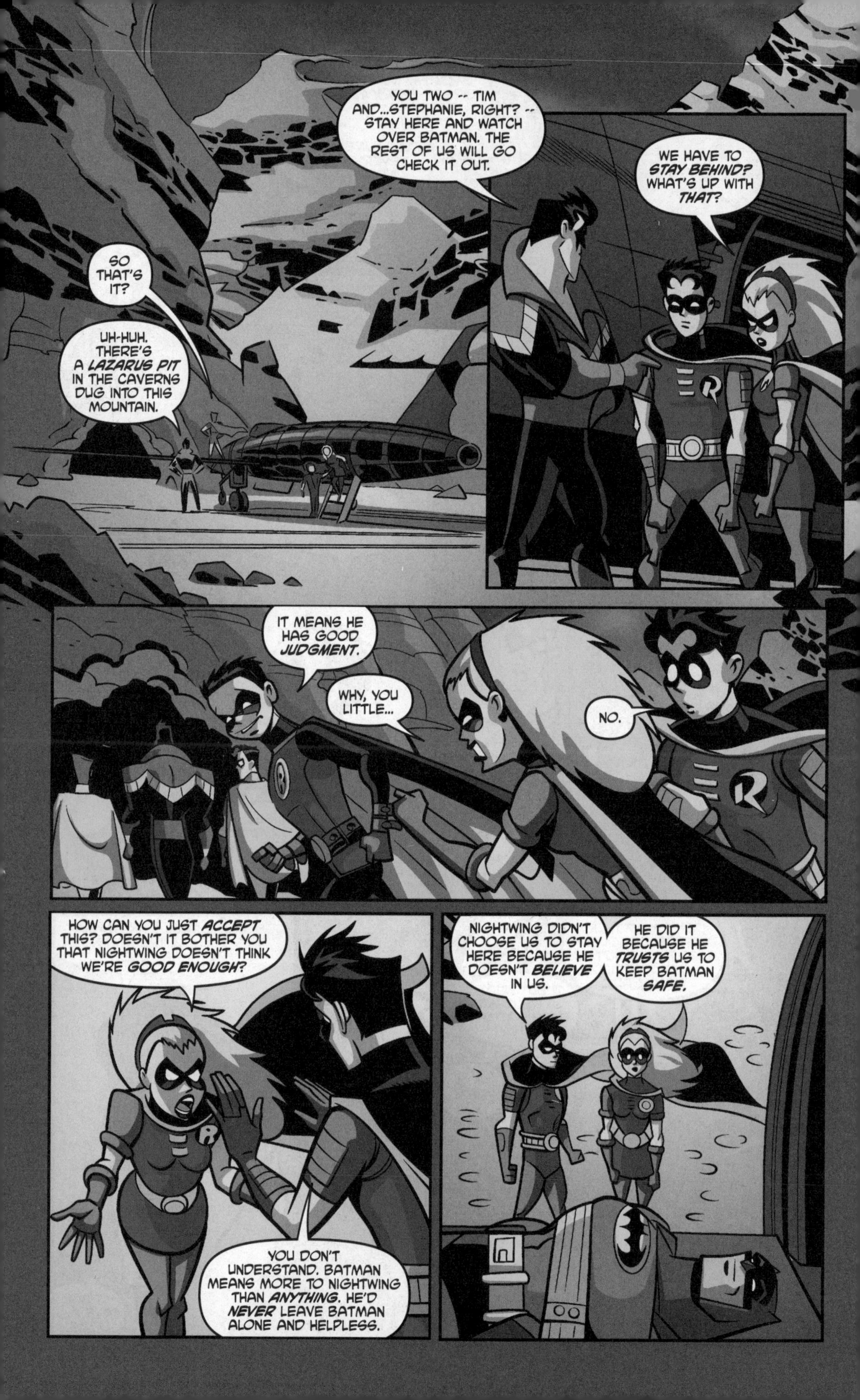
YOU TWO -- TIM AND...STEPHANIE, RIGHT? -- STAY HERE AND WATCH OVER BATMAN. THE REST OF US WILL GO CHECK IT OUT.
SO THAT'S IT?
UH-HUH. THERE'S A LAZARUS PIT IN THE CAVERNS DUG INTO THIS MOUNTAIN.
WE HAVE TO STAY BEHIND? WHAT'S UP WITH THAT?
IT MEANS HE HAS GOOD JUDGMENT.
WHY, YOU LITTLE...
NO.
HOW CAN YOU JUST ACCEPT THIS? DOESN'T IT BOTHER YOU THAT NIGHTWING DOESN'T THINK WE'RE GOOD ENOUGH?
YOU DON'T UNDERSTAND. BATMAN MEANS MORE TO NIGHTWING THAN ANYTHING. HE'D NEVER LEAVE BATMAN ALONE AND HELPLESS.
NIGHTWING DIDN'T CHOOSE US TO STAY HERE BECAUSE HE DOESN'T BELIEVE IN US.
HE DID IT BECAUSE HE TRUSTS US TO KEEP BATMAN SAFE.

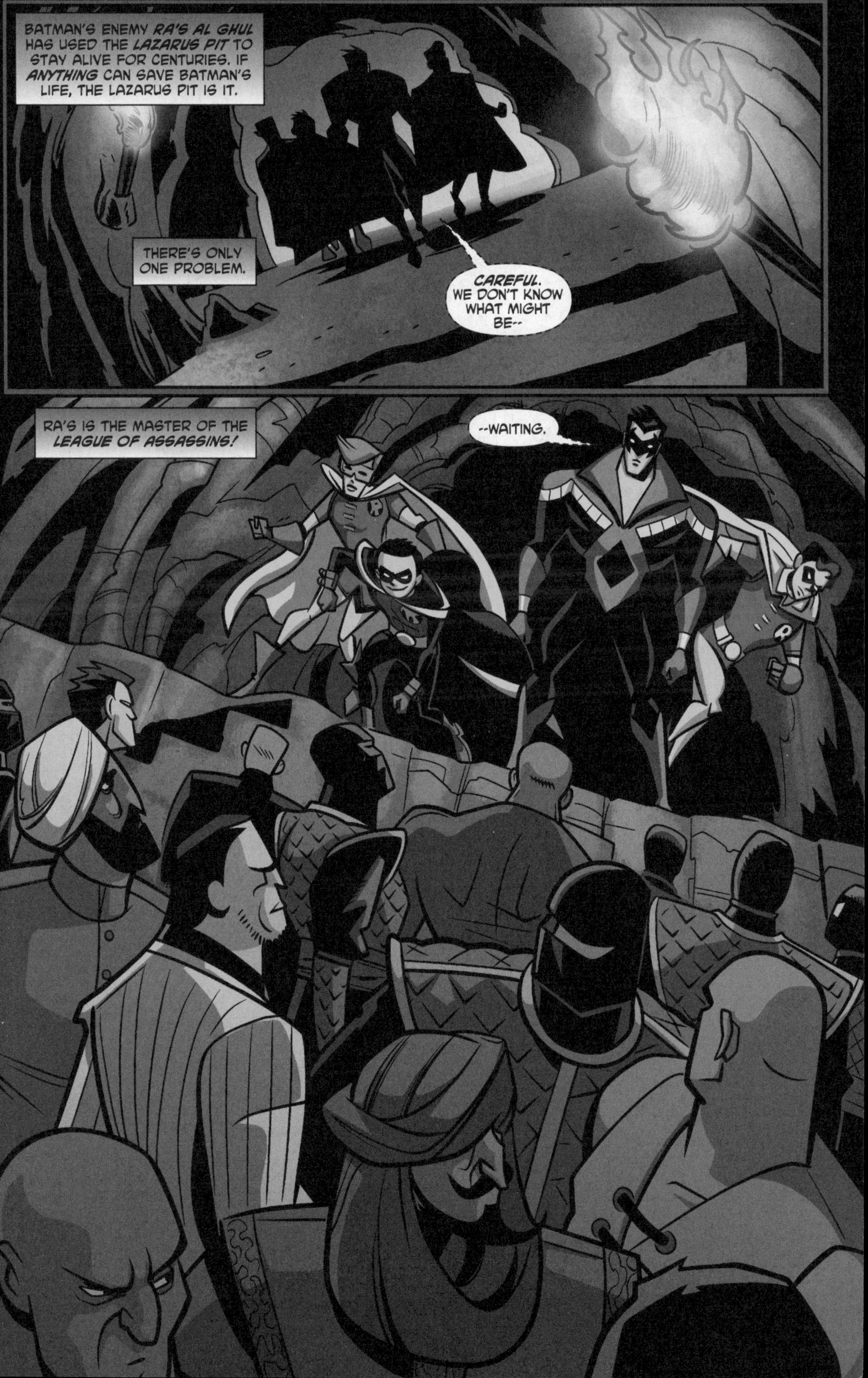
BATMAN'S ENEMY RA'S AL GHUL HAS USED THE LAZARUS PIT TO STAY ALIVE FOR CENTURIES. IF ANYTHING CAN SAVE BATMAN'S LIFE, THE LAZARUS PIT IS IT.
THERE'S ONLY ONE PROBLEM.
CAREFUL. WE DON'T KNOW WHAT MIGHT BE--
RA'S IS THE MASTER OF THE LEAGUE OF ASSASSINS!
--WAITING.

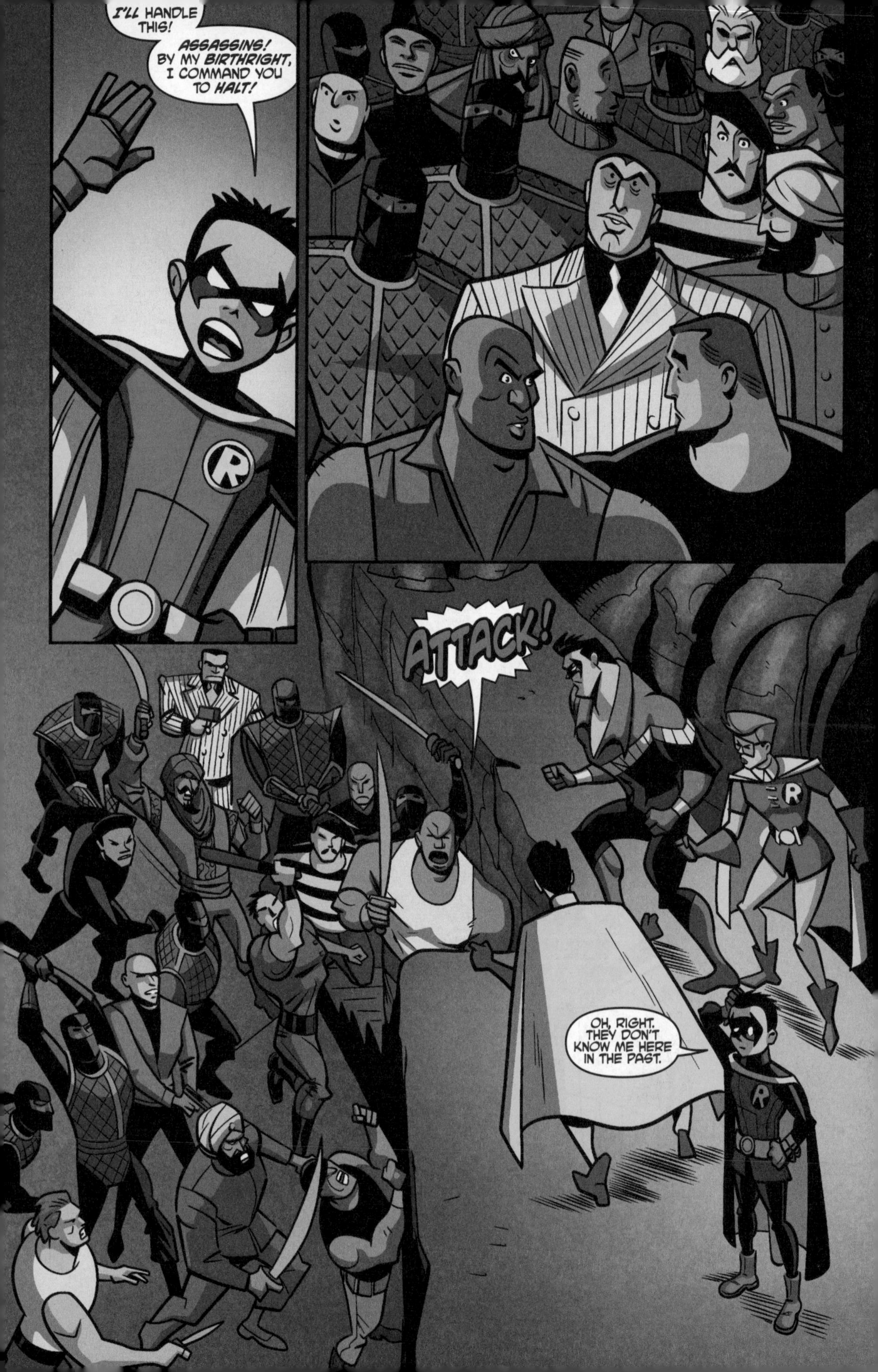
I'LL HANDLE THIS!
ASSASSINS! BY MY BIRTHRIGHT, I COMMAND YOU TO HALT!
ATTACK!
OH, RIGHT. THEY DON'T KNOW ME HERE IN THE PAST.

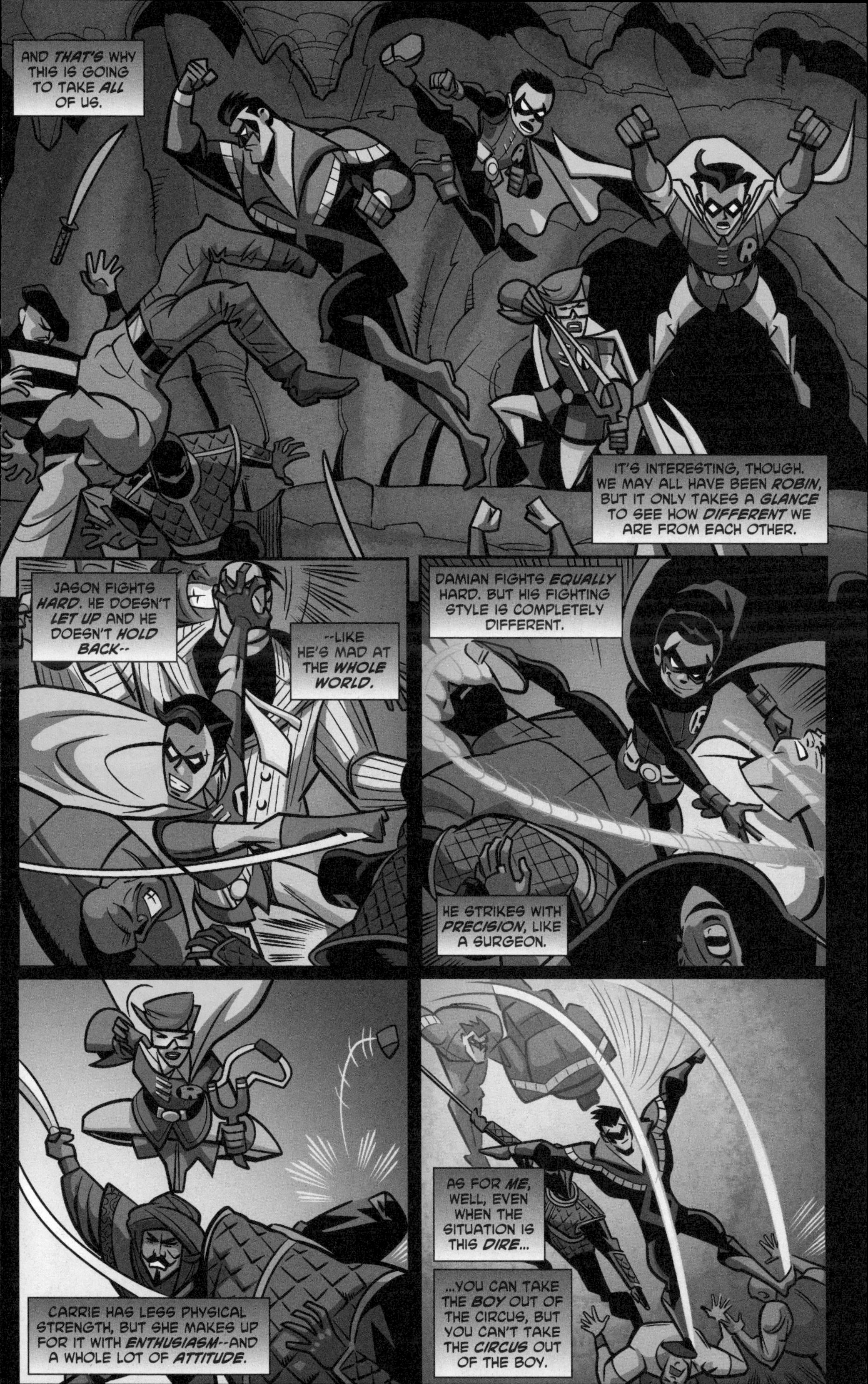
AND THAT'S WHY THIS IS GOING TO TAKE ALL OF US.
IT'S INTERESTING, THOUGH. WE MAY ALL HAVE BEEN ROBIN, BUT IT ONLY TAKES A GLANCE TO SEE HOW DIFFERENT WE ARE FROM EACH OTHER.
JASON FIGHTS HARD. HE DOESN'T LET UP AND HE DOESN'T HOLD BACK--
--LIKE HE'S MAD AT THE WHOLE WORLD.
DAMIAN FIGHTS EQUALLY HARD. BUT HIS FIGHTING STYLE IS COMPLETELY DIFFERENT.
HE STRIKES WITH PRECISION, LIKE A SURGEON.
CARRIE HAS LESS PHYSICAL STRENGTH, BUT SHE MAKES UP FOR IT WITH ENTHUSIASM--AND A WHOLE LOT OF ATTITUDE.
AS FOR ME, WELL, EVEN WHEN THE SITUATION IS THIS DIRE...
...YOU CAN TAKE THE BOY OUT OF THE CIRCUS, BUT YOU CAN'T TAKE THE CIRCUS OUT OF THE BOY.

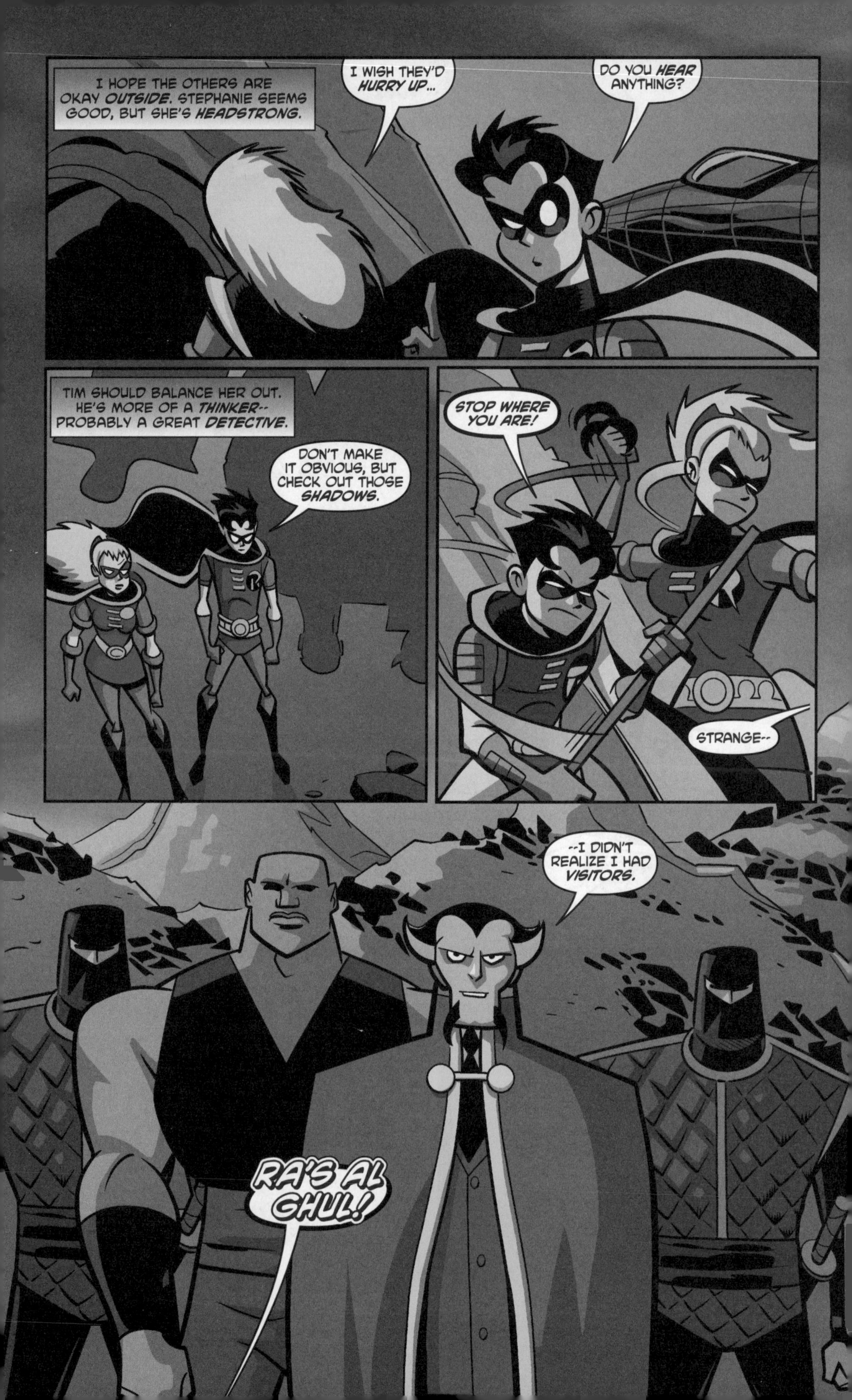
I HOPE THE OTHERS ARE OKAY OUTSIDE. STEPHANIE SEEMS GOOD, BUT SHE'S HEADSTRONG.
I WISH THEY'D HURRY UP...
DO YOU HEAR ANYTHING?
TIM SHOULD BALANCE HER OUT. HE'S MORE OF A THINKER--PROBABLY A GREAT DETECTIVE.
DON'T MAKE IT OBVIOUS, BUT CHECK OUT THOSE SHADOWS.
STOP WHERE YOU ARE!
STRANGE--
--I DIDN'T REALIZE I HAD VISITORS.
RA'S AL GHUL!

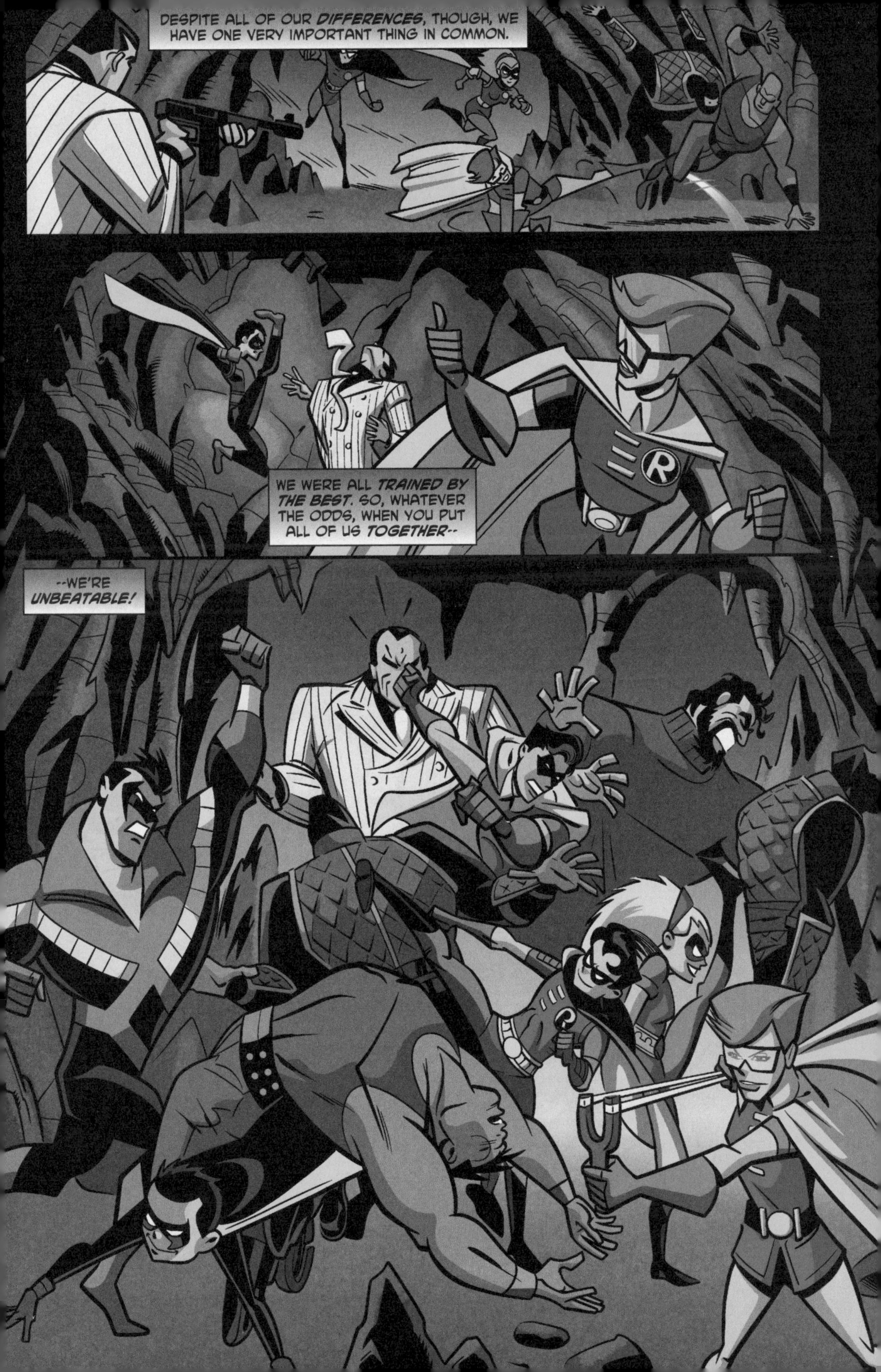
DESPITE ALL OF OUR *DIFFERENCES*, THOUGH, WE HAVE ONE VERY IMPORTANT THING IN COMMON.
WE WERE ALL *TRAINED BY THE BEST*. SO, WHATEVER THE ODDS, WHEN YOU PUT ALL OF US *TOGETHER*--
--WE'RE *UNBEATABLE!*

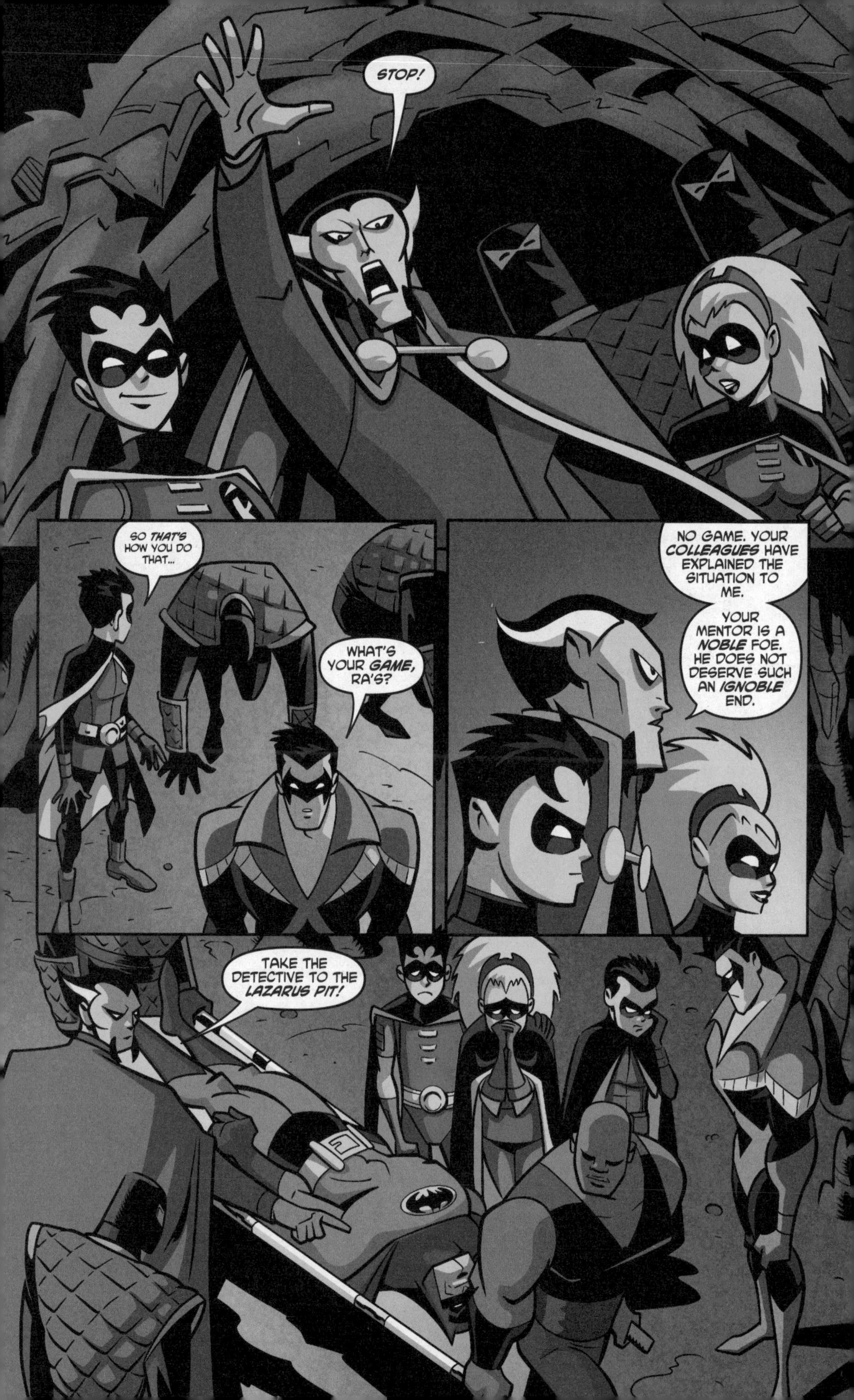
STOP!
SO THAT'S HOW YOU DO THAT...
WHAT'S YOUR GAME, RA'S?
NO GAME. YOUR COLLEAGUES HAVE EXPLAINED THE SITUATION TO ME.
YOUR MENTOR IS A NOBLE FOE. HE DOES NOT DESERVE SUCH AN IGNOBLE END.
TAKE THE DETECTIVE TO THE LAZARUS PIT!

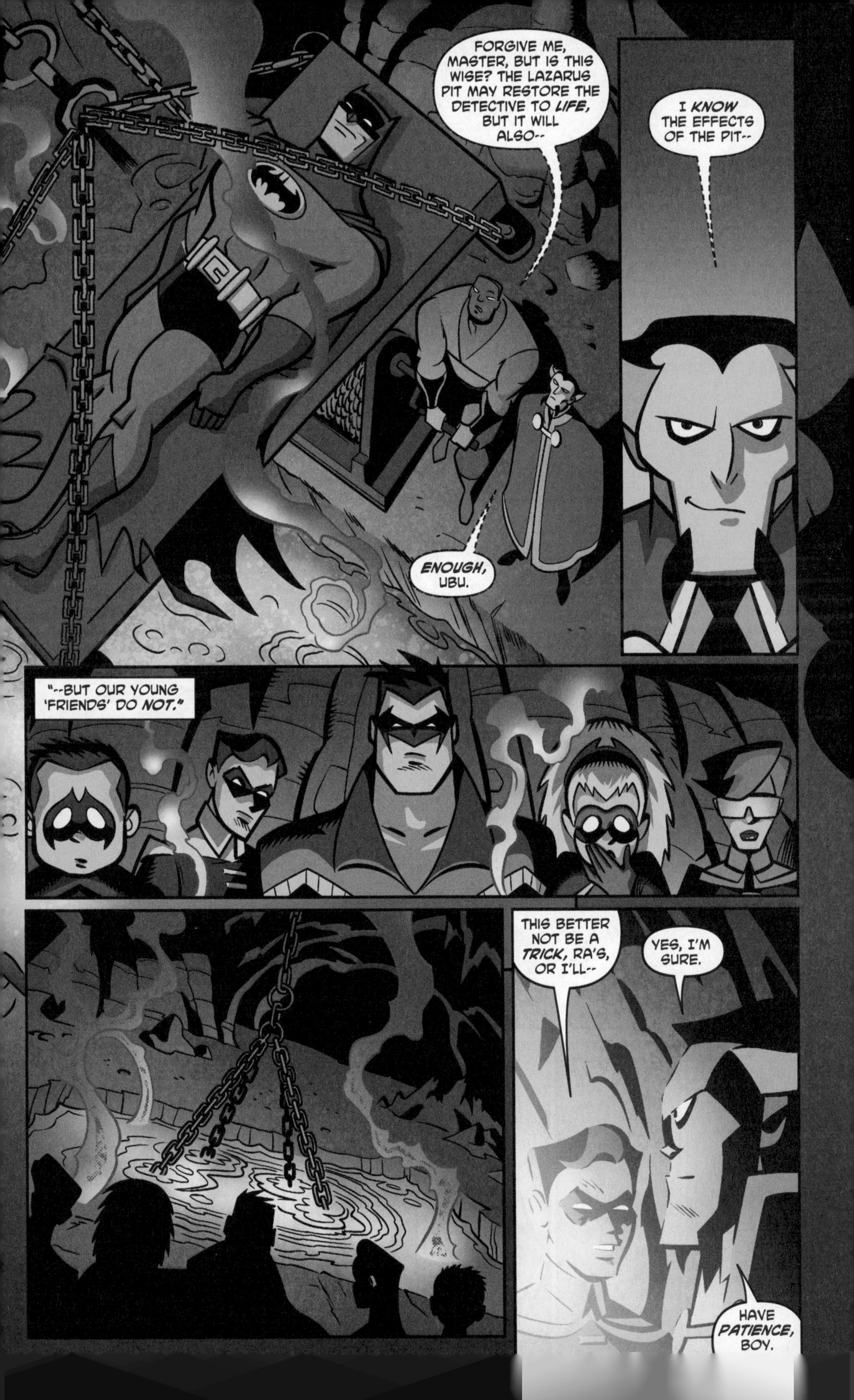
FORGIVE ME, MASTER, BUT IS THIS WISE? THE LAZARUS PIT MAY RESTORE THE DETECTIVE TO *LIFE*, BUT IT WILL ALSO--
ENOUGH, UBU.
I *KNOW* THE EFFECTS OF THE PIT--
"--BUT OUR YOUNG 'FRIENDS' DO *NOT*."
THIS BETTER NOT BE A *TRICK*, RA'S, OR I'LL--
YES, I'M SURE.
HAVE *PATIENCE,* BOY.

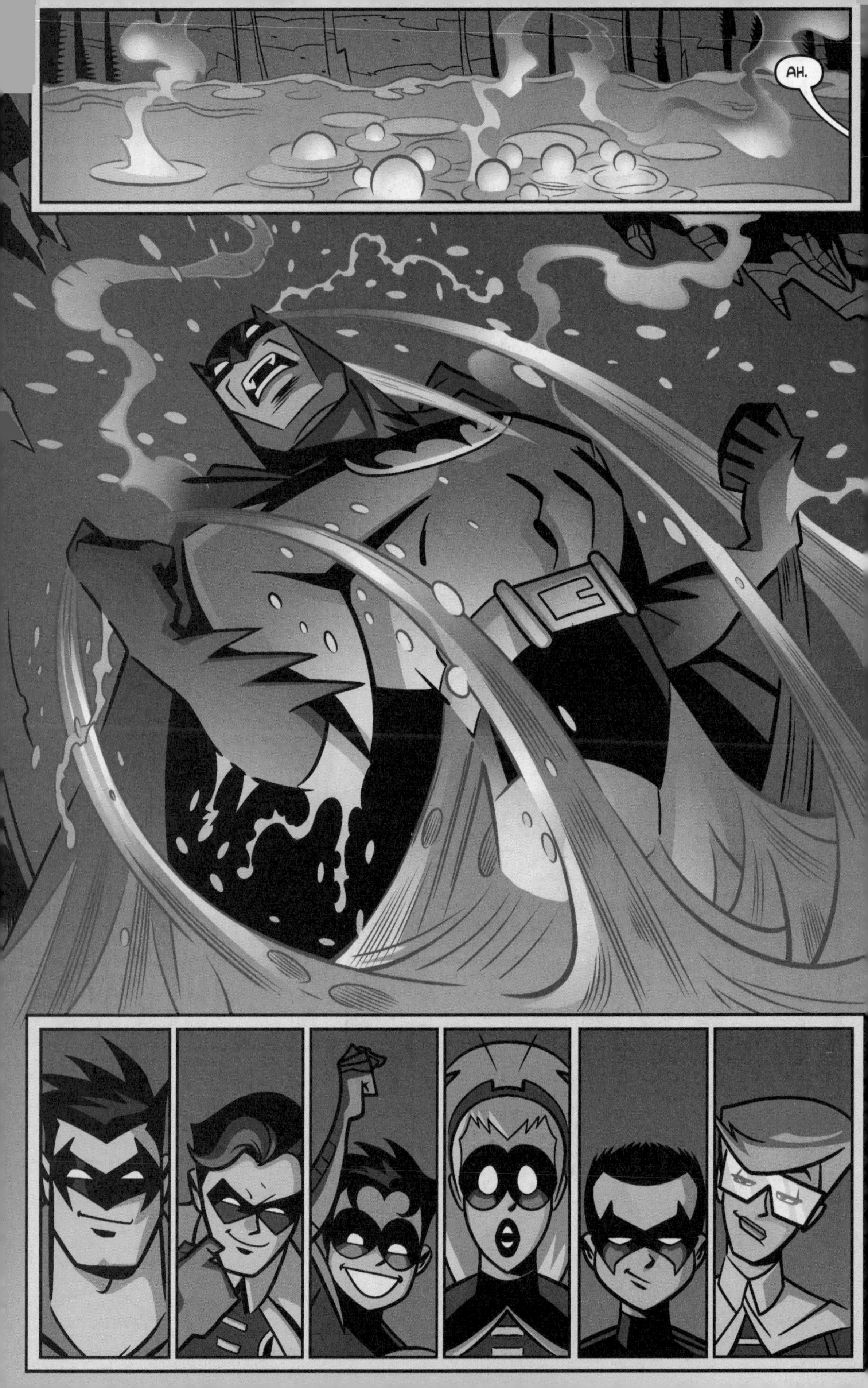
AH.

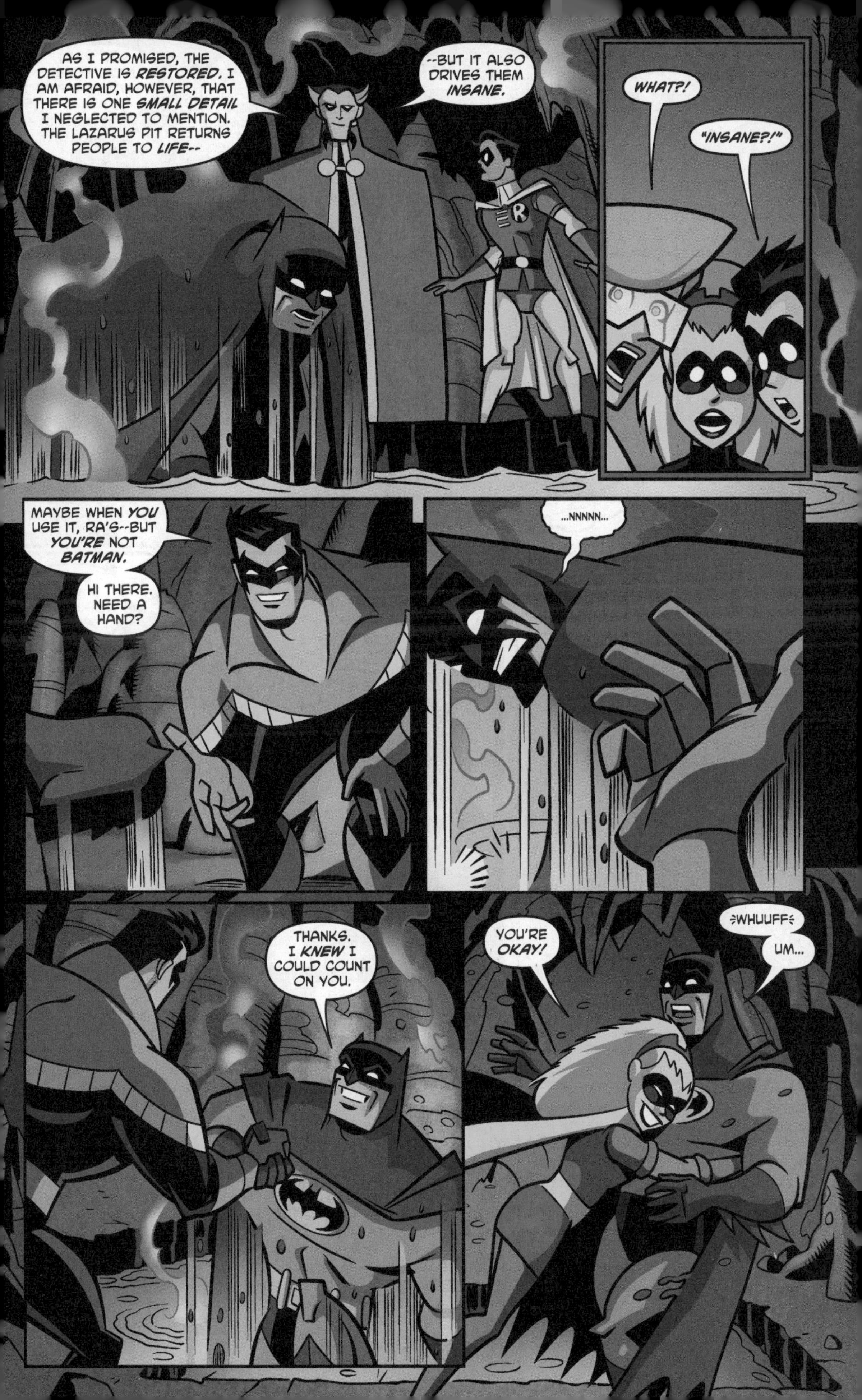
AS I PROMISED, THE DETECTIVE IS *RESTORED*. I AM AFRAID, HOWEVER, THAT THERE IS ONE *SMALL DETAIL* I NEGLECTED TO MENTION. THE LAZARUS PIT RETURNS PEOPLE TO *LIFE*--
--BUT IT ALSO DRIVES THEM *INSANE*.
WHAT?!
"INSANE?!"
MAYBE WHEN *YOU* USE IT, RA'S--BUT *YOU'RE* NOT *BATMAN*.
HI THERE. NEED A HAND?
...NNNNN...
THANKS. I *KNEW* I COULD COUNT ON YOU.
YOU'RE *OKAY!*
WHUUFF
UM...

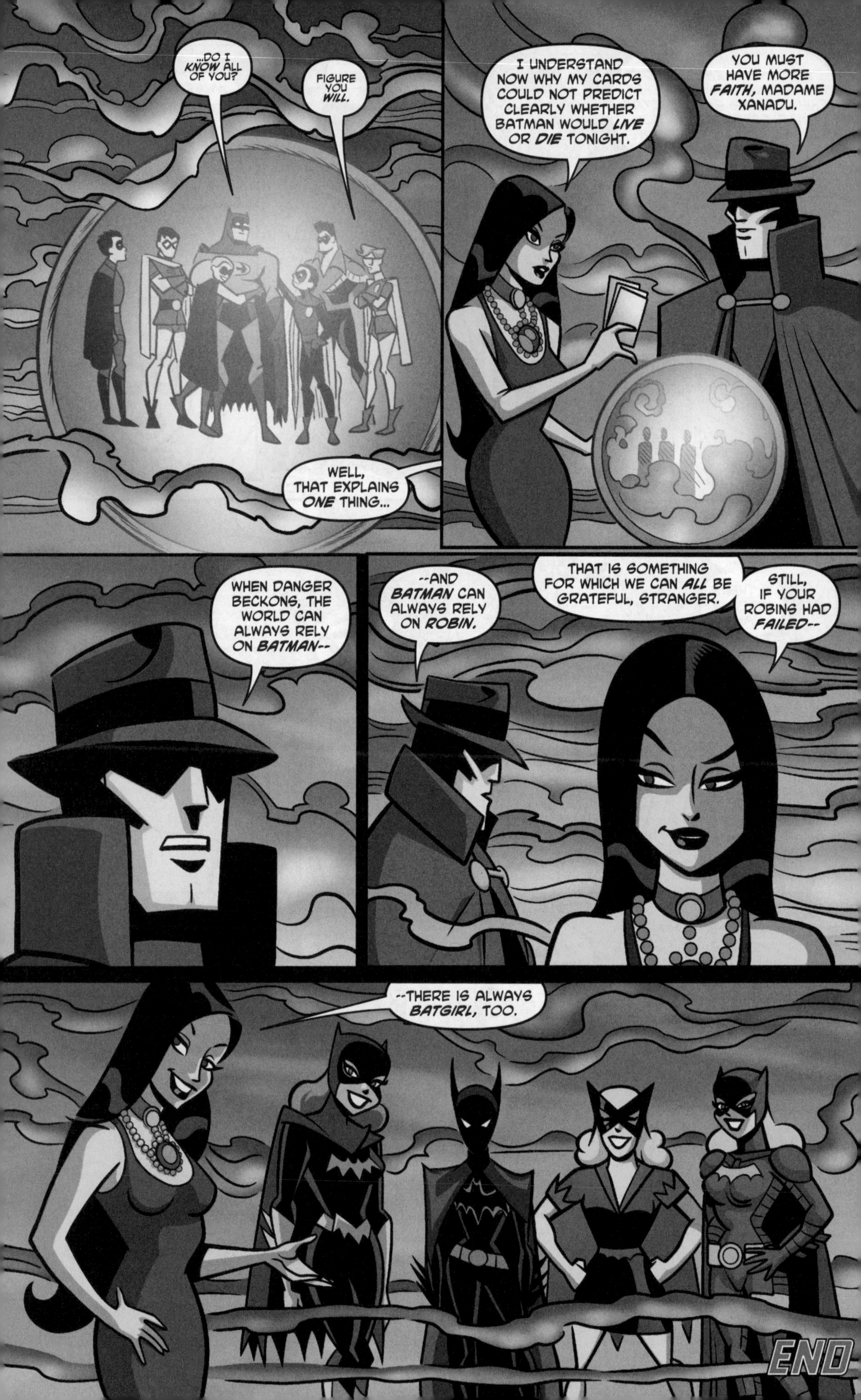
...DO I KNOW ALL OF YOU?
FIGURE YOU WILL.
WELL, THAT EXPLAINS ONE THING...
I UNDERSTAND NOW WHY MY CARDS COULD NOT PREDICT CLEARLY WHETHER BATMAN WOULD LIVE OR DIE TONIGHT.
YOU MUST HAVE MORE FAITH, MADAME XANADU.
WHEN DANGER BECKONS, THE WORLD CAN ALWAYS RELY ON BATMAN--
--AND BATMAN CAN ALWAYS RELY ON ROBIN.
THAT IS SOMETHING FOR WHICH WE CAN ALL BE GRATEFUL, STRANGER.
STILL, IF YOUR ROBINS HAD FAILED--
--THERE IS ALWAYS BATGIRL, TOO.
END

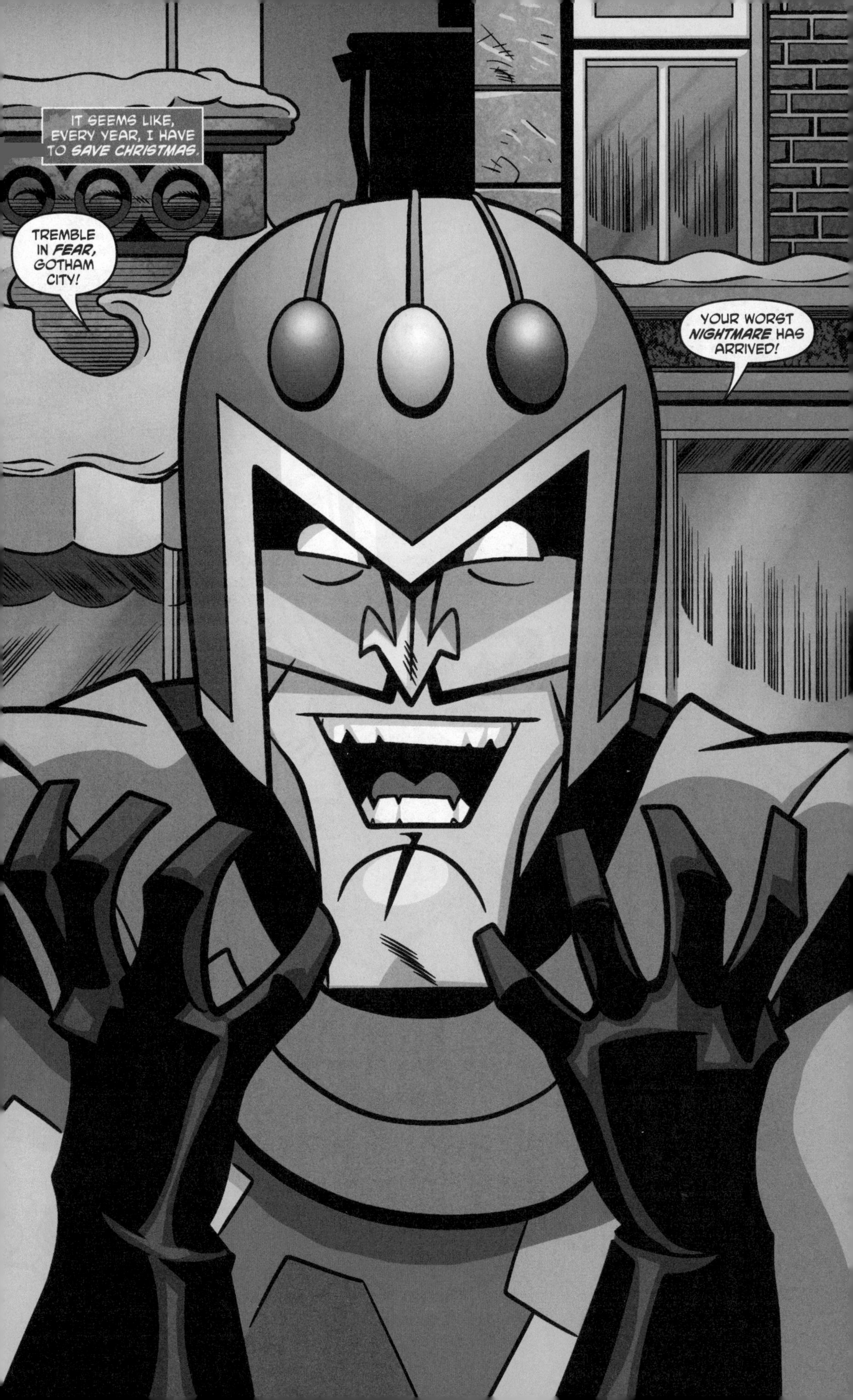
IT SEEMS LIKE, EVERY YEAR, I HAVE TO SAVE CHRISTMAS.
TREMBLE IN FEAR, GOTHAM CITY!
YOUR WORST NIGHTMARE HAS ARRIVED!

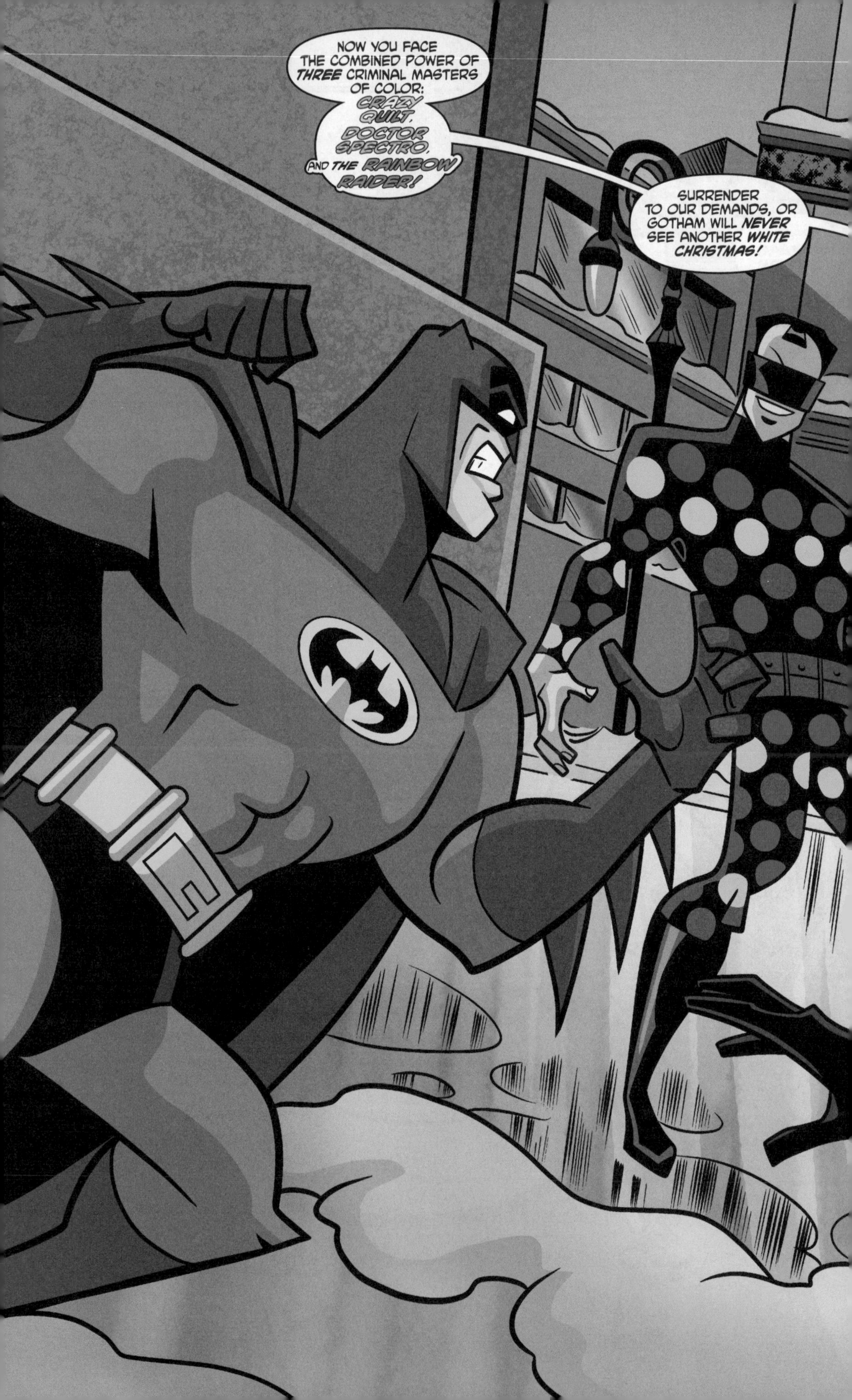
NOW YOU FACE THE COMBINED POWER OF *THREE* CRIMINAL MASTERS OF COLOR: *CRAZY QUILT*, *DOCTOR SPECTRO*, AND *THE RAINBOW RAIDER*!
SURRENDER TO OUR DEMANDS, OR GOTHAM WILL *NEVER* SEE ANOTHER *WHITE CHRISTMAS*!

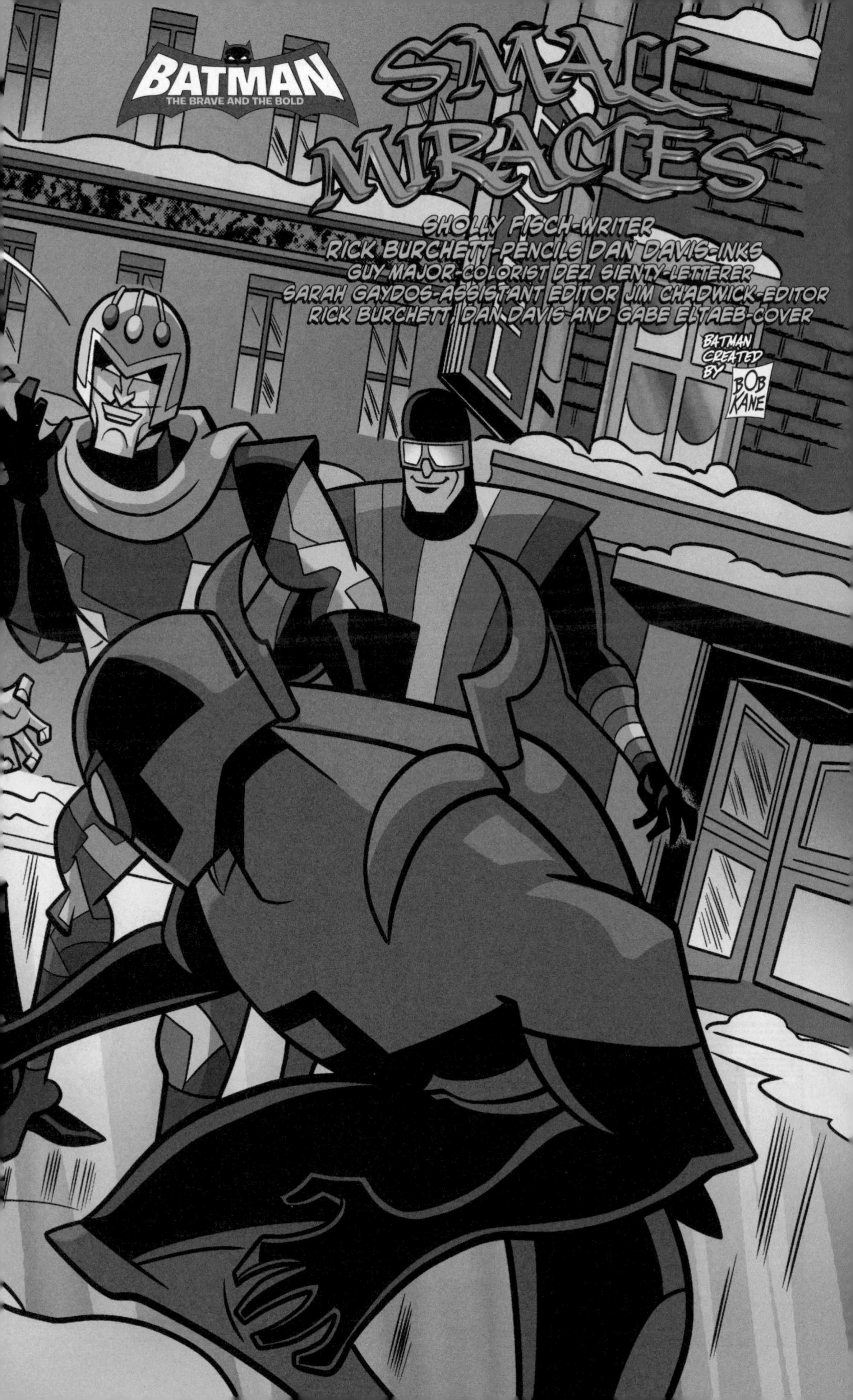
BATMAN
THE BRAVE AND THE BOLD
SMALL MIRACLES
SHOLLY FISCH-WRITER
RICK BURCHETT-PENCILS DAN DAVIS-INKS
GUY MAJOR-COLORIST DEZI SIENTY-LETTERER
SARAH GAYDOS-ASSISTANT EDITOR JIM CHADWICK-EDITOR
RICK BURCHETT, DAN DAVIS AND GABE ELTAEB-COVER
BATMAN CREATED BY BOB KANE

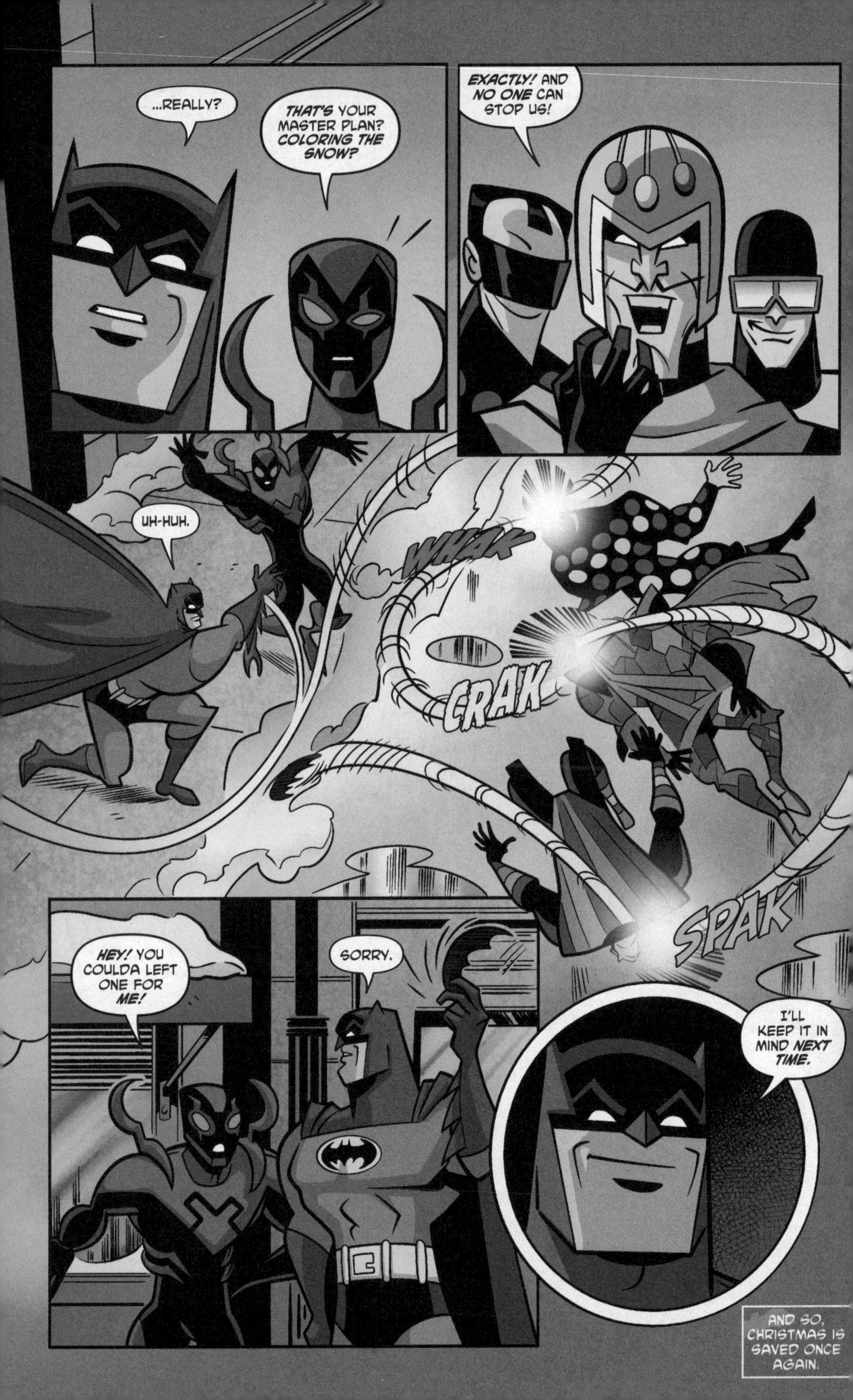
...REALLY?
THAT'S YOUR MASTER PLAN? COLORING THE SNOW?
EXACTLY! AND NO ONE CAN STOP US!
UH-HUH.
WHAK
CRAK
SPAK
HEY! YOU COULDA LEFT ONE FOR ME!
SORRY.
I'LL KEEP IT IN MIND NEXT TIME.
AND SO, CHRISTMAS IS SAVED ONCE AGAIN.

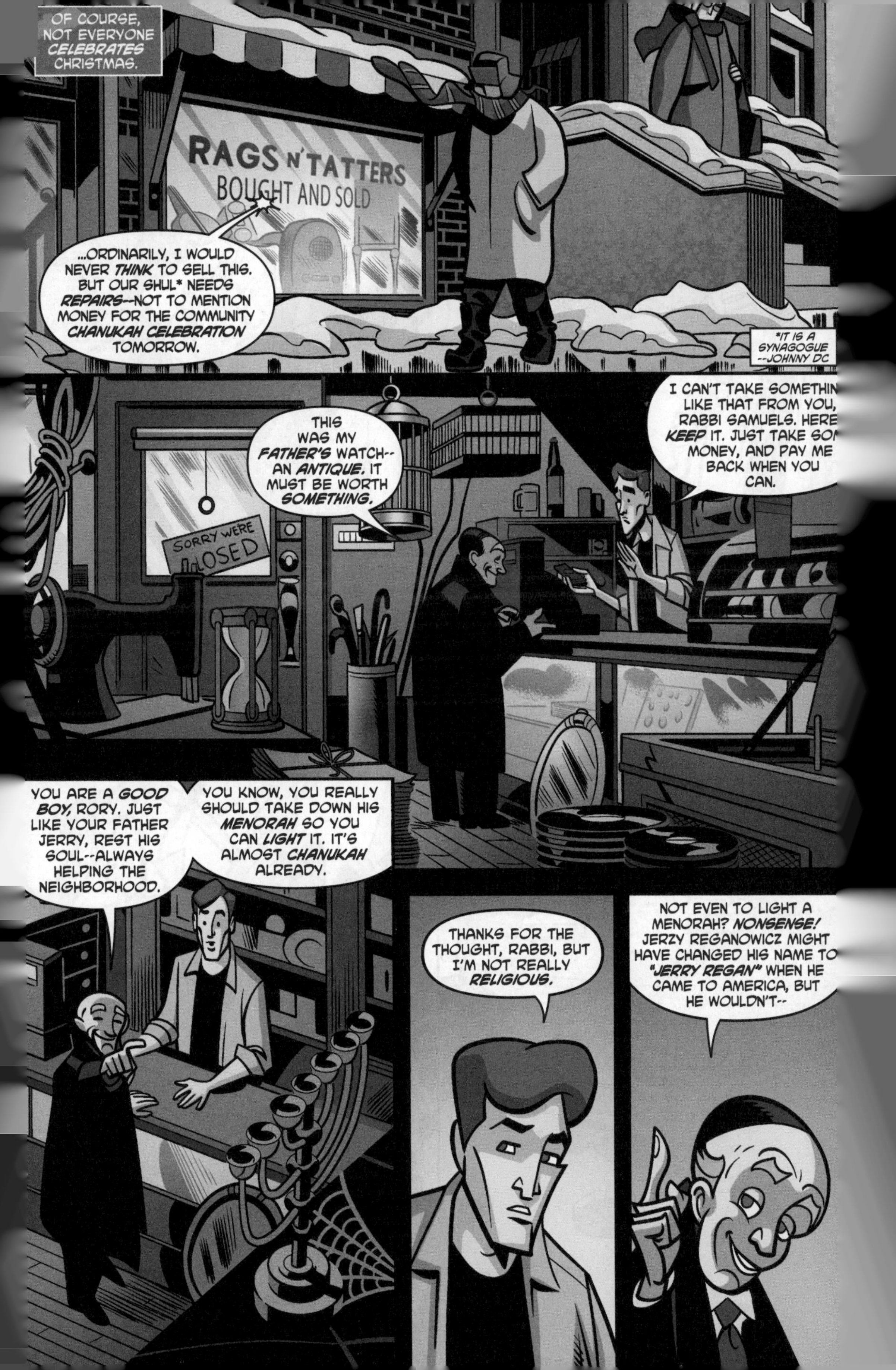
OF COURSE, NOT EVERYONE CELEBRATES CHRISTMAS.
RAGS N' TATTERS BOUGHT AND SOLD
...ORDINARILY, I WOULD NEVER THINK TO SELL THIS. BUT OUR SHUL* NEEDS REPAIRS--NOT TO MENTION MONEY FOR THE COMMUNITY CHANUKAH CELEBRATION TOMORROW.
*IT IS A SYNAGOGUE --JOHNNY DC
THIS WAS MY FATHER'S WATCH--AN ANTIQUE. IT MUST BE WORTH SOMETHING.
SORRY WERE CLOSED
I CAN'T TAKE SOMETHING LIKE THAT FROM YOU, RABBI SAMUELS. HERE, KEEP IT. JUST TAKE SOME MONEY, AND PAY ME BACK WHEN YOU CAN.
YOU ARE A GOOD BOY, RORY. JUST LIKE YOUR FATHER JERRY, REST HIS SOUL--ALWAYS HELPING THE NEIGHBORHOOD.
YOU KNOW, YOU REALLY SHOULD TAKE DOWN HIS MENORAH SO YOU CAN LIGHT IT. IT'S ALMOST CHANUKAH ALREADY.
THANKS FOR THE THOUGHT, RABBI, BUT I'M NOT REALLY RELIGIOUS.
NOT EVEN TO LIGHT A MENORAH? NONSENSE! JERZY REGANOWICZ MIGHT HAVE CHANGED HIS NAME TO "JERRY REGAN" WHEN HE CAME TO AMERICA, BUT HE WOULDN'T--

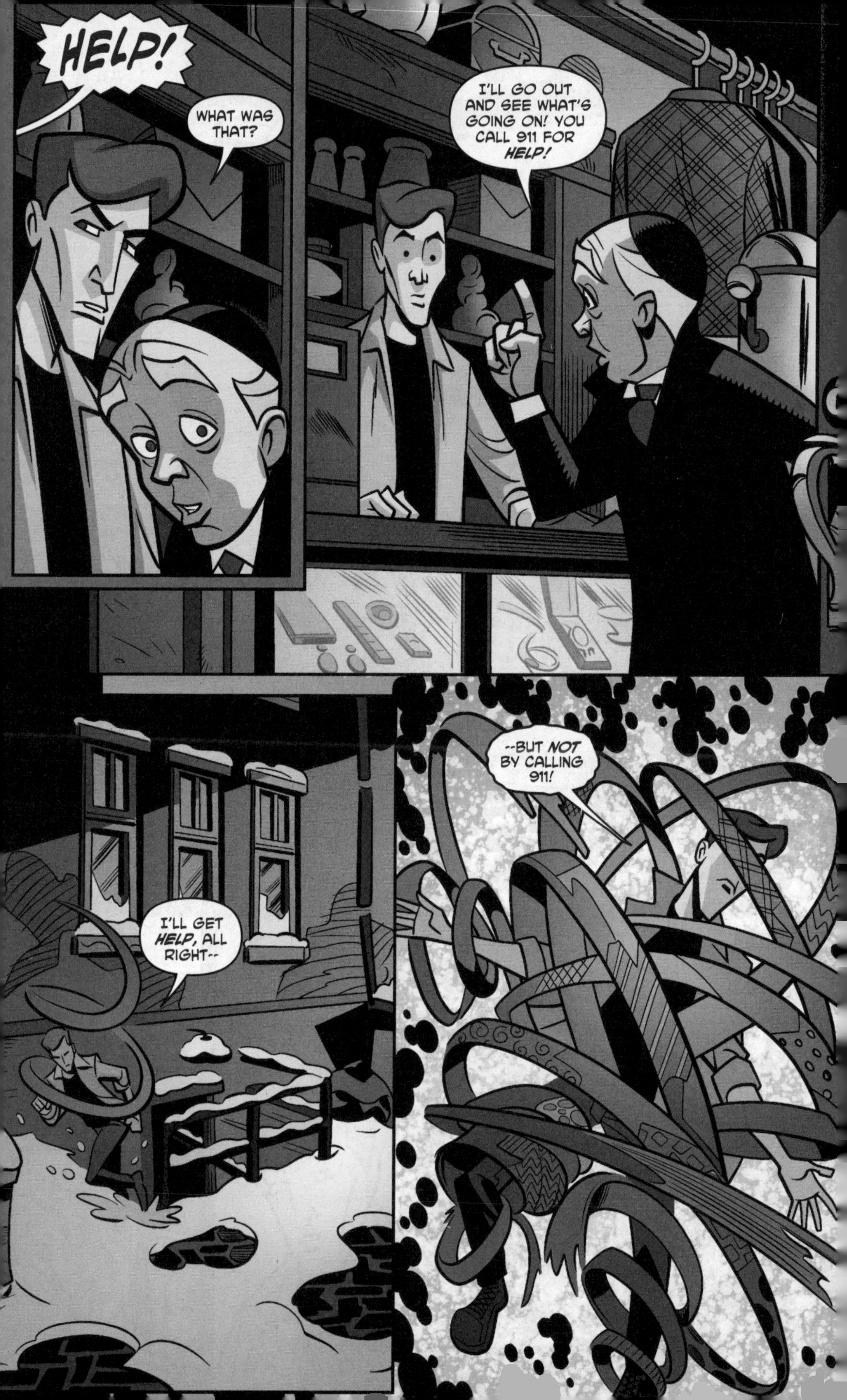
HELP!
WHAT WAS THAT?
I'LL GO OUT AND SEE WHAT'S GOING ON! YOU CALL 911 FOR HELP!
I'LL GET HELP, ALL RIGHT--
--BUT NOT BY CALLING 911!

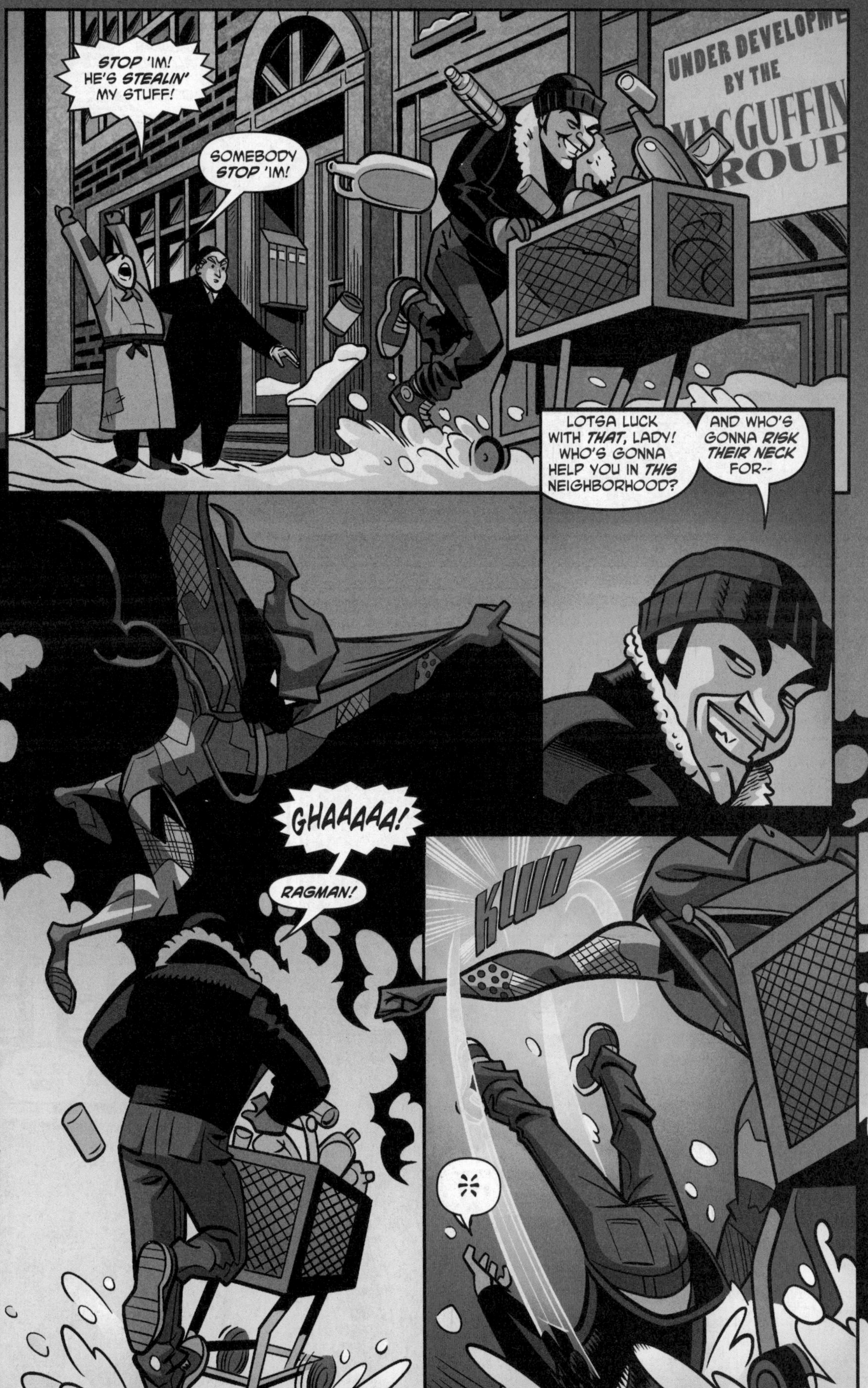
STOP 'IM! HE'S STEALIN' MY STUFF!
SOMEBODY STOP 'IM!
UNDER DEVELOPME
BY THE
MACGUFFIN
ROUP
LOTSA LUCK WITH THAT, LADY! WHO'S GONNA HELP YOU IN THIS NEIGHBORHOOD?
AND WHO'S GONNA RISK THEIR NECK FOR--
GHAAAAA!
RAGMAN!
KLUD

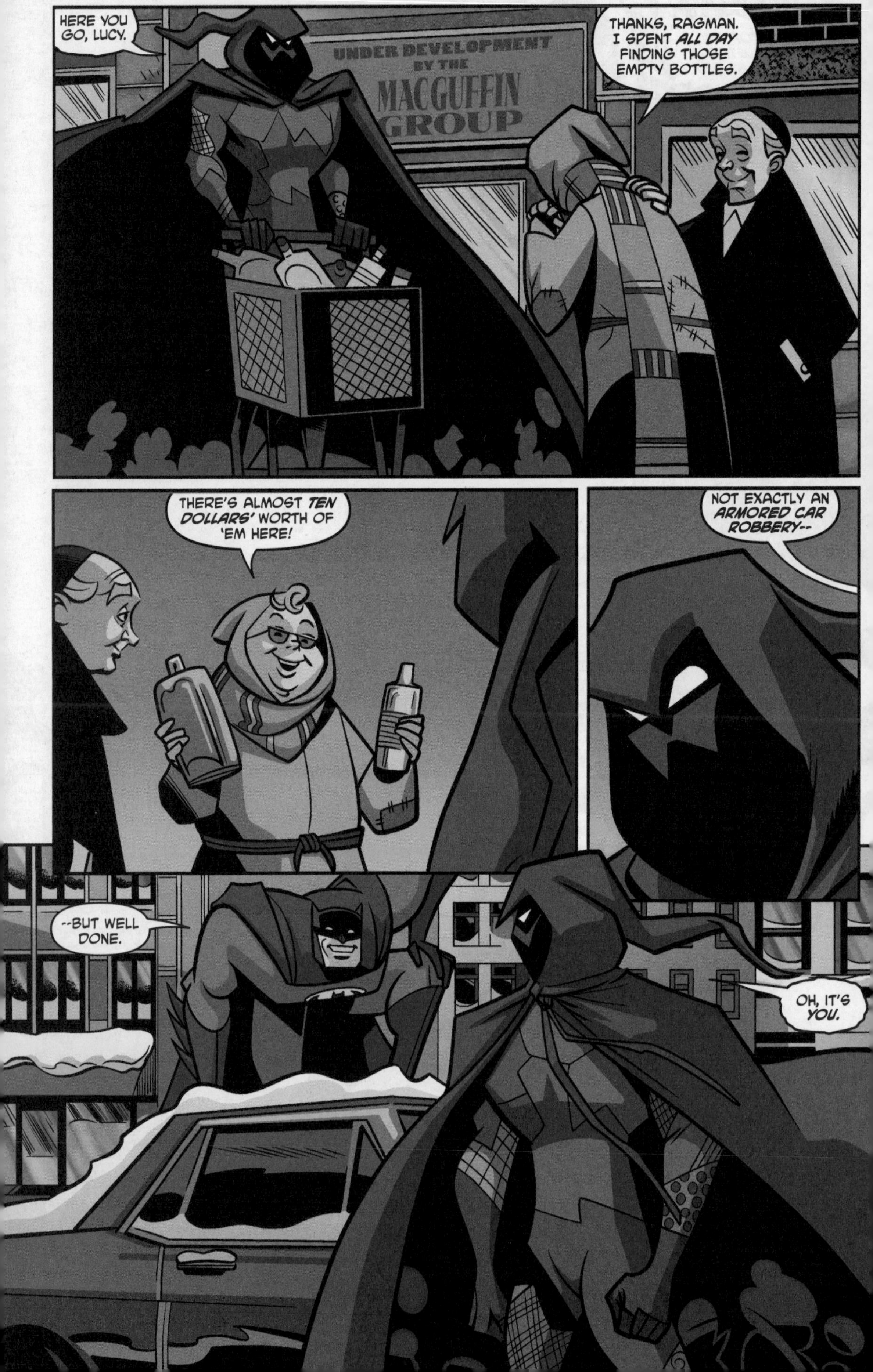
HERE YOU GO, LUCY.
UNDER DEVELOPMENT BY THE MACGUFFIN GROUP
THANKS, RAGMAN. I SPENT ALL DAY FINDING THOSE EMPTY BOTTLES.
THERE'S ALMOST TEN DOLLARS' WORTH OF 'EM HERE!
NOT EXACTLY AN ARMORED CAR ROBBERY--
--BUT WELL DONE.
OH, IT'S YOU.

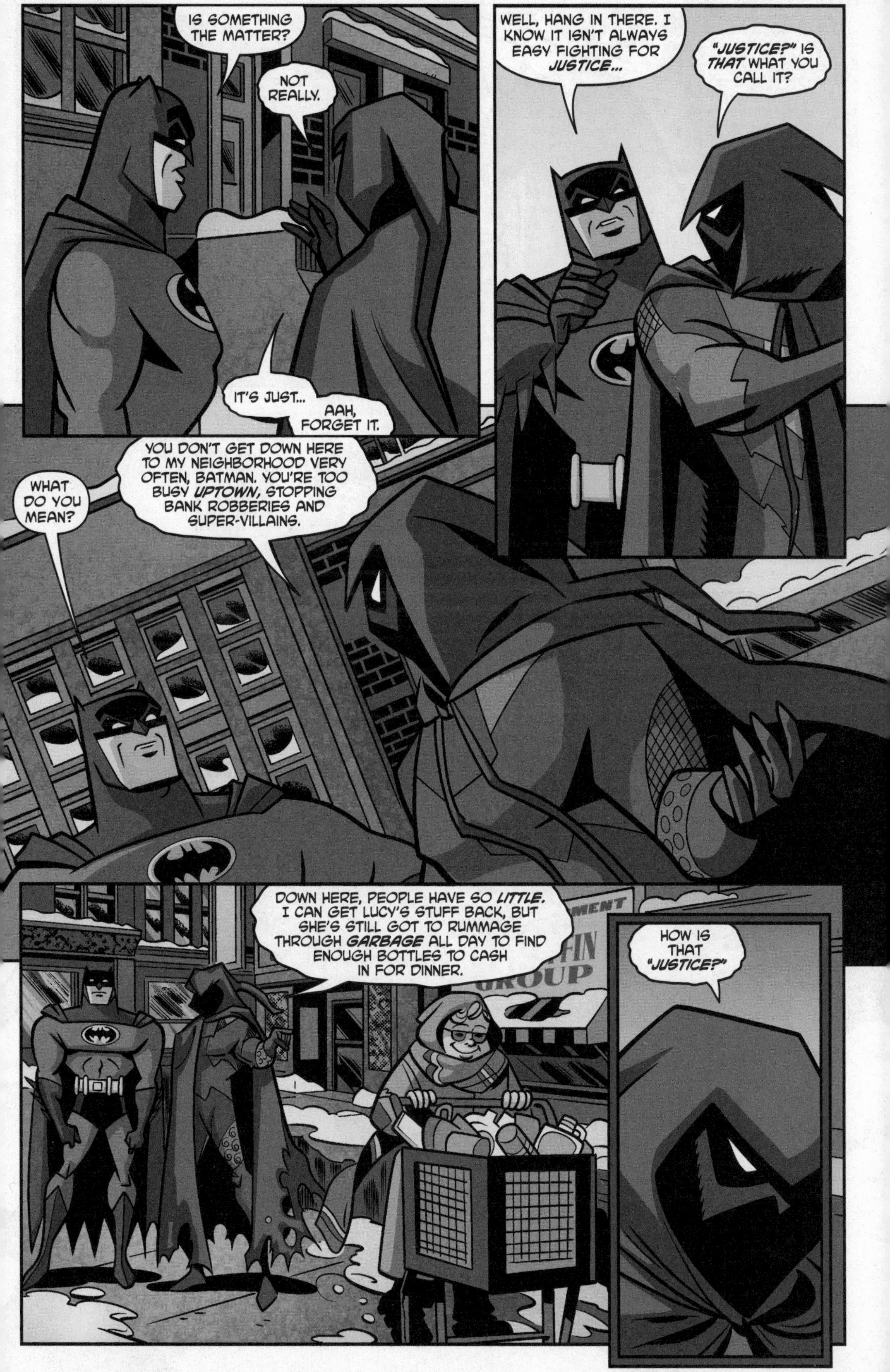

IS SOMETHING THE MATTER?
NOT REALLY.
IT'S JUST... AAH, FORGET IT.
WELL, HANG IN THERE. I KNOW IT ISN'T ALWAYS EASY FIGHTING FOR JUSTICE...
"JUSTICE?" IS THAT WHAT YOU CALL IT?
WHAT DO YOU MEAN?
YOU DON'T GET DOWN HERE TO MY NEIGHBORHOOD VERY OFTEN, BATMAN. YOU'RE TOO BUSY UPTOWN, STOPPING BANK ROBBERIES AND SUPER-VILLAINS.
DOWN HERE, PEOPLE HAVE SO LITTLE. I CAN GET LUCY'S STUFF BACK, BUT SHE'S STILL GOT TO RUMMAGE THROUGH GARBAGE ALL DAY TO FIND ENOUGH BOTTLES TO CASH IN FOR DINNER.
HOW IS THAT "JUSTICE?"

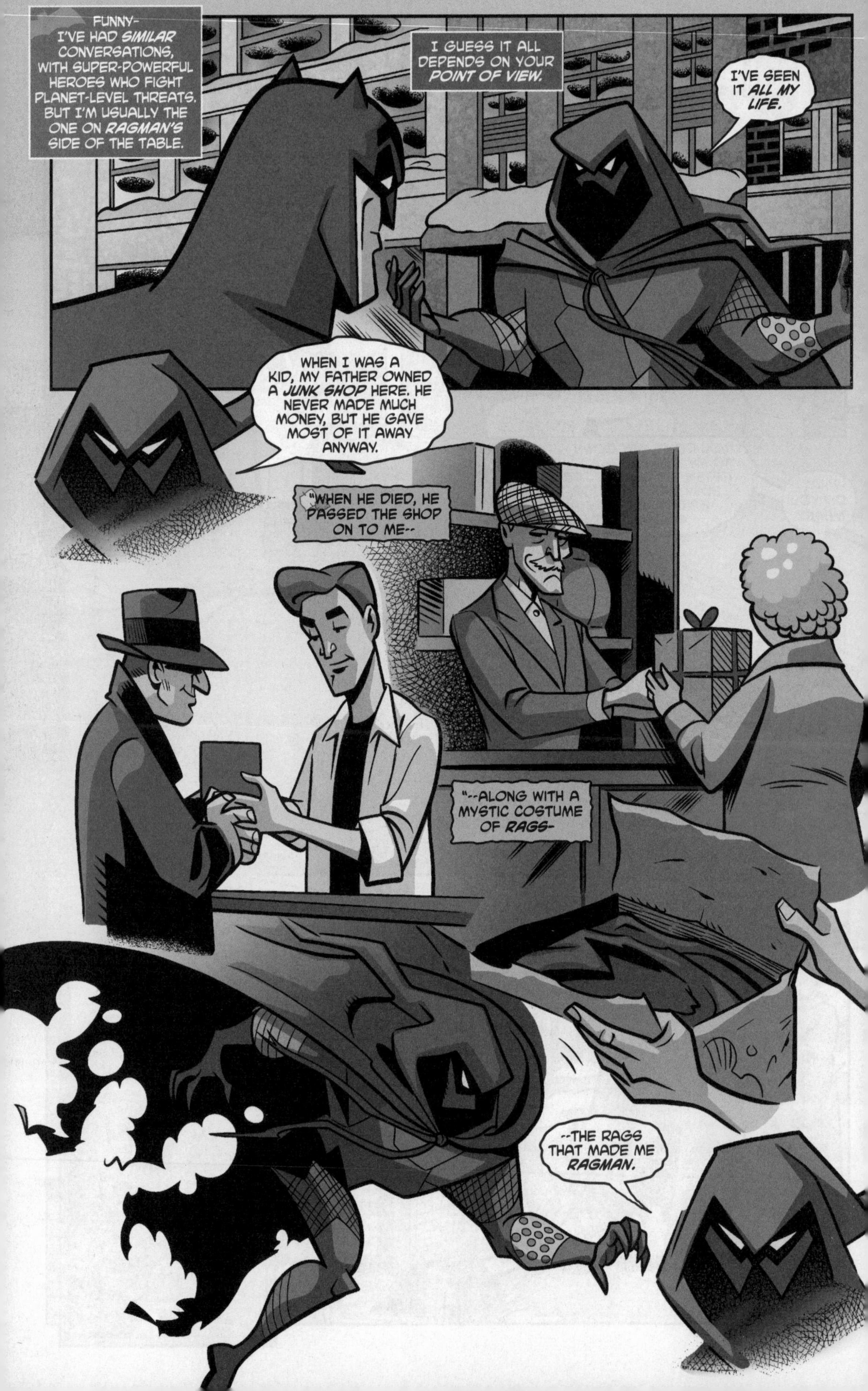
FUNNY-
I'VE HAD SIMILAR CONVERSATIONS, WITH SUPER-POWERFUL HEROES WHO FIGHT PLANET-LEVEL THREATS. BUT I'M USUALLY THE ONE ON RAGMAN'S SIDE OF THE TABLE.
I GUESS IT ALL DEPENDS ON YOUR POINT OF VIEW.
I'VE SEEN IT ALL MY LIFE.
WHEN I WAS A KID, MY FATHER OWNED A JUNK SHOP HERE. HE NEVER MADE MUCH MONEY, BUT HE GAVE MOST OF IT AWAY ANYWAY.
"WHEN HE DIED, HE PASSED THE SHOP ON TO ME--
"--ALONG WITH A MYSTIC COSTUME OF RAGS-
--THE RAGS THAT MADE ME RAGMAN.

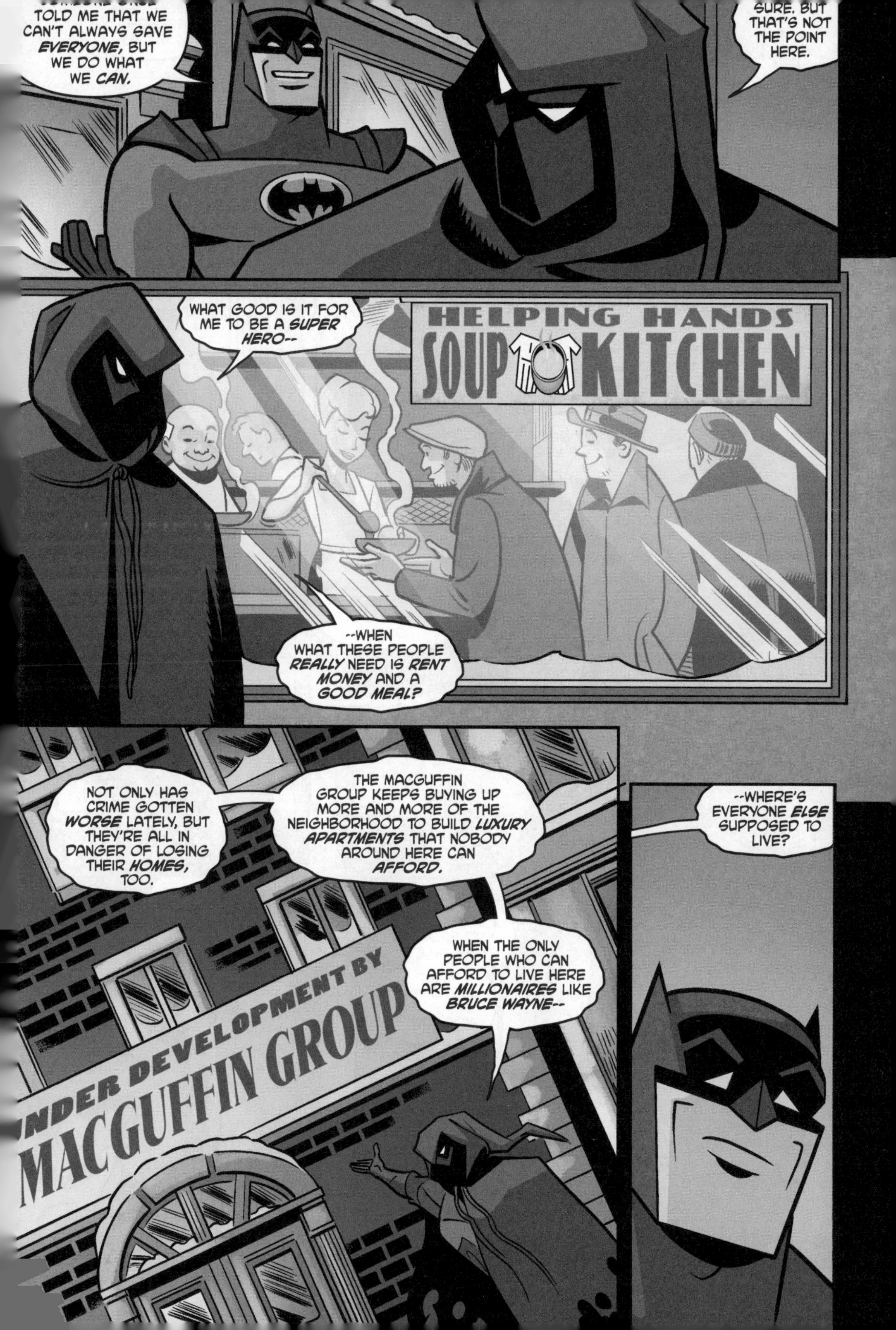
TOLD ME THAT WE CAN'T ALWAYS SAVE EVERYONE, BUT WE DO WHAT WE CAN.
SURE. BUT THAT'S NOT THE POINT HERE.
WHAT GOOD IS IT FOR ME TO BE A SUPER HERO--
HELPING HANDS
SOUP KITCHEN
--WHEN WHAT THESE PEOPLE REALLY NEED IS RENT MONEY AND A GOOD MEAL?
NOT ONLY HAS CRIME GOTTEN WORSE LATELY, BUT THEY'RE ALL IN DANGER OF LOSING THEIR HOMES, TOO.
THE MACGUFFIN GROUP KEEPS BUYING UP MORE AND MORE OF THE NEIGHBORHOOD TO BUILD LUXURY APARTMENTS THAT NOBODY AROUND HERE CAN AFFORD.
UNDER DEVELOPMENT BY
MACGUFFIN GROUP
WHEN THE ONLY PEOPLE WHO CAN AFFORD TO LIVE HERE ARE MILLIONAIRES LIKE BRUCE WAYNE--
--WHERE'S EVERYONE ELSE SUPPOSED TO LIVE?

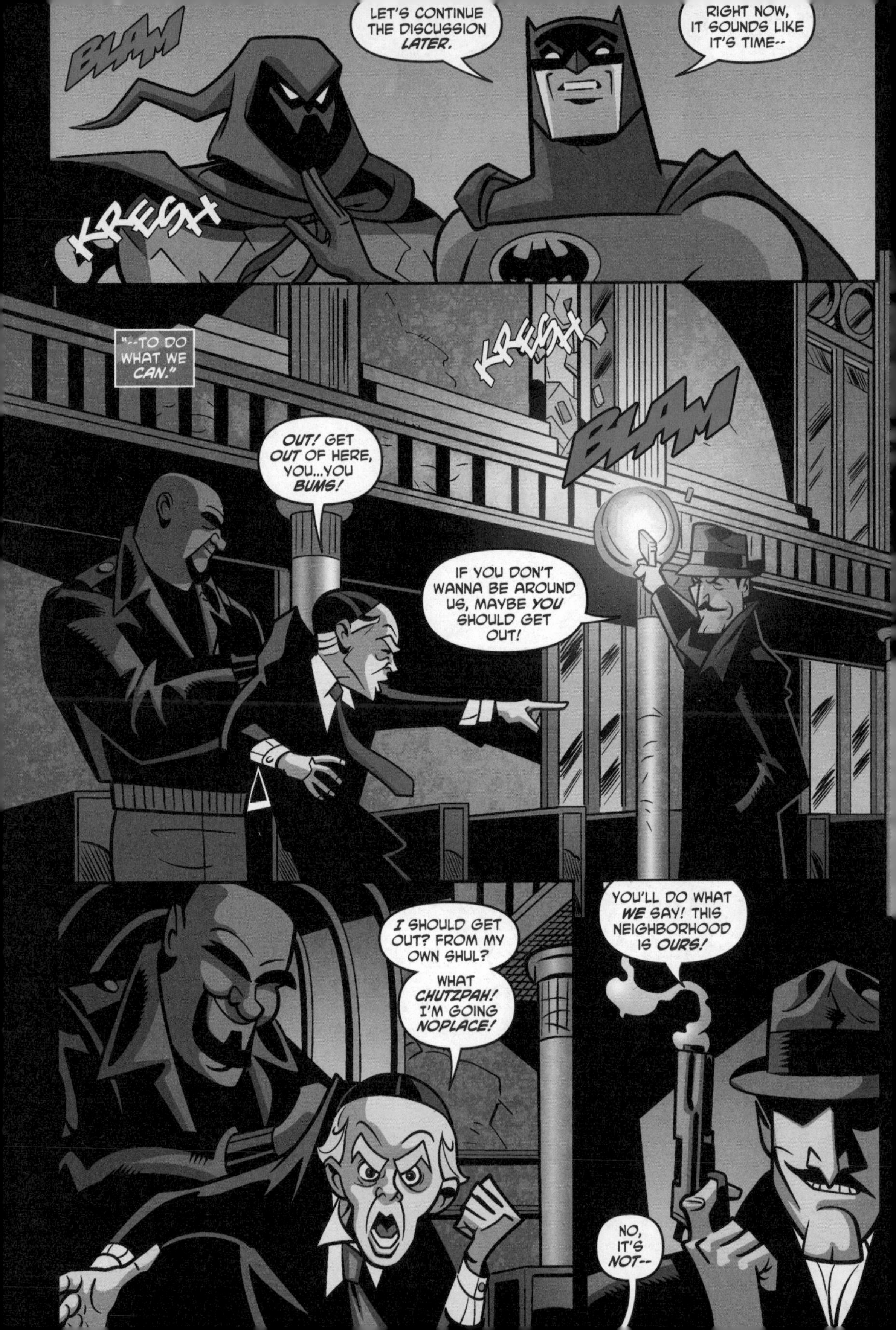
BLAM
LET'S CONTINUE THE DISCUSSION LATER.
RIGHT NOW, IT SOUNDS LIKE IT'S TIME--
KRESH
"--TO DO WHAT WE CAN."
KRESH
BLAM
OUT! GET OUT OF HERE, YOU...YOU BUMS!
IF YOU DON'T WANNA BE AROUND US, MAYBE YOU SHOULD GET OUT!
I SHOULD GET OUT? FROM MY OWN SHUL?
WHAT CHUTZPAH! I'M GOING NOPLACE!
YOU'LL DO WHAT WE SAY! THIS NEIGHBORHOOD IS OURS!
NO, IT'S NOT--

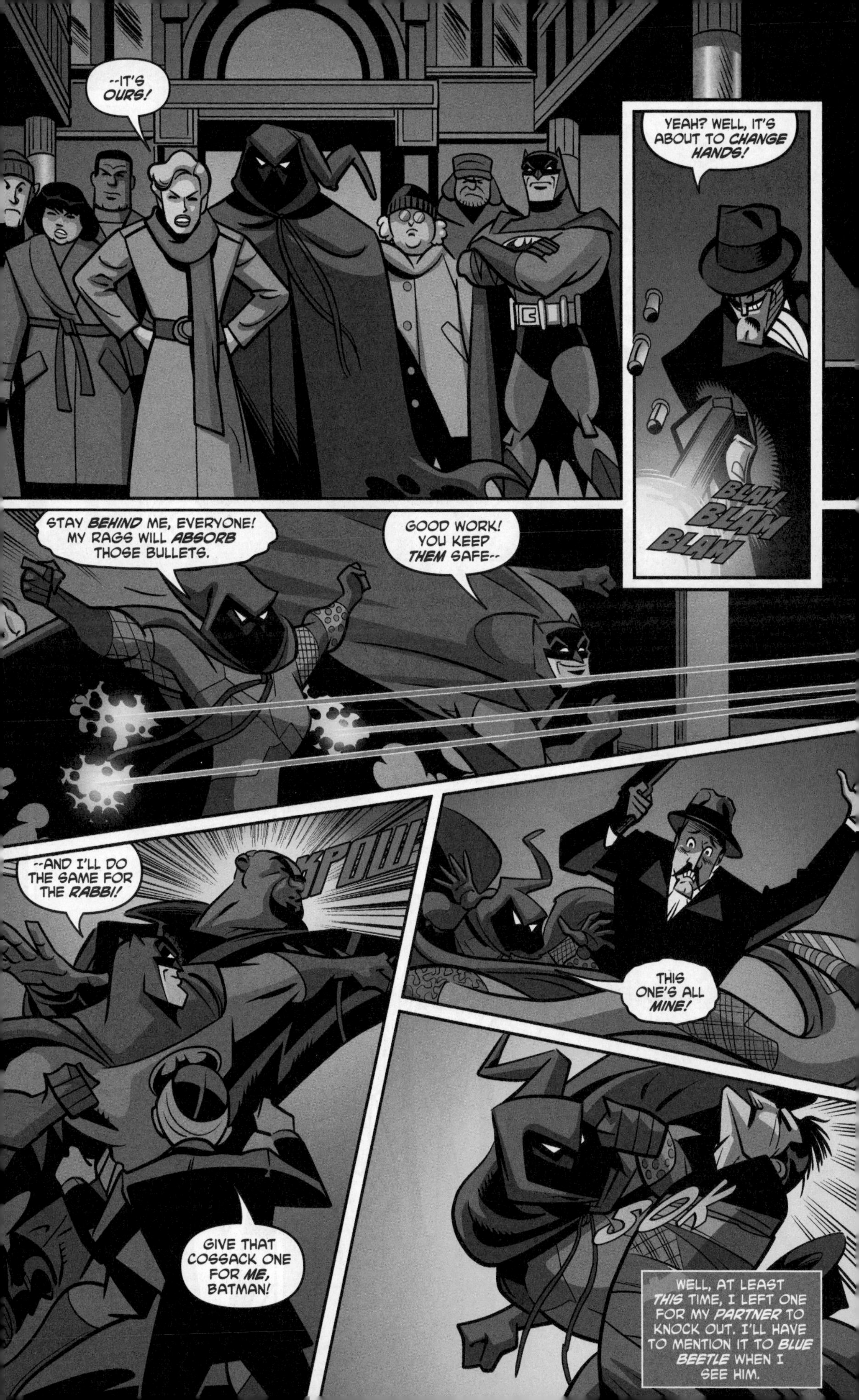
--IT'S *OURS!*
YEAH? WELL, IT'S ABOUT TO *CHANGE HANDS!*
BLAM BLAM BLAM
STAY *BEHIND* ME, EVERYONE! MY RAGS WILL *ABSORB* THOSE BULLETS.
GOOD WORK! YOU KEEP *THEM* SAFE--
--AND I'LL DO THE SAME FOR THE *RABBI!*
THIS ONE'S ALL *MINE!*
GIVE THAT COSSACK ONE FOR *ME,* BATMAN!
SOK
WELL, AT LEAST *THIS* TIME, I LEFT ONE FOR MY *PARTNER* TO KNOCK OUT. I'LL HAVE TO MENTION IT TO *BLUE BEETLE* WHEN I SEE HIM.

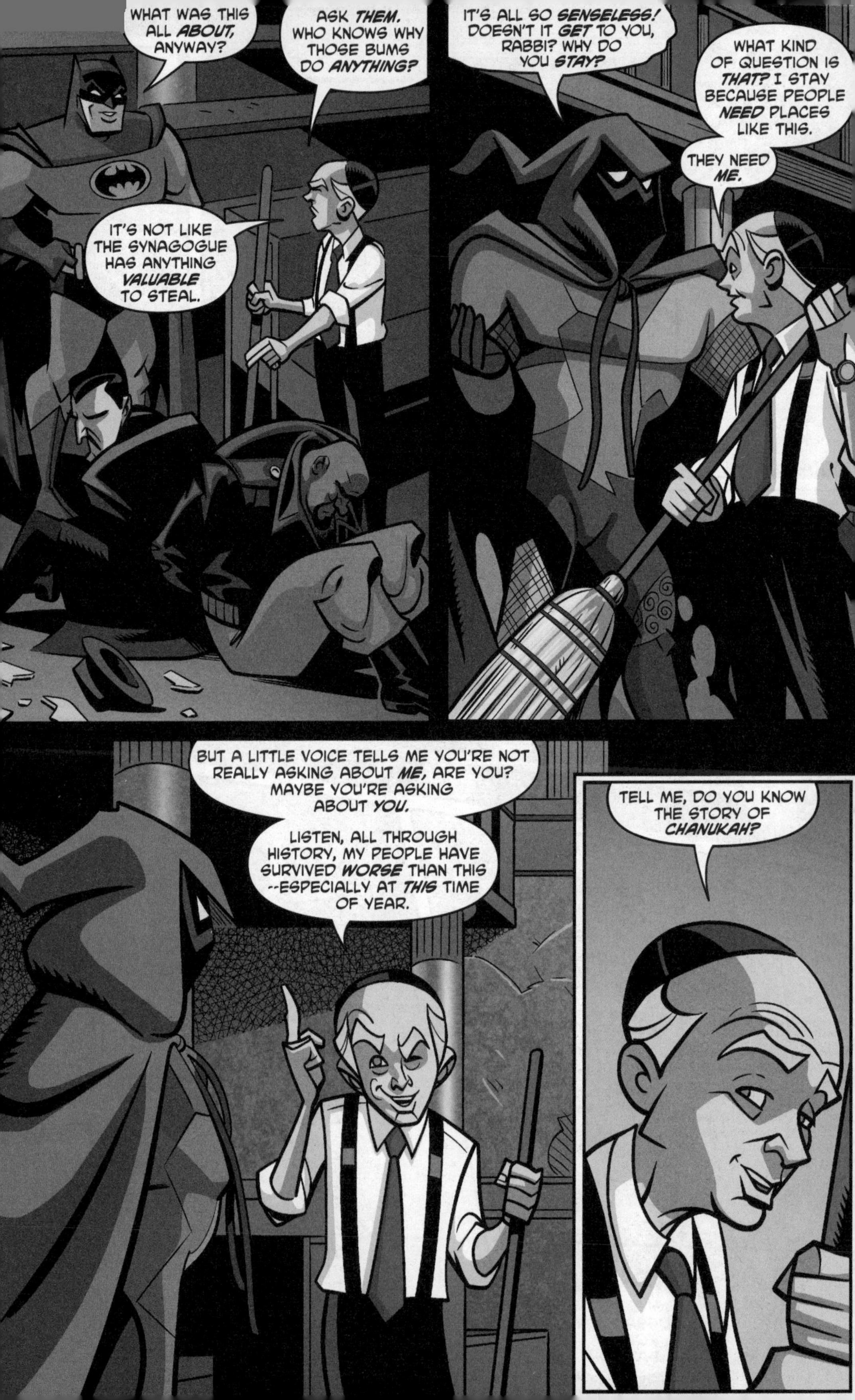
WHAT WAS THIS ALL ABOUT, ANYWAY?
ASK THEM. WHO KNOWS WHY THOSE BUMS DO ANYTHING?
IT'S NOT LIKE THE SYNAGOGUE HAS ANYTHING VALUABLE TO STEAL.
IT'S ALL SO SENSELESS! DOESN'T IT GET TO YOU, RABBI? WHY DO YOU STAY?
WHAT KIND OF QUESTION IS THAT? I STAY BECAUSE PEOPLE NEED PLACES LIKE THIS.
THEY NEED ME.
BUT A LITTLE VOICE TELLS ME YOU'RE NOT REALLY ASKING ABOUT ME, ARE YOU? MAYBE YOU'RE ASKING ABOUT YOU.
LISTEN, ALL THROUGH HISTORY, MY PEOPLE HAVE SURVIVED WORSE THAN THIS --ESPECIALLY AT THIS TIME OF YEAR.
TELL ME, DO YOU KNOW THE STORY OF CHANUKAH?

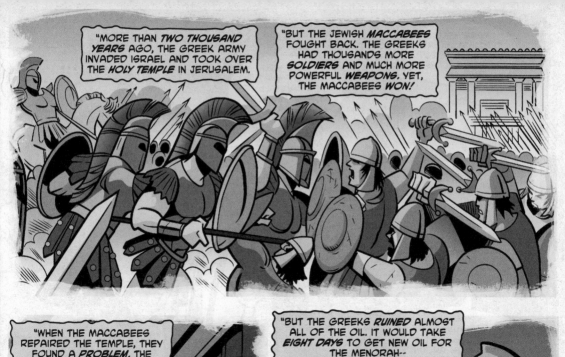

"MORE THAN *TWO THOUSAND YEARS* AGO, THE GREEK ARMY INVADED ISRAEL AND TOOK OVER THE *HOLY TEMPLE* IN JERUSALEM."

"BUT THE JEWISH *MACCABEES* FOUGHT BACK. THE GREEKS HAD THOUSANDS MORE *SOLDIERS* AND MUCH MORE POWERFUL *WEAPONS.* YET, THE MACCABEES *WON!*"

"WHEN THE MACCABEES REPAIRED THE TEMPLE, THEY FOUND A *PROBLEM.* THE TEMPLE'S *MENORAH* WAS A SYMBOL OF *FAITH,* SO IT WAS SUPPOSED TO STAY LIT *ALL THE TIME.*"

"BUT THE GREEKS *RUINED* ALMOST ALL OF THE OIL. IT WOULD TAKE *EIGHT DAYS* TO GET NEW OIL FOR THE MENORAH--"

"--AND THEY ONLY HAD ENOUGH OIL LEFT TO BURN FOR *ONE* DAY."

"THANKFULLY, THOUGH, THERE WAS A *MIRACLE.* THAT LITTLE BIT OF OIL, ONLY ENOUGH FOR *ONE* DAY--"

"--BURNED FOR *ALL EIGHT DAYS* INSTEAD!"

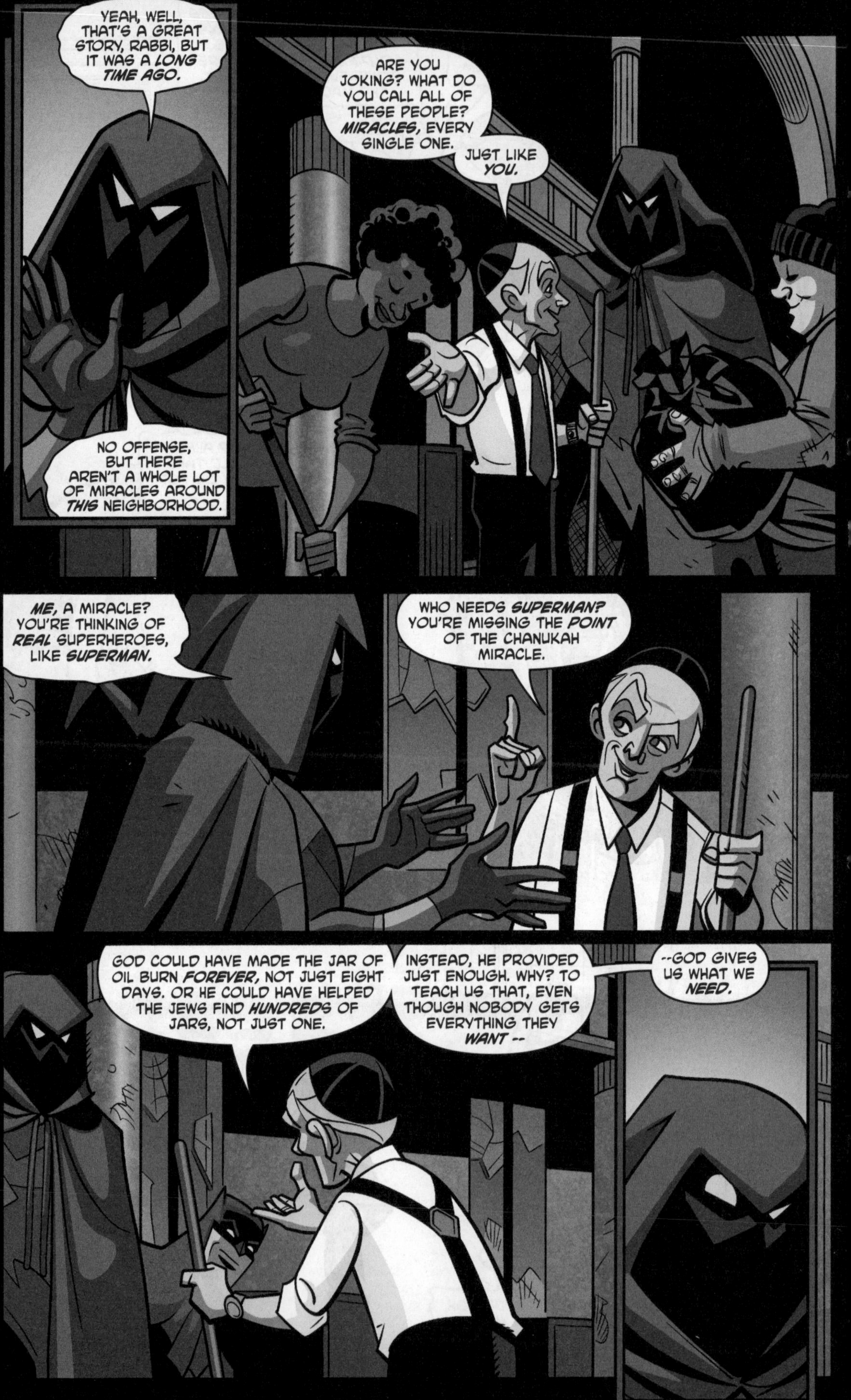
YEAH, WELL, THAT'S A GREAT STORY, RABBI, BUT IT WAS A LONG TIME AGO.
NO OFFENSE, BUT THERE AREN'T A WHOLE LOT OF MIRACLES AROUND THIS NEIGHBORHOOD.
ARE YOU JOKING? WHAT DO YOU CALL ALL OF THESE PEOPLE? MIRACLES, EVERY SINGLE ONE.
JUST LIKE YOU.
ME, A MIRACLE? YOU'RE THINKING OF REAL SUPERHEROES, LIKE SUPERMAN.
WHO NEEDS SUPERMAN? YOU'RE MISSING THE POINT OF THE CHANUKAH MIRACLE.
GOD COULD HAVE MADE THE JAR OF OIL BURN FOREVER, NOT JUST EIGHT DAYS. OR HE COULD HAVE HELPED THE JEWS FIND HUNDREDS OF JARS, NOT JUST ONE.
INSTEAD, HE PROVIDED JUST ENOUGH. WHY? TO TEACH US THAT, EVEN THOUGH NOBODY GETS EVERYTHING THEY WANT --
--GOD GIVES US WHAT WE NEED.

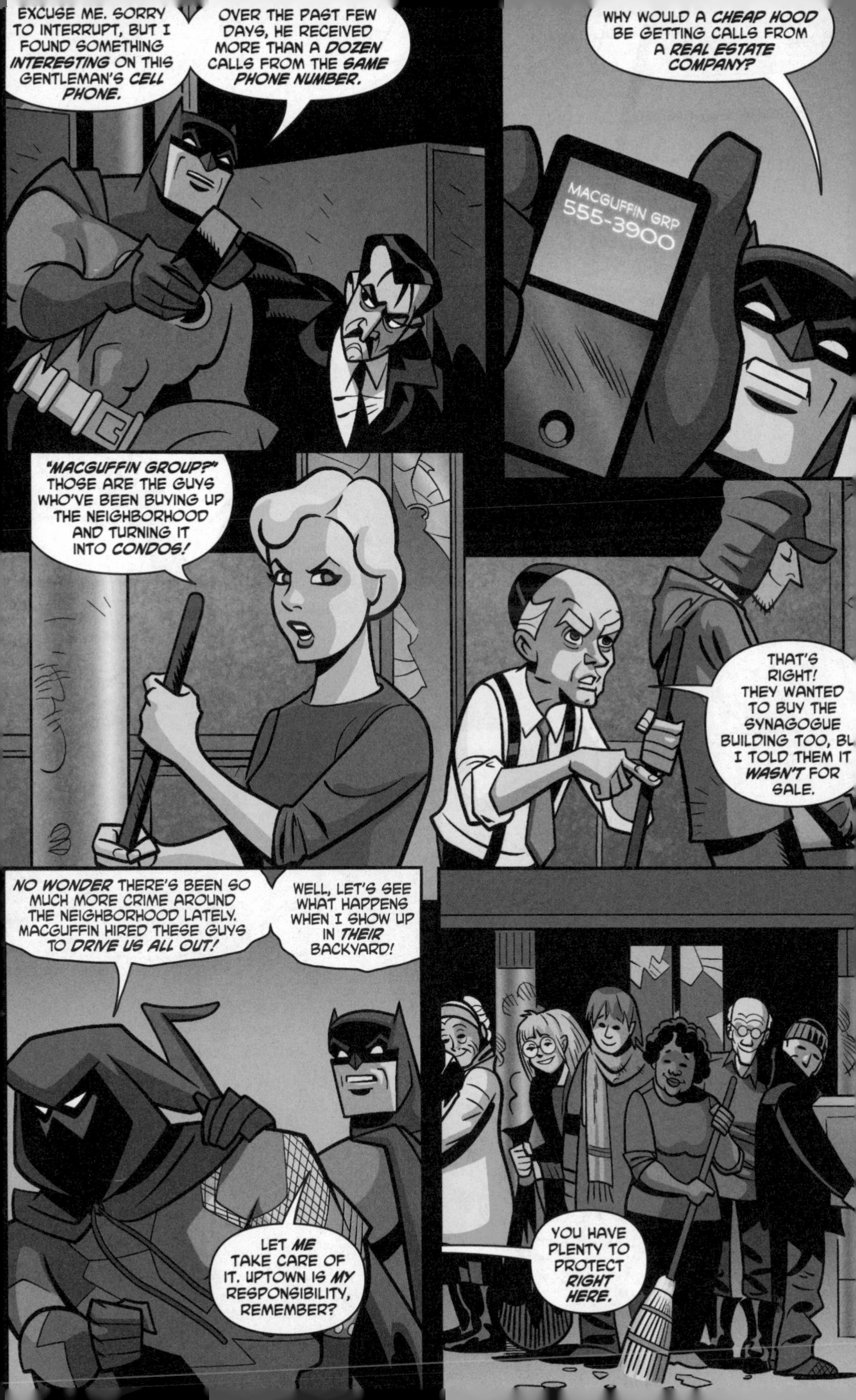
EXCUSE ME. SORRY TO INTERRUPT, BUT I FOUND SOMETHING INTERESTING ON THIS GENTLEMAN'S CELL PHONE.
OVER THE PAST FEW DAYS, HE RECEIVED MORE THAN A DOZEN CALLS FROM THE SAME PHONE NUMBER.
MACGUFFIN GRP
555-3900
WHY WOULD A CHEAP HOOD BE GETTING CALLS FROM A REAL ESTATE COMPANY?
"MACGUFFIN GROUP?" THOSE ARE THE GUYS WHO'VE BEEN BUYING UP THE NEIGHBORHOOD AND TURNING IT INTO CONDOS!
THAT'S RIGHT! THEY WANTED TO BUY THE SYNAGOGUE BUILDING TOO, BU I TOLD THEM IT WASN'T FOR SALE.
NO WONDER THERE'S BEEN SO MUCH MORE CRIME AROUND THE NEIGHBORHOOD LATELY. MACGUFFIN HIRED THESE GUYS TO DRIVE US ALL OUT!
WELL, LET'S SEE WHAT HAPPENS WHEN I SHOW UP IN THEIR BACKYARD!
LET ME TAKE CARE OF IT. UPTOWN IS MY RESPONSIBILITY, REMEMBER?
YOU HAVE PLENTY TO PROTECT RIGHT HERE.

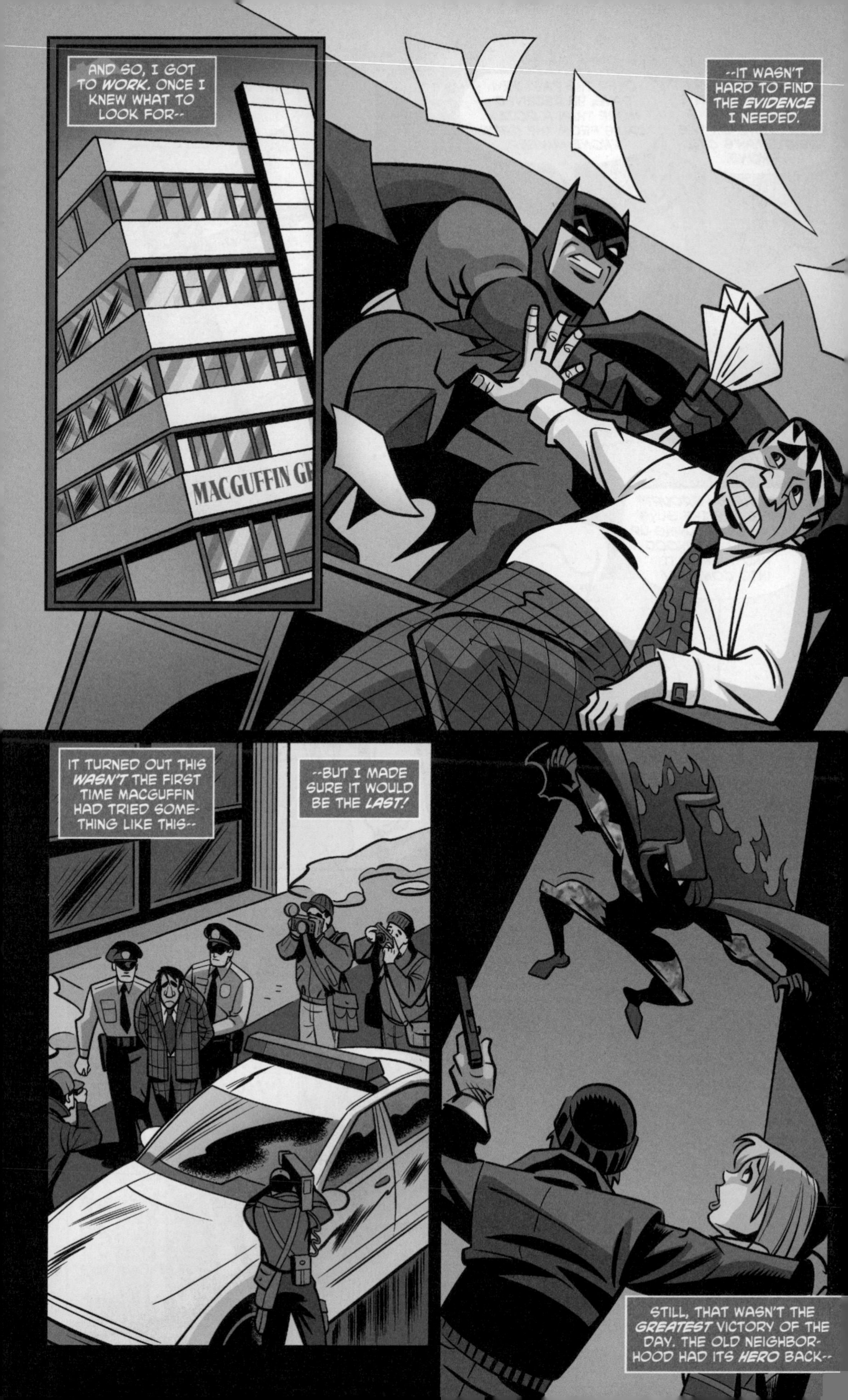
AND SO, I GOT TO *WORK*. ONCE I KNEW WHAT TO LOOK FOR--
MACGUFFIN GR
--IT WASN'T HARD TO FIND THE *EVIDENCE* I NEEDED.
IT TURNED OUT THIS *WASN'T* THE FIRST TIME MACGUFFIN HAD TRIED SOME-THING LIKE THIS--
--BUT I MADE SURE IT WOULD BE THE *LAST!*
STILL, THAT WASN'T THE *GREATEST* VICTORY OF THE DAY. THE OLD NEIGHBOR-HOOD HAD ITS *HERO* BACK--

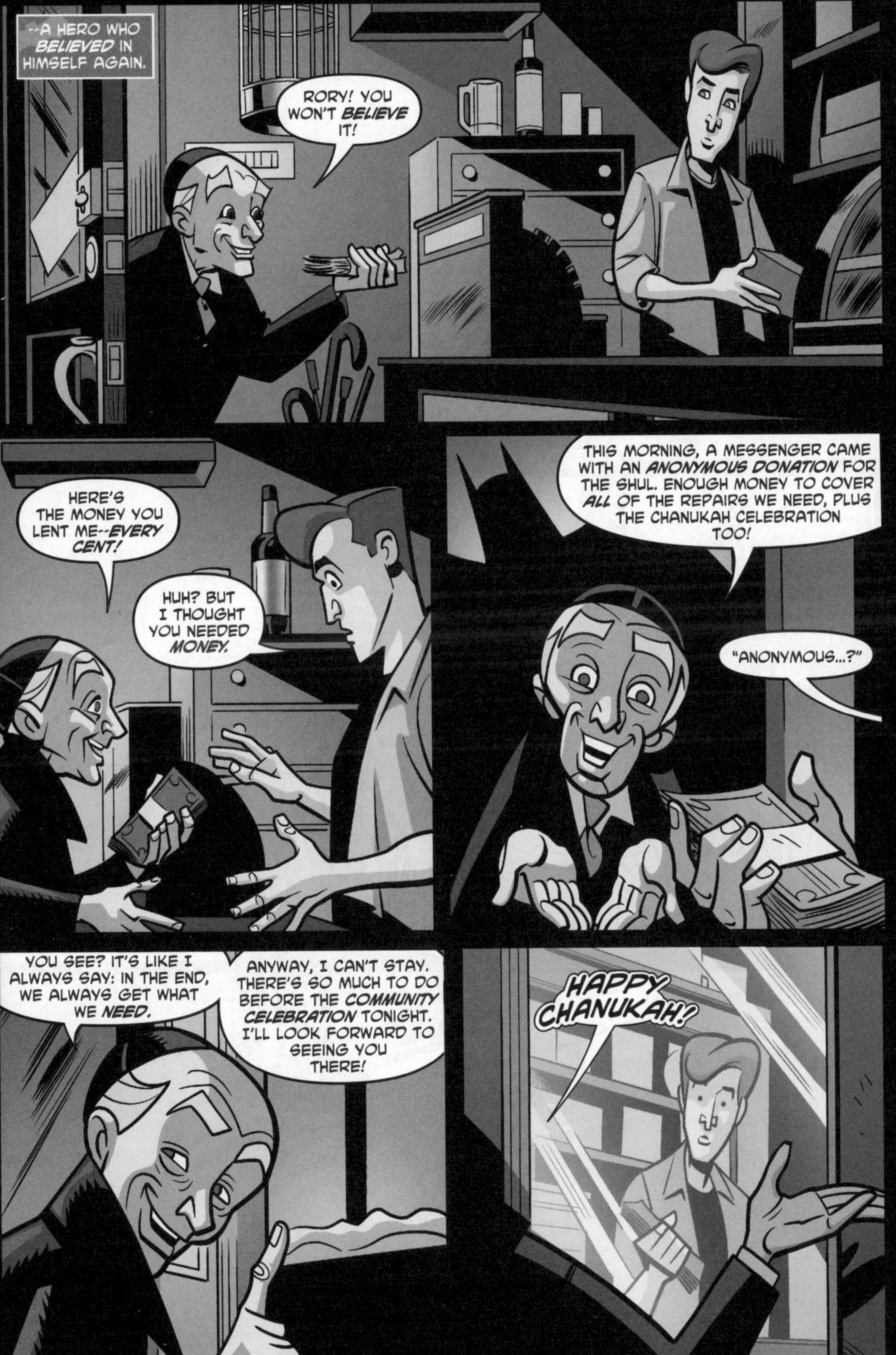
--A HERO WHO BELIEVED IN HIMSELF AGAIN.
RORY! YOU WON'T BELIEVE IT!
HERE'S THE MONEY YOU LENT ME--EVERY CENT!
HUH? BUT I THOUGHT YOU NEEDED MONEY.
THIS MORNING, A MESSENGER CAME WITH AN ANONYMOUS DONATION FOR THE SHUL. ENOUGH MONEY TO COVER ALL OF THE REPAIRS WE NEED, PLUS THE CHANUKAH CELEBRATION TOO!
"ANONYMOUS...?"
YOU SEE? IT'S LIKE I ALWAYS SAY: IN THE END, WE ALWAYS GET WHAT WE NEED.
ANYWAY, I CAN'T STAY. THERE'S SO MUCH TO DO BEFORE THE COMMUNITY CELEBRATION TONIGHT. I'LL LOOK FORWARD TO SEEING YOU THERE!
HAPPY CHANUKAH!

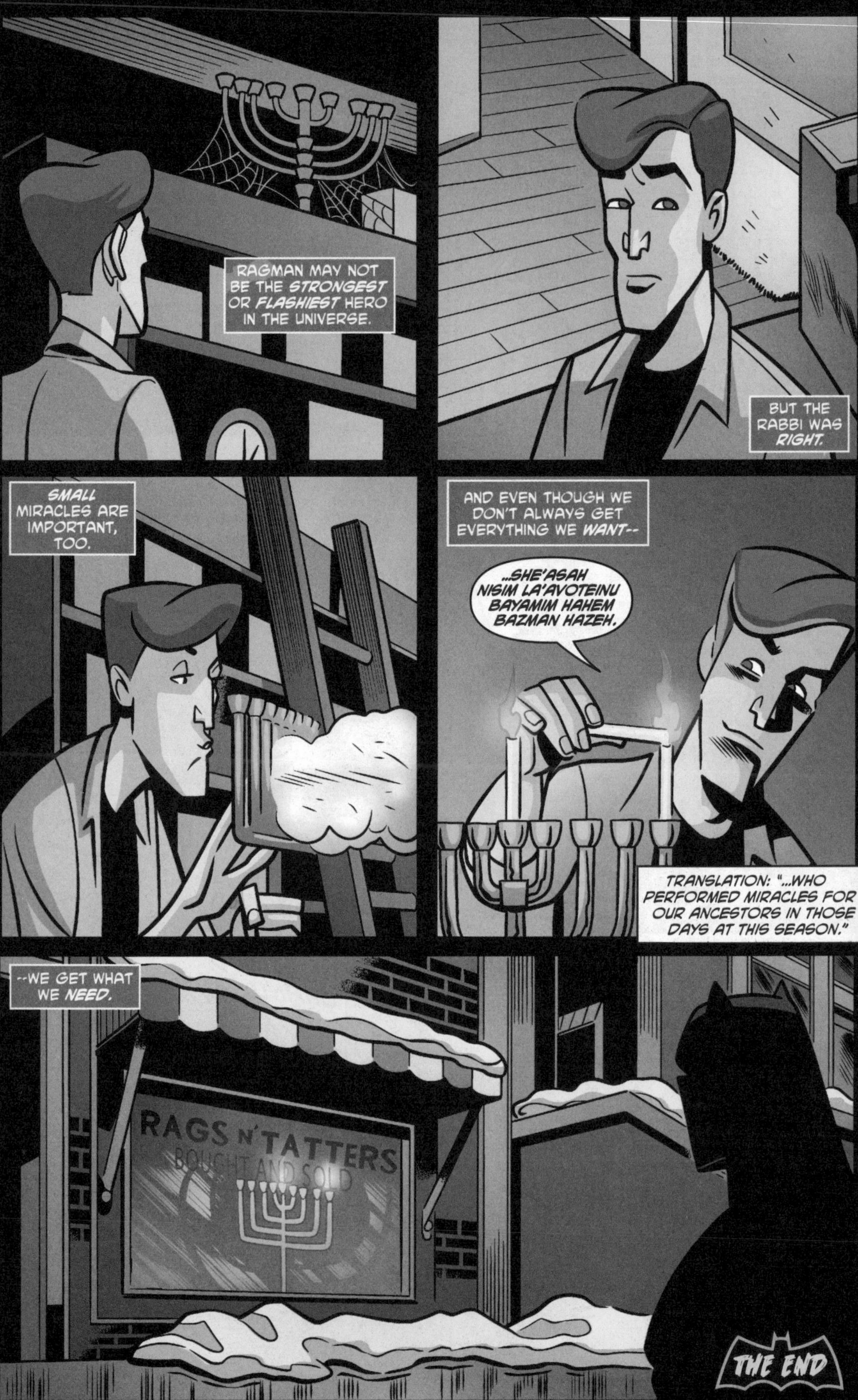
RAGMAN MAY NOT BE THE STRONGEST OR FLASHIEST HERO IN THE UNIVERSE.
BUT THE RABBI WAS RIGHT.
SMALL MIRACLES ARE IMPORTANT, TOO.
AND EVEN THOUGH WE DON'T ALWAYS GET EVERYTHING WE WANT--
...SHE'ASAH NISIM LA'AVOTEINU BAYAMIM HAHEM BAZMAN HAZEH.
TRANSLATION: "...WHO PERFORMED MIRACLES FOR OUR ANCESTORS IN THOSE DAYS AT THIS SEASON."
--WE GET WHAT WE NEED.
RAGS N' TATTERS
BOUGHT AND SOLD
THE END

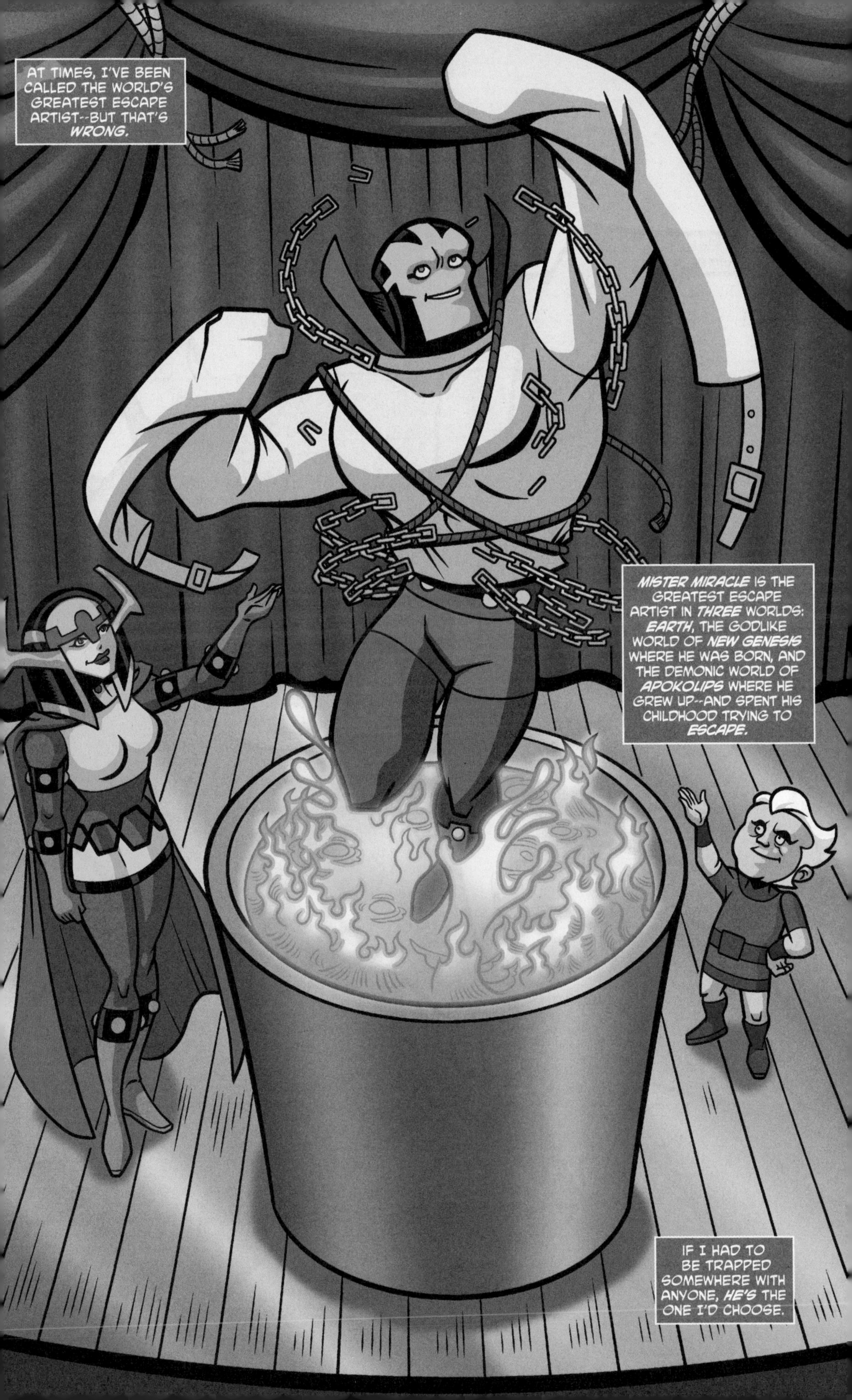
AT TIMES, I'VE BEEN CALLED THE WORLD'S GREATEST ESCAPE ARTIST--BUT THAT'S *WRONG.*
MISTER MIRACLE IS THE GREATEST ESCAPE ARTIST IN *THREE* WORLDS: *EARTH*, THE GODLIKE WORLD OF *NEW GENESIS* WHERE HE WAS BORN, AND THE DEMONIC WORLD OF *APOKOLIPS* WHERE HE GREW UP--AND SPENT HIS CHILDHOOD TRYING TO *ESCAPE.*
IF I HAD TO BE TRAPPED SOMEWHERE WITH ANYONE, *HE'S* THE ONE I'D CHOOSE.

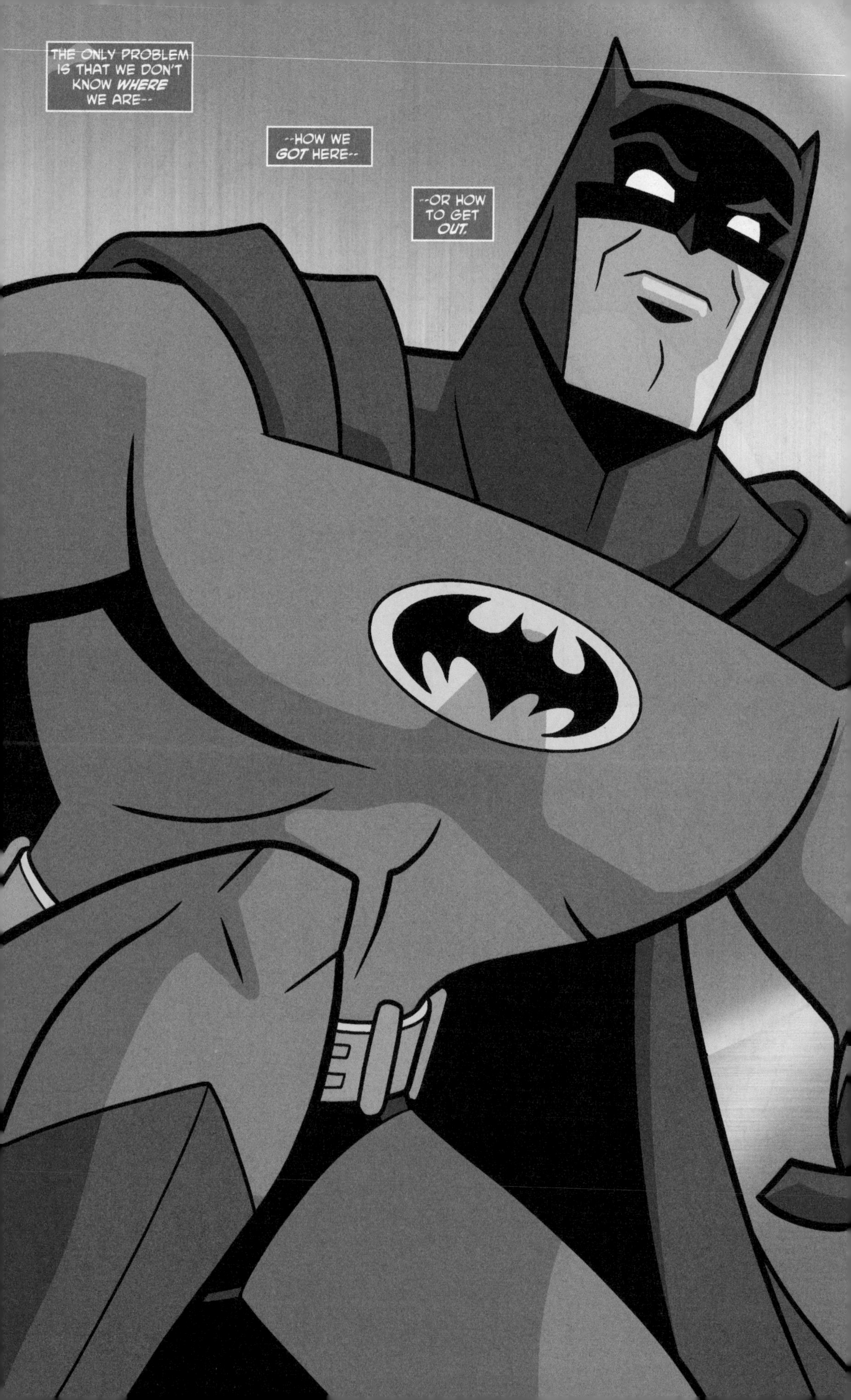
THE ONLY PROBLEM IS THAT WE DON'T KNOW *WHERE* WE ARE--
--HOW WE *GOT* HERE--
--OR HOW TO GET *OUT.*

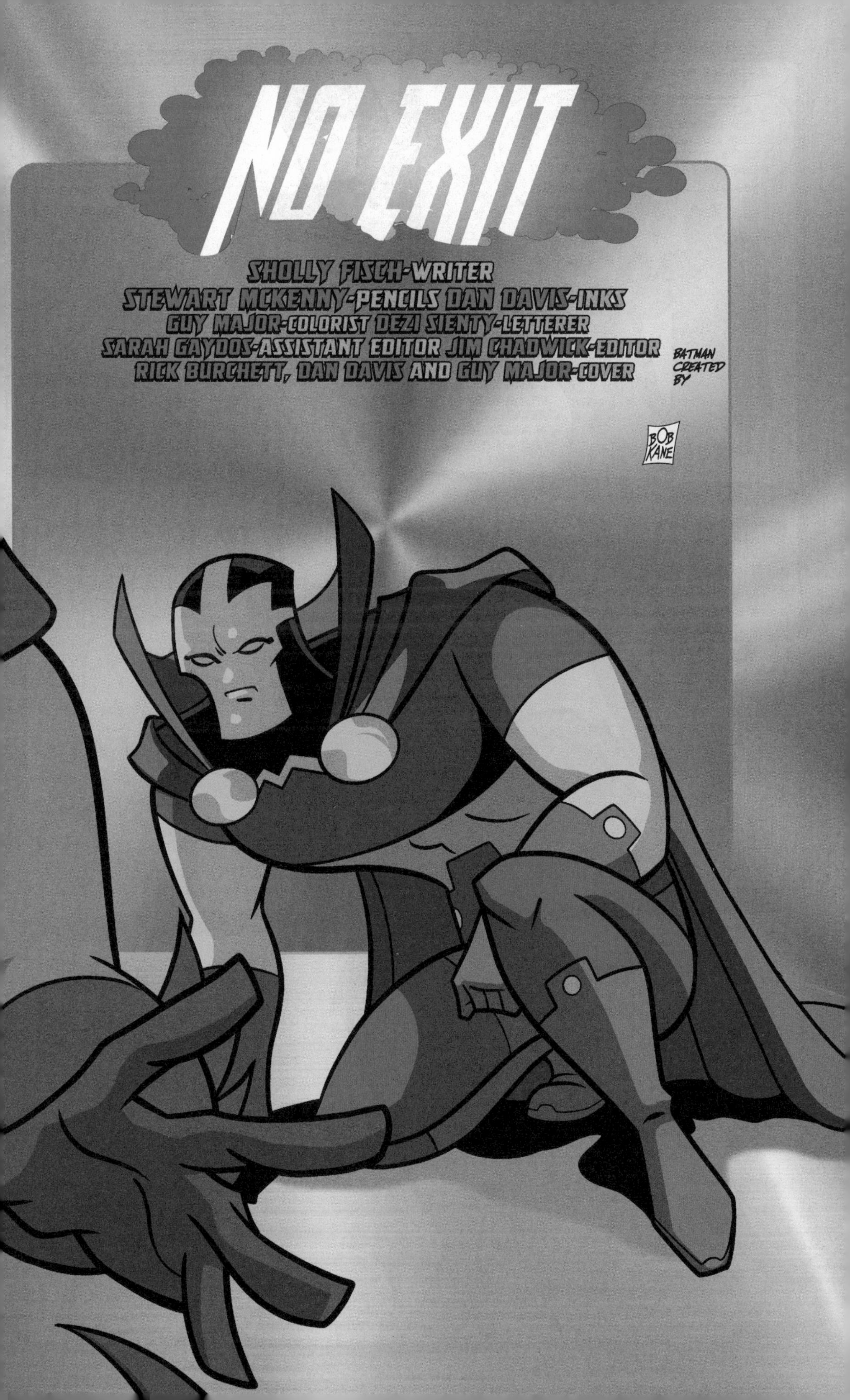

NO EXIT
SHOLLY FISCH-WRITER
STEWART MCKENNY-PENCILS DAN DAVIS-INKS
GUY MAJOR-COLORIST DEZI SIENTY-LETTERER
SARAH GAYDOS-ASSISTANT EDITOR JIM CHADWICK-EDITOR
RICK BURCHETT, DAN DAVIS AND GUY MAJOR-COVER
BATMAN CREATED BY
BOB KANE

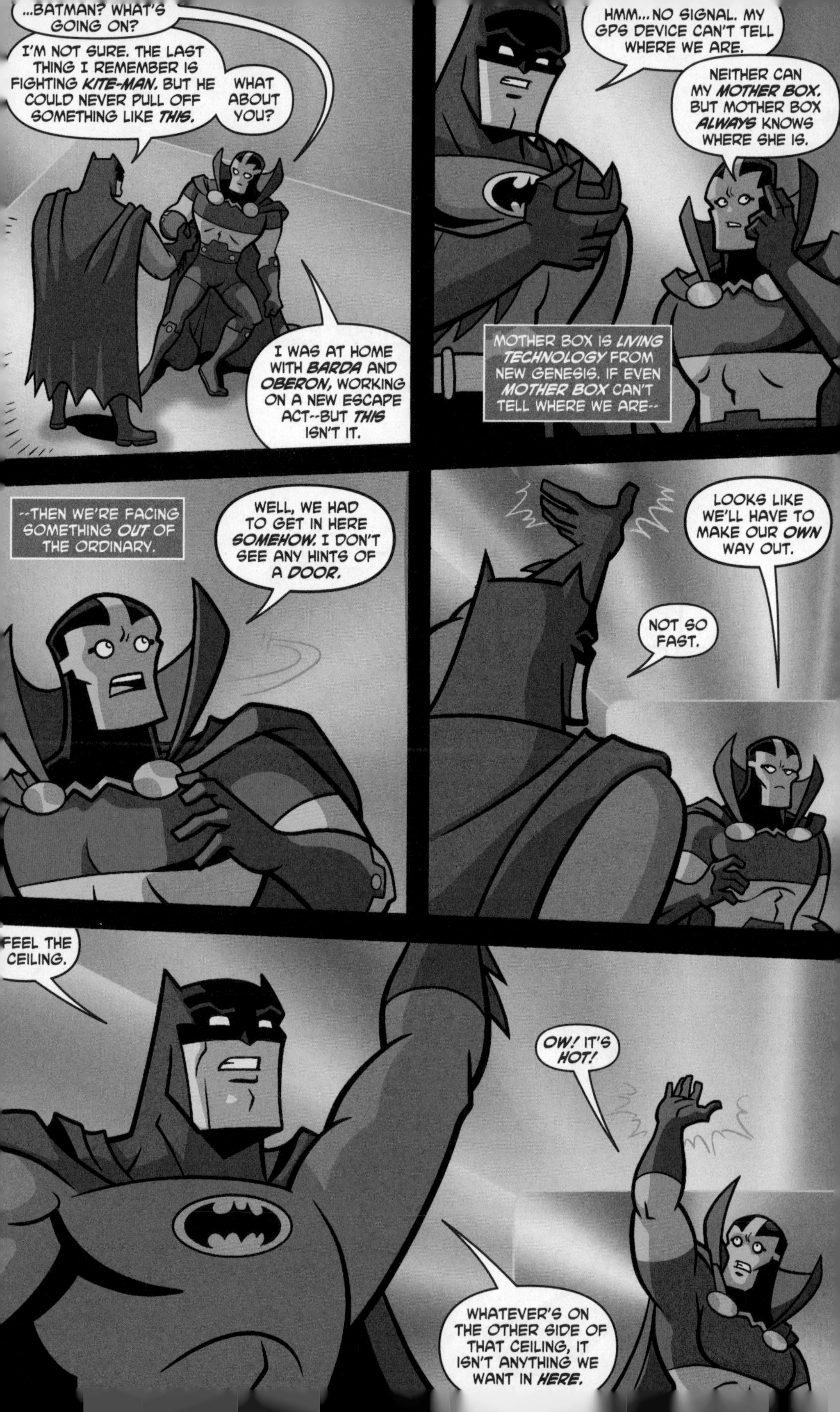
...BATMAN? WHAT'S GOING ON?
I'M NOT SURE. THE LAST THING I REMEMBER IS FIGHTING KITE-MAN. BUT HE COULD NEVER PULL OFF SOMETHING LIKE THIS.
WHAT ABOUT YOU?
I WAS AT HOME WITH BARDA AND OBERON, WORKING ON A NEW ESCAPE ACT--BUT THIS ISN'T IT.
HMM... NO SIGNAL. MY GPS DEVICE CAN'T TELL WHERE WE ARE.
NEITHER CAN MY MOTHER BOX. BUT MOTHER BOX ALWAYS KNOWS WHERE SHE IS.
MOTHER BOX IS LIVING TECHNOLOGY FROM NEW GENESIS. IF EVEN MOTHER BOX CAN'T TELL WHERE WE ARE--
--THEN WE'RE FACING SOMETHING OUT OF THE ORDINARY.
WELL, WE HAD TO GET IN HERE SOMEHOW. I DON'T SEE ANY HINTS OF A DOOR.
LOOKS LIKE WE'LL HAVE TO MAKE OUR OWN WAY OUT.
NOT SO FAST.
FEEL THE CEILING.
OW! IT'S HOT!
WHATEVER'S ON THE OTHER SIDE OF THAT CEILING, IT ISN'T ANYTHING WE WANT IN HERE.

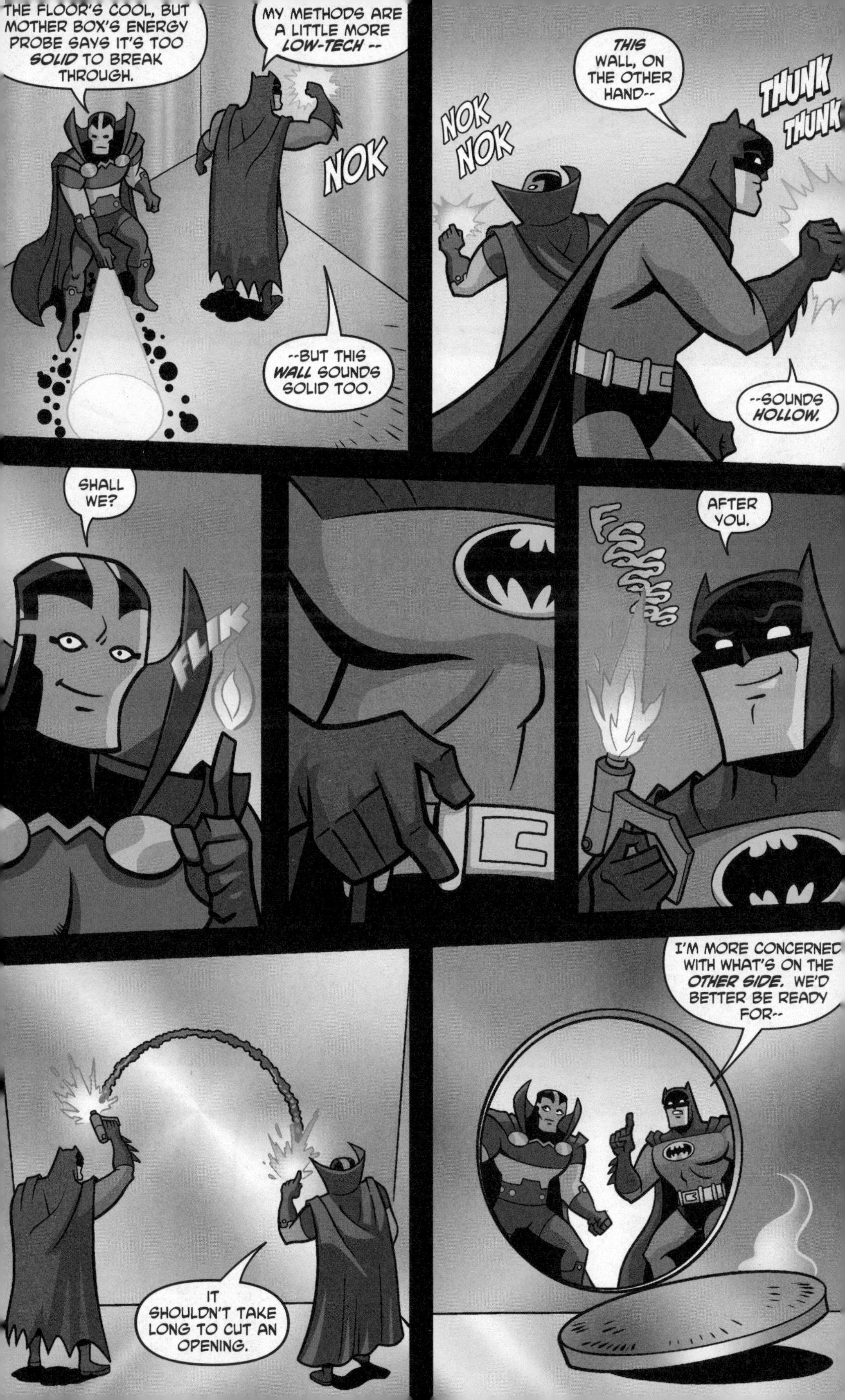
THE FLOOR'S COOL, BUT MOTHER BOX'S ENERGY PROBE SAYS IT'S TOO *SOLID* TO BREAK THROUGH.
MY METHODS ARE A LITTLE MORE *LOW-TECH* --
NOK
--BUT THIS *WALL* SOUNDS SOLID TOO.
NOK NOK
THIS WALL, ON THE OTHER HAND--
THUNK THUNK
--SOUNDS *HOLLOW.*
SHALL WE?
FLIK
AFTER YOU.
FSSSSSS
IT SHOULDN'T TAKE LONG TO CUT AN OPENING.
I'M MORE CONCERNED WITH WHAT'S ON THE *OTHER SIDE.* WE'D BETTER BE READY FOR--

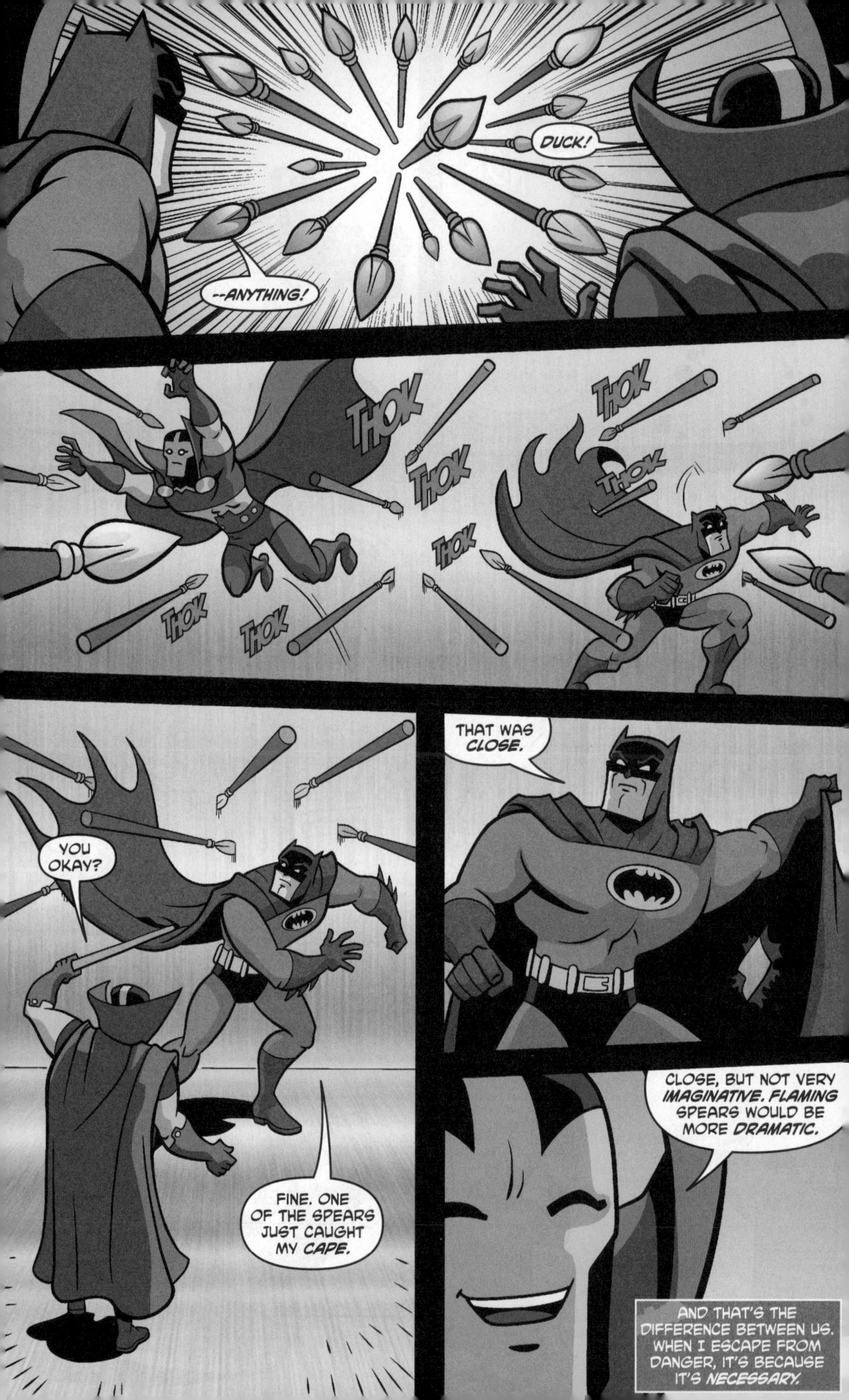
DUCK!
--ANYTHING!
THOK
THOK
THOK
THOK
THOK
THOK
THOK
THAT WAS CLOSE.
YOU OKAY?
FINE. ONE OF THE SPEARS JUST CAUGHT MY CAPE.
CLOSE, BUT NOT VERY IMAGINATIVE. FLAMING SPEARS WOULD BE MORE DRAMATIC.
AND THAT'S THE DIFFERENCE BETWEEN US. WHEN I ESCAPE FROM DANGER, IT'S BECAUSE IT'S NECESSARY.

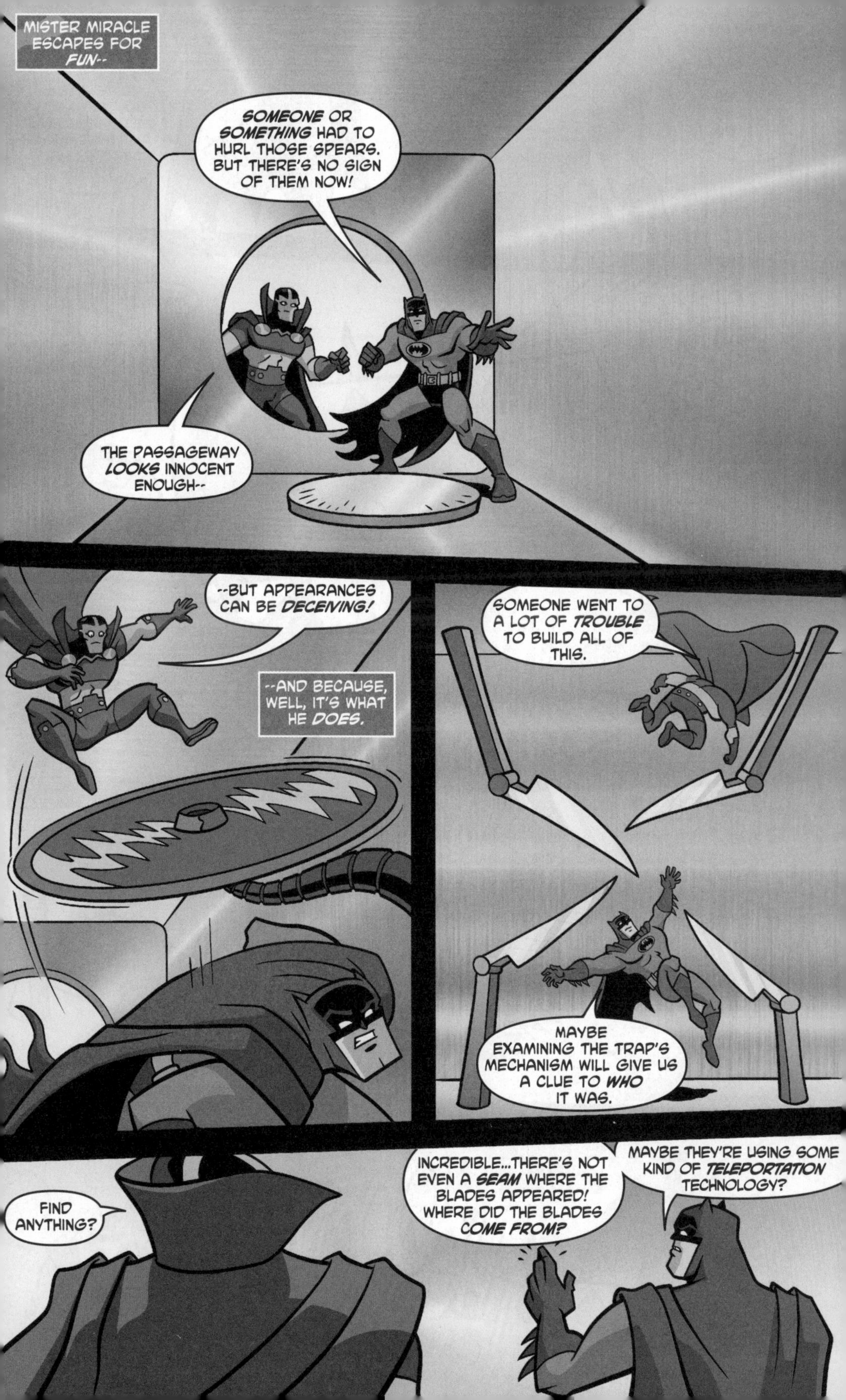
MISTER MIRACLE ESCAPES FOR FUN--
SOMEONE OR SOMETHING HAD TO HURL THOSE SPEARS. BUT THERE'S NO SIGN OF THEM NOW!
THE PASSAGEWAY LOOKS INNOCENT ENOUGH--
--BUT APPEARANCES CAN BE DECEIVING!
--AND BECAUSE, WELL, IT'S WHAT HE DOES.
SOMEONE WENT TO A LOT OF TROUBLE TO BUILD ALL OF THIS.
MAYBE EXAMINING THE TRAP'S MECHANISM WILL GIVE US A CLUE TO WHO IT WAS.
FIND ANYTHING?
INCREDIBLE...THERE'S NOT EVEN A SEAM WHERE THE BLADES APPEARED! WHERE DID THE BLADES COME FROM?
MAYBE THEY'RE USING SOME KIND OF TELEPORTATION TECHNOLOGY?

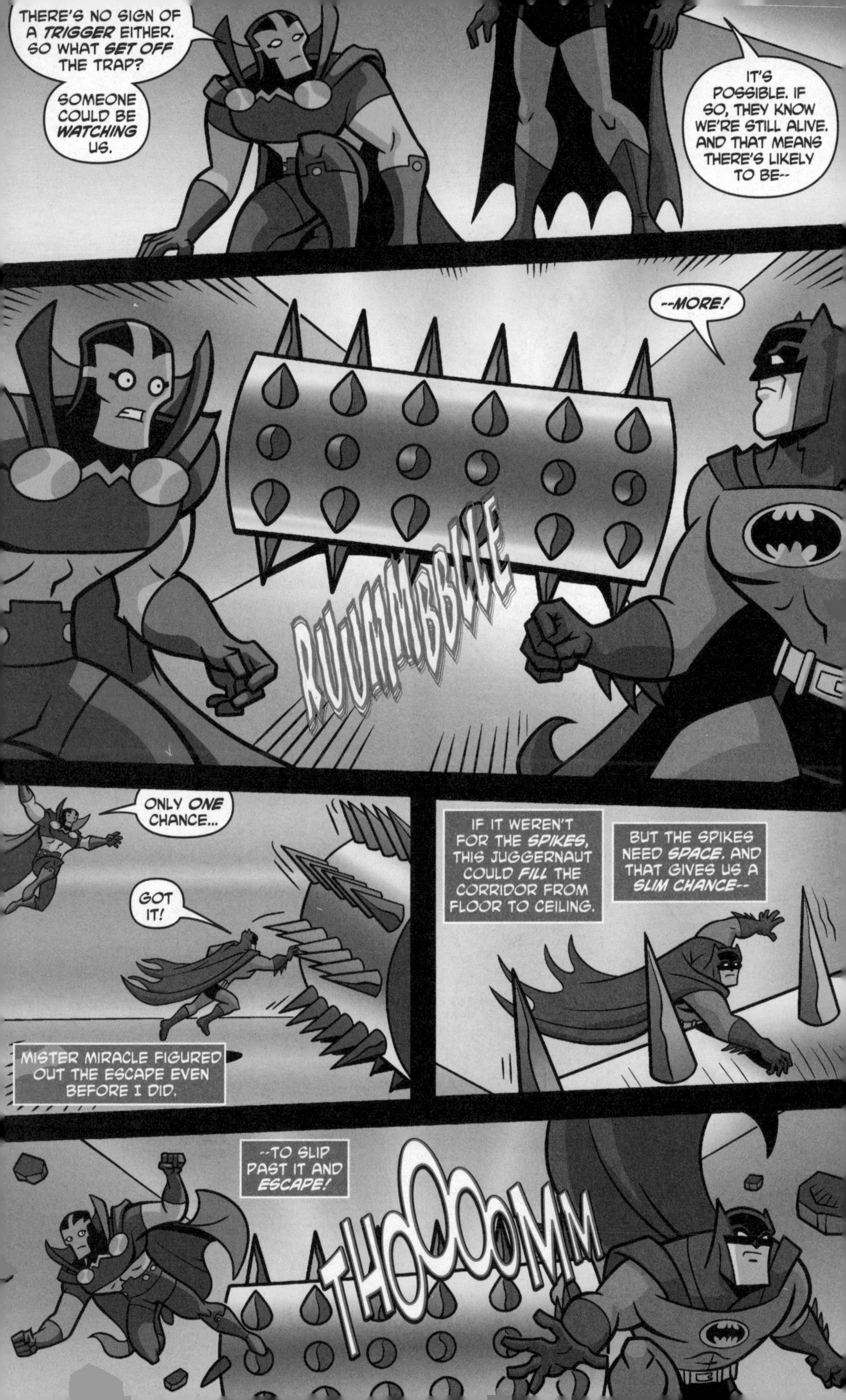
THERE'S NO SIGN OF A TRIGGER EITHER. SO WHAT SET OFF THE TRAP?
SOMEONE COULD BE WATCHING US.
IT'S POSSIBLE. IF SO, THEY KNOW WE'RE STILL ALIVE. AND THAT MEANS THERE'S LIKELY TO BE--
--MORE!
RUUMMBBLLE
ONLY ONE CHANCE...
GOT IT!
MISTER MIRACLE FIGURED OUT THE ESCAPE EVEN BEFORE I DID.
IF IT WEREN'T FOR THE SPIKES, THIS JUGGERNAUT COULD FILL THE CORRIDOR FROM FLOOR TO CEILING.
BUT THE SPIKES NEED SPACE. AND THAT GIVES US A SLIM CHANCE--
--TO SLIP PAST IT AND ESCAPE!
THOOOOMM

THAT COULD HAVE BEEN *BAD*.

BUT IT WOULD HAVE LOOKED AMAZING ON STAGE!

A *BOMB?*

00:02

WE HAVE TO *DEFUSE* IT!

IN *TWO SECONDS?* THERE'S *NO* TIME!

COME HERE!

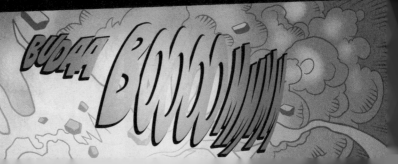

BUDAA *L-L* BOOOOMMM

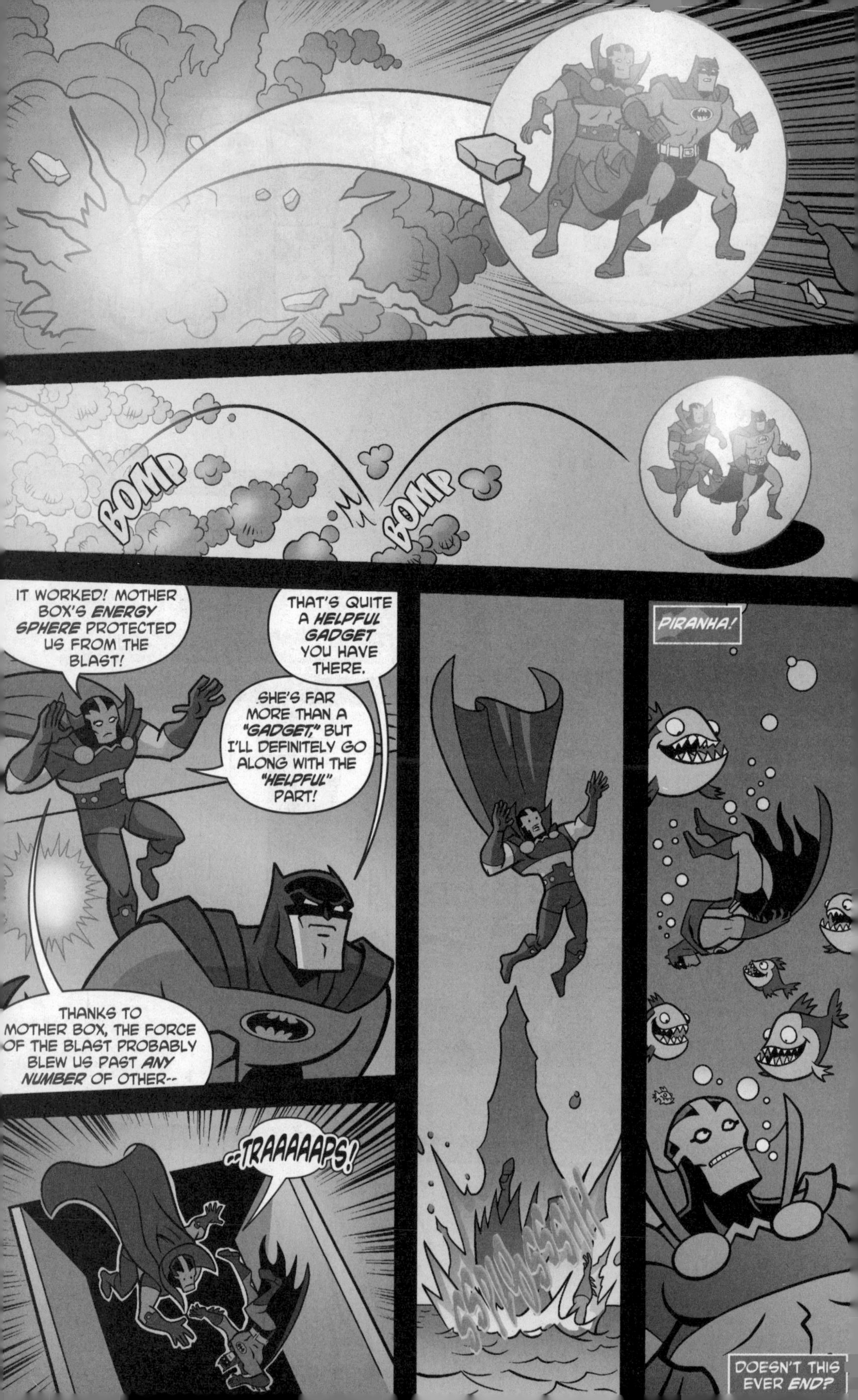
BOMP
BOMP
IT WORKED! MOTHER BOX'S ENERGY SPHERE PROTECTED US FROM THE BLAST!
THAT'S QUITE A HELPFUL GADGET YOU HAVE THERE.
SHE'S FAR MORE THAN A "GADGET," BUT I'LL DEFINITELY GO ALONG WITH THE "HELPFUL" PART!
THANKS TO MOTHER BOX, THE FORCE OF THE BLAST PROBABLY BLEW US PAST ANY NUMBER OF OTHER--
--TRAAAAAPS!
SPLOOSSSH!
PIRANHA!
DOESN'T THIS EVER END?

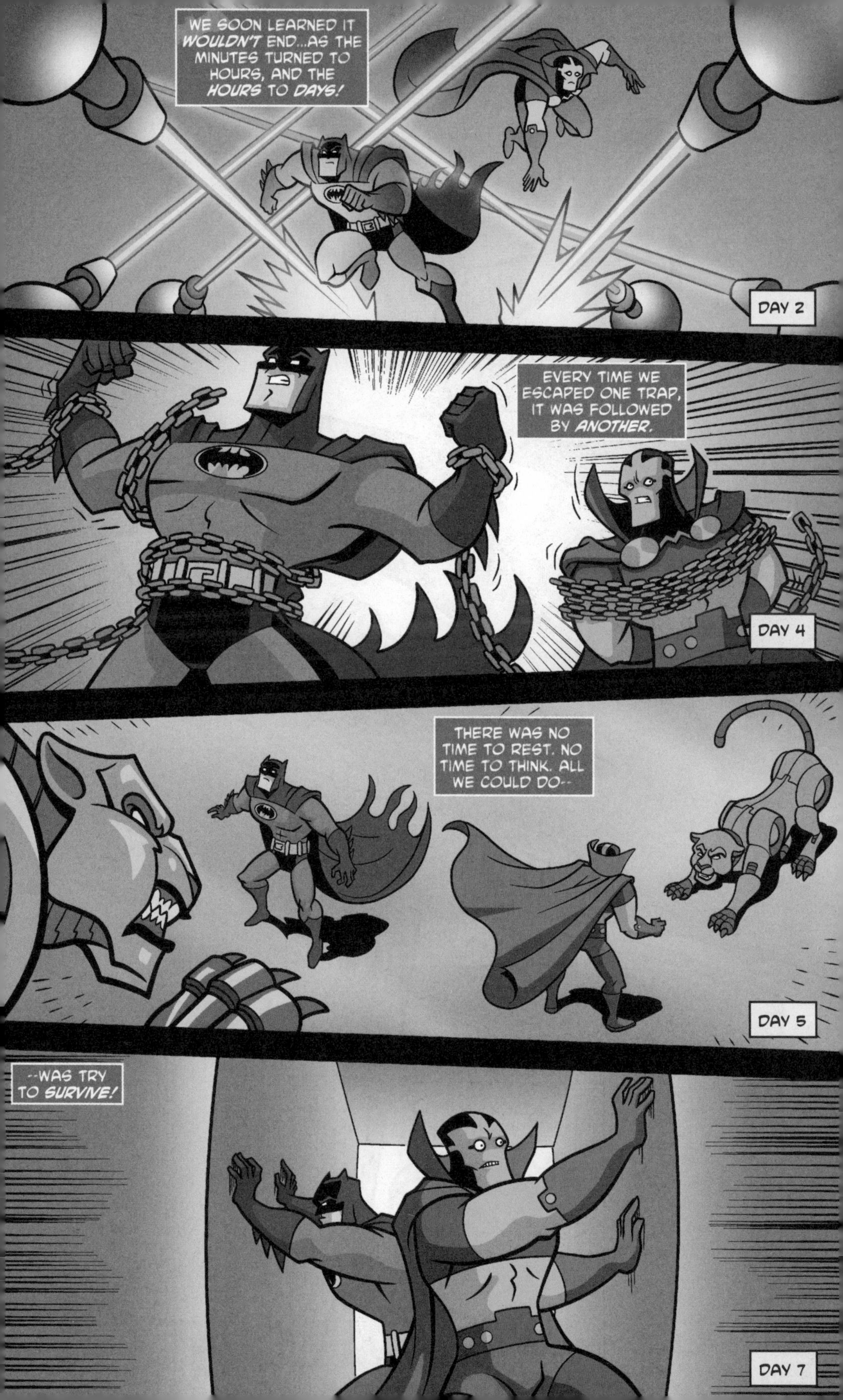
WE SOON LEARNED IT WOULDN'T END...AS THE MINUTES TURNED TO HOURS, AND THE HOURS TO DAYS!
DAY 2
EVERY TIME WE ESCAPED ONE TRAP, IT WAS FOLLOWED BY ANOTHER.
DAY 4
THERE WAS NO TIME TO REST. NO TIME TO THINK. ALL WE COULD DO--
DAY 5
--WAS TRY TO SURVIVE!
DAY 7

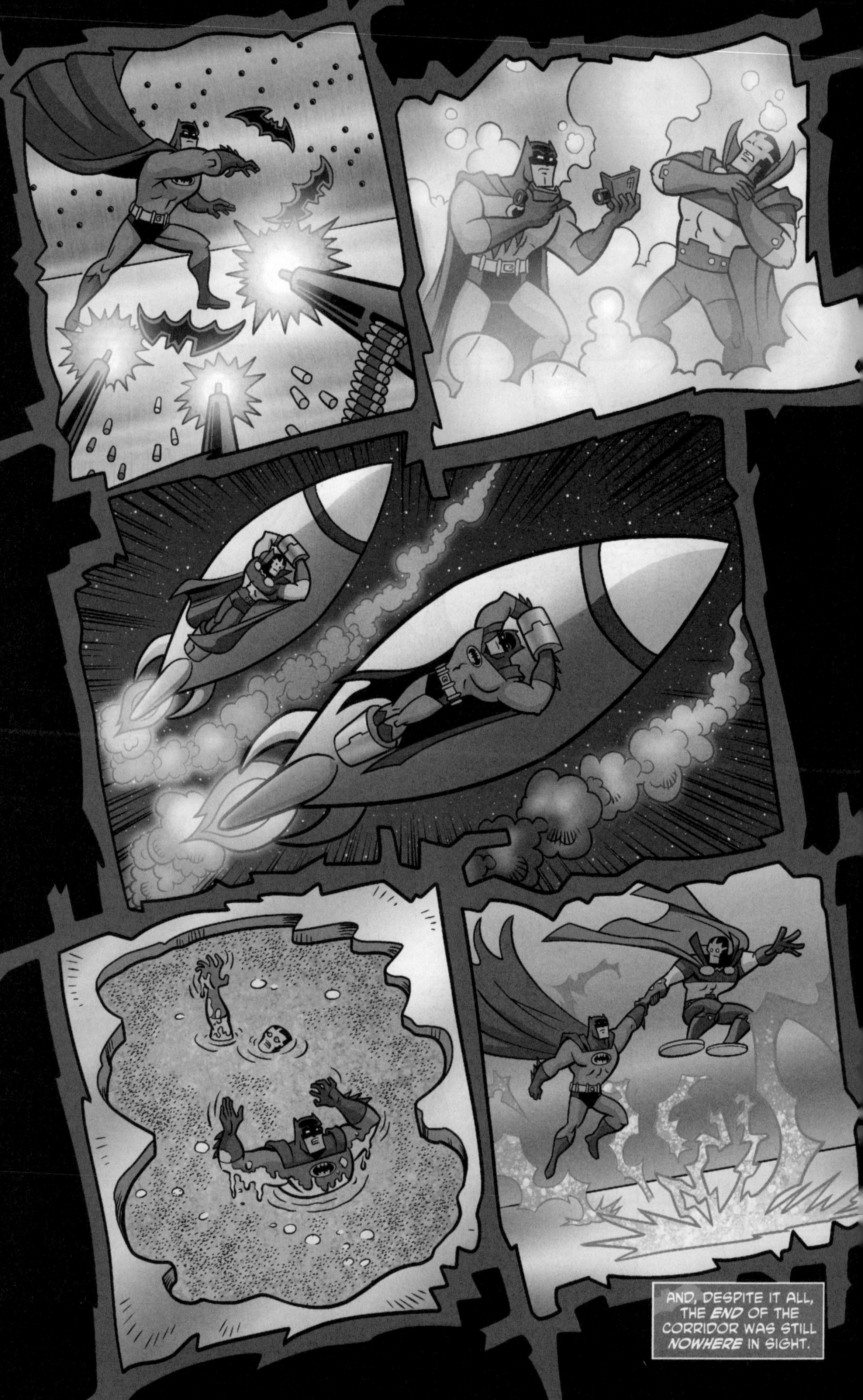
AND, DESPITE IT ALL, THE END OF THE CORRIDOR WAS STILL NOWHERE IN SIGHT.

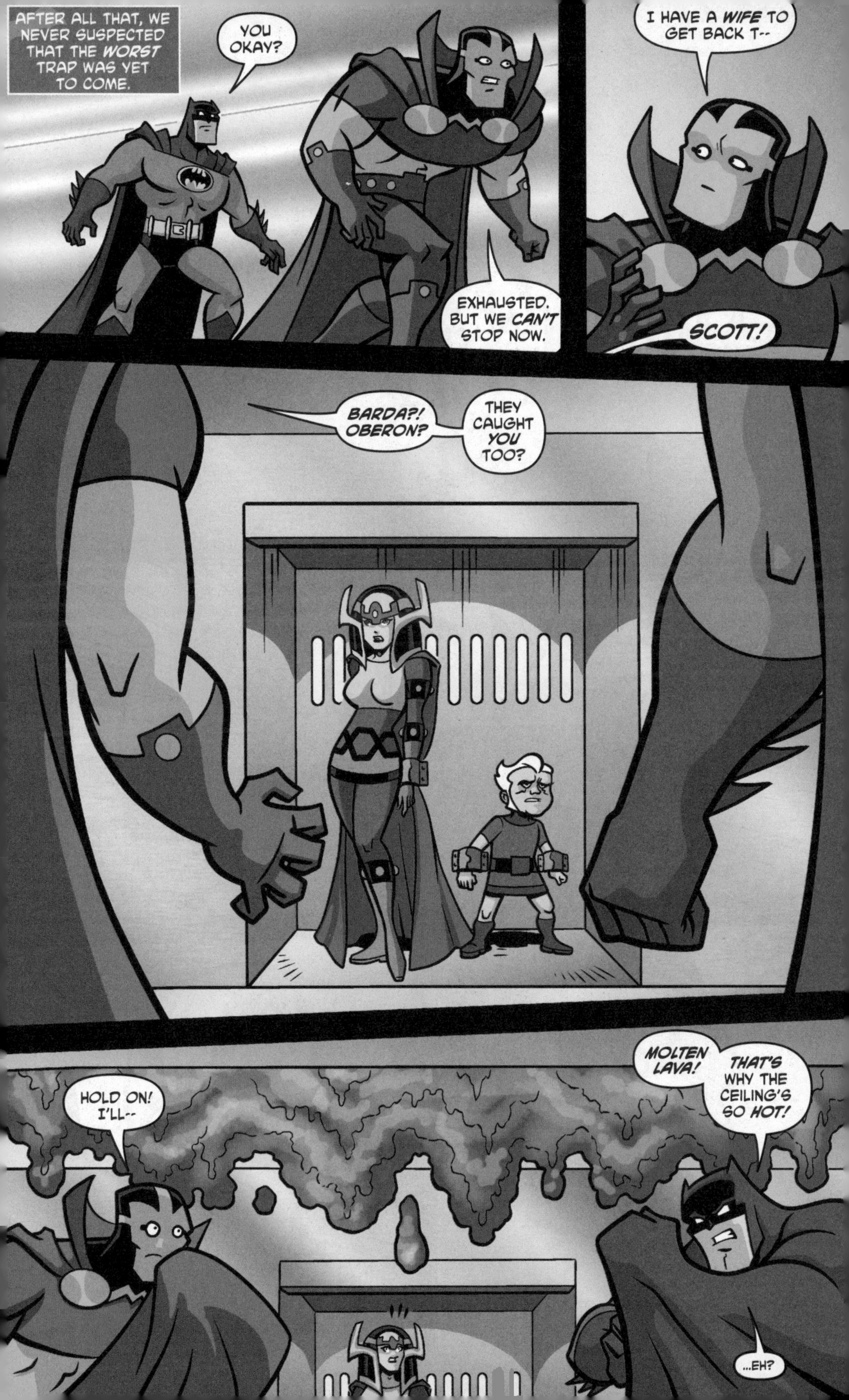
AFTER ALL THAT, WE NEVER SUSPECTED THAT THE WORST TRAP WAS YET TO COME.
YOU OKAY?
EXHAUSTED. BUT WE CAN'T STOP NOW.
I HAVE A WIFE TO GET BACK T--
SCOTT!
BARDA?! OBERON?
THEY CAUGHT YOU TOO?
HOLD ON! I'LL--
MOLTEN LAVA!
THAT'S WHY THE CEILING'S SO HOT!
...EH?

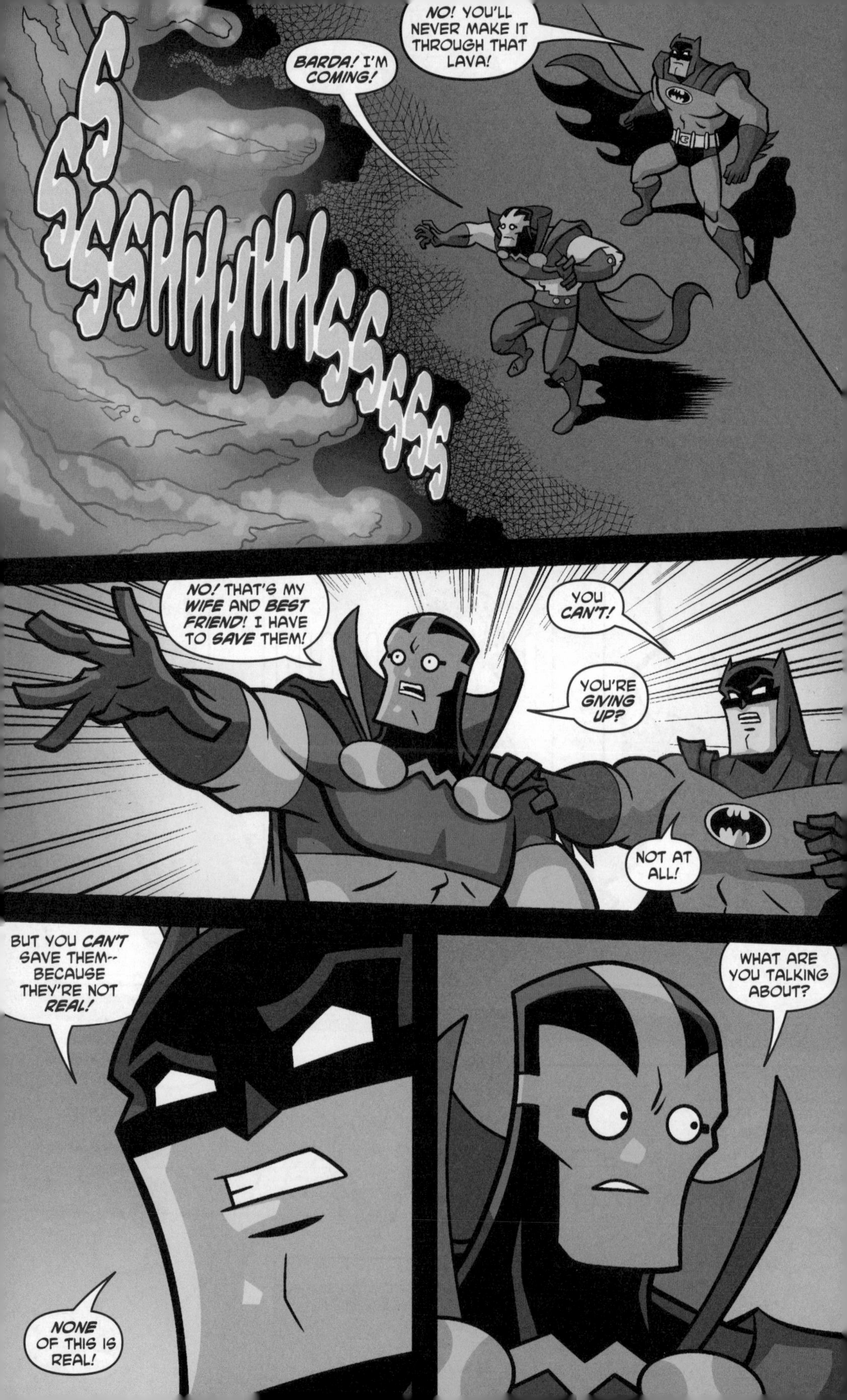

BARDA! I'M COMING!
NO! YOU'LL NEVER MAKE IT THROUGH THAT LAVA!
SSSSHHHHHHSSSSSS
NO! THAT'S MY WIFE AND BEST FRIEND! I HAVE TO SAVE THEM!
YOU CAN'T!
YOU'RE GIVING UP?
NOT AT ALL!
BUT YOU CAN'T SAVE THEM-- BECAUSE THEY'RE NOT REAL!
NONE OF THIS IS REAL!
WHAT ARE YOU TALKING ABOUT?

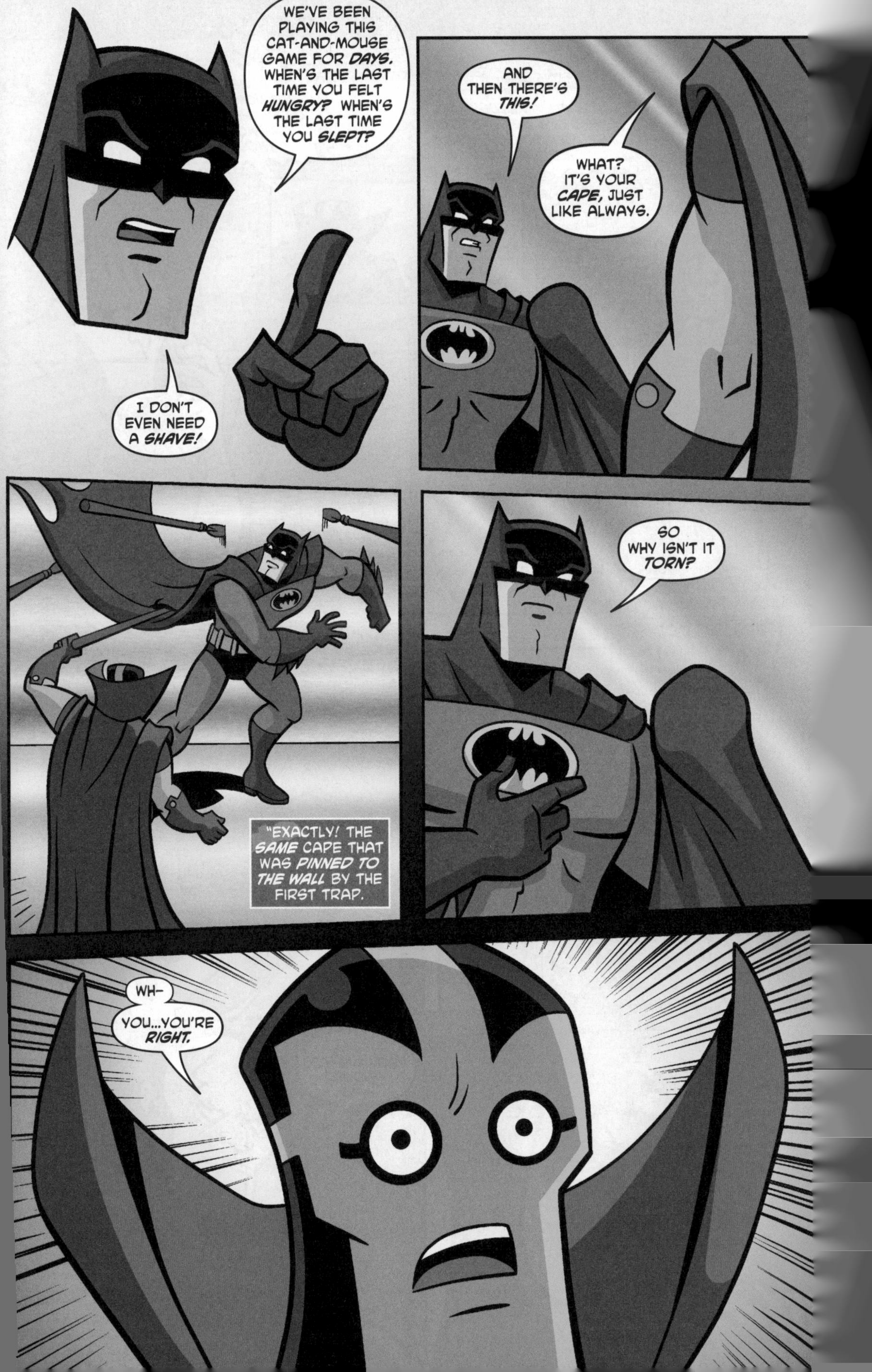
WE'VE BEEN PLAYING THIS CAT-AND-MOUSE GAME FOR DAYS. WHEN'S THE LAST TIME YOU FELT HUNGRY? WHEN'S THE LAST TIME YOU SLEPT?
I DON'T EVEN NEED A SHAVE!
AND THEN THERE'S THIS!
WHAT? IT'S YOUR CAPE, JUST LIKE ALWAYS.
"EXACTLY! THE SAME CAPE THAT WAS PINNED TO THE WALL BY THE FIRST TRAP.
SO WHY ISN'T IT TORN?
WH-
YOU...YOU'RE RIGHT.

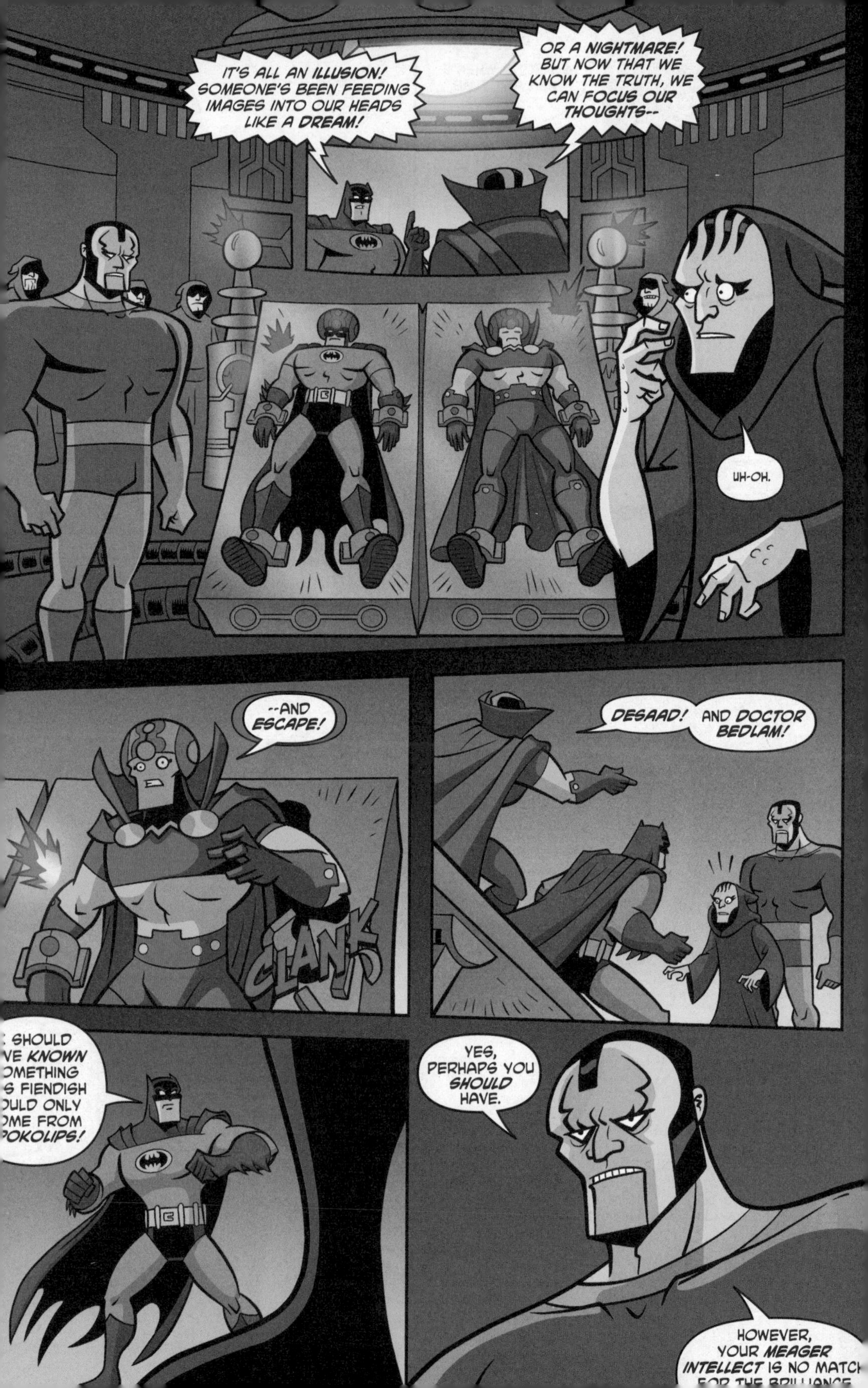
IT'S ALL AN ILLUSION! SOMEONE'S BEEN FEEDING IMAGES INTO OUR HEADS LIKE A DREAM!
OR A NIGHTMARE! BUT NOW THAT WE KNOW THE TRUTH, WE CAN FOCUS OUR THOUGHTS--
UH-OH.
--AND ESCAPE!
CLANK
DESAAD!
AND DOCTOR BEDLAM!
YES, PERHAPS YOU SHOULD HAVE.
HOWEVER, YOUR MEAGER INTELLECT IS NO MATC

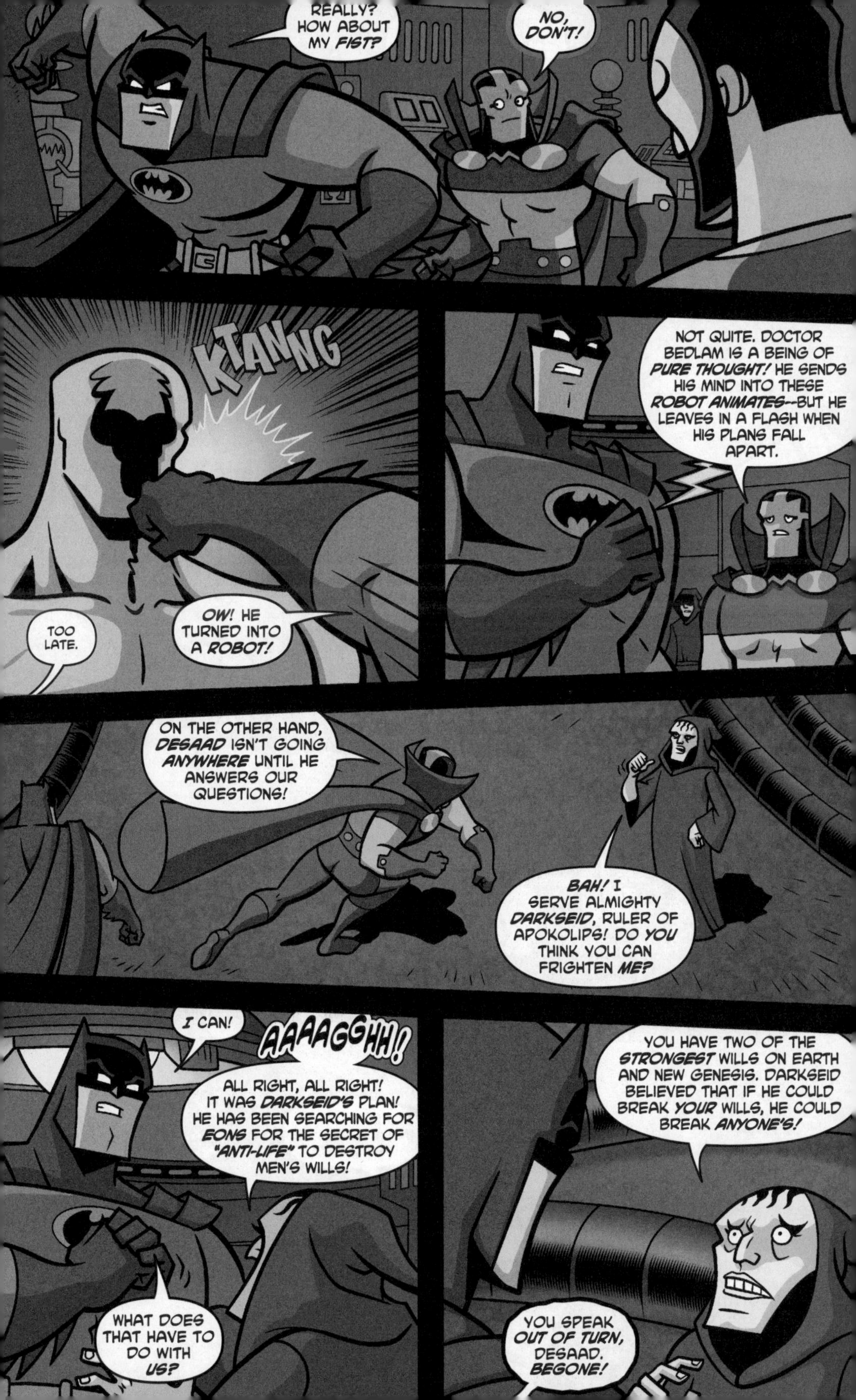
REALLY? HOW ABOUT MY FIST?
NO, DON'T!
KTANNG
TOO LATE.
OW! HE TURNED INTO A ROBOT!
NOT QUITE. DOCTOR BEDLAM IS A BEING OF PURE THOUGHT! HE SENDS HIS MIND INTO THESE ROBOT ANIMATES--BUT HE LEAVES IN A FLASH WHEN HIS PLANS FALL APART.
ON THE OTHER HAND, DESAAD ISN'T GOING ANYWHERE UNTIL HE ANSWERS OUR QUESTIONS!
BAH! I SERVE ALMIGHTY DARKSEID, RULER OF APOKOLIPS! DO YOU THINK YOU CAN FRIGHTEN ME?
I CAN!
AAAAGGHH!
ALL RIGHT, ALL RIGHT! IT WAS DARKSEID'S PLAN! HE HAS BEEN SEARCHING FOR EONS FOR THE SECRET OF "ANTI-LIFE" TO DESTROY MEN'S WILLS!
WHAT DOES THAT HAVE TO DO WITH US?
YOU HAVE TWO OF THE STRONGEST WILLS ON EARTH AND NEW GENESIS. DARKSEID BELIEVED THAT IF HE COULD BREAK YOUR WILLS, HE COULD BREAK ANYONE'S!
YOU SPEAK OUT OF TURN, DESAAD. BEGONE!

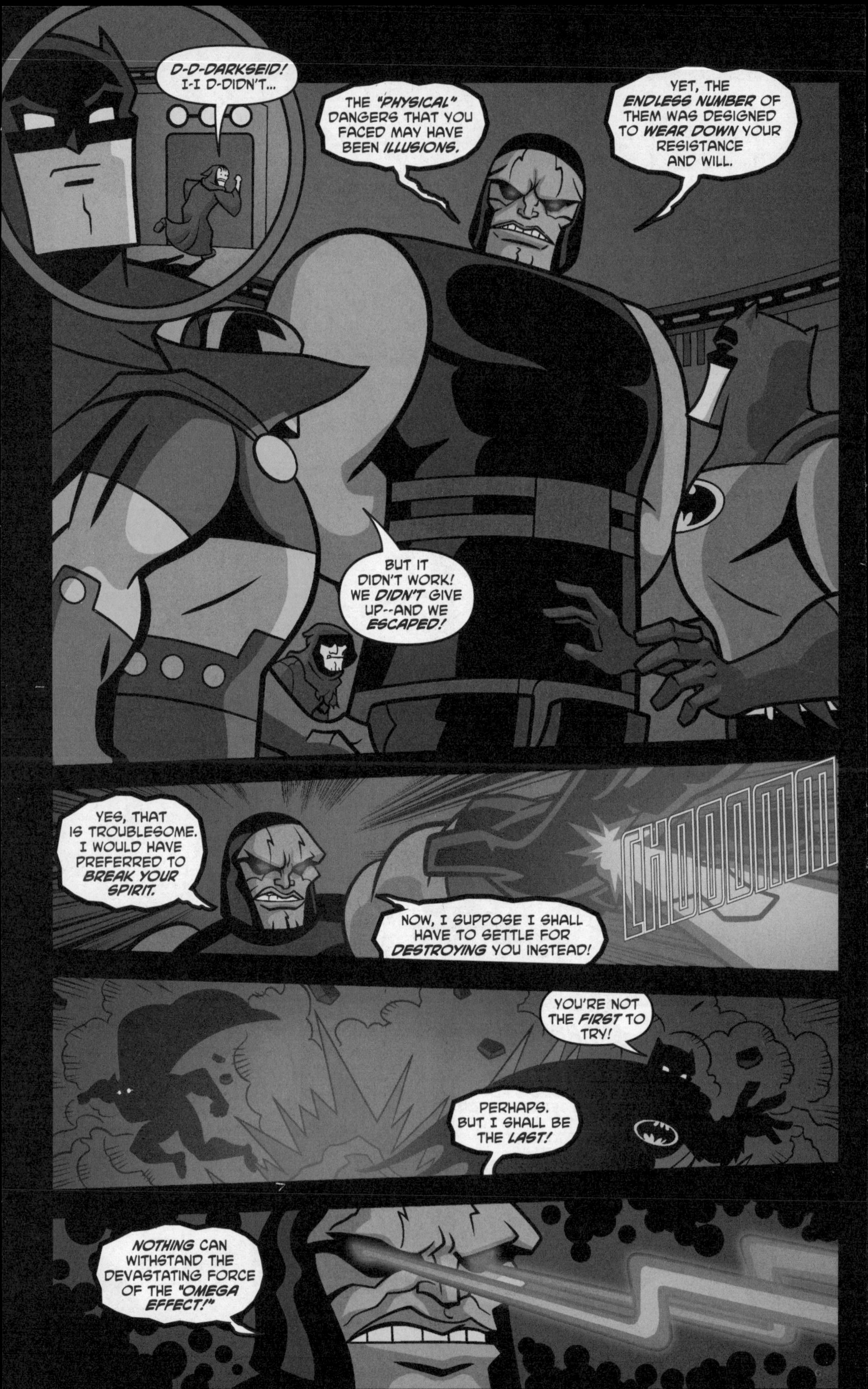

D-D-DARKSEID! I-I D-DIDN'T...
THE "PHYSICAL" DANGERS THAT YOU FACED MAY HAVE BEEN ILLUSIONS.
YET, THE ENDLESS NUMBER OF THEM WAS DESIGNED TO WEAR DOWN YOUR RESISTANCE AND WILL.
BUT IT DIDN'T WORK! WE DIDN'T GIVE UP--AND WE ESCAPED!
YES, THAT IS TROUBLESOME. I WOULD HAVE PREFERRED TO BREAK YOUR SPIRIT.
NOW, I SUPPOSE I SHALL HAVE TO SETTLE FOR DESTROYING YOU INSTEAD!
CHOOOMM
YOU'RE NOT THE FIRST TO TRY!
PERHAPS. BUT I SHALL BE THE LAST!
NOTHING CAN WITHSTAND THE DEVASTATING FORCE OF THE "OMEGA EFFECT!"

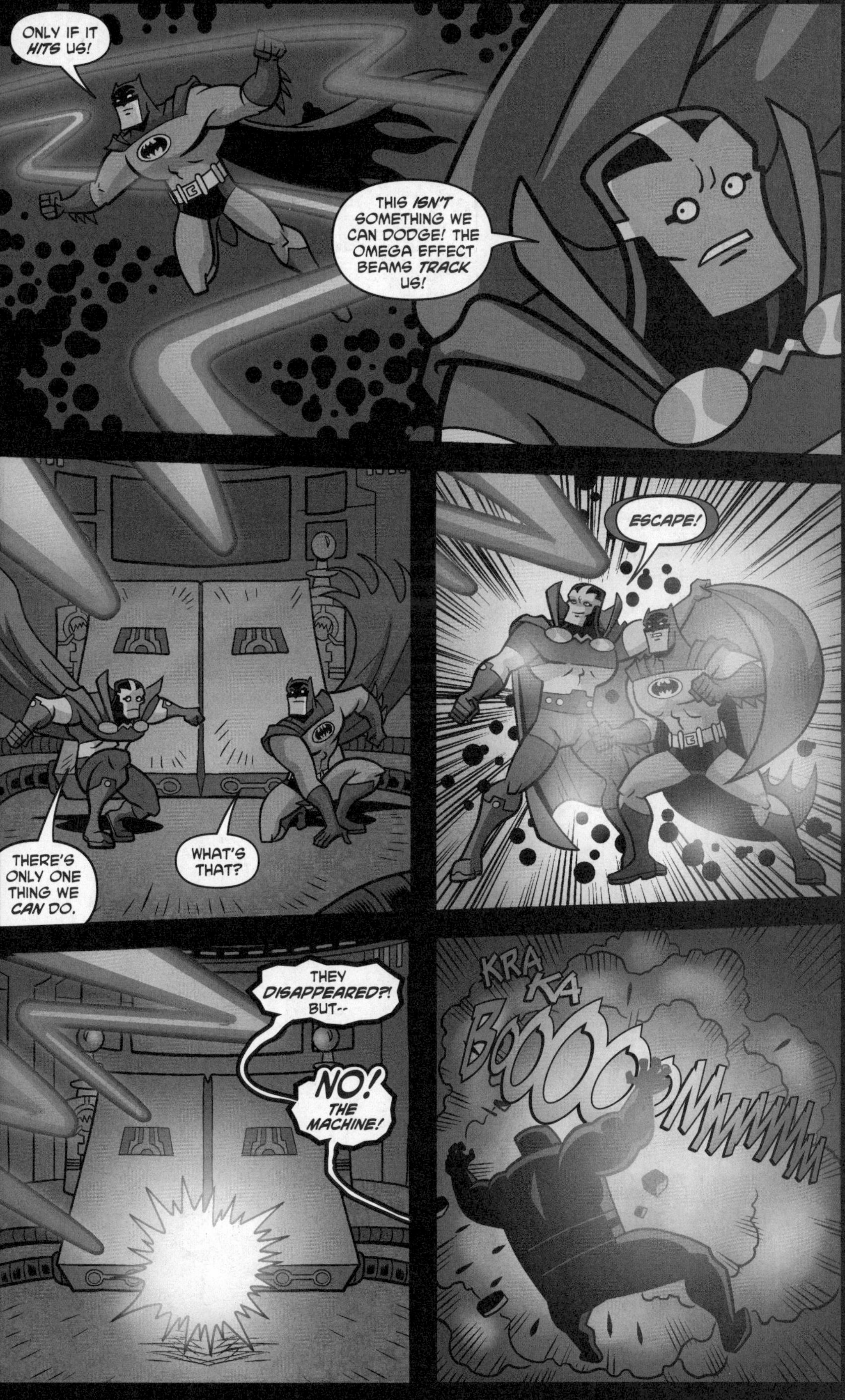

ONLY IF IT HITS US!
THIS ISN'T SOMETHING WE CAN DODGE! THE OMEGA EFFECT BEAMS TRACK US!
THERE'S ONLY ONE THING WE CAN DO.
WHAT'S THAT?
ESCAPE!
THEY DISAPPEARED?! BUT--
NO! THE MACHINE!
KRA KA BOOOOOMMMMMM

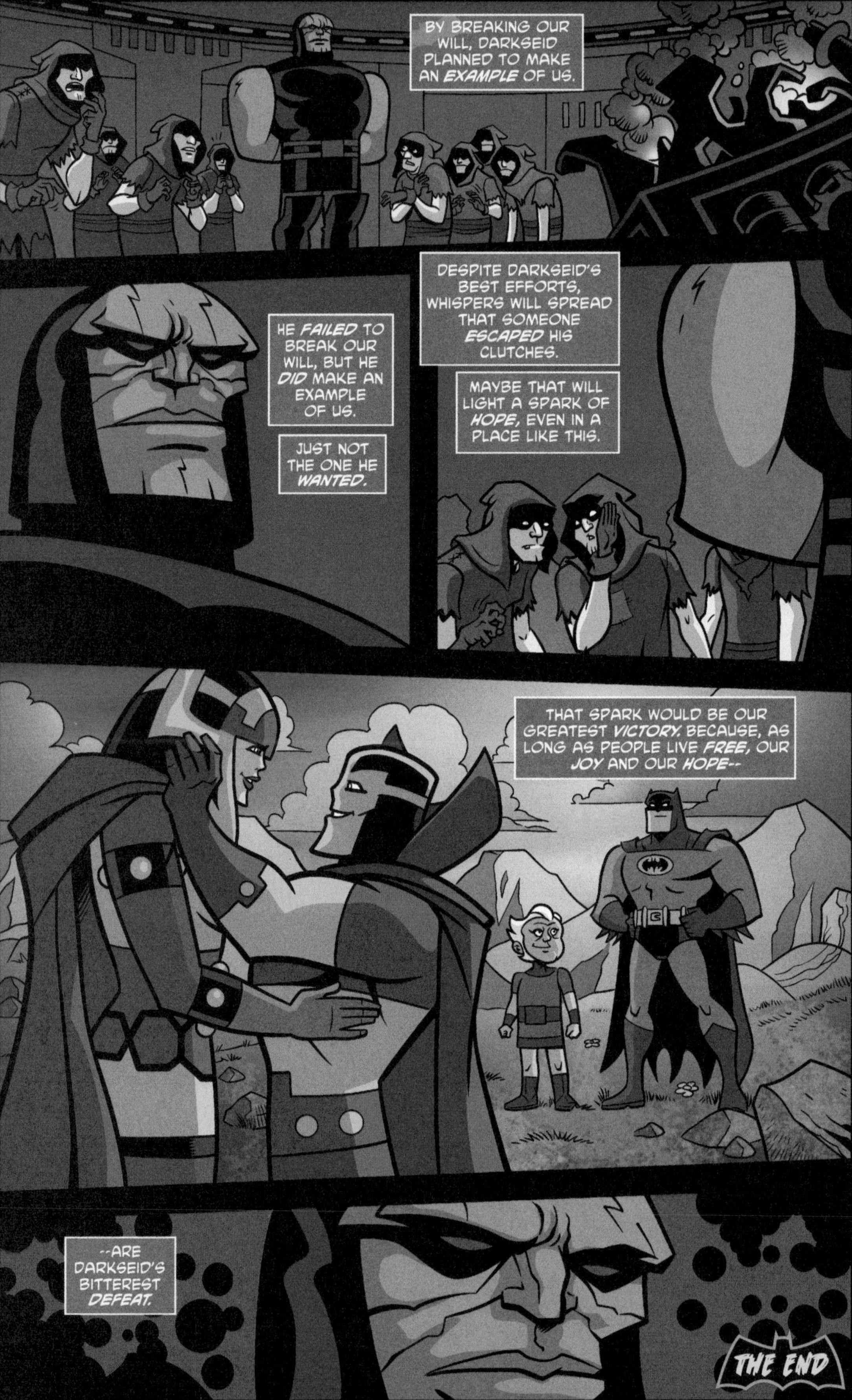

BY BREAKING OUR WILL, DARKSEID PLANNED TO MAKE AN EXAMPLE OF US.
HE FAILED TO BREAK OUR WILL, BUT HE DID MAKE AN EXAMPLE OF US.
JUST NOT THE ONE HE WANTED.
DESPITE DARKSEID'S BEST EFFORTS, WHISPERS WILL SPREAD THAT SOMEONE ESCAPED HIS CLUTCHES.
MAYBE THAT WILL LIGHT A SPARK OF HOPE, EVEN IN A PLACE LIKE THIS.
THAT SPARK WOULD BE OUR GREATEST VICTORY. BECAUSE, AS LONG AS PEOPLE LIVE FREE, OUR JOY AND OUR HOPE--
--ARE DARKSEID'S BITTEREST DEFEAT.
THE END

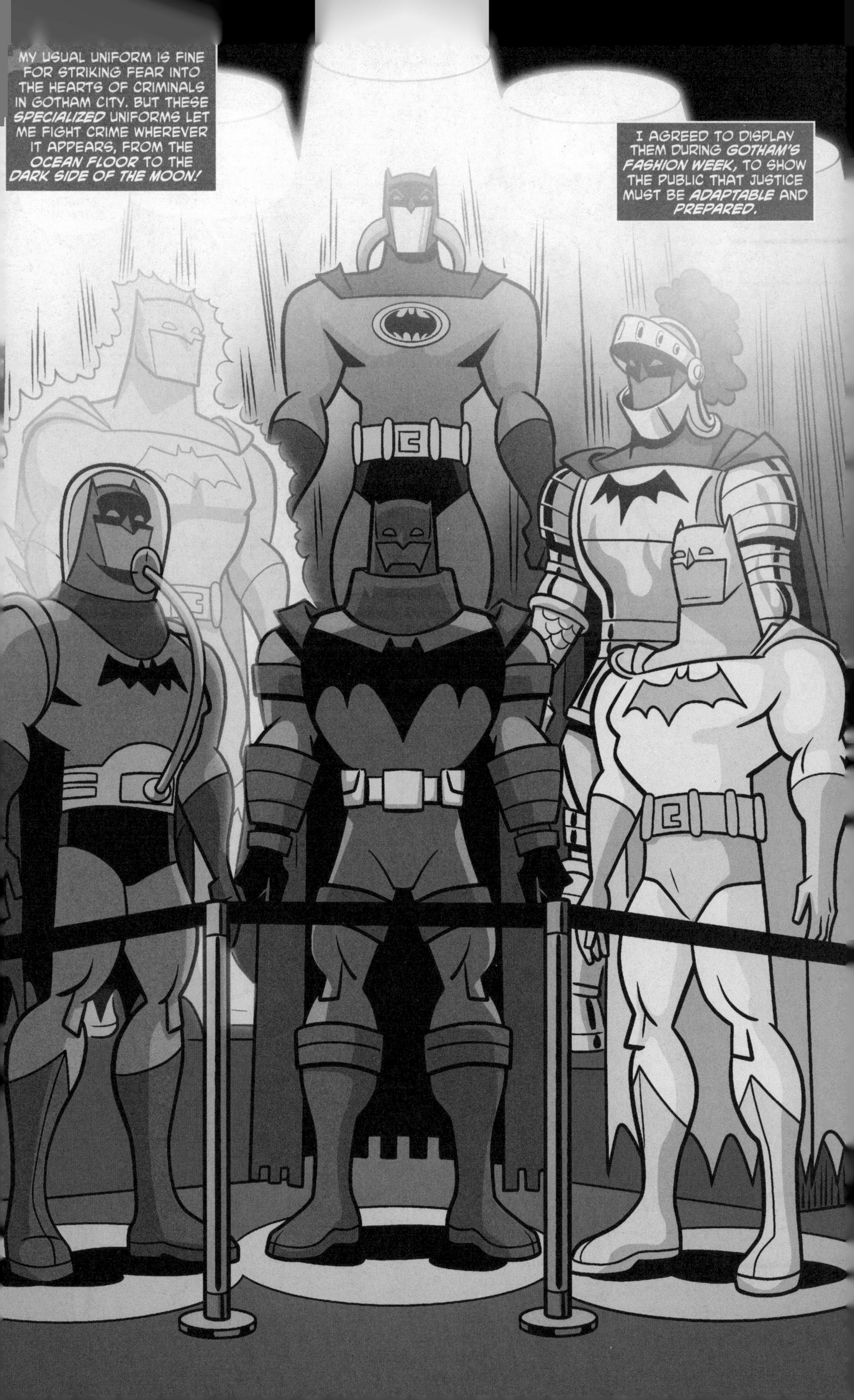
MY USUAL UNIFORM IS FINE FOR STRIKING FEAR INTO THE HEARTS OF CRIMINALS IN GOTHAM CITY. BUT THESE *SPECIALIZED* UNIFORMS LET ME FIGHT CRIME WHEREVER IT APPEARS, FROM THE *OCEAN FLOOR* TO THE *DARK SIDE OF THE MOON!*
I AGREED TO DISPLAY THEM DURING *GOTHAM'S FASHION WEEK,* TO SHOW THE PUBLIC THAT JUSTICE MUST BE *ADAPTABLE* AND *PREPARED.*

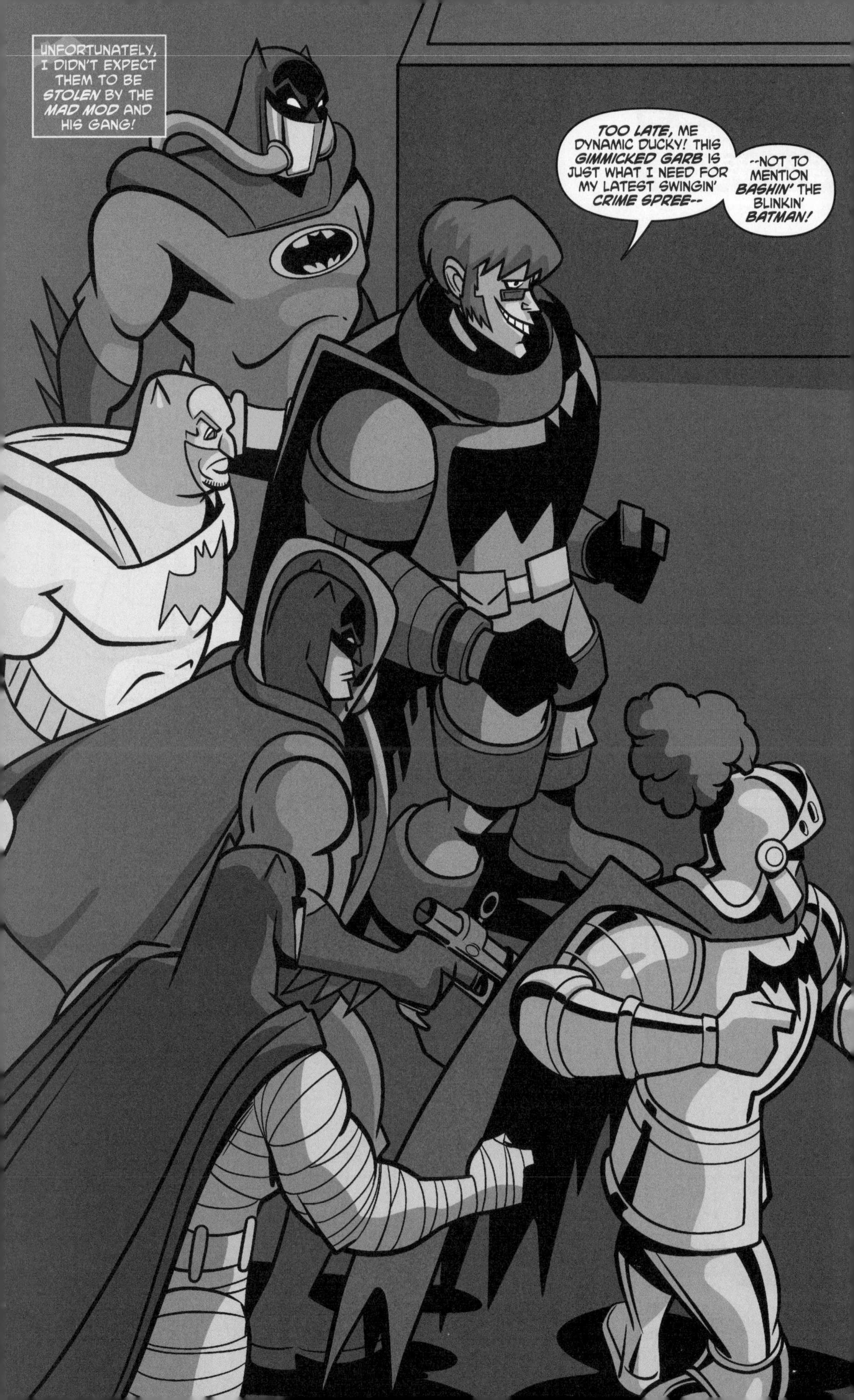
UNFORTUNATELY, I DIDN'T EXPECT THEM TO BE STOLEN BY THE MAD MOD AND HIS GANG!
TOO LATE, ME DYNAMIC DUCKY! THIS GIMMICKED GARB IS JUST WHAT I NEED FOR MY LATEST SWINGIN' CRIME SPREE--
--NOT TO MENTION BASHIN' THE BLINKIN' BATMAN!

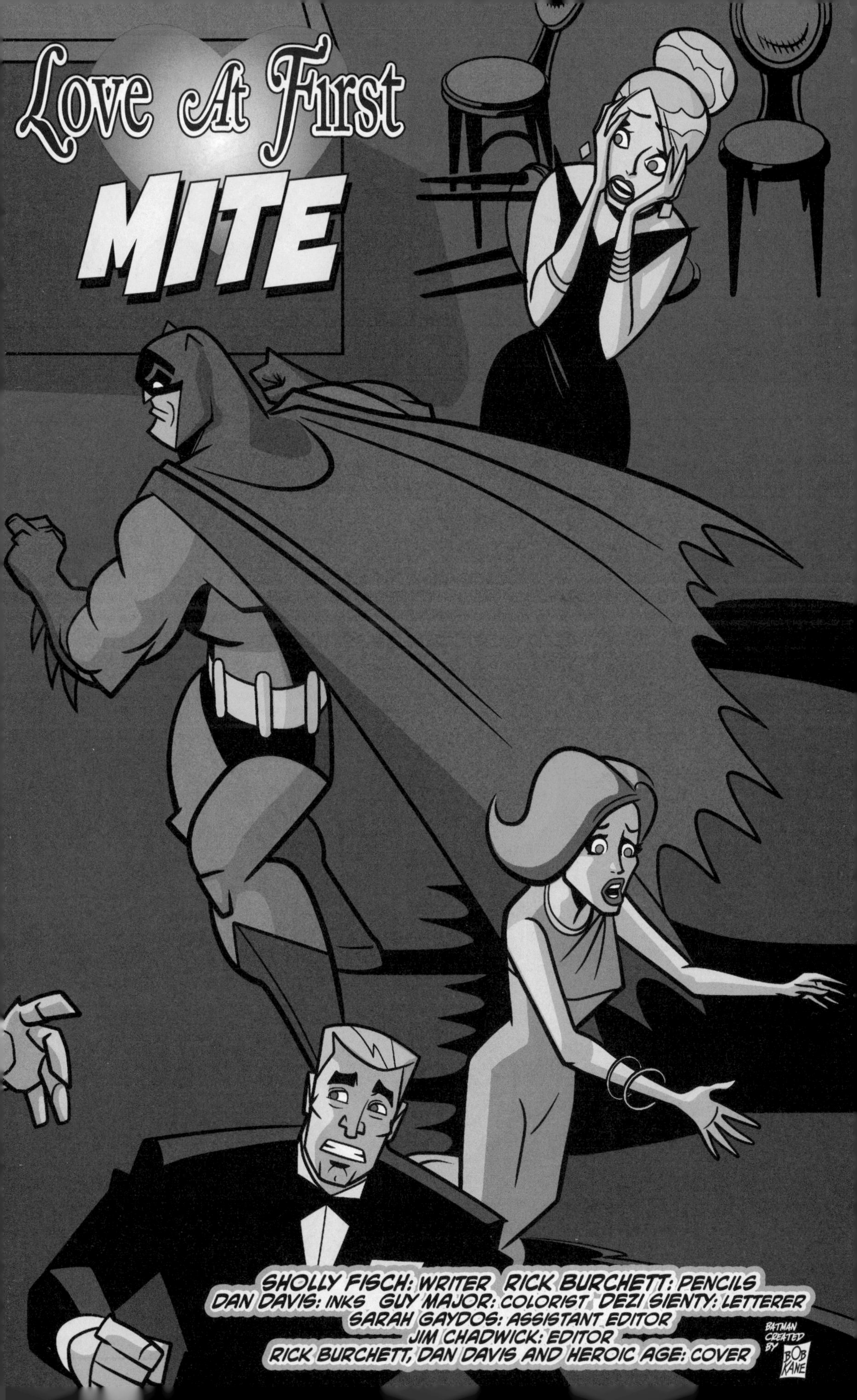
Love At First
MITE
SHOLLY FISCH: WRITER RICK BURCHETT: PENCILS
DAN DAVIS: INKS GUY MAJOR: COLORIST DEZI SIENTY: LETTERER
SARAH GAYDOS: ASSISTANT EDITOR
JIM CHADWICK: EDITOR
RICK BURCHETT, DAN DAVIS AND HEROIC AGE: COVER
BATMAN CREATED BY BOB KANE

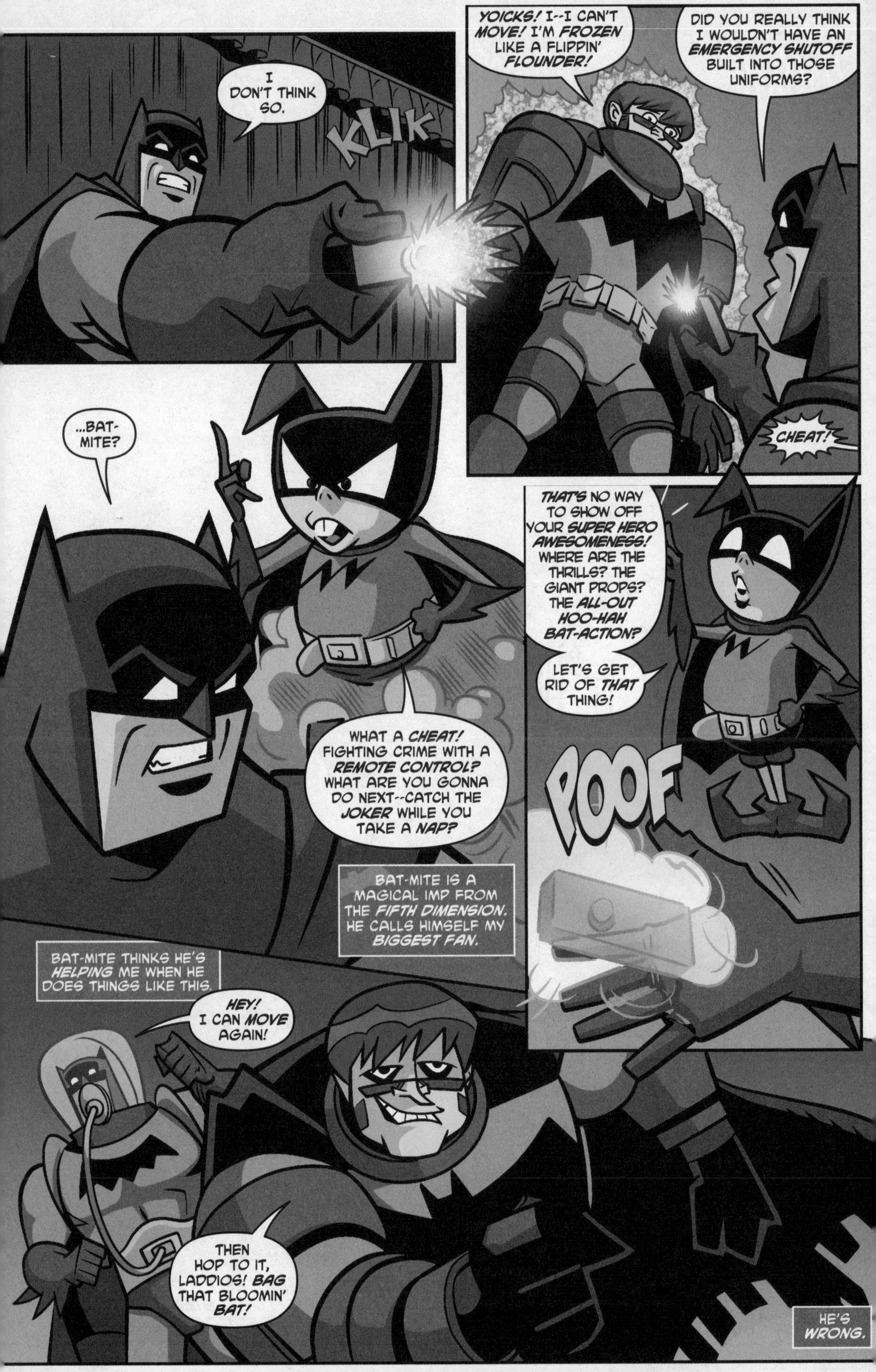
I DON'T THINK SO.
KLIK
YOICKS! I--I CAN'T MOVE! I'M FROZEN LIKE A FLIPPIN' FLOUNDER!
DID YOU REALLY THINK I WOULDN'T HAVE AN EMERGENCY SHUTOFF BUILT INTO THOSE UNIFORMS?
CHEAT!
...BAT-MITE?
WHAT A CHEAT! FIGHTING CRIME WITH A REMOTE CONTROL? WHAT ARE YOU GONNA DO NEXT--CATCH THE JOKER WHILE YOU TAKE A NAP?
BAT-MITE IS A MAGICAL IMP FROM THE FIFTH DIMENSION. HE CALLS HIMSELF MY BIGGEST FAN.
THAT'S NO WAY TO SHOW OFF YOUR SUPER HERO AWESOMENESS! WHERE ARE THE THRILLS? THE GIANT PROPS? THE ALL-OUT HOO-HAH BAT-ACTION?
LET'S GET RID OF THAT THING!
POOF
BAT-MITE THINKS HE'S HELPING ME WHEN HE DOES THINGS LIKE THIS.
HEY! I CAN MOVE AGAIN!
THEN HOP TO IT, LADDIOS! BAG THAT BLOOMIN' BAT!
HE'S WRONG.

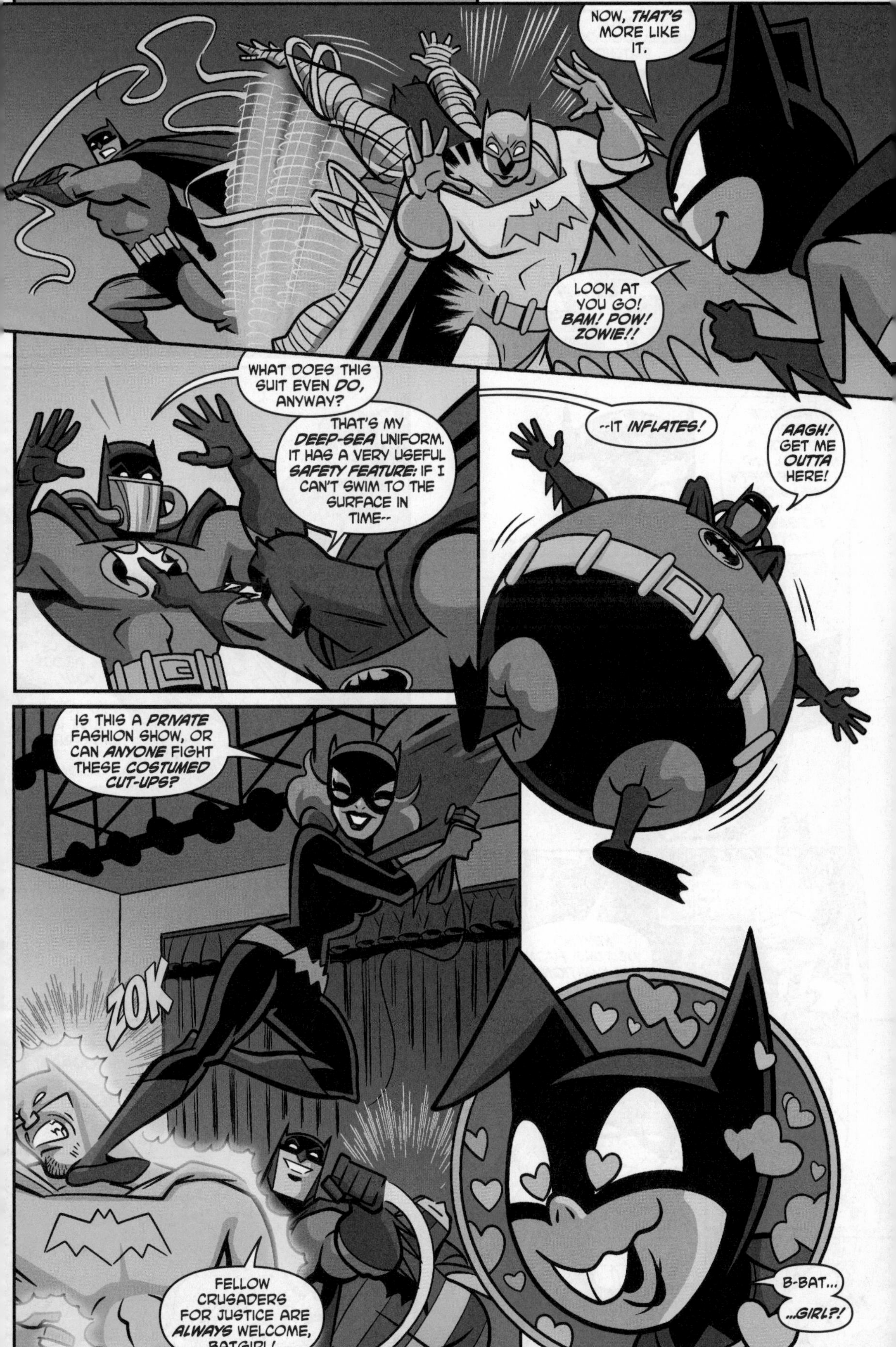
NOW, THAT'S MORE LIKE IT.
LOOK AT YOU GO! BAM! POW! ZOWIE!!
WHAT DOES THIS SUIT EVEN DO, ANYWAY?
THAT'S MY DEEP-SEA UNIFORM. IT HAS A VERY USEFUL SAFETY FEATURE: IF I CAN'T SWIM TO THE SURFACE IN TIME--
--IT INFLATES!
AAGH! GET ME OUTTA HERE!
IS THIS A PRIVATE FASHION SHOW, OR CAN ANYONE FIGHT THESE COSTUMED CUT-UPS?
ZOK
FELLOW CRUSADERS FOR JUSTICE ARE ALWAYS WELCOME, BATGIRL!
B-BAT...
...GIRL?!

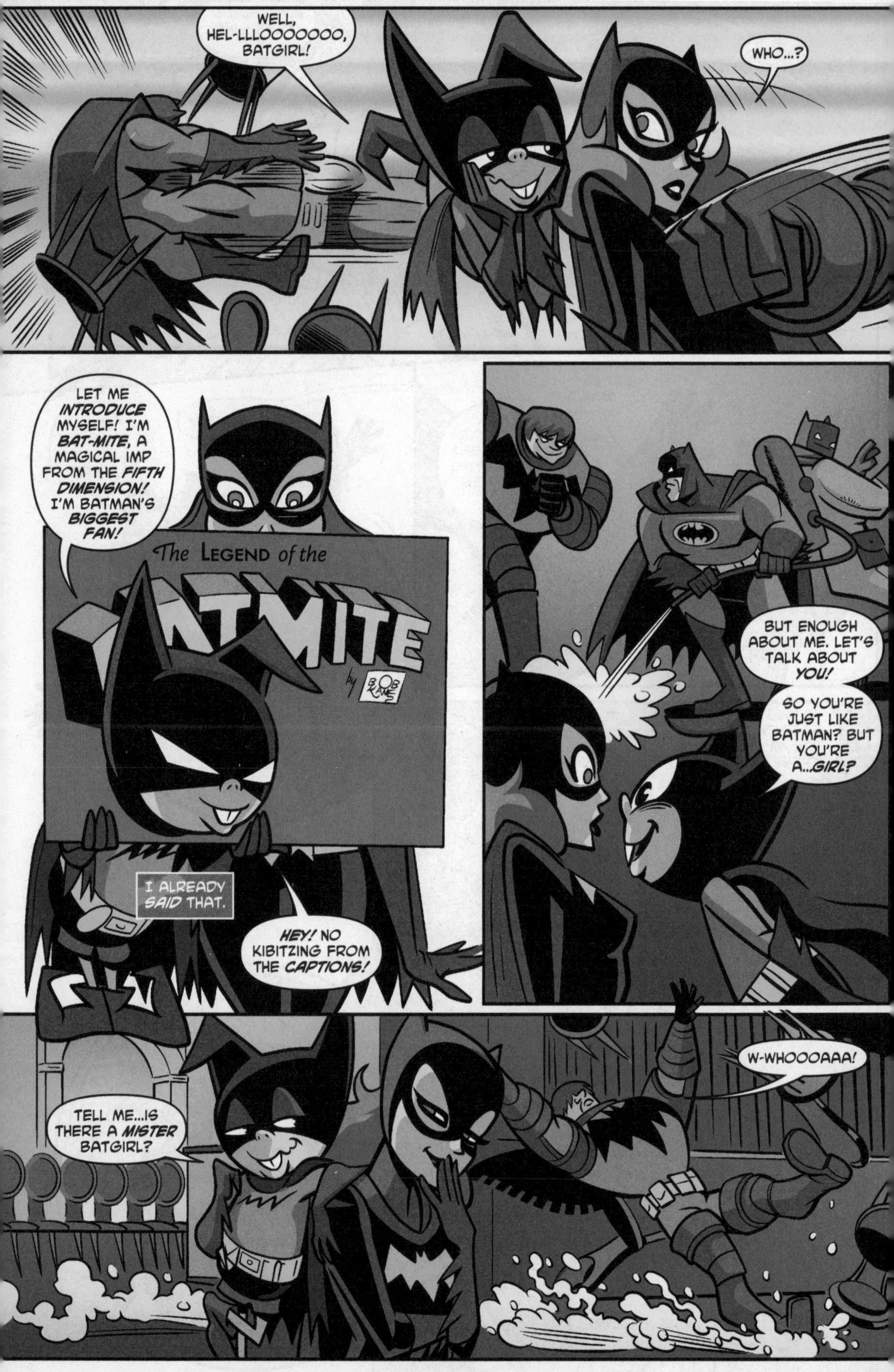
WELL, HEL-LLLOOOOOOO, BATGIRL!
WHO...?
LET ME INTRODUCE MYSELF! I'M BAT-MITE, A MAGICAL IMP FROM THE FIFTH DIMENSION! I'M BATMAN'S BIGGEST FAN!
The LEGEND of the BATMITE
by BOB KANE
I ALREADY SAID THAT.
HEY! NO KIBITZING FROM THE CAPTIONS!
BUT ENOUGH ABOUT ME. LET'S TALK ABOUT YOU!
SO YOU'RE JUST LIKE BATMAN? BUT YOU'RE A...GIRL?
W-WHOOOAAA!
TELL ME...IS THERE A MISTER BATGIRL?

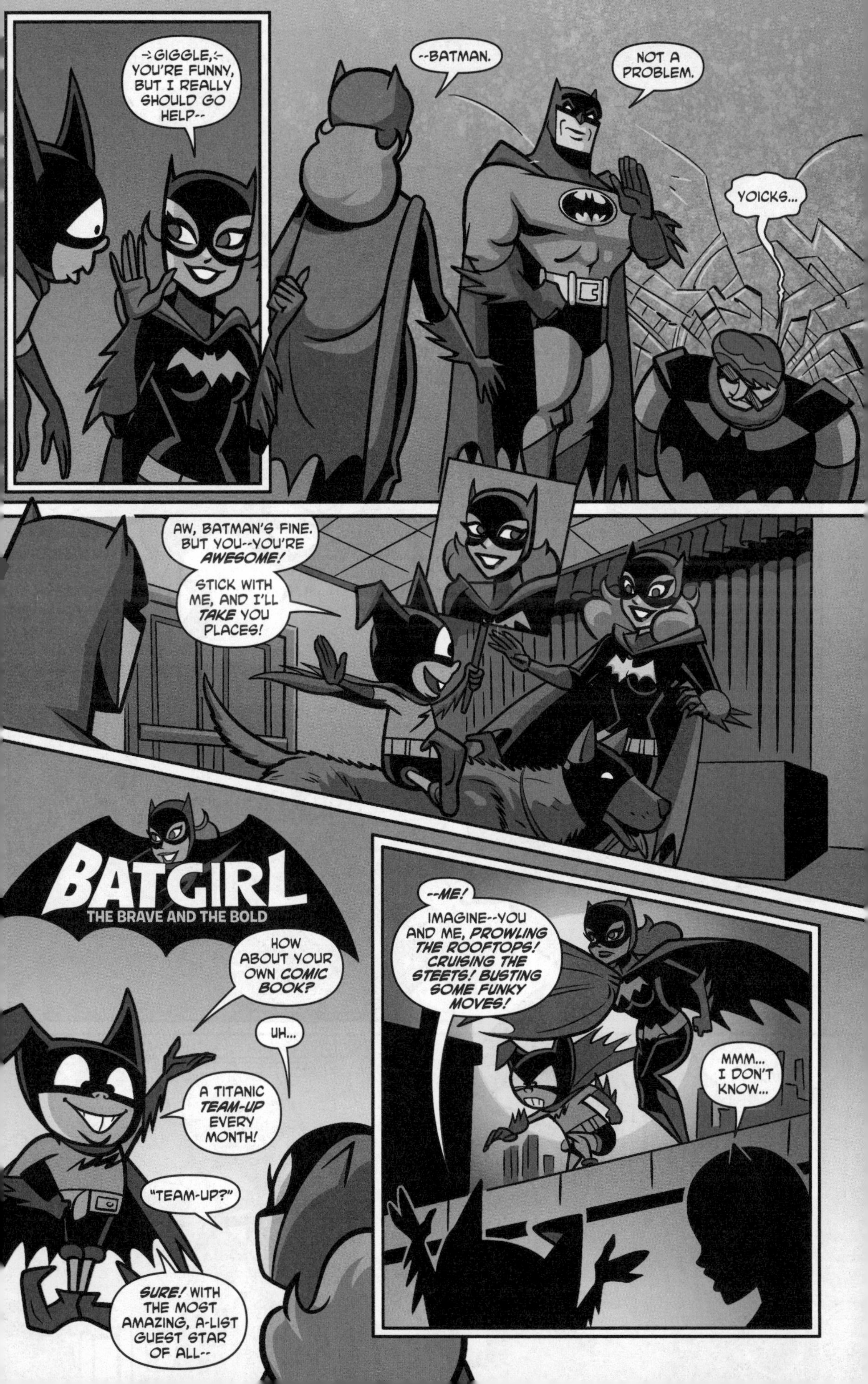

-:-GIGGLE,-:- YOU'RE FUNNY, BUT I REALLY SHOULD GO HELP--
--BATMAN.
NOT A PROBLEM.
YOICKS...
AW, BATMAN'S FINE. BUT YOU--YOU'RE AWESOME!
STICK WITH ME, AND I'LL TAKE YOU PLACES!
BATGIRL
THE BRAVE AND THE BOLD
HOW ABOUT YOUR OWN COMIC BOOK?
UH...
A TITANIC TEAM-UP EVERY MONTH!
"TEAM-UP?"
SURE! WITH THE MOST AMAZING, A-LIST GUEST STAR OF ALL--
--ME!
IMAGINE--YOU AND ME, PROWLING THE ROOFTOPS! CRUISING THE STEETS! BUSTING SOME FUNKY MOVES!
MMM... I DON'T KNOW...

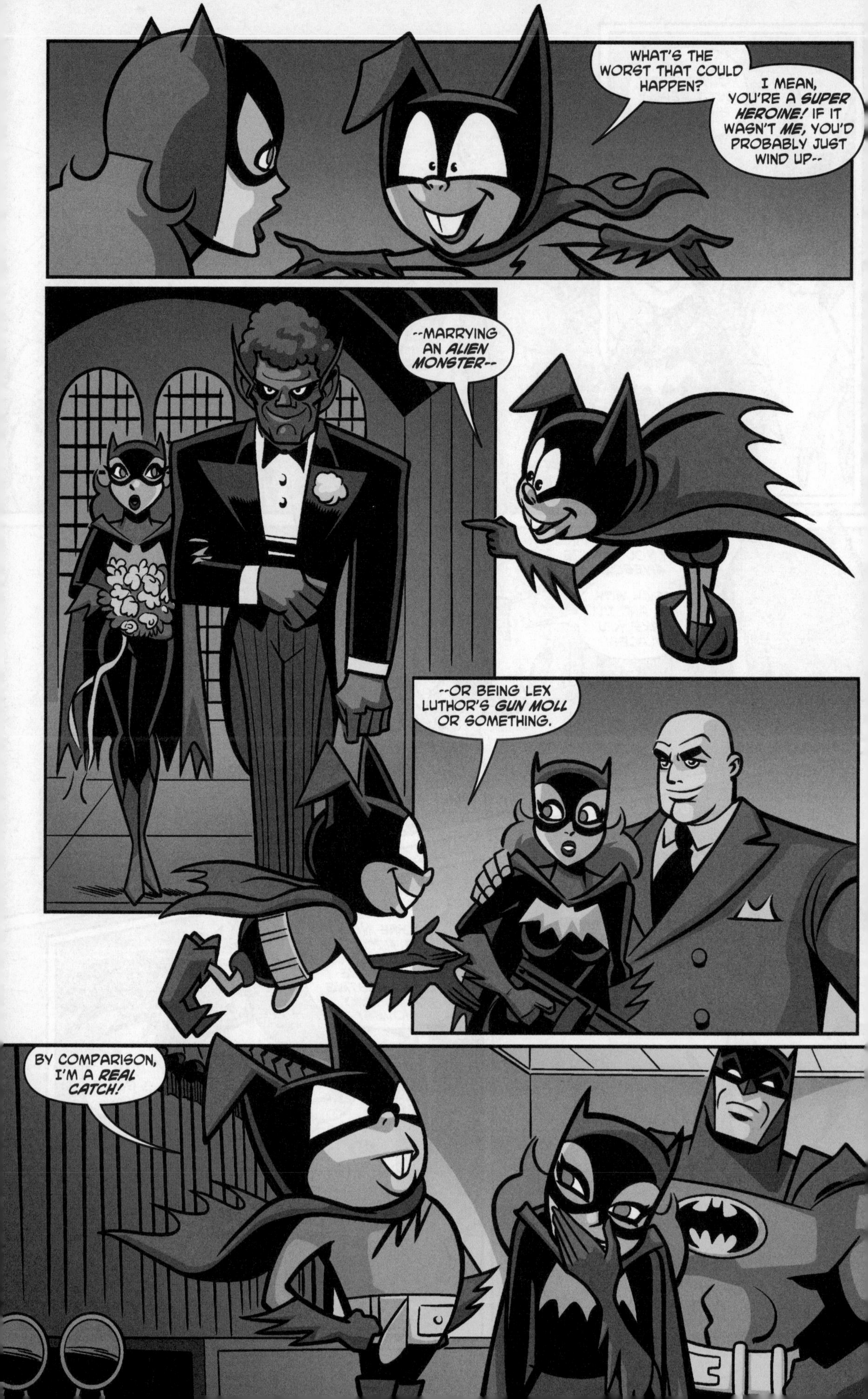
WHAT'S THE WORST THAT COULD HAPPEN?
I MEAN, YOU'RE A *SUPER HEROINE!* IF IT WASN'T *ME,* YOU'D PROBABLY JUST WIND UP--
--MARRYING AN *ALIEN MONSTER*--
--OR BEING LEX LUTHOR'S *GUN MOLL* OR SOMETHING.
BY COMPARISON, I'M A *REAL CATCH!*

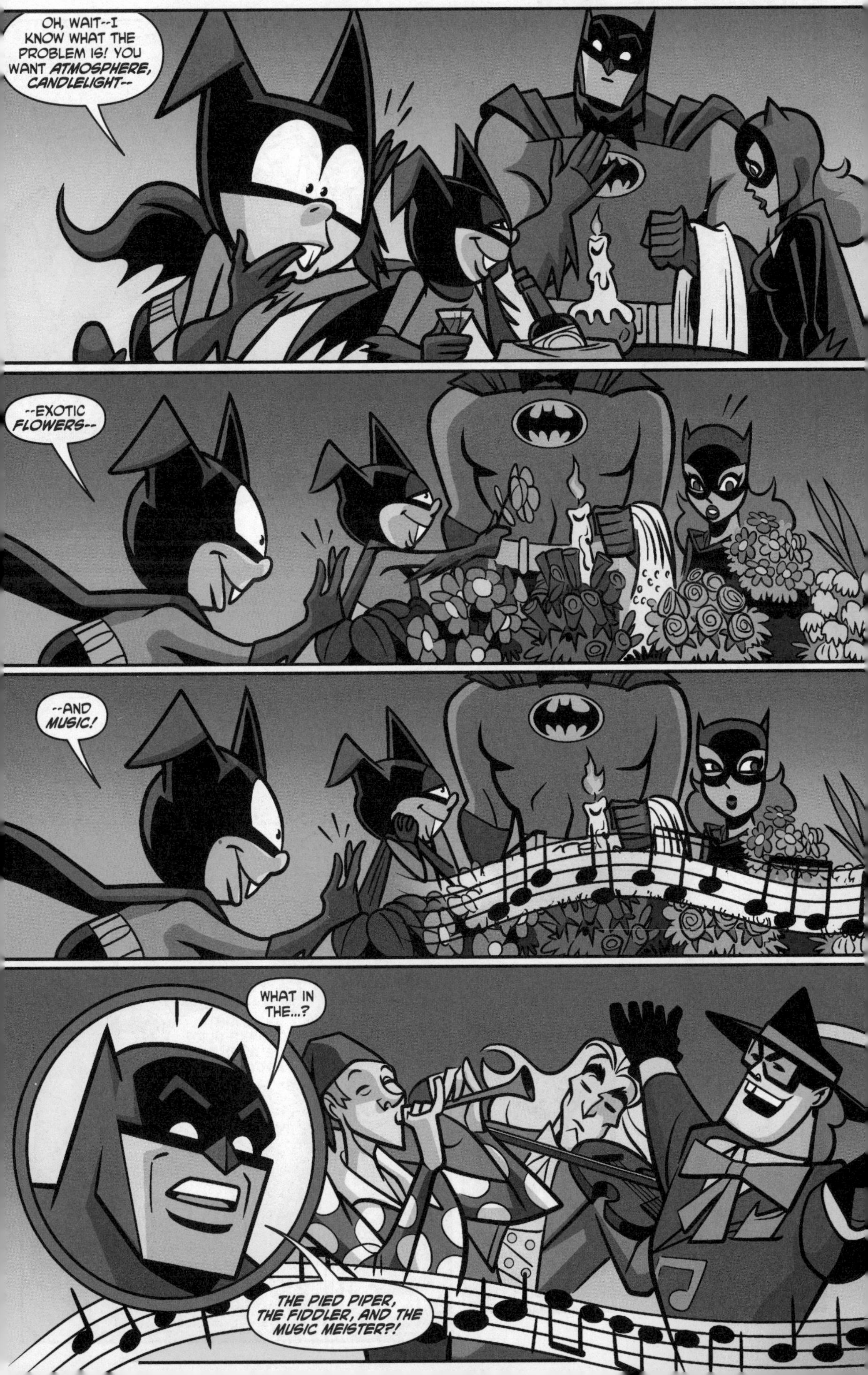
OH, WAIT--I KNOW WHAT THE PROBLEM IS! YOU WANT ATMOSPHERE, CANDLELIGHT--
--EXOTIC FLOWERS--
--AND MUSIC!
WHAT IN THE...?
THE PIED PIPER, THE FIDDLER, AND THE MUSIC MEISTER?!

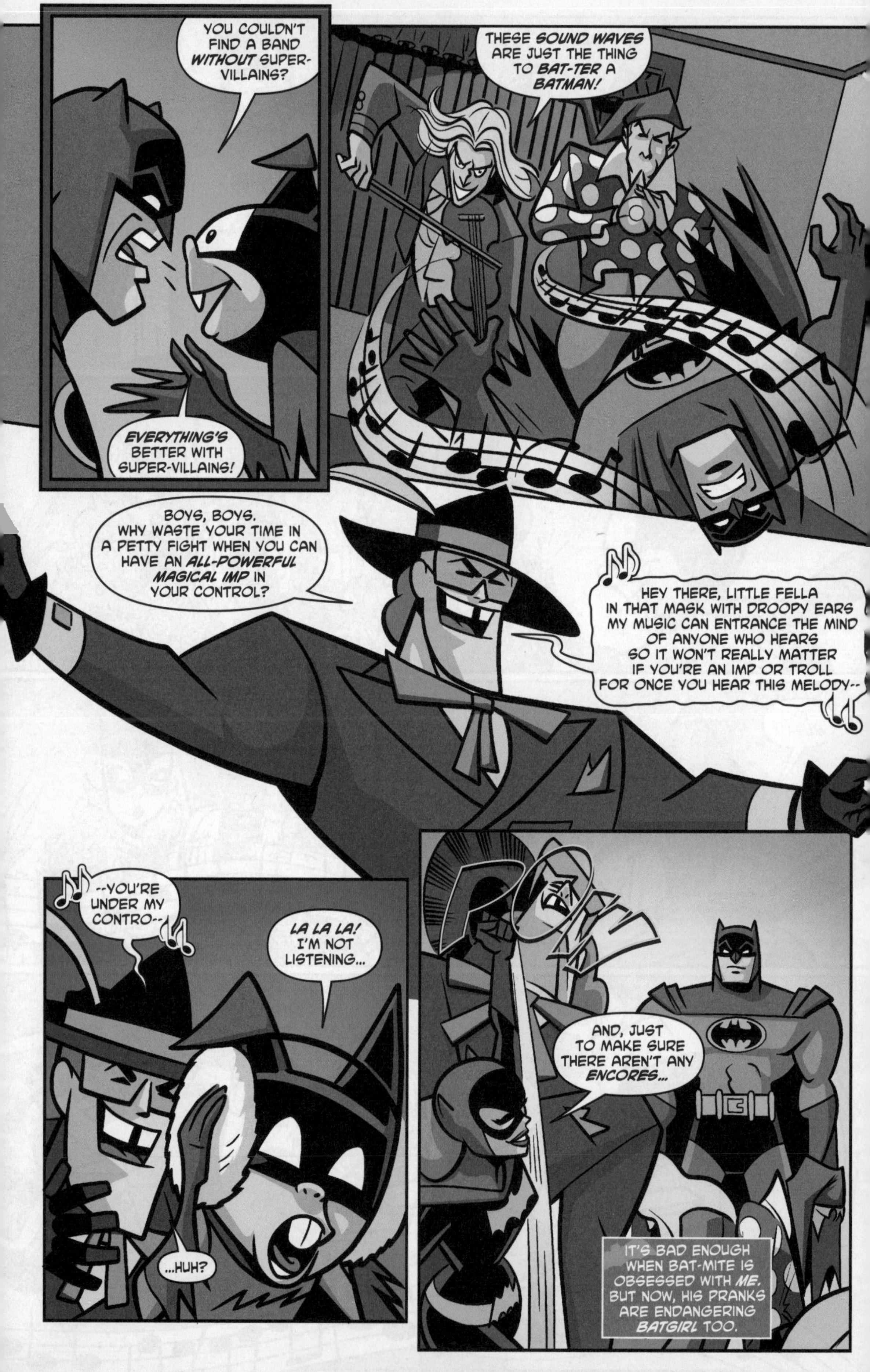

YOU COULDN'T FIND A BAND WITHOUT SUPER-VILLAINS?
EVERYTHING'S BETTER WITH SUPER-VILLAINS!
THESE SOUND WAVES ARE JUST THE THING TO BAT-TER A BATMAN!
BOYS, BOYS. WHY WASTE YOUR TIME IN A PETTY FIGHT WHEN YOU CAN HAVE AN ALL-POWERFUL MAGICAL IMP IN YOUR CONTROL?
HEY THERE, LITTLE FELLA IN THAT MASK WITH DROOPY EARS MY MUSIC CAN ENTRANCE THE MIND OF ANYONE WHO HEARS SO IT WON'T REALLY MATTER IF YOU'RE AN IMP OR TROLL FOR ONCE YOU HEAR THIS MELODY--
--YOU'RE UNDER MY CONTRO--
LA LA LA! I'M NOT LISTENING...
...HUH?
AND, JUST TO MAKE SURE THERE AREN'T ANY ENCORES...
IT'S BAD ENOUGH WHEN BAT-MITE IS OBSESSED WITH ME. BUT NOW, HIS PRANKS ARE ENDANGERING BATGIRL TOO.

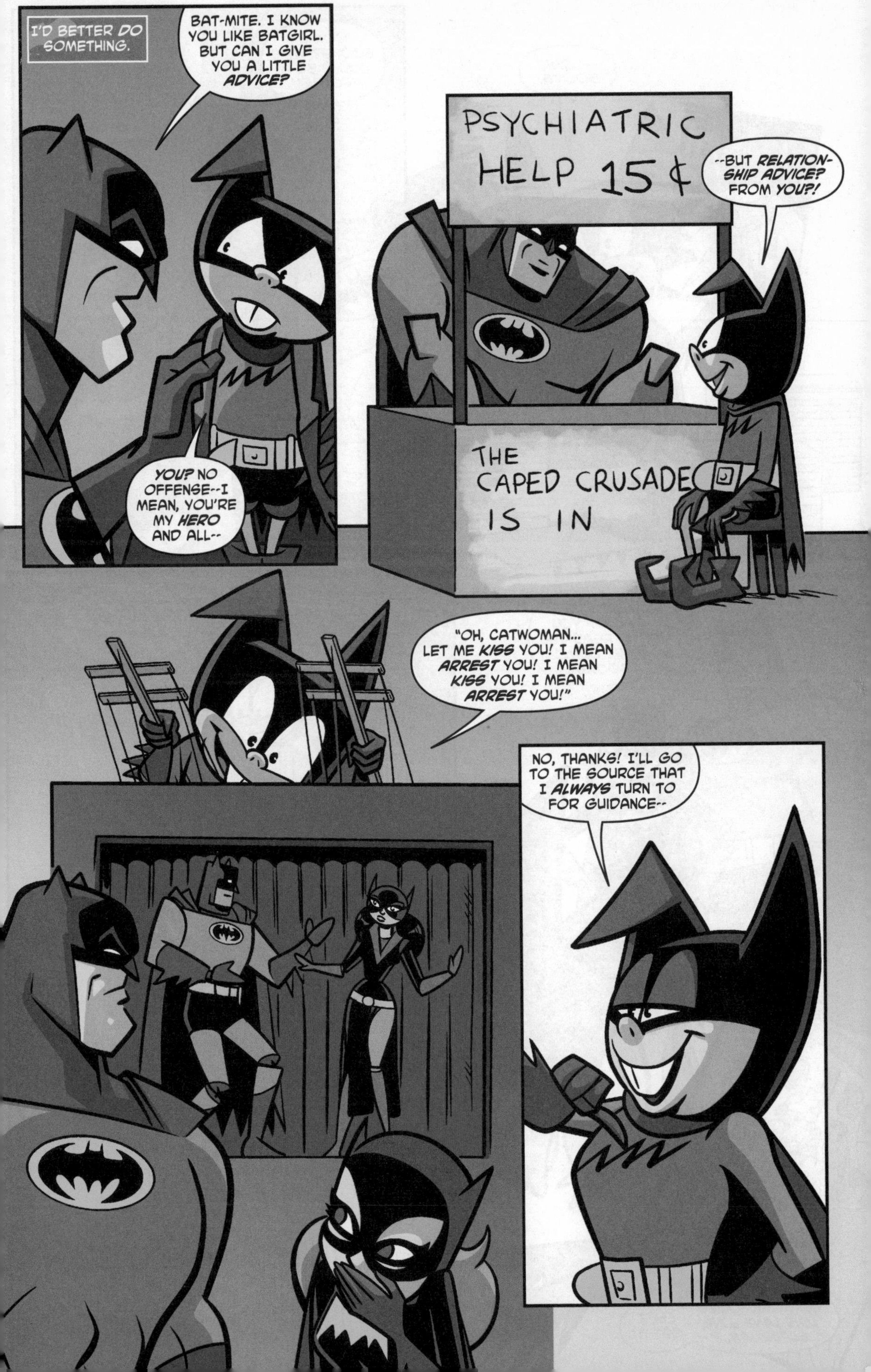
I'D BETTER DO SOMETHING.
BAT-MITE. I KNOW YOU LIKE BATGIRL. BUT CAN I GIVE YOU A LITTLE ADVICE?
YOU? NO OFFENSE--I MEAN, YOU'RE MY HERO AND ALL--
PSYCHIATRIC HELP 15¢
THE CAPED CRUSADE IS IN
--BUT RELATIONSHIP ADVICE? FROM YOU?!
"OH, CATWOMAN... LET ME KISS YOU! I MEAN ARREST YOU! I MEAN KISS YOU! I MEAN ARREST YOU!"
NO, THANKS! I'LL GO TO THE SOURCE THAT I ALWAYS TURN TO FOR GUIDANCE--

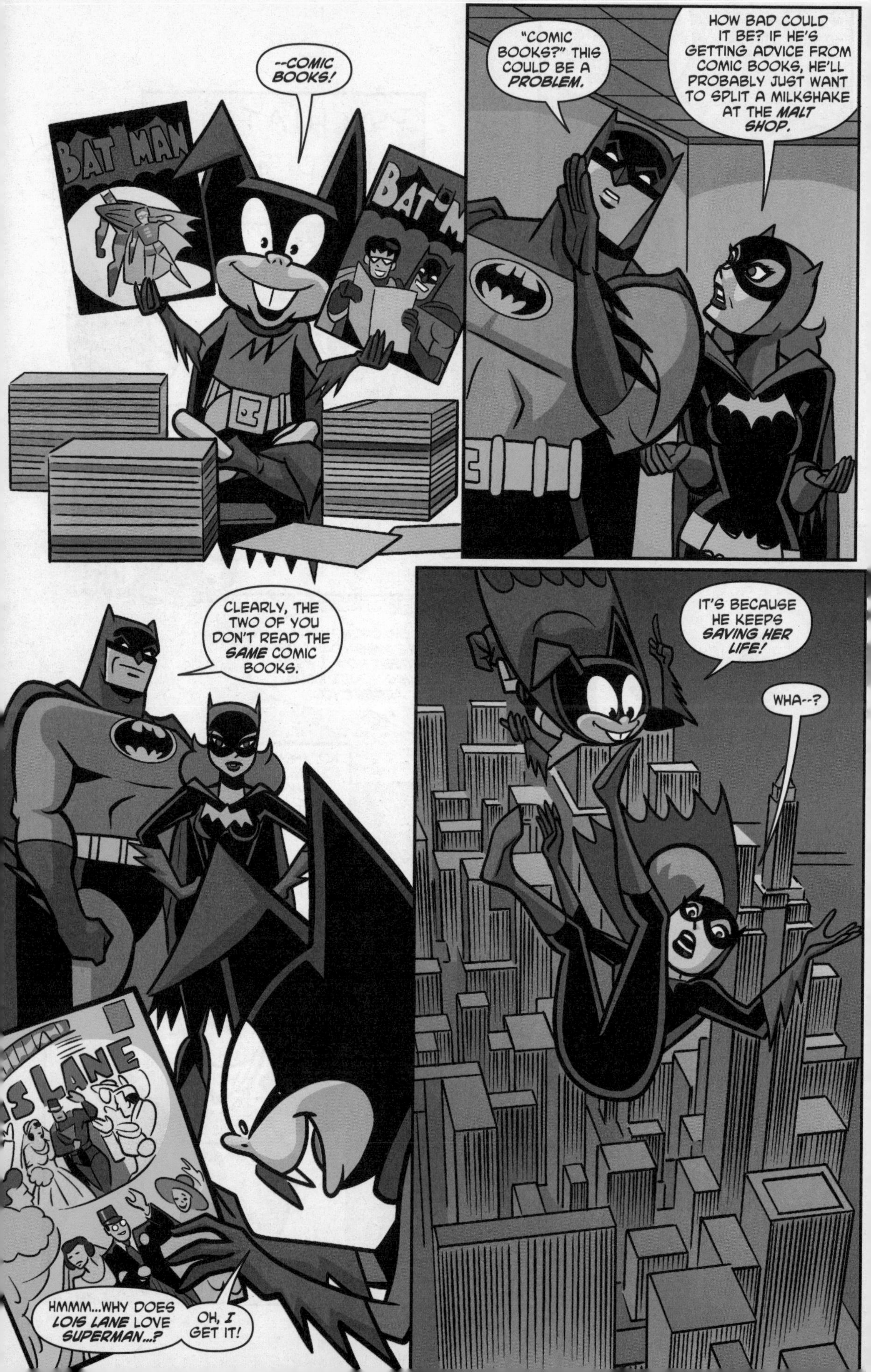
BAT MAN
BAT M
--*COMIC BOOKS!*
"COMIC BOOKS?" THIS COULD BE A *PROBLEM.*
HOW BAD COULD IT BE? IF HE'S GETTING ADVICE FROM COMIC BOOKS, HE'LL PROBABLY JUST WANT TO SPLIT A MILKSHAKE AT THE *MALT SHOP.*
CLEARLY, THE TWO OF YOU DON'T READ THE *SAME* COMIC BOOKS.
IS LANE
HMMM...WHY DOES *LOIS LANE* LOVE *SUPERMAN...?*
OH, *I* GET IT!
IT'S BECAUSE HE KEEPS *SAVING HER LIFE!*
WHA--?

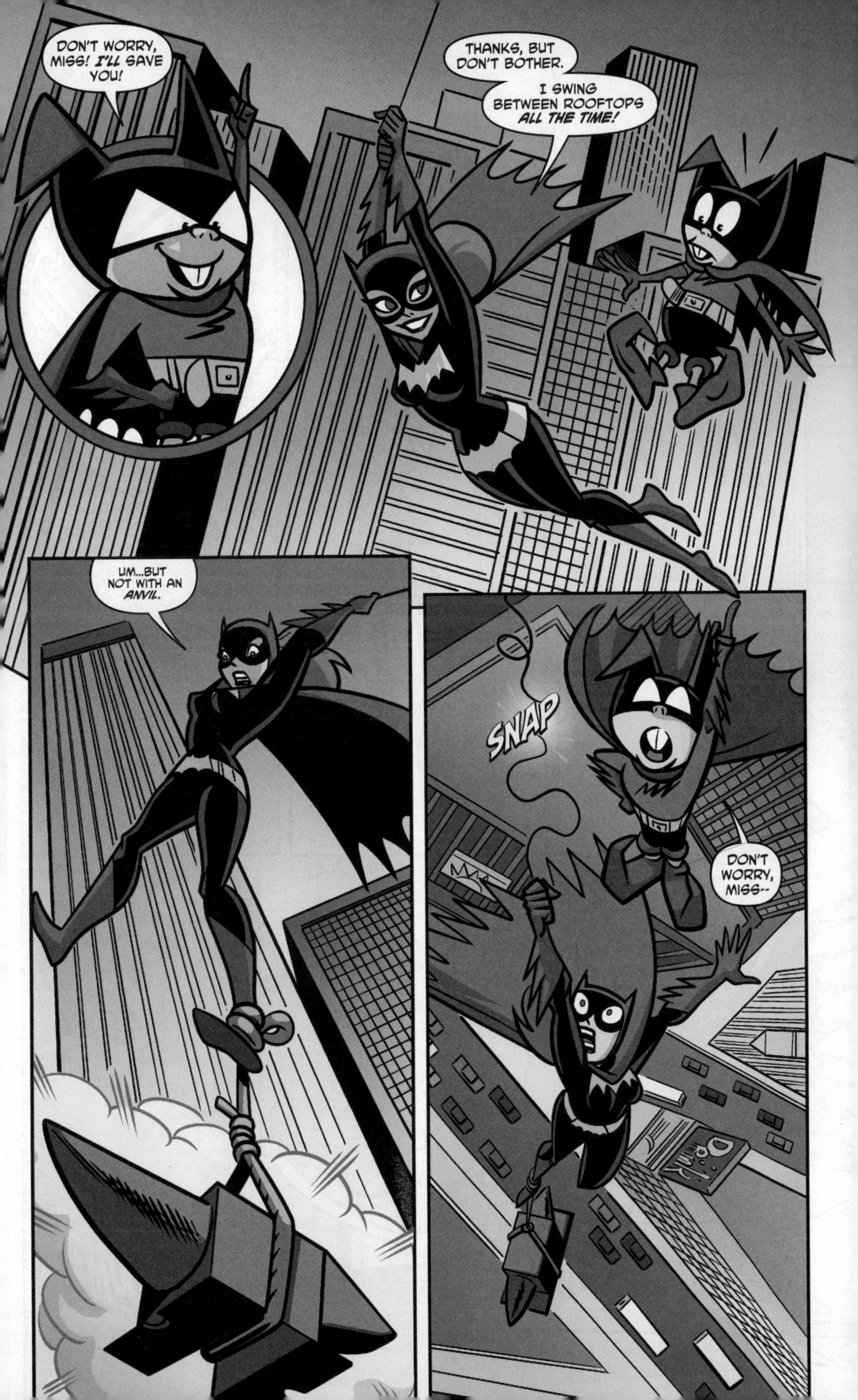
DON'T WORRY, MISS! I'LL SAVE YOU!
THANKS, BUT DON'T BOTHER.
I SWING BETWEEN ROOFTOPS ALL THE TIME!
UM...BUT NOT WITH AN ANVIL.
SNAP
DON'T WORRY, MISS--

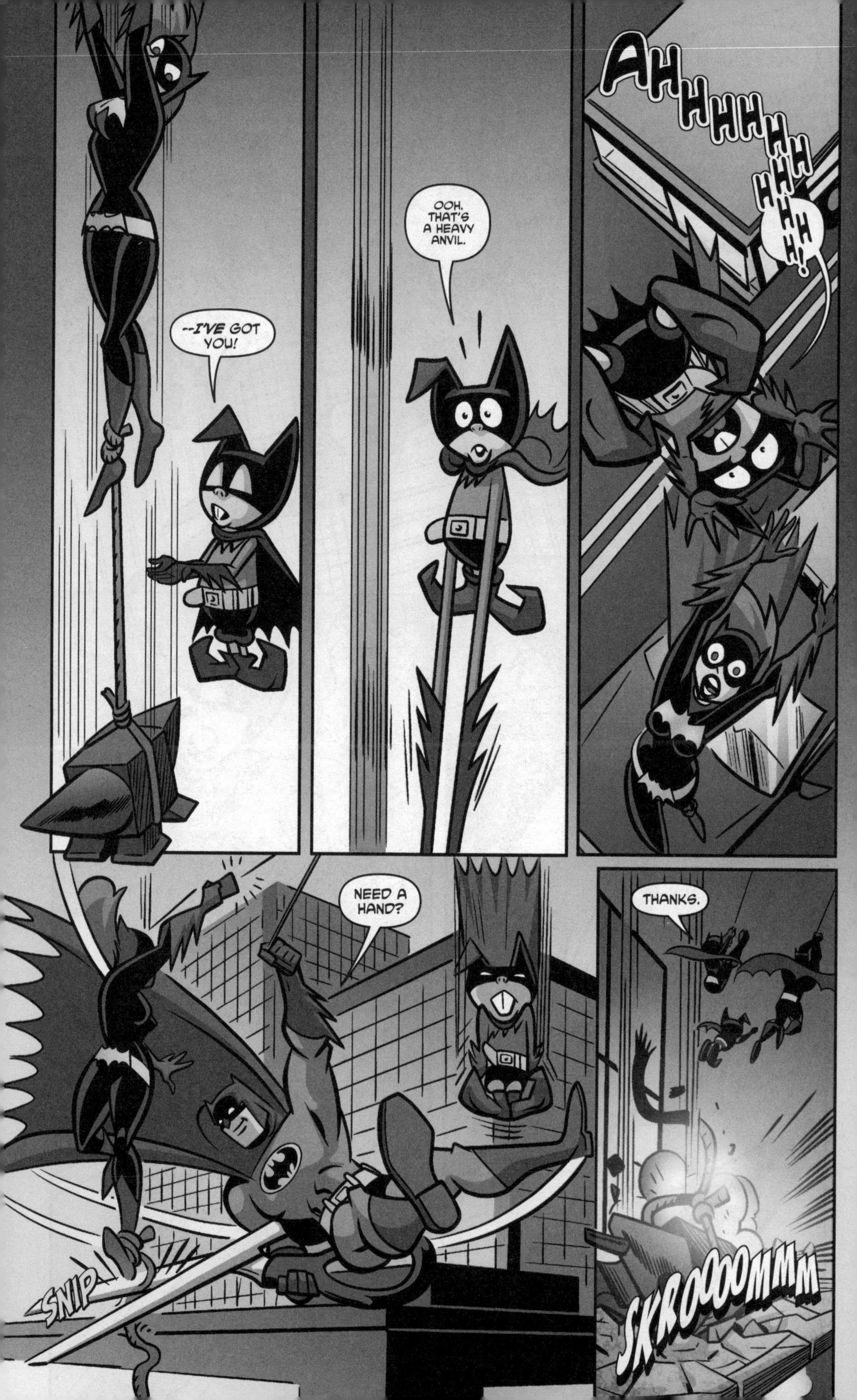
--I'VE GOT YOU!
OOH. THAT'S A HEAVY ANVIL.
AHHHHHHHHHHHHH!
NEED A HAND?
SNIP
THANKS.
SKROOOOMMM

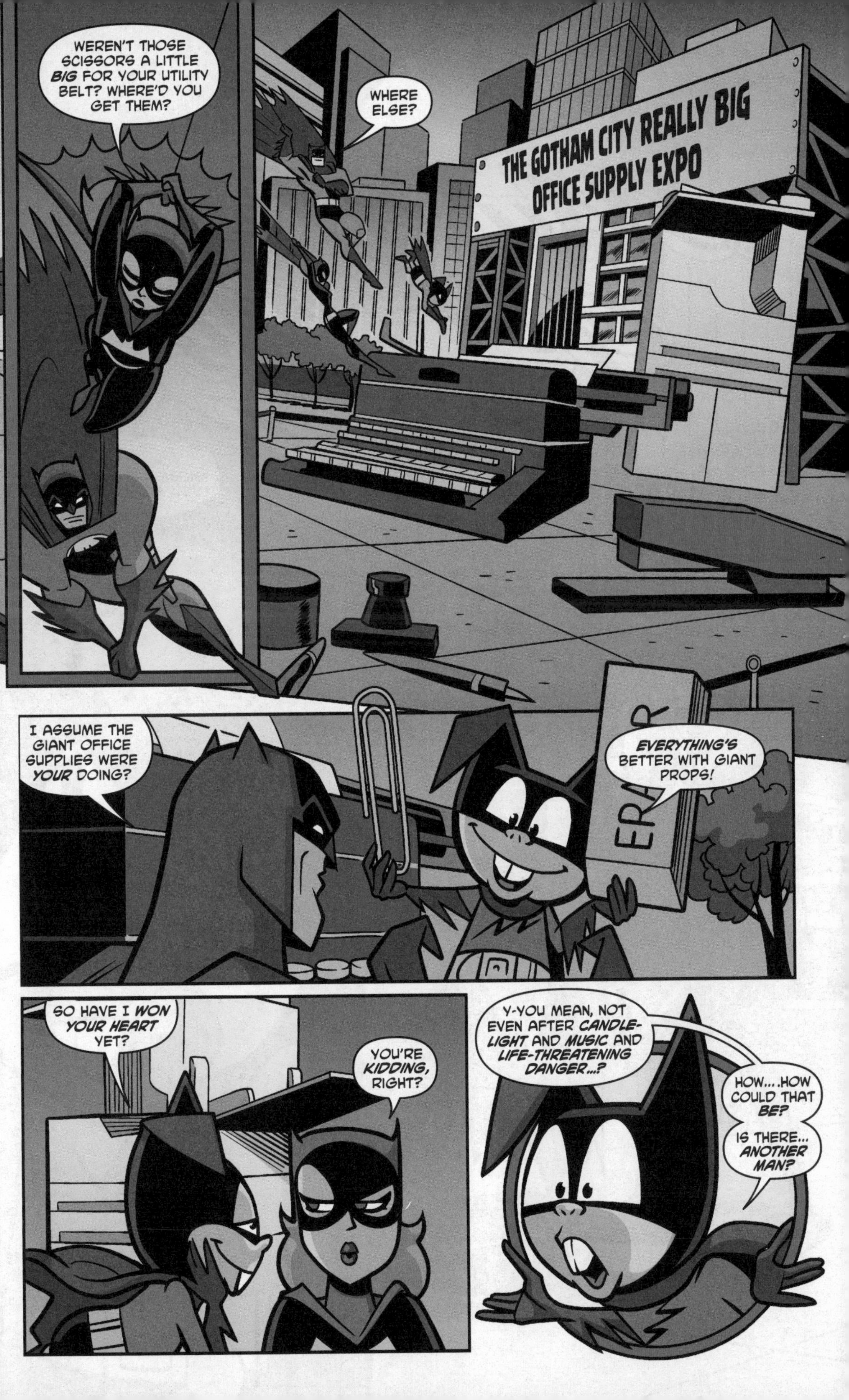
WEREN'T THOSE SCISSORS A LITTLE *BIG* FOR YOUR UTILITY BELT? WHERE'D YOU GET THEM?
WHERE ELSE?
THE GOTHAM CITY REALLY BIG OFFICE SUPPLY EXPO
I ASSUME THE GIANT OFFICE SUPPLIES WERE *YOUR* DOING?
EVERYTHING'S BETTER WITH GIANT PROPS!
ERA
SO HAVE I *WON YOUR HEART* YET?
YOU'RE *KIDDING,* RIGHT?
Y-YOU MEAN, NOT EVEN AFTER *CANDLE-LIGHT* AND *MUSIC* AND *LIFE-THREATENING DANGER...?*
HOW....HOW COULD THAT *BE?*
IS THERE... *ANOTHER MAN?*

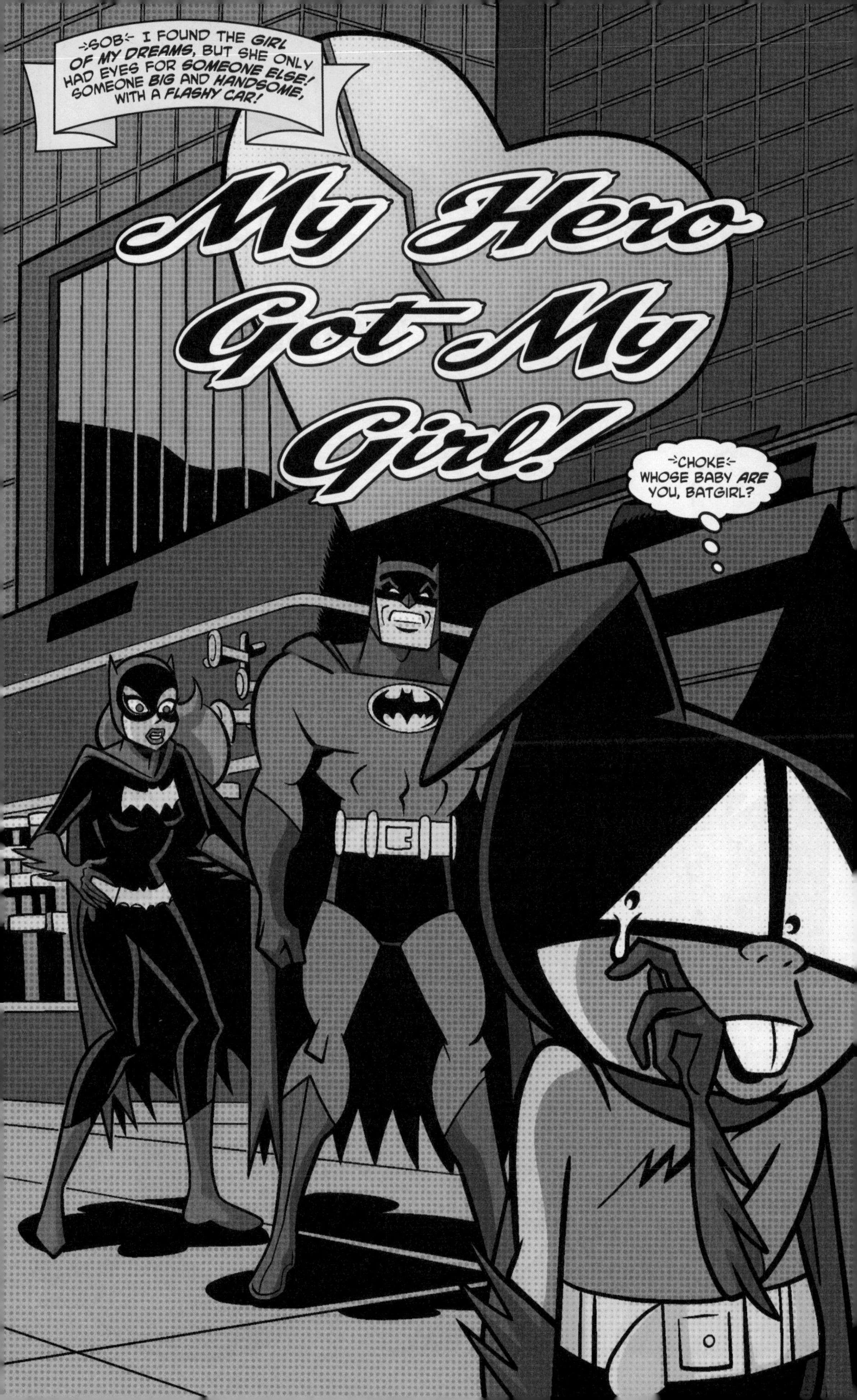

-SOB- I FOUND THE GIRL OF MY DREAMS, BUT SHE ONLY HAD EYES FOR SOMEONE ELSE! SOMEONE BIG AND HANDSOME, WITH A FLASHY CAR!
My Hero Got My Girl!
-CHOKE- WHOSE BABY ARE YOU, BATGIRL?

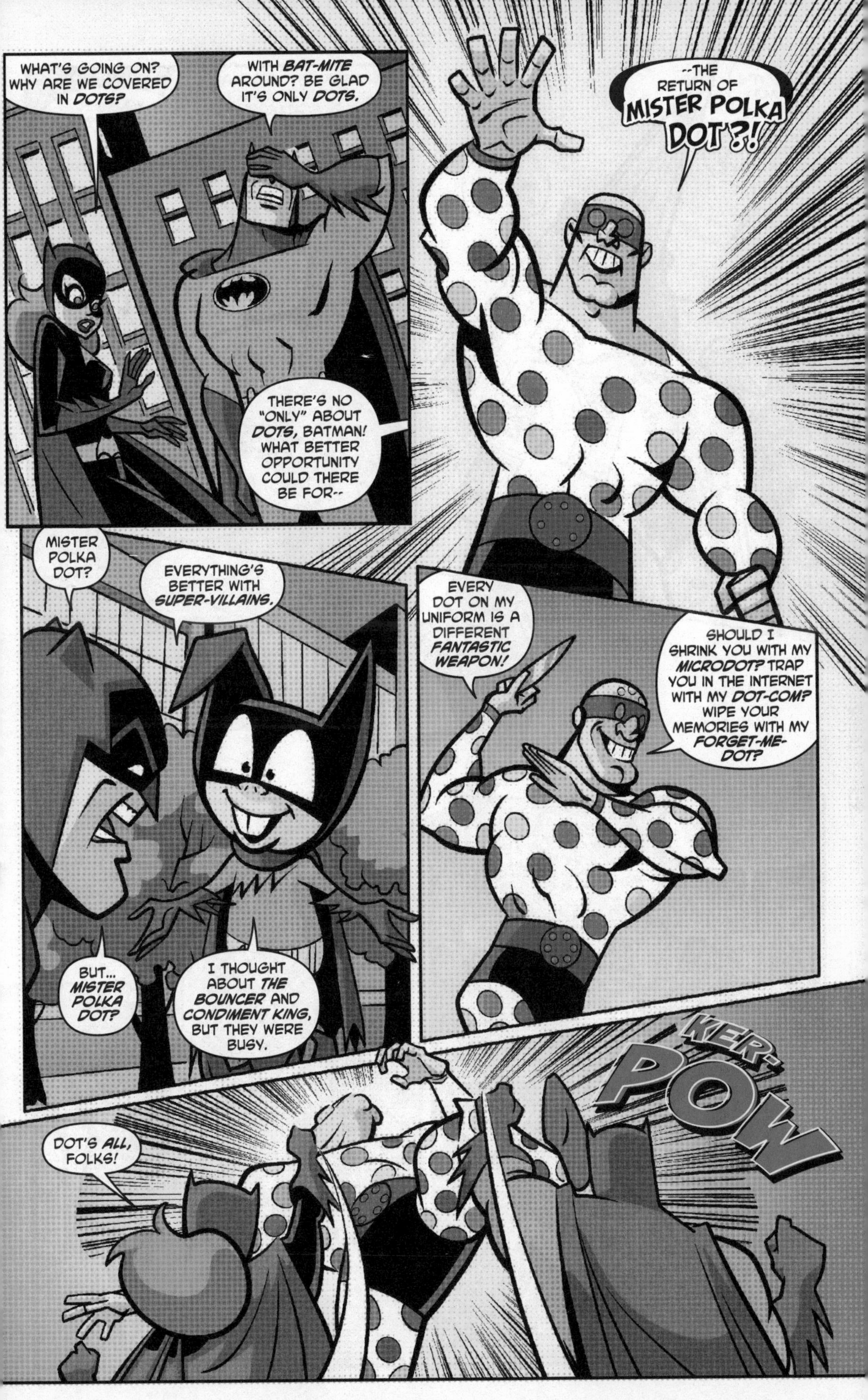
WHAT'S GOING ON? WHY ARE WE COVERED IN *DOTS?*
WITH *BAT-MITE* AROUND? BE GLAD IT'S ONLY *DOTS.*
THERE'S NO "ONLY" ABOUT *DOTS,* BATMAN! WHAT BETTER OPPORTUNITY COULD THERE BE FOR--
--THE RETURN OF MISTER POLKA DOT?!
MISTER POLKA DOT?
EVERYTHING'S BETTER WITH *SUPER-VILLAINS.*
BUT... *MISTER POLKA DOT?*
I THOUGHT ABOUT *THE BOUNCER* AND *CONDIMENT KING,* BUT THEY WERE BUSY.
EVERY DOT ON MY UNIFORM IS A DIFFERENT *FANTASTIC WEAPON!*
SHOULD I SHRINK YOU WITH MY *MICRODOT?* TRAP YOU IN THE INTERNET WITH MY *DOT-COM?* WIPE YOUR MEMORIES WITH MY *FORGET-ME-DOT?*
KER-POW
DOT'S *ALL,* FOLKS!

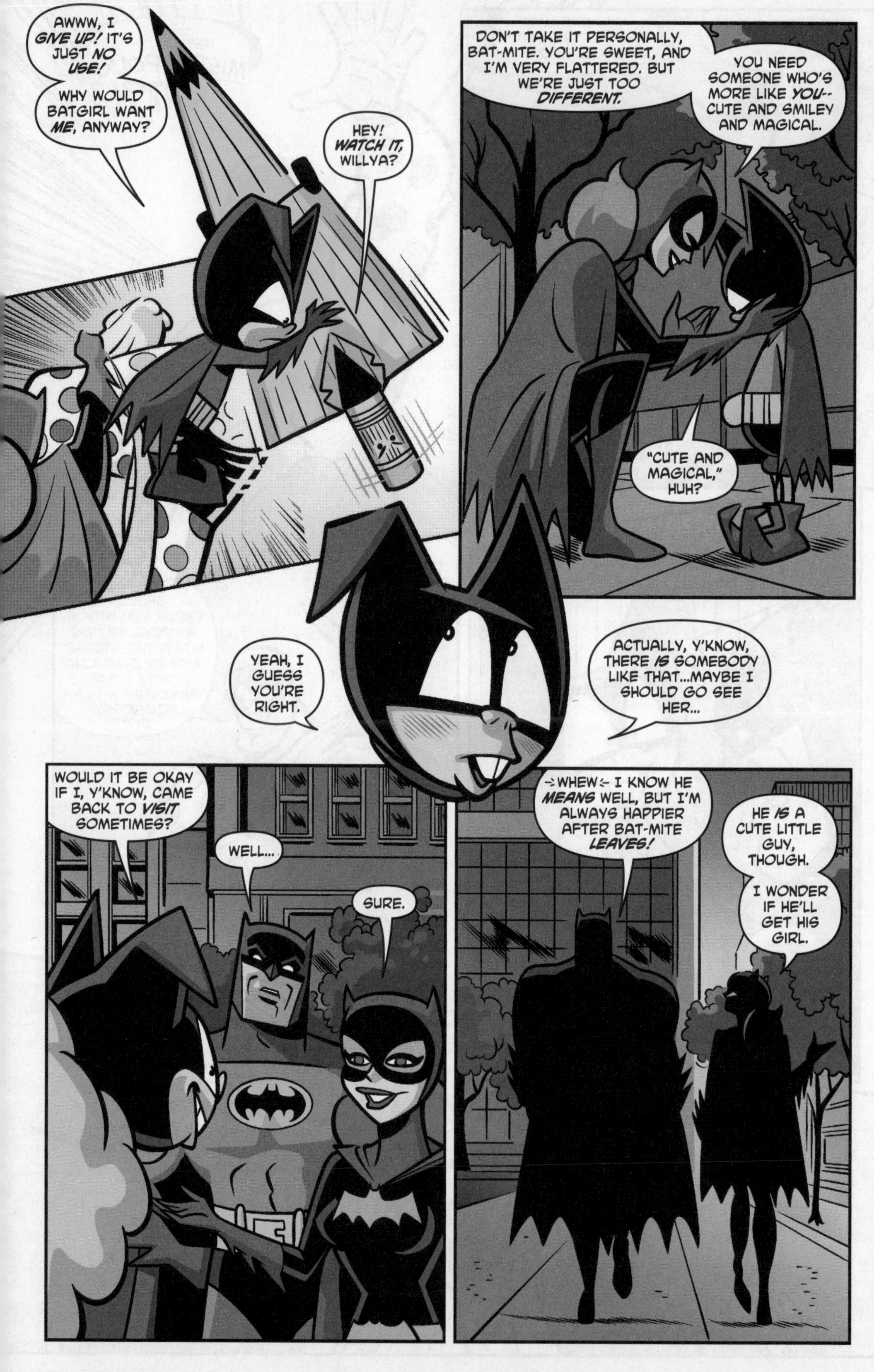
AWWW, I GIVE UP! IT'S JUST NO USE!
WHY WOULD BATGIRL WANT ME, ANYWAY?
HEY! WATCH IT, WILLYA?
DON'T TAKE IT PERSONALLY, BAT-MITE. YOU'RE SWEET, AND I'M VERY FLATTERED. BUT WE'RE JUST TOO DIFFERENT.
YOU NEED SOMEONE WHO'S MORE LIKE YOU--CUTE AND SMILEY AND MAGICAL.
"CUTE AND MAGICAL," HUH?
YEAH, I GUESS YOU'RE RIGHT.
ACTUALLY, Y'KNOW, THERE IS SOMEBODY LIKE THAT...MAYBE I SHOULD GO SEE HER...
WOULD IT BE OKAY IF I, Y'KNOW, CAME BACK TO VISIT SOMETIMES?
WELL...
SURE.
WHEW I KNOW HE MEANS WELL, BUT I'M ALWAYS HAPPIER AFTER BAT-MITE LEAVES!
HE IS A CUTE LITTLE GUY, THOUGH.
I WONDER IF HE'LL GET HIS GIRL.

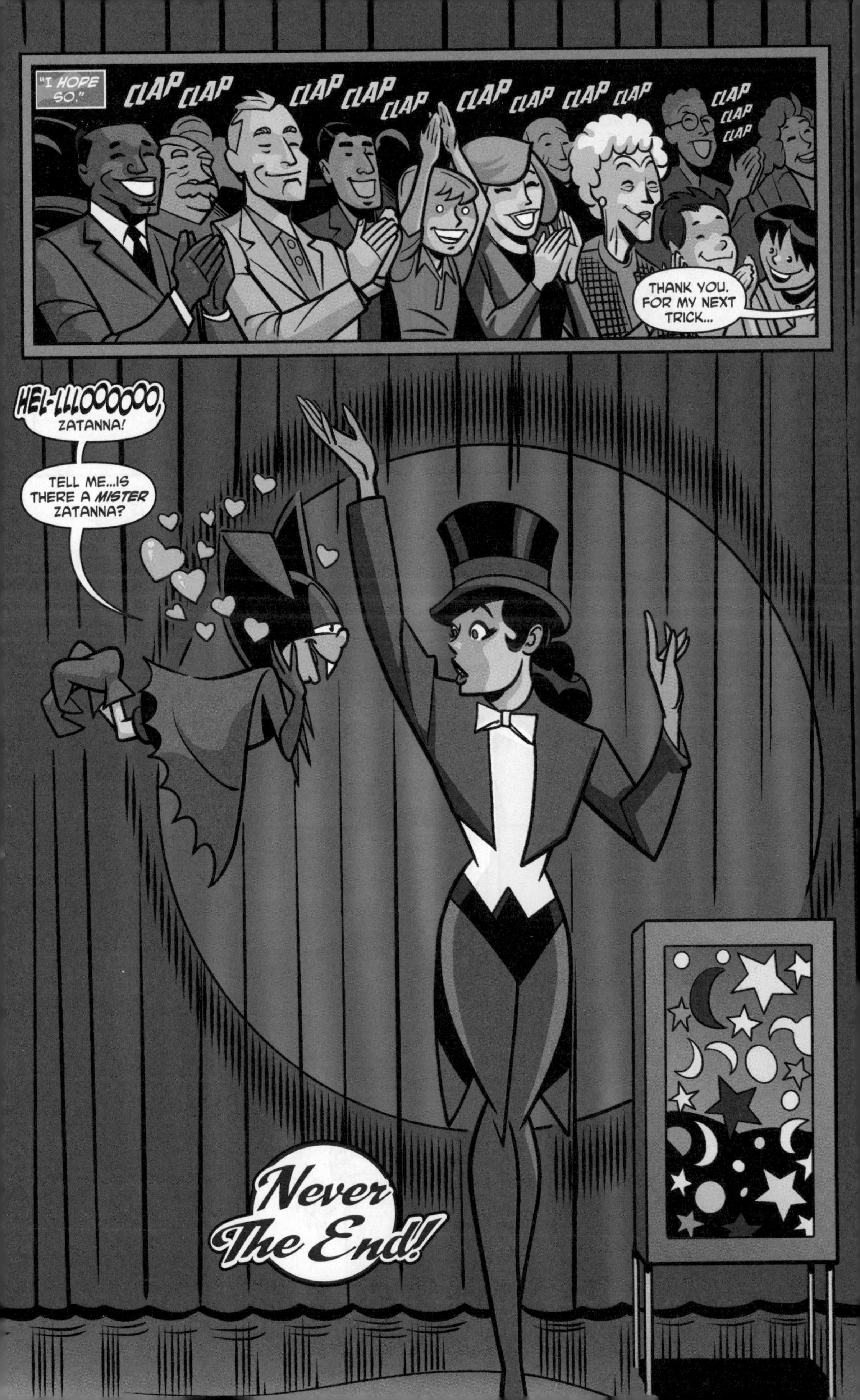
"I HOPE SO."
CLAP CLAP
CLAP CLAP CLAP
CLAP CLAP CLAP CLAP
CLAP CLAP CLAP
THANK YOU. FOR MY NEXT TRICK...
HEL-LLLOOOOOO, ZATANNA!
TELL ME...IS THERE A MISTER ZATANNA?
Never The End!

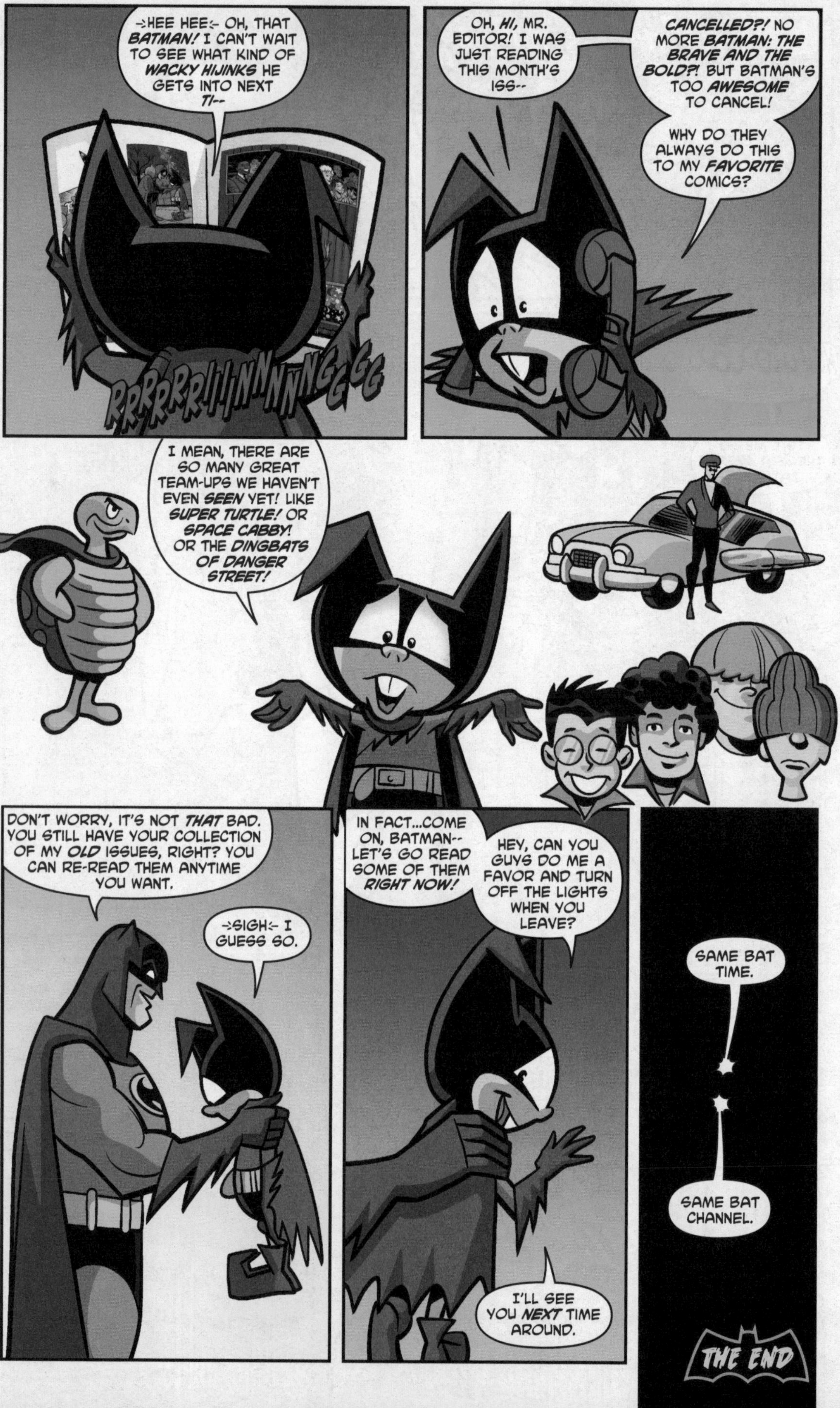

~HEE HEE~ OH, THAT BATMAN! I CAN'T WAIT TO SEE WHAT KIND OF WACKY HIJINKS HE GETS INTO NEXT TI--
RRRRRIIINNNNNGGGG
OH, HI, MR. EDITOR! I WAS JUST READING THIS MONTH'S ISS--
CANCELLED?! NO MORE BATMAN: THE BRAVE AND THE BOLD?! BUT BATMAN'S TOO AWESOME TO CANCEL!
WHY DO THEY ALWAYS DO THIS TO MY FAVORITE COMICS?
I MEAN, THERE ARE SO MANY GREAT TEAM-UPS WE HAVEN'T EVEN SEEN YET! LIKE SUPER TURTLE! OR SPACE CABBY! OR THE DINGBATS OF DANGER STREET!
DON'T WORRY, IT'S NOT THAT BAD. YOU STILL HAVE YOUR COLLECTION OF MY OLD ISSUES, RIGHT? YOU CAN RE-READ THEM ANYTIME YOU WANT.
~SIGH~ I GUESS SO.
IN FACT...COME ON, BATMAN-- LET'S GO READ SOME OF THEM RIGHT NOW!
HEY, CAN YOU GUYS DO ME A FAVOR AND TURN OFF THE LIGHTS WHEN YOU LEAVE?
I'LL SEE YOU NEXT TIME AROUND.
SAME BAT TIME.
SAME BAT CHANNEL.
THE END

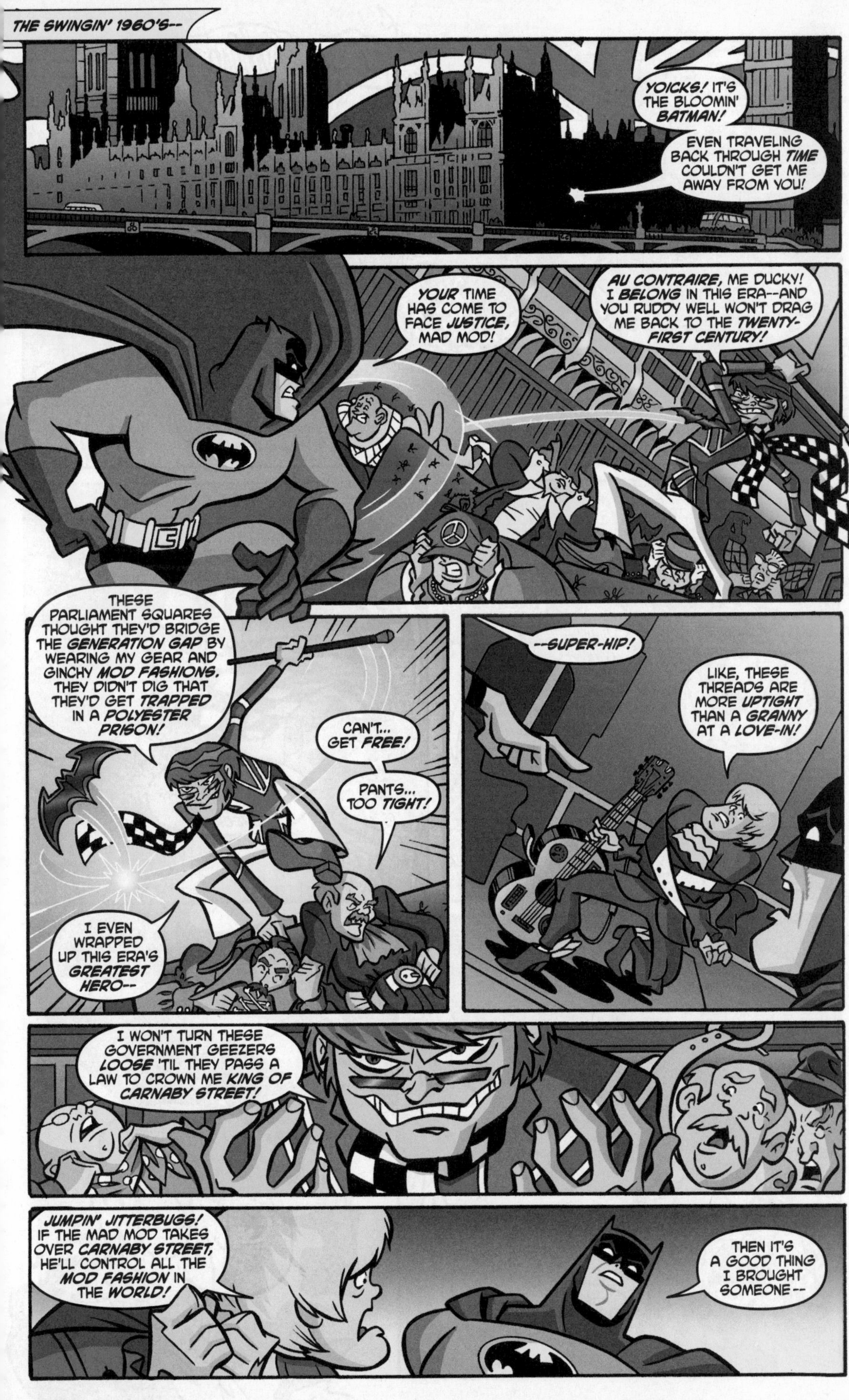
THE SWINGIN' 1960'S--
YOICKS! IT'S THE BLOOMIN' BATMAN!
EVEN TRAVELING BACK THROUGH TIME COULDN'T GET ME AWAY FROM YOU!
YOUR TIME HAS COME TO FACE JUSTICE, MAD MOD!
AU CONTRAIRE, ME DUCKY! I BELONG IN THIS ERA--AND YOU RUDDY WELL WON'T DRAG ME BACK TO THE TWENTY-FIRST CENTURY!
THESE PARLIAMENT SQUARES THOUGHT THEY'D BRIDGE THE GENERATION GAP BY WEARING MY GEAR AND GINCHY MOD FASHIONS. THEY DIDN'T DIG THAT THEY'D GET TRAPPED IN A POLYESTER PRISON!
CAN'T... GET FREE!
PANTS... TOO TIGHT!
I EVEN WRAPPED UP THIS ERA'S GREATEST HERO--
--SUPER-HIP!
LIKE, THESE THREADS ARE MORE UPTIGHT THAN A GRANNY AT A LOVE-IN!
I WON'T TURN THESE GOVERNMENT GEEZERS LOOSE 'TIL THEY PASS A LAW TO CROWN ME KING OF CARNABY STREET!
JUMPIN' JITTERBUGS! IF THE MAD MOD TAKES OVER CARNABY STREET, HE'LL CONTROL ALL THE MOD FASHION IN THE WORLD!
THEN IT'S A GOOD THING I BROUGHT SOMEONE --

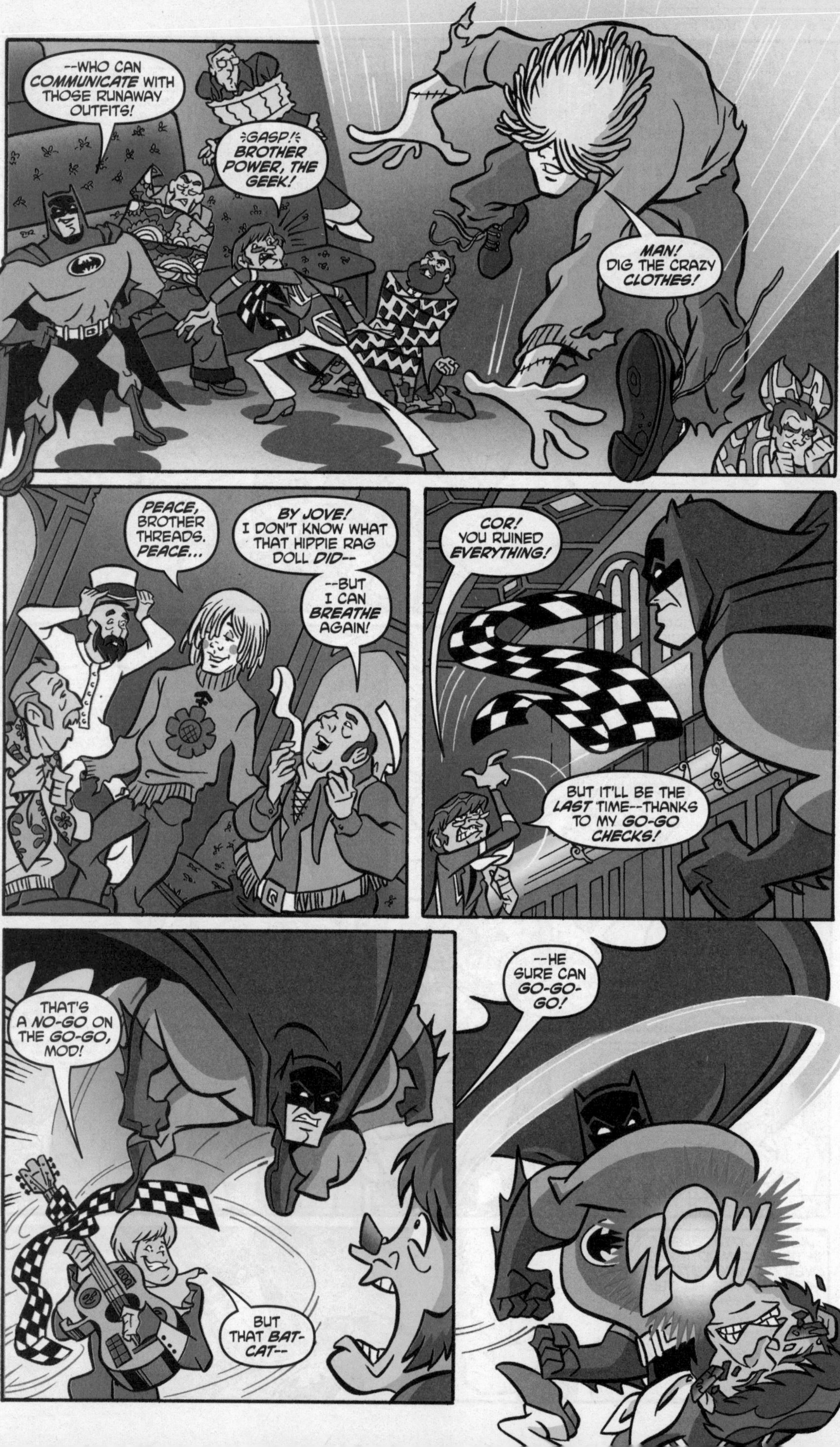
--WHO CAN COMMUNICATE WITH THOSE RUNAWAY OUTFITS!
GASP! BROTHER POWER, THE GEEK!
MAN! DIG THE CRAZY CLOTHES!
PEACE, BROTHER THREADS. PEACE...
BY JOVE! I DON'T KNOW WHAT THAT HIPPIE RAG DOLL DID--
--BUT I CAN BREATHE AGAIN!
COR! YOU RUINED EVERYTHING!
BUT IT'LL BE THE LAST TIME--THANKS TO MY GO-GO CHECKS!
THAT'S A NO-GO ON THE GO-GO, MOD!
BUT THAT BAT-CAT--
--HE SURE CAN GO-GO-GO!
ZOW

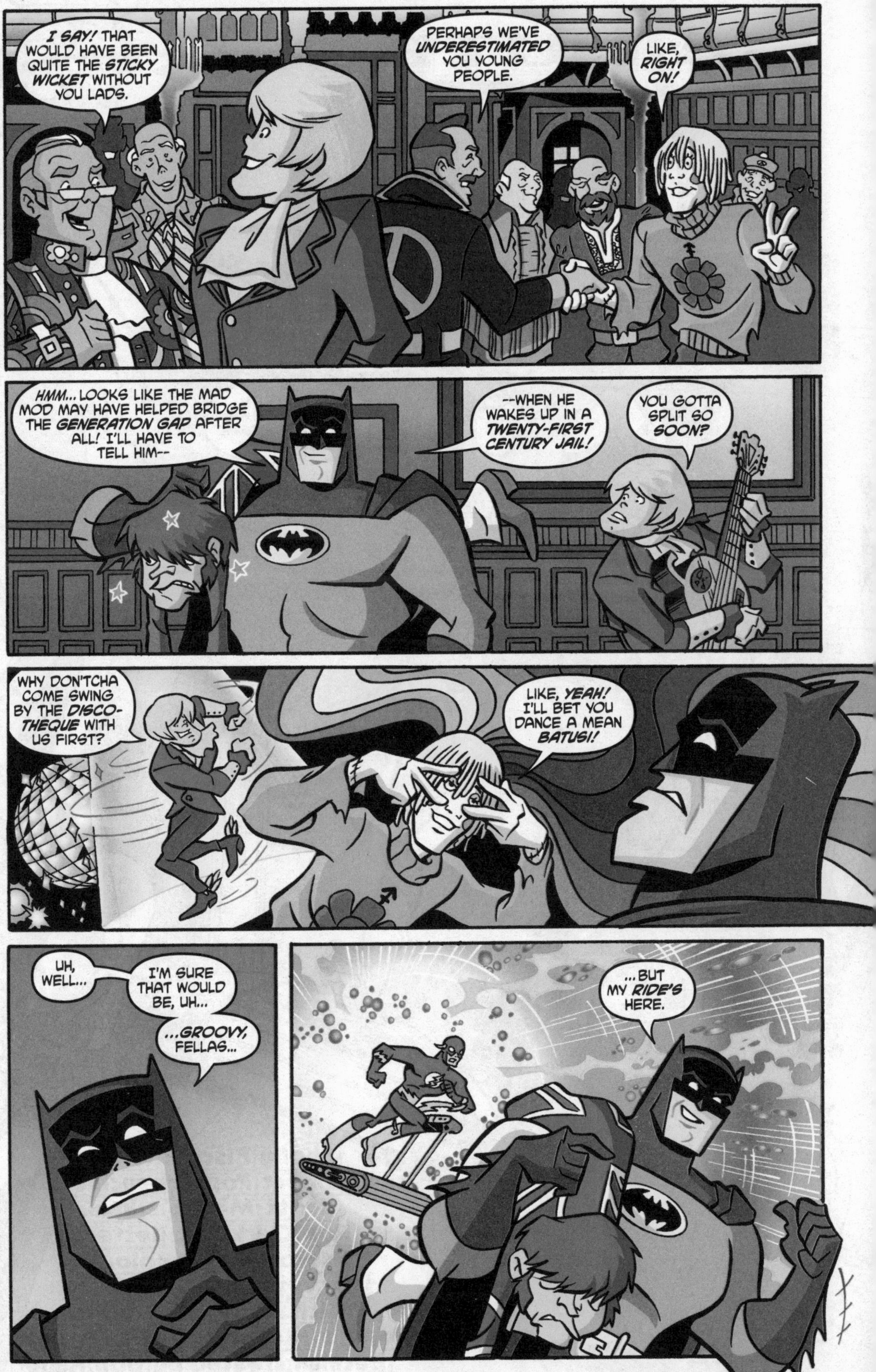
I SAY! THAT WOULD HAVE BEEN QUITE THE STICKY WICKET WITHOUT YOU LADS.
PERHAPS WE'VE UNDERESTIMATED YOU YOUNG PEOPLE.
LIKE, RIGHT ON!
HMM... LOOKS LIKE THE MAD MOD MAY HAVE HELPED BRIDGE THE GENERATION GAP AFTER ALL! I'LL HAVE TO TELL HIM--
--WHEN HE WAKES UP IN A TWENTY-FIRST CENTURY JAIL!
YOU GOTTA SPLIT SO SOON?
WHY DON'TCHA COME SWING BY THE DISCO-THEQUE WITH US FIRST?
LIKE, YEAH! I'LL BET YOU DANCE A MEAN BATUSI!
UH, WELL...
I'M SURE THAT WOULD BE, UH...
...GROOVY, FELLAS...
...BUT MY RIDE'S HERE.

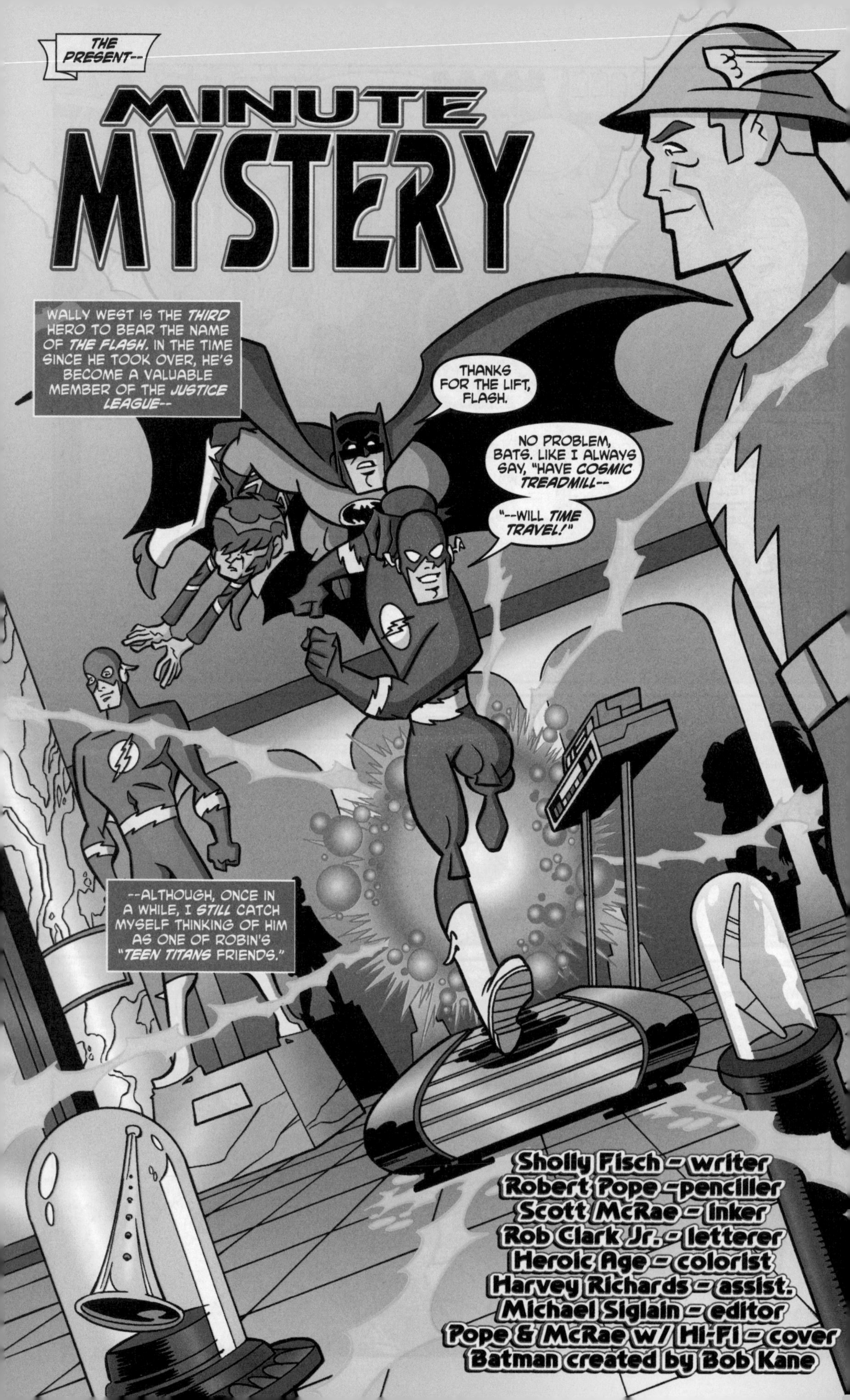
THE PRESENT--
MINUTE MYSTERY
WALLY WEST IS THE THIRD HERO TO BEAR THE NAME OF THE FLASH. IN THE TIME SINCE HE TOOK OVER, HE'S BECOME A VALUABLE MEMBER OF THE JUSTICE LEAGUE--
THANKS FOR THE LIFT, FLASH.
NO PROBLEM, BATS. LIKE I ALWAYS SAY, "HAVE COSMIC TREADMILL--
"--WILL TIME TRAVEL!"
--ALTHOUGH, ONCE IN A WHILE, I STILL CATCH MYSELF THINKING OF HIM AS ONE OF ROBIN'S "TEEN TITANS FRIENDS."
Sholly Fisch - writer
Robert Pope - penciller
Scott McRae - inker
Rob Clark Jr. - letterer
Heroic Age - colorist
Harvey Richards - assist.
Michael Siglain - editor
Pope & McRae w/ Hi-Fi - cover
Batman created by Bob Kane

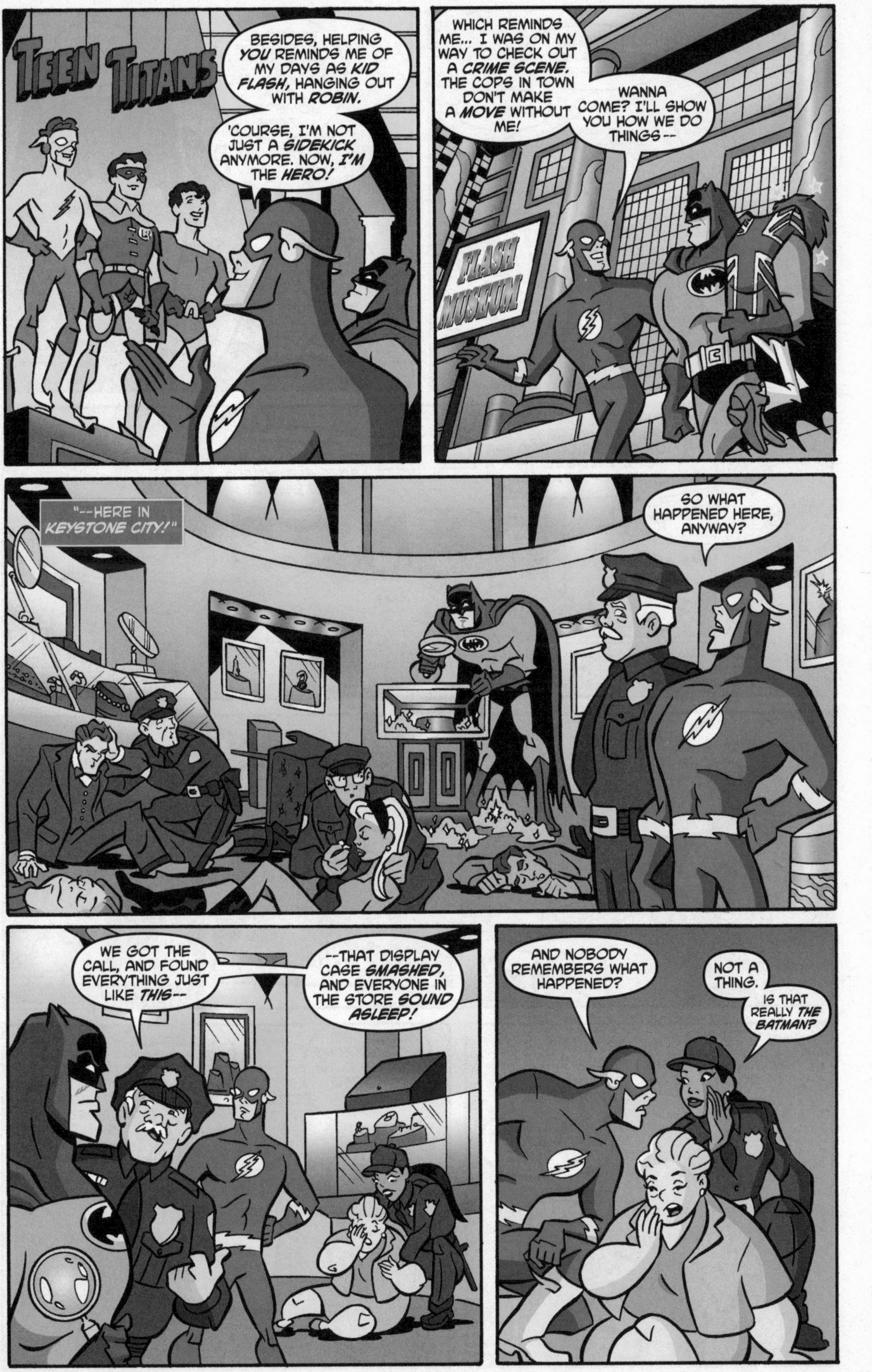
TEEN TITANS
BESIDES, HELPING YOU REMINDS ME OF MY DAYS AS KID FLASH, HANGING OUT WITH ROBIN.
'COURSE, I'M NOT JUST A SIDEKICK ANYMORE. NOW, I'M THE HERO!
WHICH REMINDS ME... I WAS ON MY WAY TO CHECK OUT A CRIME SCENE. THE COPS IN TOWN DON'T MAKE A MOVE WITHOUT ME!
WANNA COME? I'LL SHOW YOU HOW WE DO THINGS--
FLASH MUSEUM
"--HERE IN KEYSTONE CITY!"
SO WHAT HAPPENED HERE, ANYWAY?
WE GOT THE CALL, AND FOUND EVERYTHING JUST LIKE THIS--
--THAT DISPLAY CASE SMASHED, AND EVERYONE IN THE STORE SOUND ASLEEP!
AND NOBODY REMEMBERS WHAT HAPPENED?
NOT A THING.
IS THAT REALLY THE BATMAN?

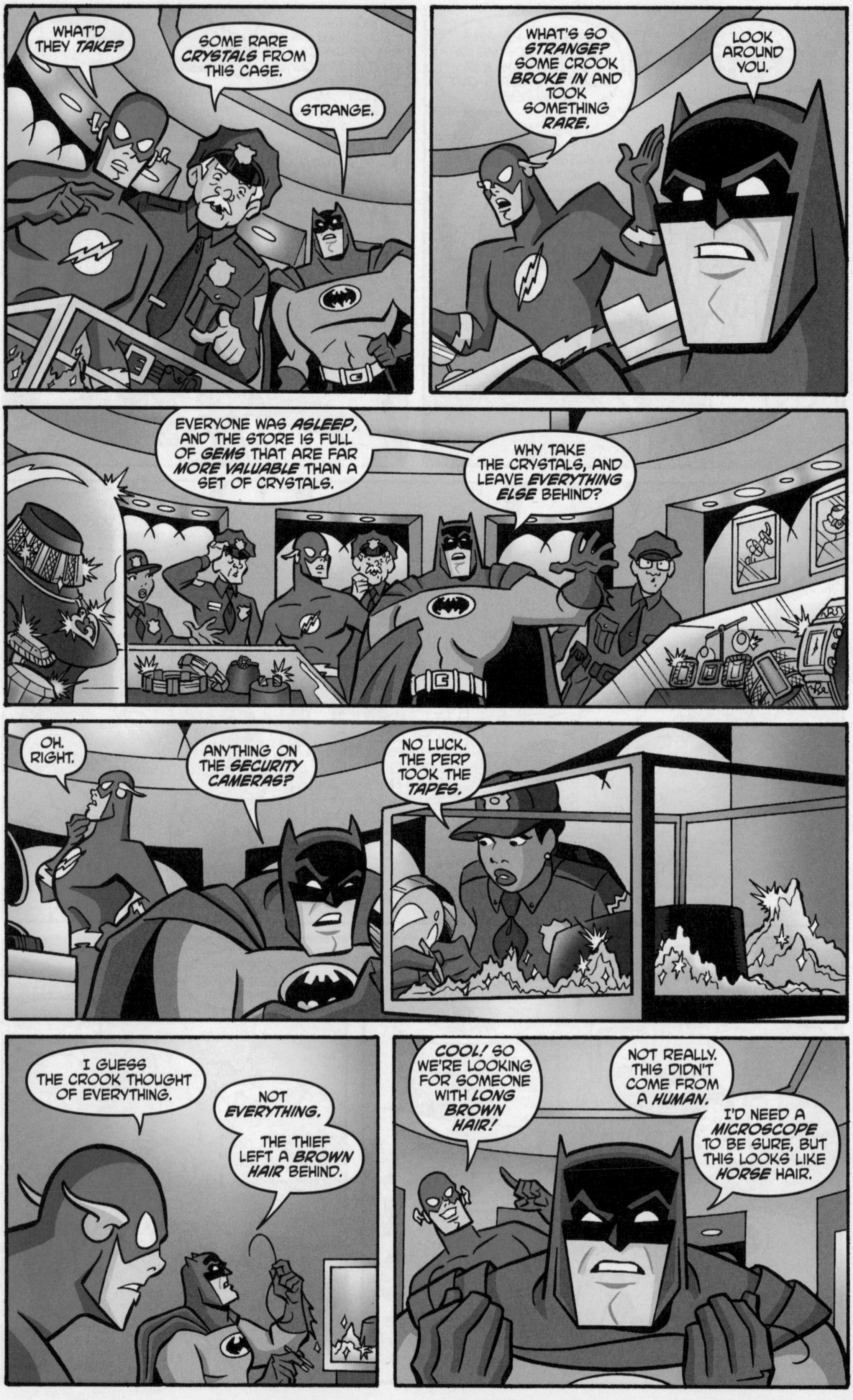
WHAT'D THEY TAKE?
SOME RARE CRYSTALS FROM THIS CASE.
STRANGE.
WHAT'S SO STRANGE? SOME CROOK BROKE IN AND TOOK SOMETHING RARE.
LOOK AROUND YOU.
EVERYONE WAS ASLEEP, AND THE STORE IS FULL OF GEMS THAT ARE FAR MORE VALUABLE THAN A SET OF CRYSTALS.
WHY TAKE THE CRYSTALS, AND LEAVE EVERYTHING ELSE BEHIND?
OH. RIGHT.
ANYTHING ON THE SECURITY CAMERAS?
NO LUCK. THE PERP TOOK THE TAPES.
I GUESS THE CROOK THOUGHT OF EVERYTHING.
NOT EVERYTHING.
THE THIEF LEFT A BROWN HAIR BEHIND.
COOL! SO WE'RE LOOKING FOR SOMEONE WITH LONG BROWN HAIR!
NOT REALLY. THIS DIDN'T COME FROM A HUMAN.
I'D NEED A MICROSCOPE TO BE SURE, BUT THIS LOOKS LIKE HORSE HAIR.

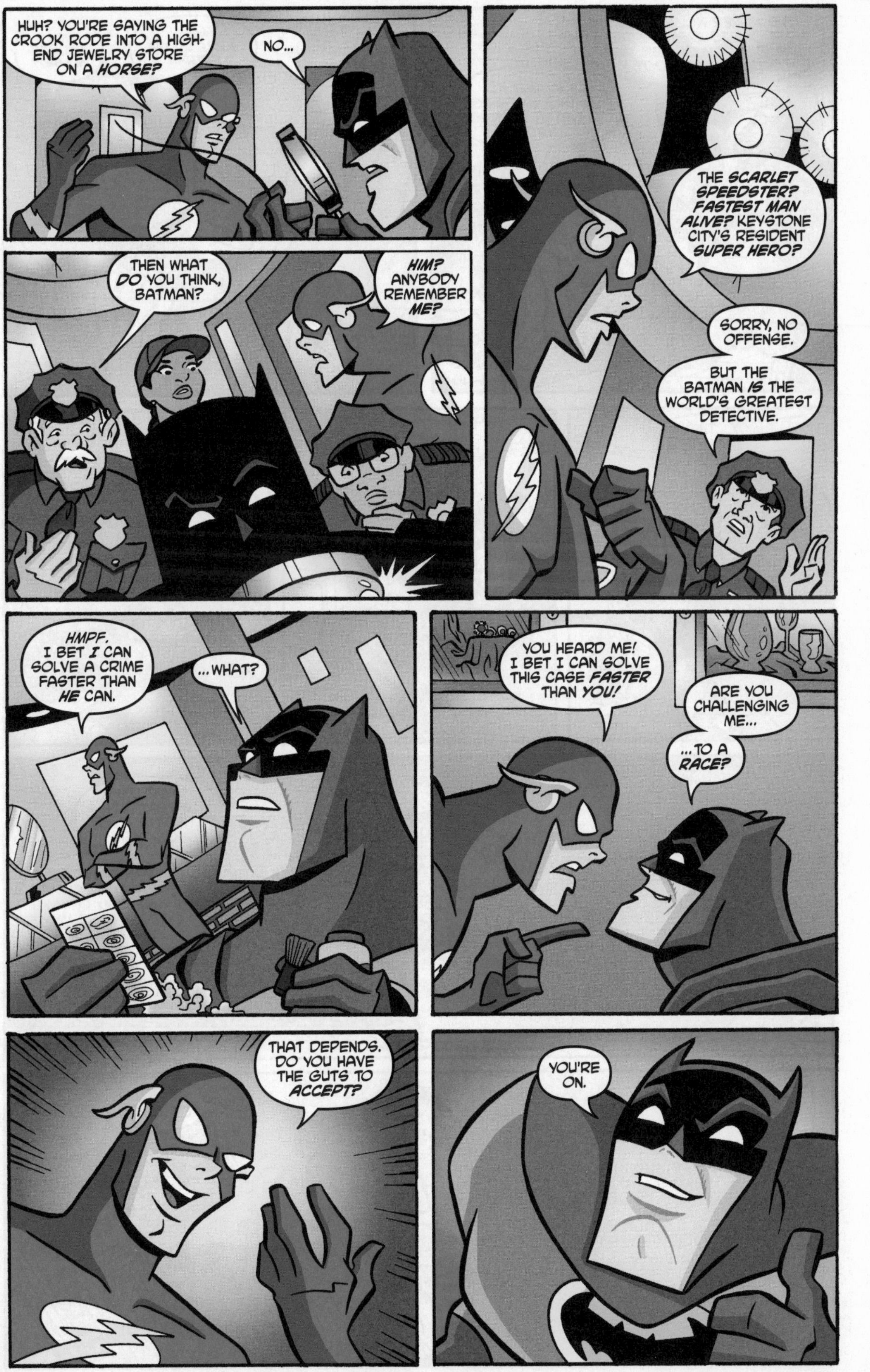

HUH? YOU'RE SAYING THE CROOK RODE INTO A HIGH-END JEWELRY STORE ON A HORSE?
NO...
THEN WHAT DO YOU THINK, BATMAN?
HIM? ANYBODY REMEMBER ME?
THE SCARLET SPEEDSTER? FASTEST MAN ALIVE? KEYSTONE CITY'S RESIDENT SUPER HERO?
SORRY, NO OFFENSE.
BUT THE BATMAN IS THE WORLD'S GREATEST DETECTIVE.
HMPF. I BET I CAN SOLVE A CRIME FASTER THAN HE CAN.
...WHAT?
YOU HEARD ME! I BET I CAN SOLVE THIS CASE FASTER THAN YOU!
ARE YOU CHALLENGING ME...
...TO A RACE?
THAT DEPENDS. DO YOU HAVE THE GUTS TO ACCEPT?
YOU'RE ON.

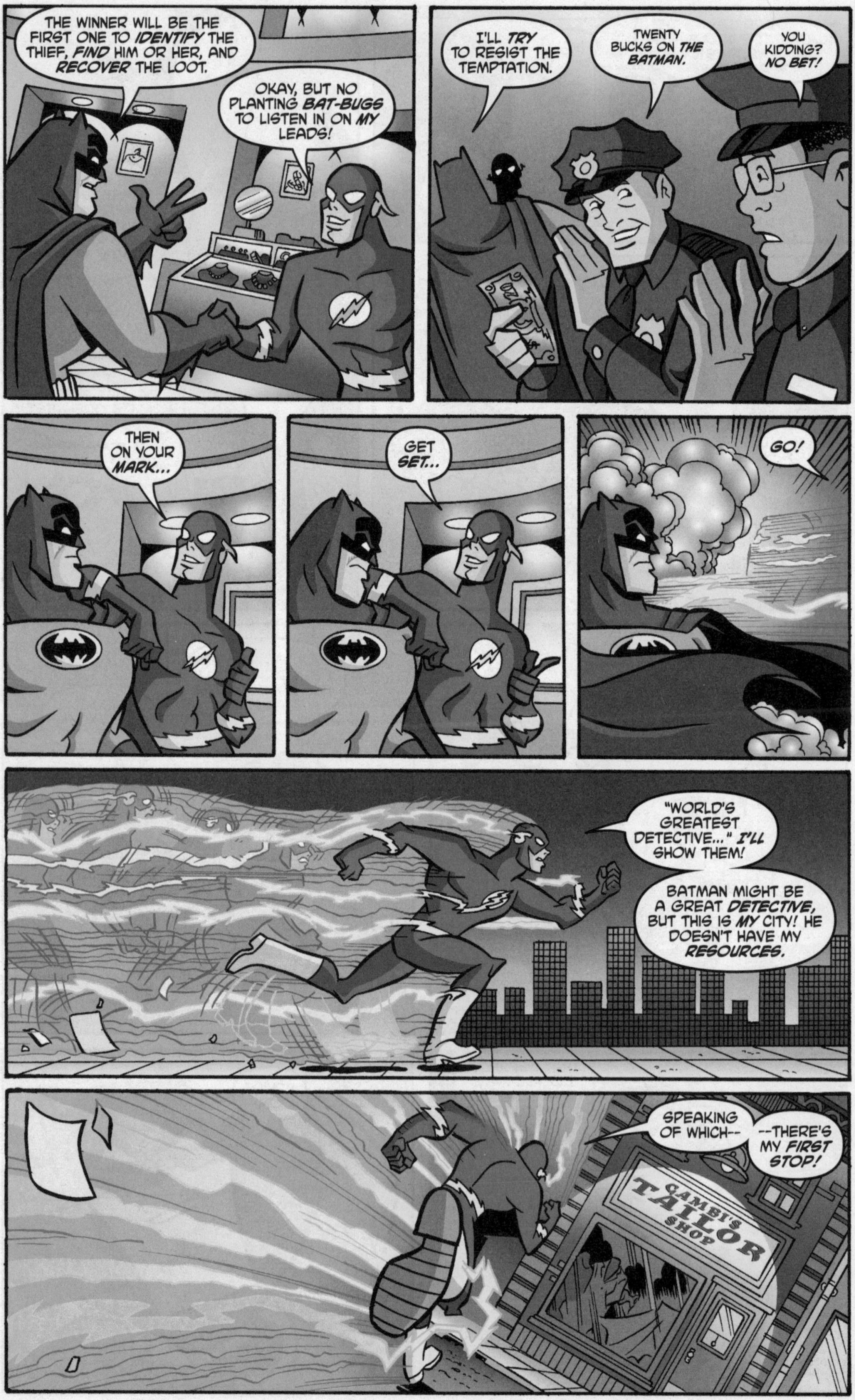
THE WINNER WILL BE THE FIRST ONE TO IDENTIFY THE THIEF, FIND HIM OR HER, AND RECOVER THE LOOT.
OKAY, BUT NO PLANTING BAT-BUGS TO LISTEN IN ON MY LEADS!
I'LL TRY TO RESIST THE TEMPTATION.
TWENTY BUCKS ON THE BATMAN.
YOU KIDDING? NO BET!
THEN ON YOUR MARK...
GET SET...
GO!
"WORLD'S GREATEST DETECTIVE..." I'LL SHOW THEM!
BATMAN MIGHT BE A GREAT DETECTIVE, BUT THIS IS MY CITY! HE DOESN'T HAVE MY RESOURCES.
SPEAKING OF WHICH--
--THERE'S MY FIRST STOP!
GAMBI'S TAILOR SHOP

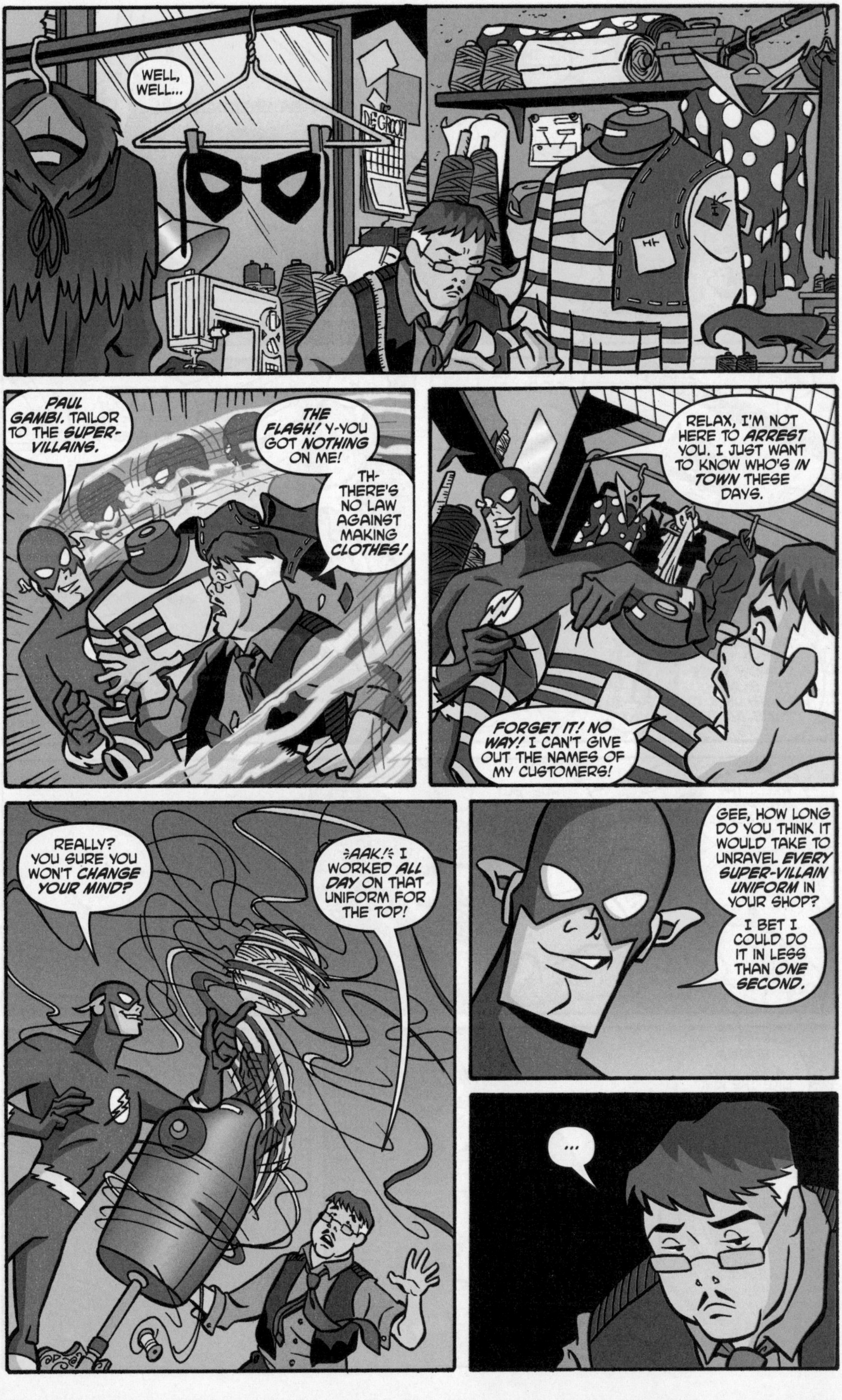
WELL, WELL...
PAUL GAMBI. TAILOR TO THE SUPER-VILLAINS.
THE FLASH! Y-YOU GOT NOTHING ON ME!
TH-THERE'S NO LAW AGAINST MAKING CLOTHES!
RELAX, I'M NOT HERE TO ARREST YOU. I JUST WANT TO KNOW WHO'S IN TOWN THESE DAYS.
FORGET IT! NO WAY! I CAN'T GIVE OUT THE NAMES OF MY CUSTOMERS!
REALLY? YOU SURE YOU WON'T CHANGE YOUR MIND?
AAK! I WORKED ALL DAY ON THAT UNIFORM FOR THE TOP!
GEE, HOW LONG DO YOU THINK IT WOULD TAKE TO UNRAVEL EVERY SUPER-VILLAIN UNIFORM IN YOUR SHOP?
I BET I COULD DO IT IN LESS THAN ONE SECOND.
...

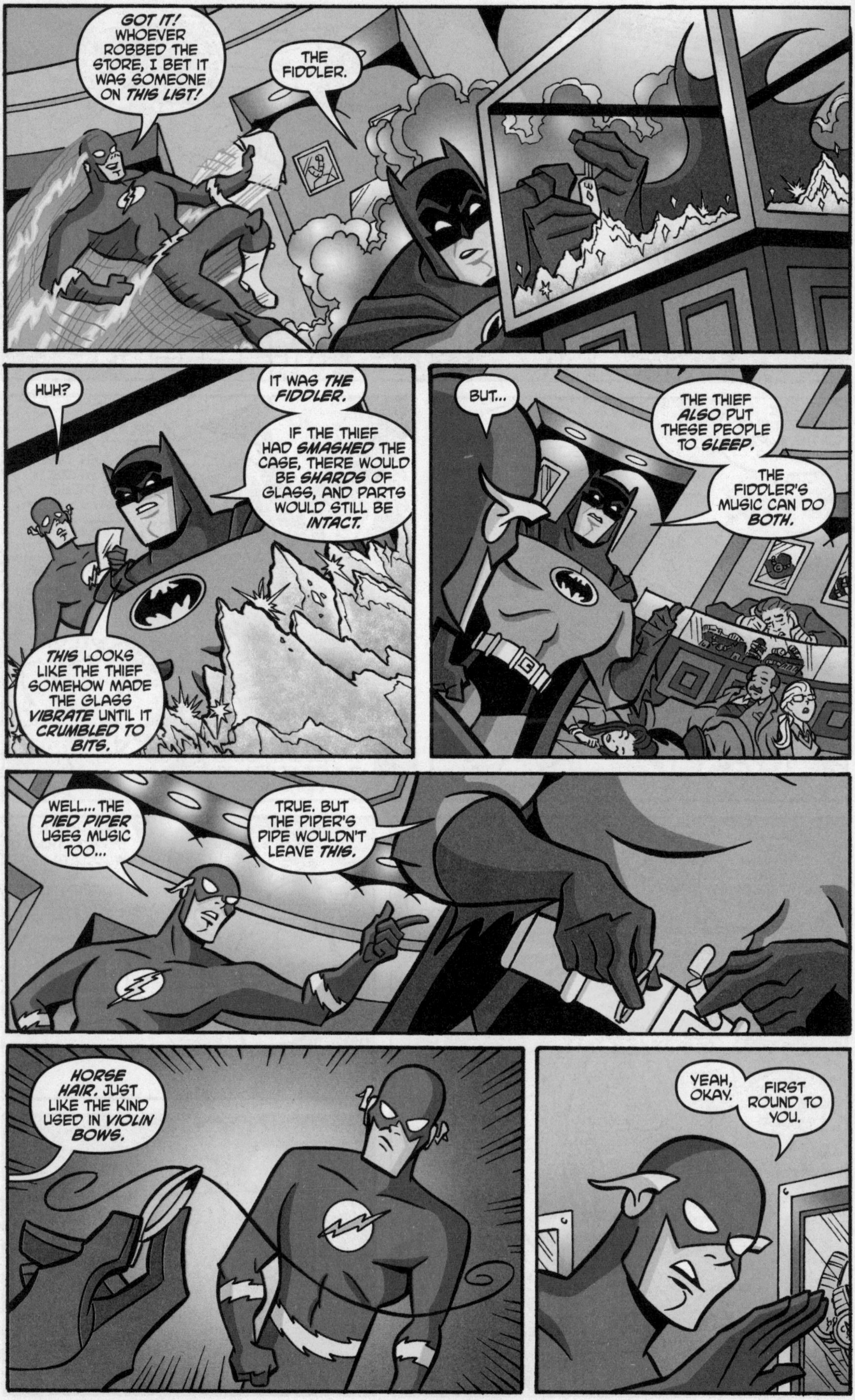
GOT IT! WHOEVER ROBBED THE STORE, I BET IT WAS SOMEONE ON THIS LIST!
THE FIDDLER.
HUH?
IT WAS THE FIDDLER.
IF THE THIEF HAD SMASHED THE CASE, THERE WOULD BE SHARDS OF GLASS, AND PARTS WOULD STILL BE INTACT.
THIS LOOKS LIKE THE THIEF SOMEHOW MADE THE GLASS VIBRATE UNTIL IT CRUMBLED TO BITS.
BUT...
THE THIEF ALSO PUT THESE PEOPLE TO SLEEP.
THE FIDDLER'S MUSIC CAN DO BOTH.
WELL... THE PIED PIPER USES MUSIC TOO...
TRUE. BUT THE PIPER'S PIPE WOULDN'T LEAVE THIS.
HORSE HAIR. JUST LIKE THE KIND USED IN VIOLIN BOWS.
YEAH, OKAY.
FIRST ROUND TO YOU.

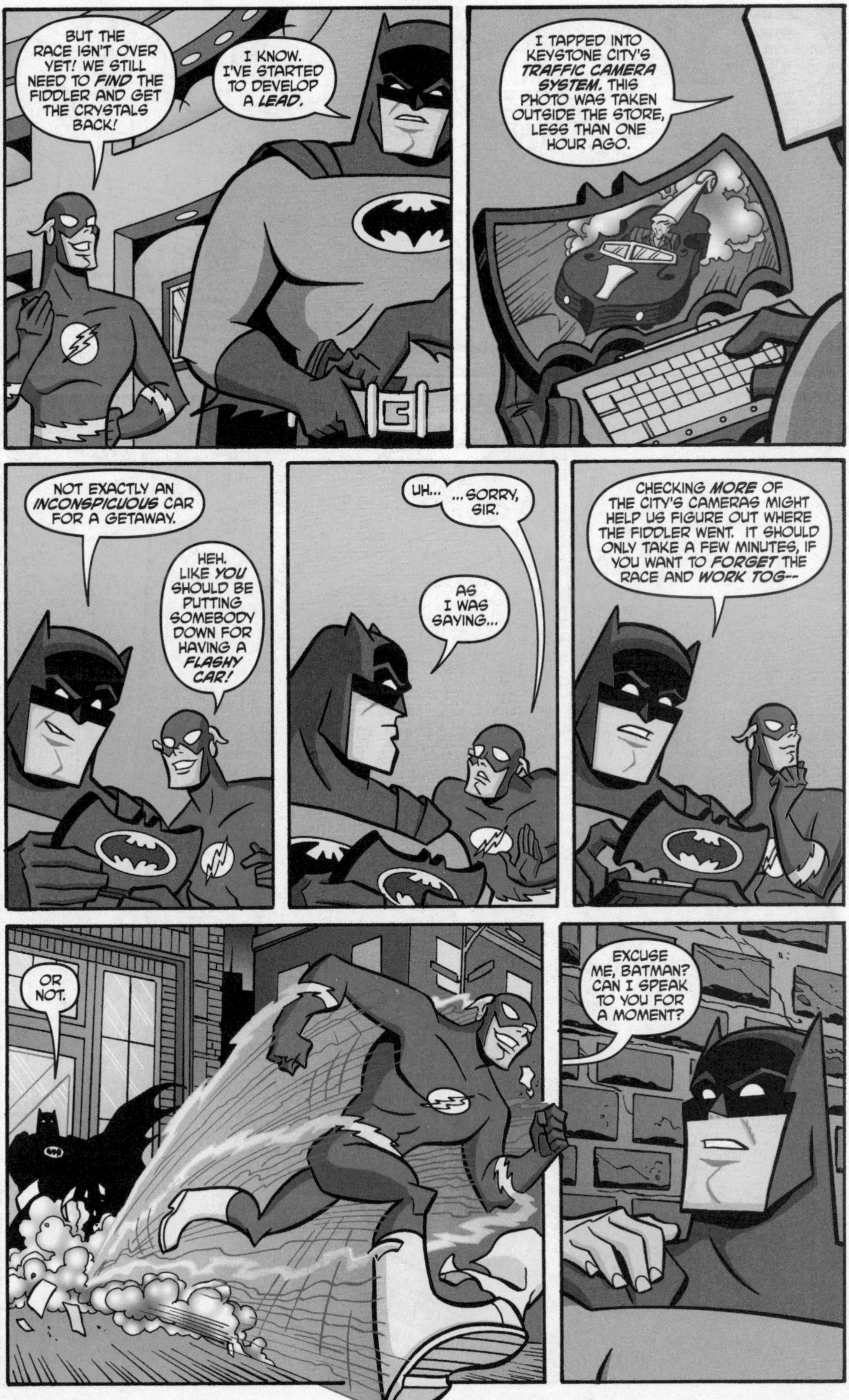
BUT THE RACE ISN'T OVER YET! WE STILL NEED TO *FIND* THE FIDDLER AND GET THE CRYSTALS BACK!
I KNOW. I'VE STARTED TO DEVELOP A *LEAD.*
I TAPPED INTO KEYSTONE CITY'S *TRAFFIC CAMERA SYSTEM.* THIS PHOTO WAS TAKEN OUTSIDE THE STORE, LESS THAN ONE HOUR AGO.
NOT EXACTLY AN *INCONSPICUOUS* CAR FOR A GETAWAY.
HEH. LIKE *YOU* SHOULD BE PUTTING SOMEBODY DOWN FOR HAVING A *FLASHY CAR!*
UH...
...SORRY, SIR.
AS I WAS SAYING...
CHECKING *MORE* OF THE CITY'S CAMERAS MIGHT HELP US FIGURE OUT WHERE THE FIDDLER WENT. IT SHOULD ONLY TAKE A FEW MINUTES, IF YOU WANT TO *FORGET* THE RACE AND *WORK TOG--*
OR NOT.
EXCUSE ME, BATMAN? CAN I SPEAK TO YOU FOR A MOMENT?

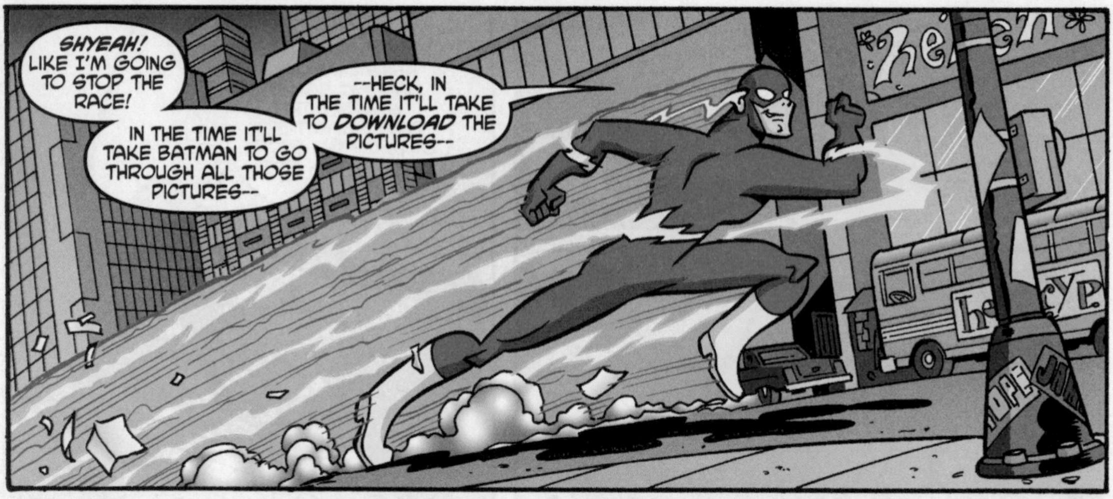
SHYEAH! LIKE I'M GOING TO STOP THE RACE!
IN THE TIME IT'LL TAKE BATMAN TO GO THROUGH ALL THOSE PICTURES--
--HECK, IN THE TIME IT'LL TAKE TO *DOWNLOAD* THE PICTURES--

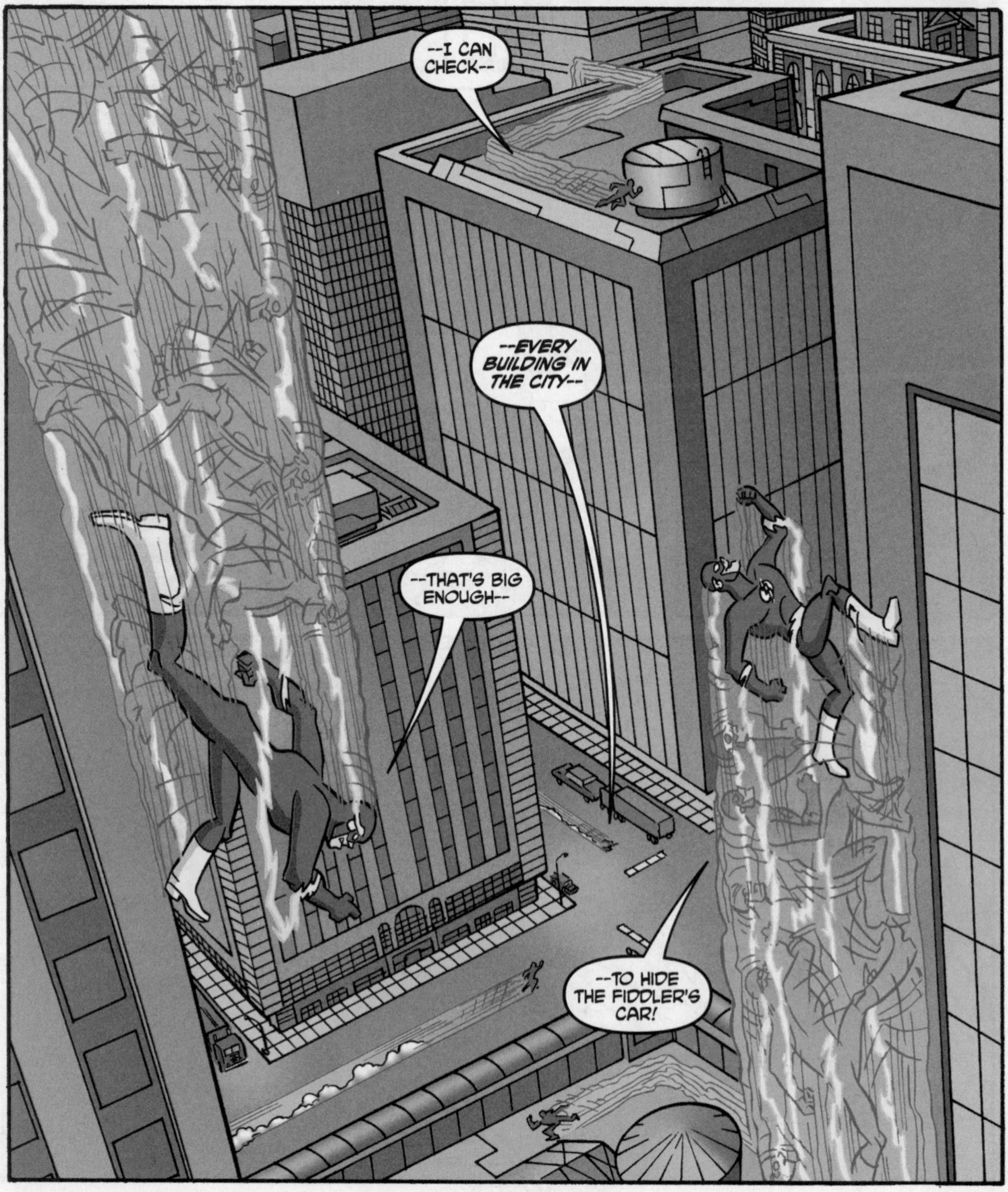
--I CAN CHECK--
--EVERY BUILDING IN THE CITY--
--THAT'S BIG ENOUGH--
--TO HIDE THE FIDDLER'S CAR!

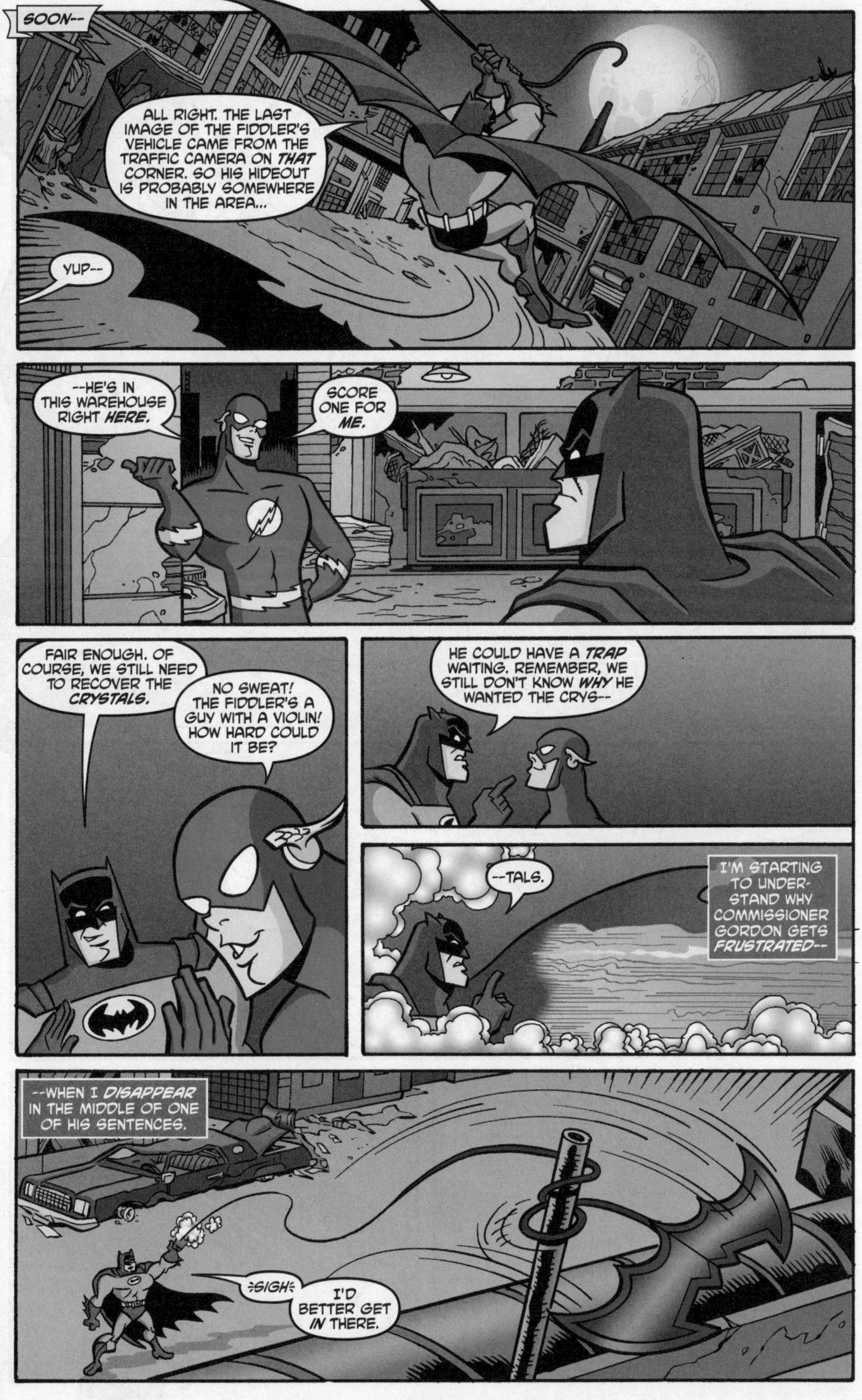
SOON--
ALL RIGHT. THE LAST IMAGE OF THE FIDDLER'S VEHICLE CAME FROM THE TRAFFIC CAMERA ON *THAT* CORNER. SO HIS HIDEOUT IS PROBABLY SOMEWHERE IN THE AREA...
YUP--
--HE'S IN THIS WAREHOUSE RIGHT *HERE.*
SCORE ONE FOR *ME.*
FAIR ENOUGH. OF COURSE, WE STILL NEED TO RECOVER THE *CRYSTALS.*
NO SWEAT! THE FIDDLER'S A GUY WITH A VIOLIN! HOW HARD COULD IT BE?
HE COULD HAVE A *TRAP* WAITING. REMEMBER, WE STILL DON'T KNOW *WHY* HE WANTED THE CRYS--
--TALS.
I'M STARTING TO UNDER-STAND WHY COMMISSIONER GORDON GETS *FRUSTRATED*--
--WHEN I *DISAPPEAR* IN THE MIDDLE OF ONE OF HIS SENTENCES.
SIGH
I'D BETTER GET *IN* THERE.

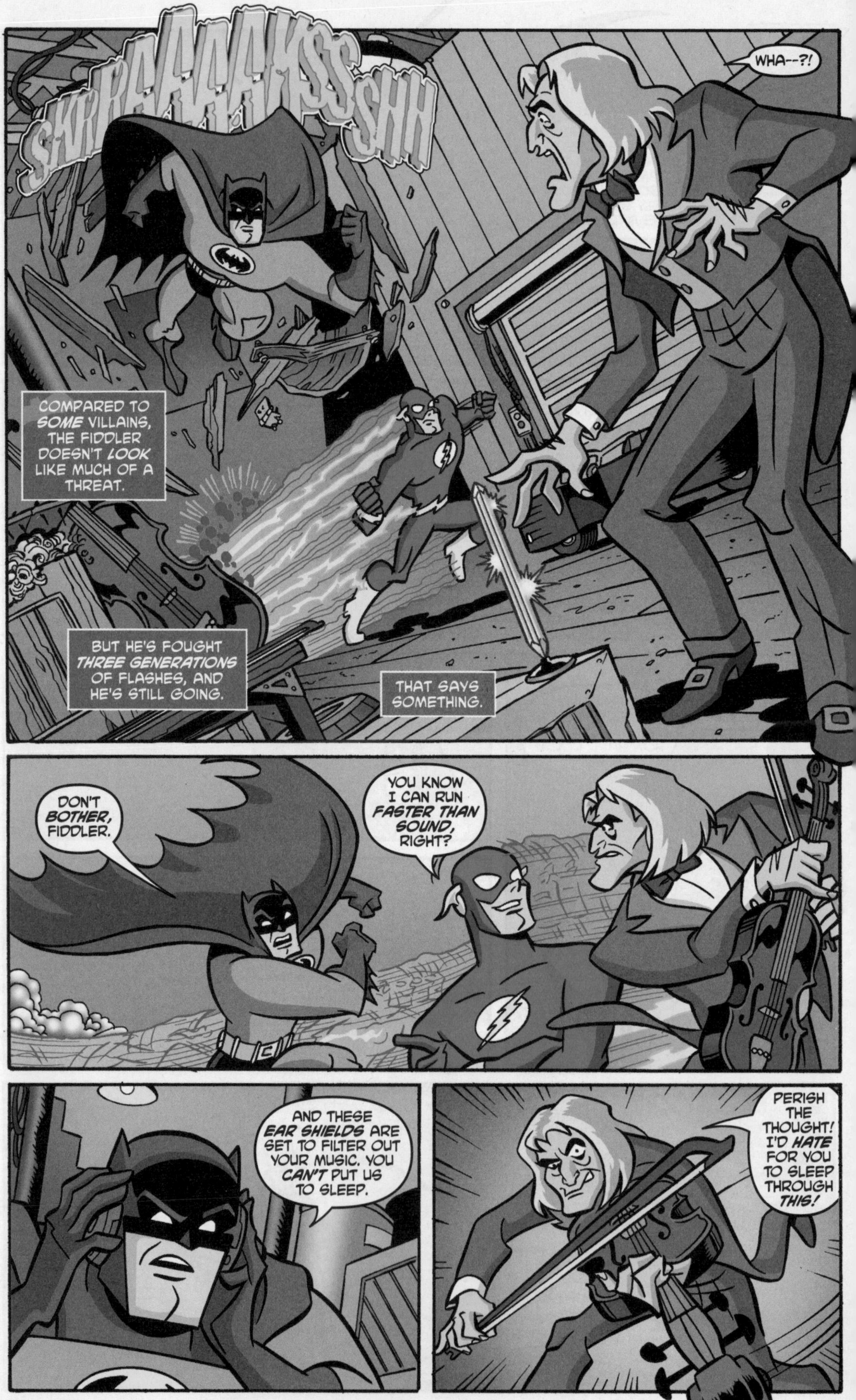
SKRRAAAAKSSSHH
WHA--?!
COMPARED TO SOME VILLAINS, THE FIDDLER DOESN'T LOOK LIKE MUCH OF A THREAT.
BUT HE'S FOUGHT THREE GENERATIONS OF FLASHES, AND HE'S STILL GOING.
THAT SAYS SOMETHING.
DON'T BOTHER, FIDDLER.
YOU KNOW I CAN RUN FASTER THAN SOUND, RIGHT?
AND THESE EAR SHIELDS ARE SET TO FILTER OUT YOUR MUSIC. YOU CAN'T PUT US TO SLEEP.
PERISH THE THOUGHT! I'D HATE FOR YOU TO SLEEP THROUGH THIS!

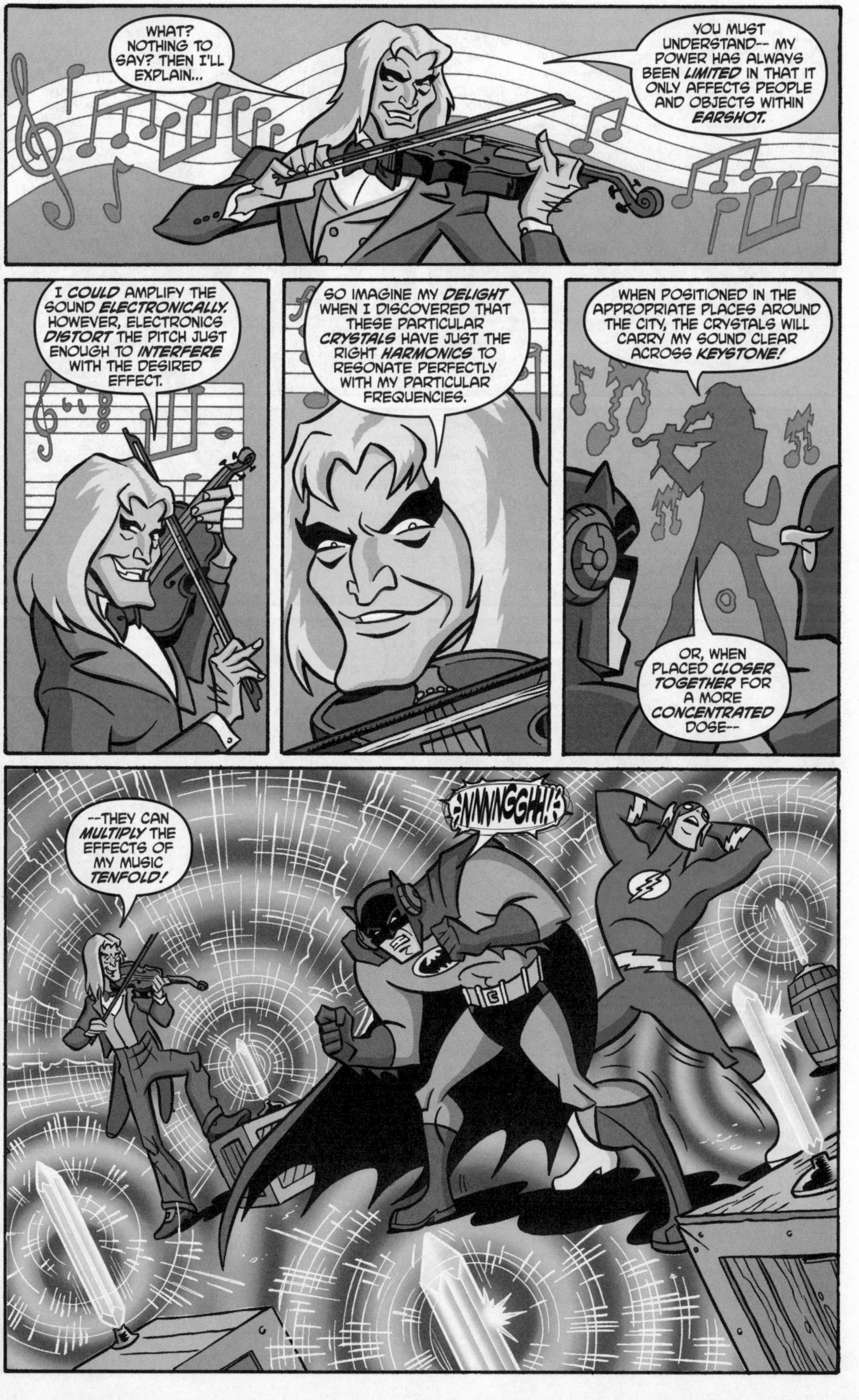
WHAT? NOTHING TO SAY? THEN I'LL EXPLAIN...
YOU MUST UNDERSTAND-- MY POWER HAS ALWAYS BEEN LIMITED IN THAT IT ONLY AFFECTS PEOPLE AND OBJECTS WITHIN EARSHOT.
I COULD AMPLIFY THE SOUND ELECTRONICALLY. HOWEVER, ELECTRONICS DISTORT THE PITCH JUST ENOUGH TO INTERFERE WITH THE DESIRED EFFECT.
SO IMAGINE MY DELIGHT WHEN I DISCOVERED THAT THESE PARTICULAR CRYSTALS HAVE JUST THE RIGHT HARMONICS TO RESONATE PERFECTLY WITH MY PARTICULAR FREQUENCIES.
WHEN POSITIONED IN THE APPROPRIATE PLACES AROUND THE CITY, THE CRYSTALS WILL CARRY MY SOUND CLEAR ACROSS KEYSTONE!
OR, WHEN PLACED CLOSER TOGETHER FOR A MORE CONCENTRATED DOSE--
--THEY CAN MULTIPLY THE EFFECTS OF MY MUSIC TENFOLD!
NNNNGGHH!

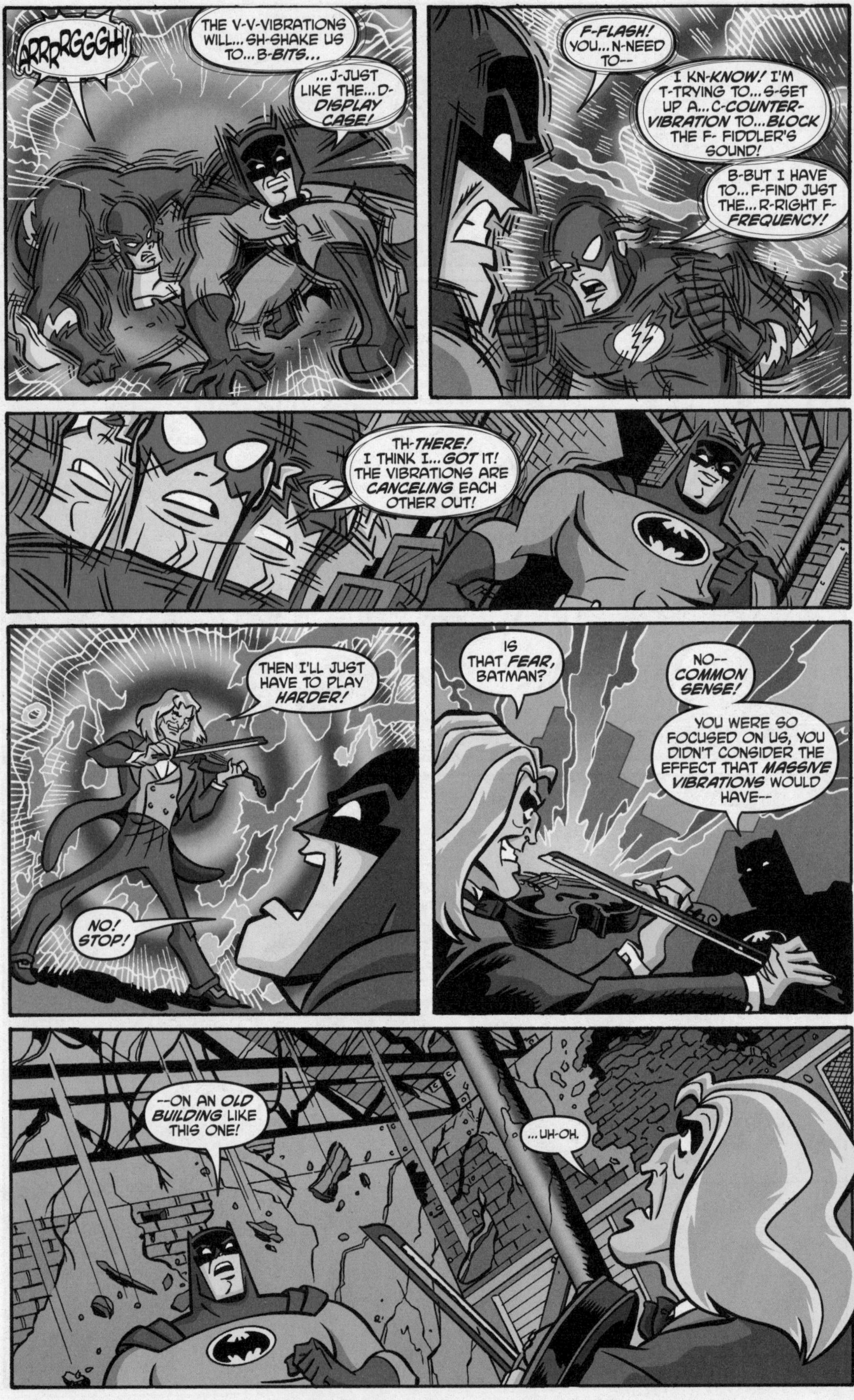
ARRRRGGGH!
THE V-V-VIBRATIONS WILL... SH-SHAKE US TO... B-BITS...
...J-JUST LIKE THE... D-DISPLAY CASE!
F-FLASH! YOU... N-NEED TO--
I KN-KNOW! I'M T-TRYING TO... S-SET UP A... C-COUNTER-VIBRATION TO... BLOCK THE F- FIDDLER'S SOUND!
B-BUT I HAVE TO... F-FIND JUST THE... R-RIGHT F-FREQUENCY!
TH-THERE! I THINK I... GOT IT! THE VIBRATIONS ARE CANCELING EACH OTHER OUT!
THEN I'LL JUST HAVE TO PLAY HARDER!
NO! STOP!
IS THAT FEAR, BATMAN?
NO-- COMMON SENSE!
YOU WERE SO FOCUSED ON US, YOU DIDN'T CONSIDER THE EFFECT THAT MASSIVE VIBRATIONS WOULD HAVE--
--ON AN OLD BUILDING LIKE THIS ONE!
...UH-OH.

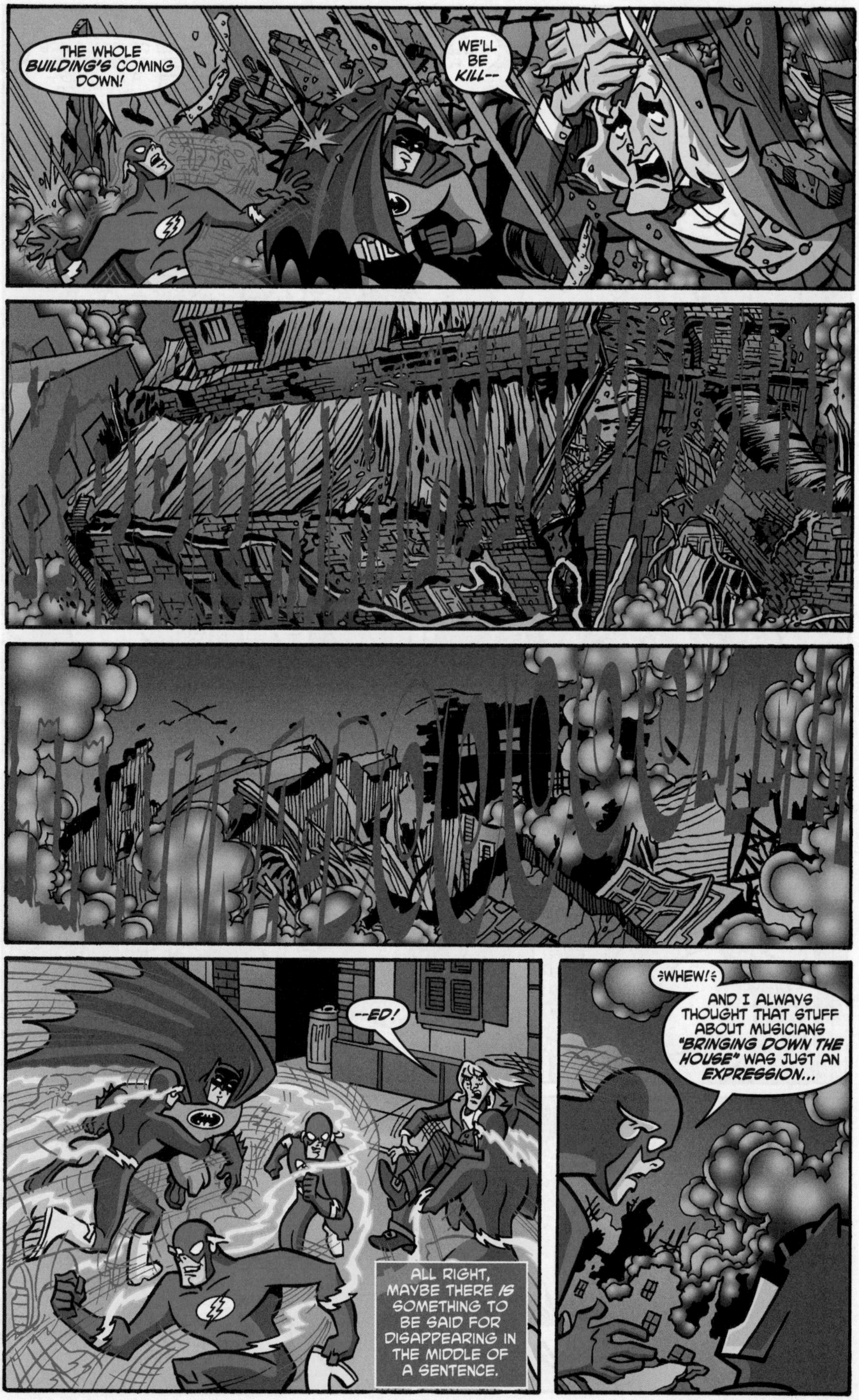
THE WHOLE *BUILDING'S* COMING DOWN!
WE'LL BE *KILL--*
--ED!
ALL RIGHT, MAYBE THERE *IS* SOMETHING TO BE SAID FOR DISAPPEARING IN THE MIDDLE OF A SENTENCE.
WHEW!
AND I ALWAYS THOUGHT THAT STUFF ABOUT MUSICIANS *"BRINGING DOWN THE HOUSE"* WAS JUST AN *EXPRESSION...*

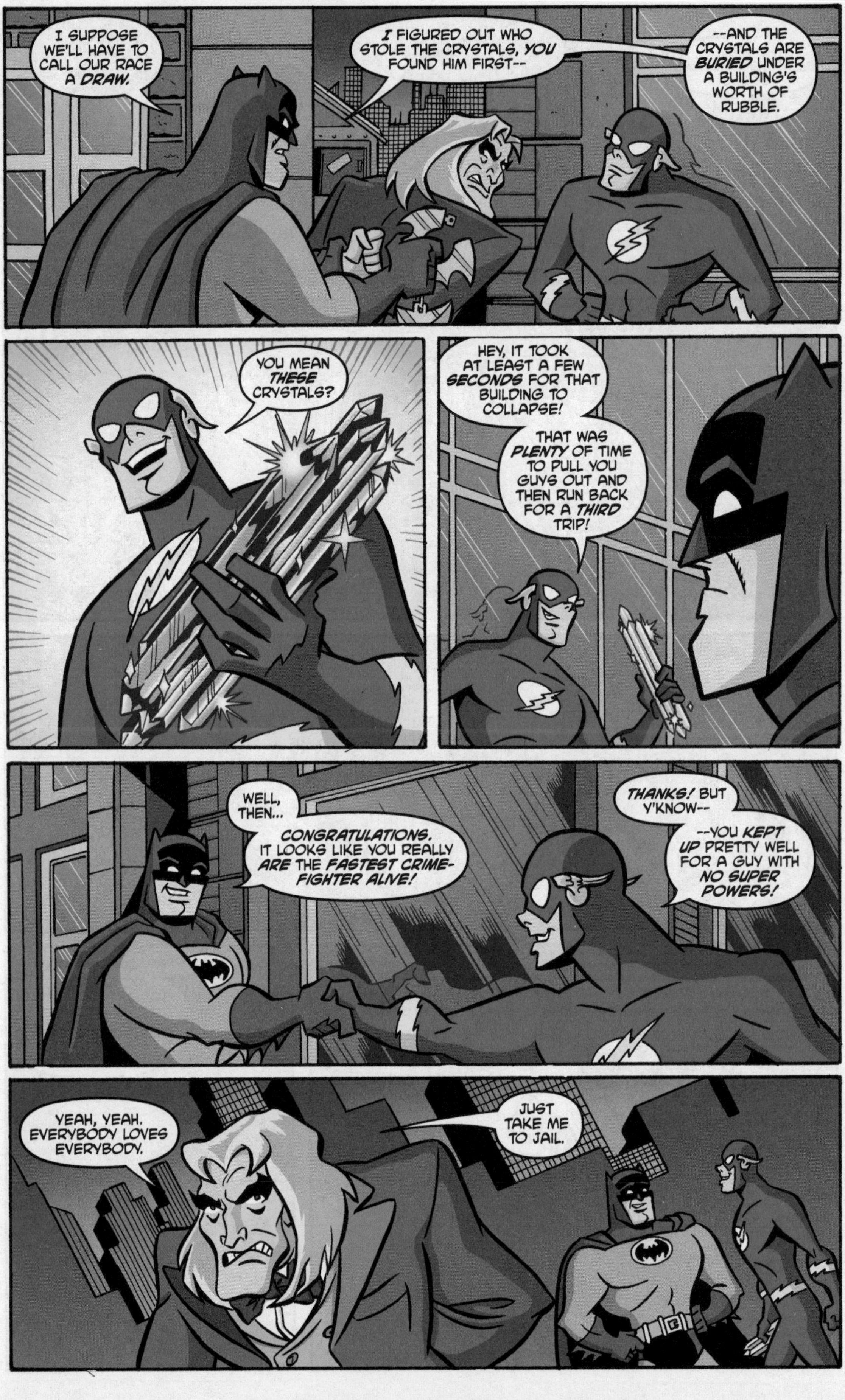
I SUPPOSE WE'LL HAVE TO CALL OUR RACE A *DRAW.*
I FIGURED OUT WHO STOLE THE CRYSTALS, *YOU* FOUND HIM FIRST--
--AND THE CRYSTALS ARE *BURIED* UNDER A BUILDING'S WORTH OF RUBBLE.
YOU MEAN *THESE* CRYSTALS?
HEY, IT TOOK AT LEAST A FEW *SECONDS* FOR THAT BUILDING TO COLLAPSE!
THAT WAS *PLENTY* OF TIME TO PULL YOU GUYS OUT AND THEN RUN BACK FOR A *THIRD* TRIP!
WELL, THEN...
CONGRATULATIONS. IT LOOKS LIKE YOU REALLY *ARE* THE *FASTEST CRIME-FIGHTER ALIVE!*
THANKS! BUT Y'KNOW--
--YOU *KEPT UP* PRETTY WELL FOR A GUY WITH *NO SUPER POWERS!*
YEAH, YEAH. EVERYBODY LOVES EVERYBODY.
JUST TAKE ME TO JAIL.

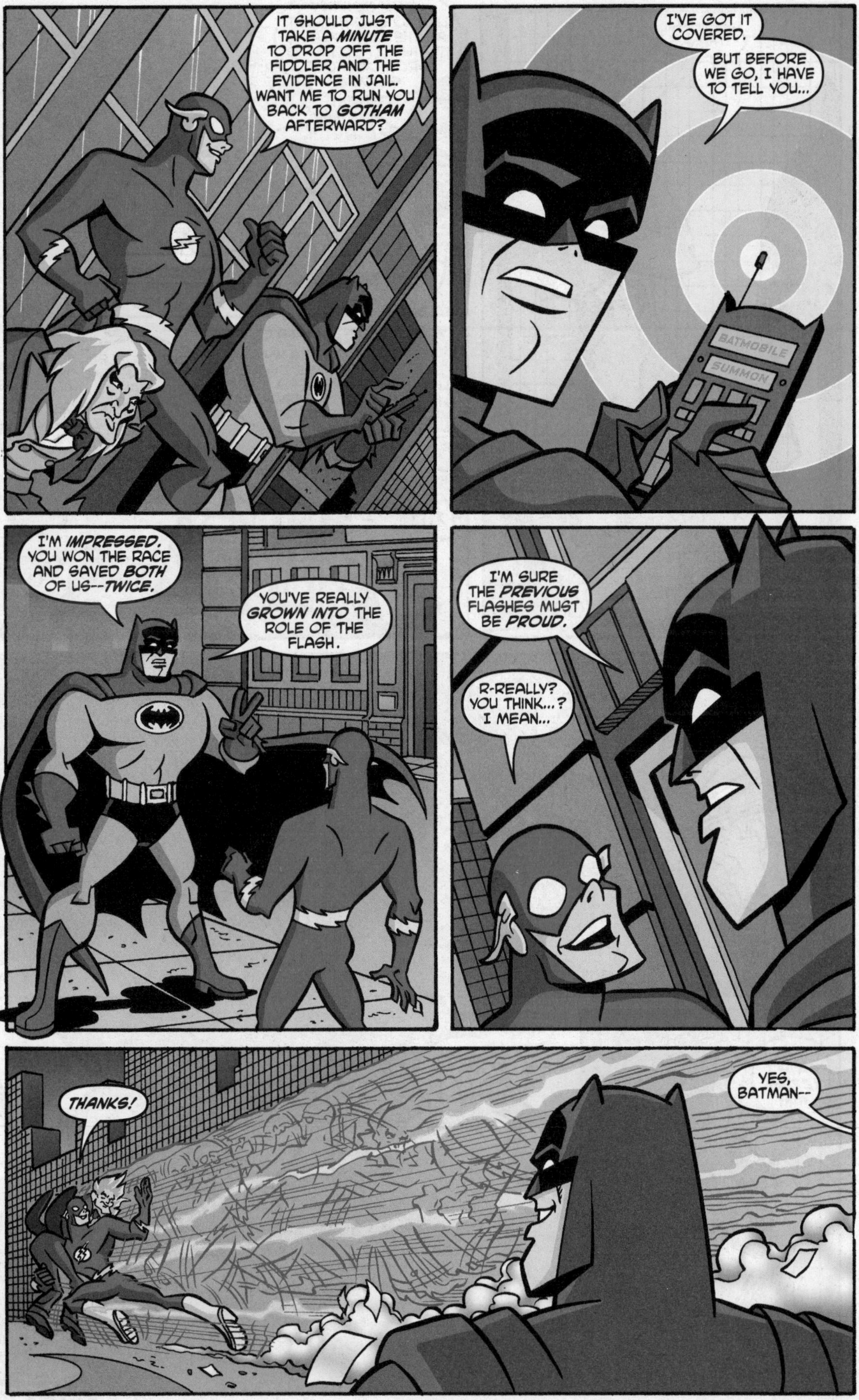
IT SHOULD JUST TAKE A *MINUTE* TO DROP OFF THE FIDDLER AND THE EVIDENCE IN JAIL. WANT ME TO RUN YOU BACK TO *GOTHAM* AFTERWARD?
I'VE GOT IT COVERED.
BUT BEFORE WE GO, I HAVE TO TELL YOU...
BATMOBILE
SUMMON
I'M *IMPRESSED.* YOU WON THE RACE AND SAVED *BOTH* OF US--*TWICE.*
YOU'VE REALLY *GROWN INTO* THE ROLE OF THE FLASH.
I'M SURE THE *PREVIOUS* FLASHES MUST BE *PROUD.*
R-REALLY? YOU THINK...? I MEAN...
THANKS!
YES, BATMAN--

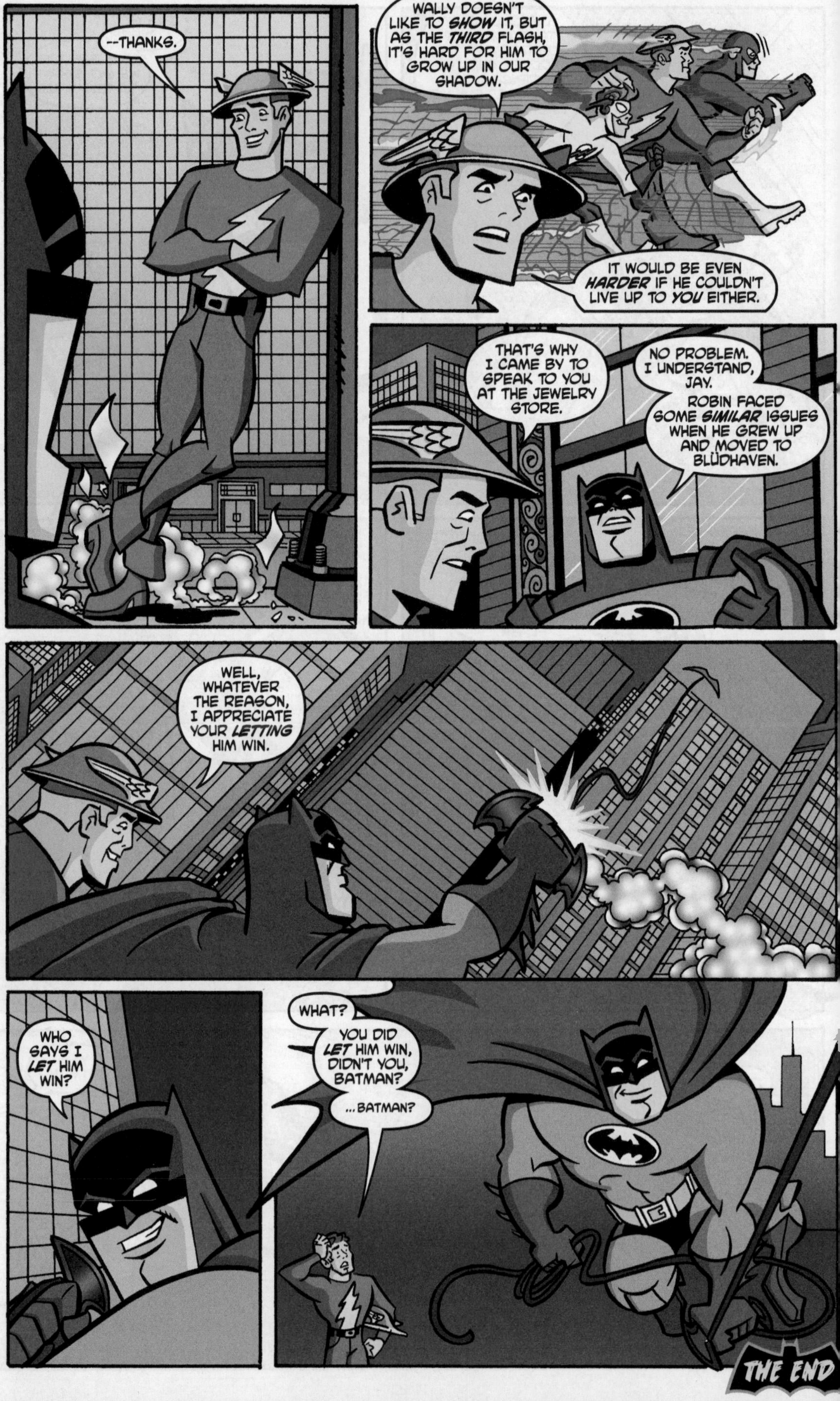
--THANKS.
WALLY DOESN'T LIKE TO SHOW IT, BUT AS THE THIRD FLASH, IT'S HARD FOR HIM TO GROW UP IN OUR SHADOW.
IT WOULD BE EVEN HARDER IF HE COULDN'T LIVE UP TO YOU EITHER.
THAT'S WHY I CAME BY TO SPEAK TO YOU AT THE JEWELRY STORE.
NO PROBLEM. I UNDERSTAND, JAY.
ROBIN FACED SOME SIMILAR ISSUES WHEN HE GREW UP AND MOVED TO BLÜDHAVEN.
WELL, WHATEVER THE REASON, I APPRECIATE YOUR LETTING HIM WIN.
WHO SAYS I LET HIM WIN?
WHAT?
YOU DID LET HIM WIN, DIDN'T YOU, BATMAN?
...BATMAN?
THE END

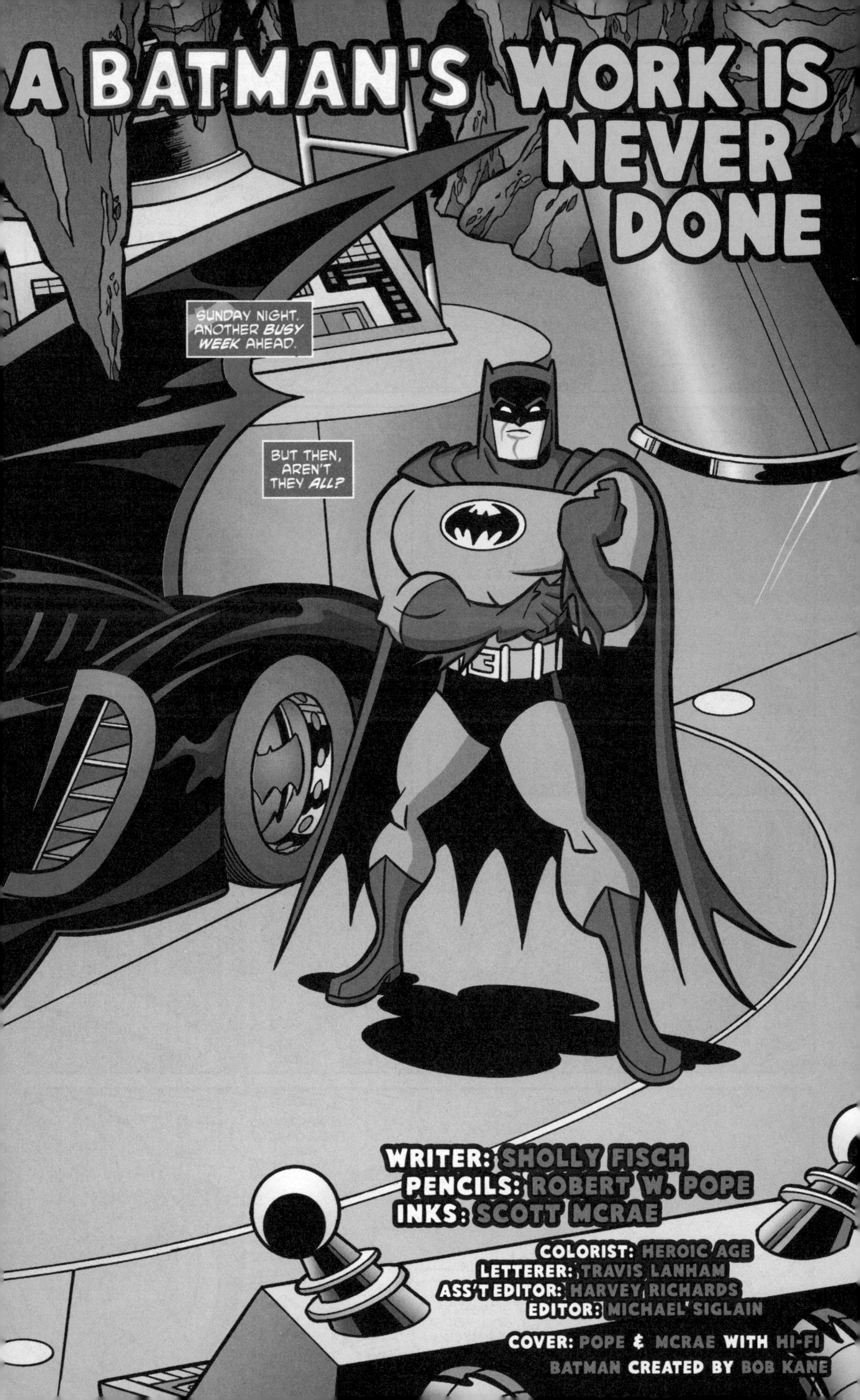
A BATMAN'S WORK IS NEVER DONE
SUNDAY NIGHT. ANOTHER BUSY WEEK AHEAD.
BUT THEN, AREN'T THEY ALL?
WRITER: SHOLLY FISCH
PENCILS: ROBERT W. POPE
INKS: SCOTT MCRAE
COLORIST: HEROIC AGE
LETTERER: TRAVIS LANHAM
ASS'T EDITOR: HARVEY RICHARDS
EDITOR: MICHAEL SIGLAIN
COVER: POPE & MCRAE WITH HI-FI
BATMAN CREATED BY BOB KANE

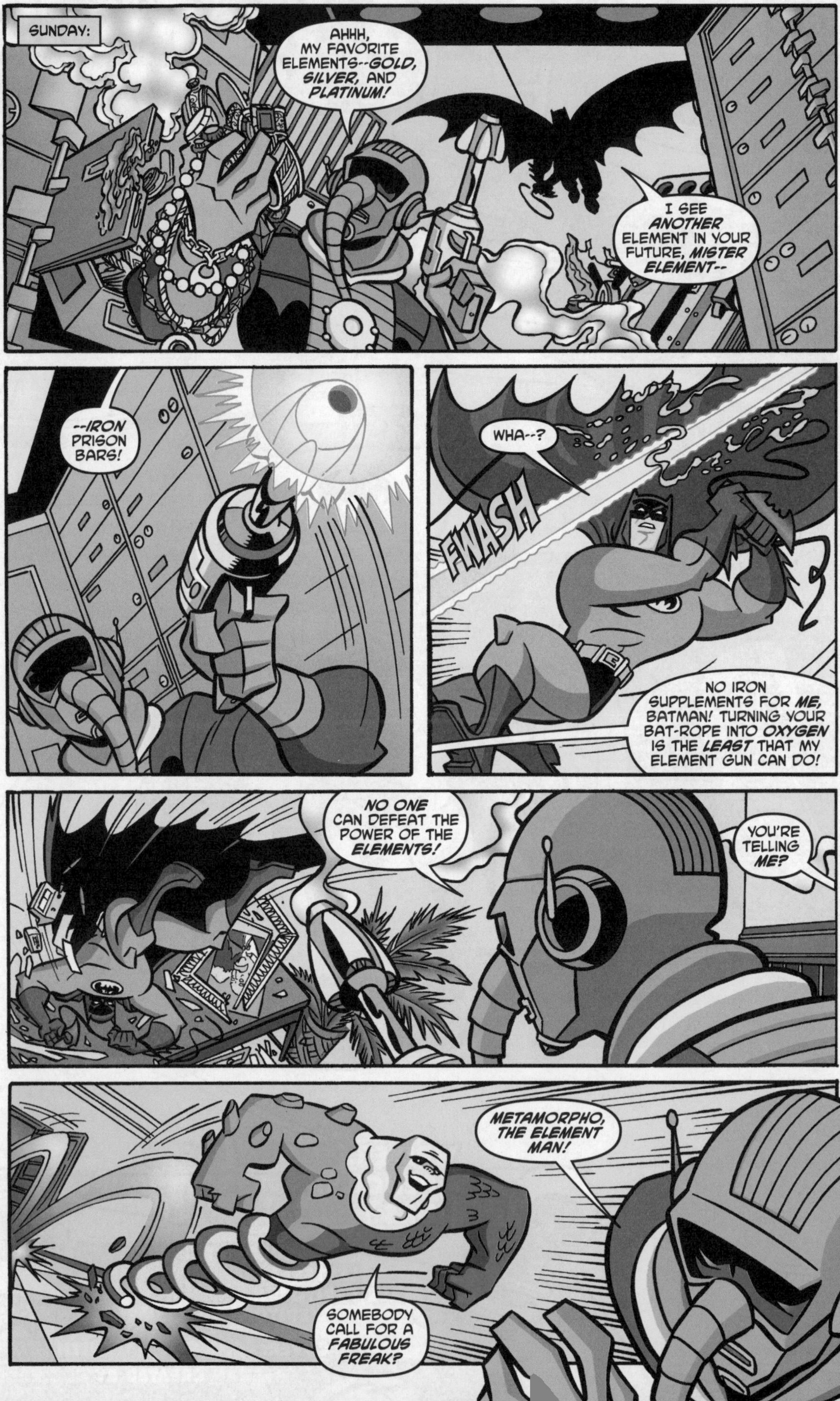
SUNDAY:
AHHH, MY FAVORITE ELEMENTS--GOLD, SILVER, AND PLATINUM!
I SEE ANOTHER ELEMENT IN YOUR FUTURE, MISTER ELEMENT--
--IRON PRISON BARS!
WHA--?
FWASH
NO IRON SUPPLEMENTS FOR ME, BATMAN! TURNING YOUR BAT-ROPE INTO OXYGEN IS THE LEAST THAT MY ELEMENT GUN CAN DO!
NO ONE CAN DEFEAT THE POWER OF THE ELEMENTS!
YOU'RE TELLING ME?
METAMORPHO, THE ELEMENT MAN!
SOMEBODY CALL FOR A FABULOUS FREAK?

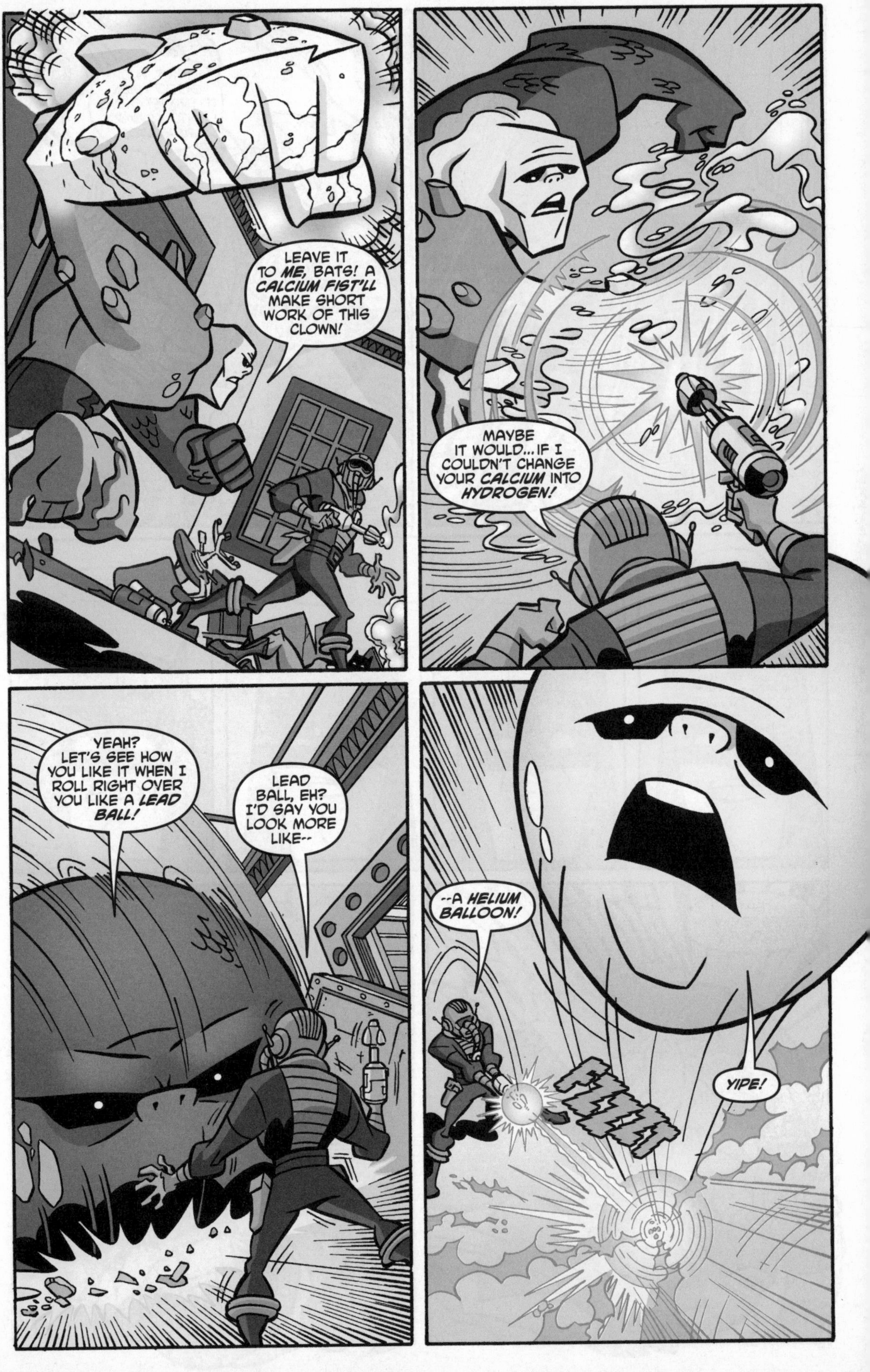
LEAVE IT TO *ME*, BATS! A *CALCIUM FIST'LL* MAKE SHORT WORK OF THIS CLOWN!
MAYBE IT WOULD... IF I COULDN'T CHANGE YOUR *CALCIUM* INTO *HYDROGEN!*
YEAH? LET'S SEE HOW YOU LIKE IT WHEN I ROLL RIGHT OVER YOU LIKE A *LEAD BALL!*
LEAD BALL, EH? I'D SAY YOU LOOK MORE LIKE--
--A *HELIUM BALLOON!*
YIPE!

VERY CUTE. BUT A *TITANIUM* CAGE--

--ISN'T MUCH GOOD WHEN IT TRANSFORMS INTO *LIQUID MERCURY!*

...FRIGID BLAST OF *FREON...*

...WARM IT UP WITH *PHOSPHOROUS...*

...COBALT HAMMER...

...NITROGEN...

EAT *TUNGSTEN,* YO--=OOOF!=

RIGHT HOOK!

SOMETIMES, THE *SIMPLE* WAYS ARE BEST.

MONDAY:

QUITE A *GETAWAY*, MONGUL--ACROSS *THREE* GALAXIES AND *TWENTY-SEVEN* LIGHT YEARS--

--BUT DID YOU REALLY THINK I WOULDN'T *TRACK YOU DOWN?*

I'M TAKING YOU BACK TO EARTH-- TO FACE *JUSTICE!*

BACK...

...TO *EARTH?*

HAHAHAHAHA!!

YOU MUST BE JOKING!

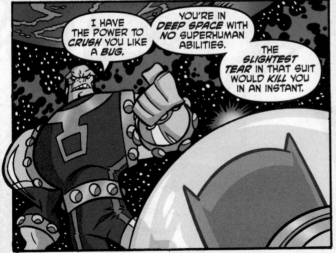

I HAVE THE POWER TO *CRUSH* YOU LIKE A BUG.

YOU'RE IN *DEEP SPACE* WITH NO SUPERHUMAN ABILITIES.

THE *SLIGHTEST TEAR* IN THAT SUIT WOULD *KILL* YOU IN AN INSTANT.

YOU MUST BE *INSANE* TO FOLLOW ME OUT HERE...

...*ALONE...?*

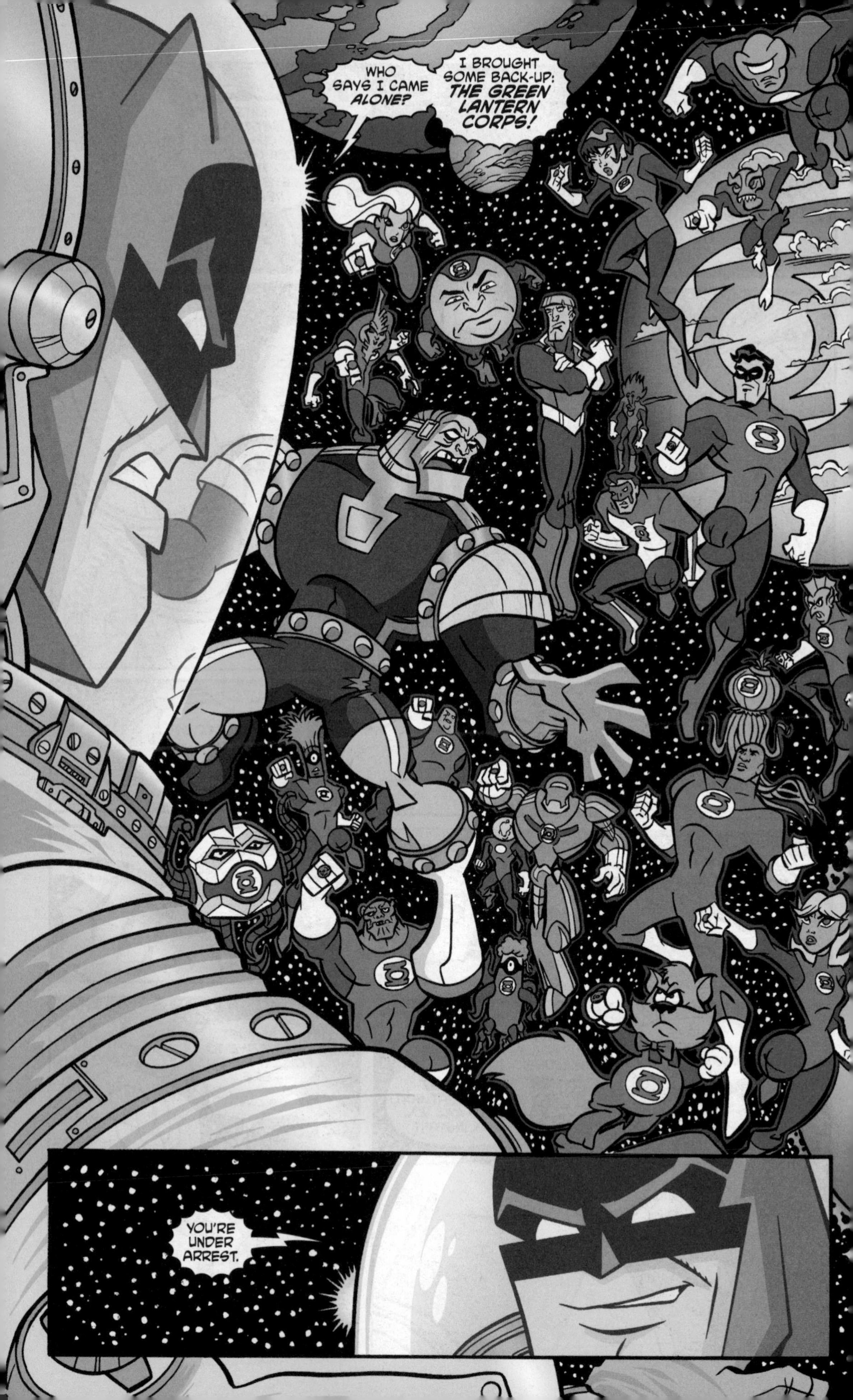
WHO SAYS I CAME *ALONE?*
I BROUGHT SOME BACK-UP: ***THE GREEN LANTERN CORPS!***
YOU'RE UNDER ARREST.

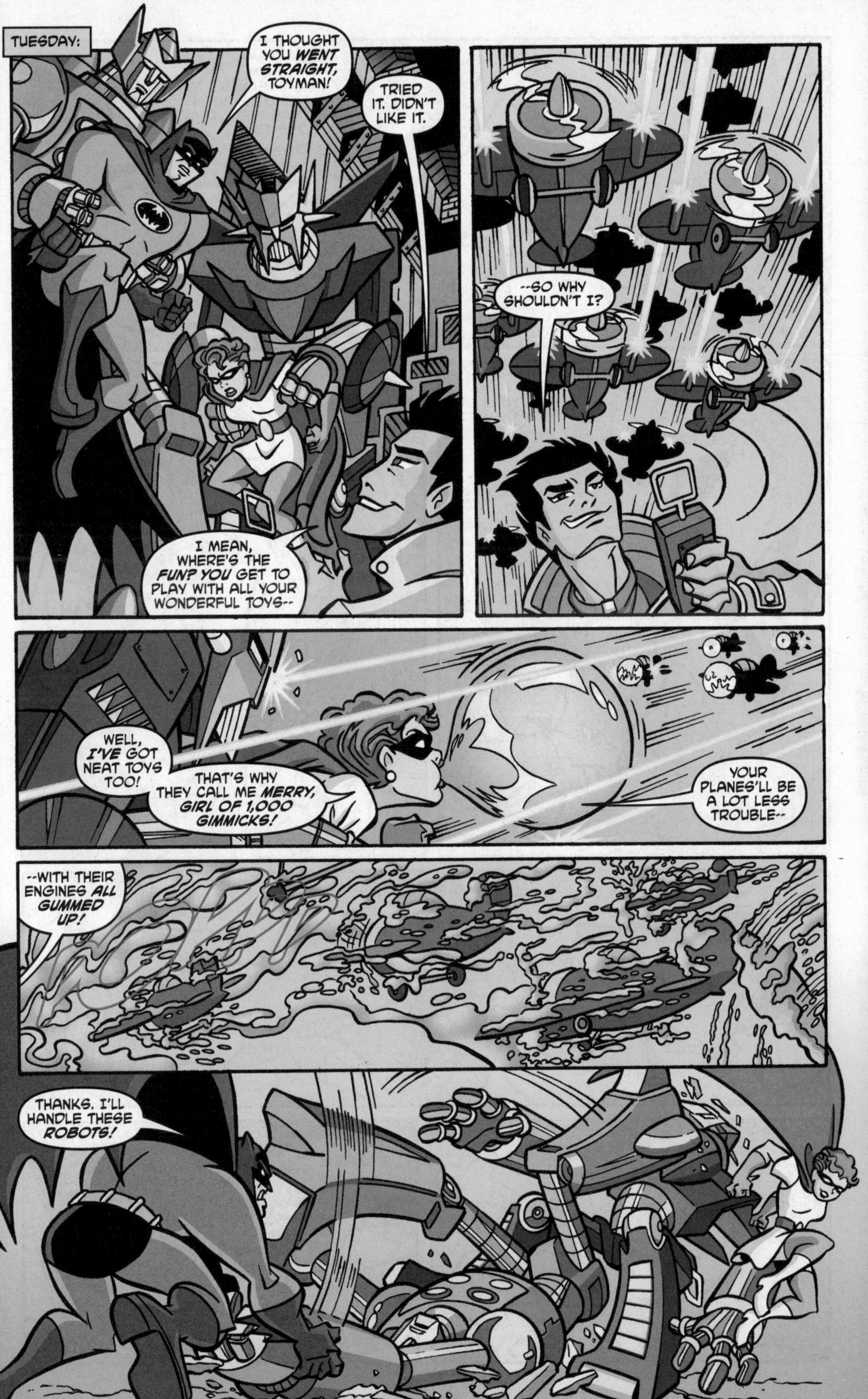
TUESDAY:
I THOUGHT YOU WENT STRAIGHT, TOYMAN!
TRIED IT. DIDN'T LIKE IT.
I MEAN, WHERE'S THE FUN? YOU GET TO PLAY WITH ALL YOUR WONDERFUL TOYS--
--SO WHY SHOULDN'T I?
WELL, I'VE GOT NEAT TOYS TOO!
THAT'S WHY THEY CALL ME MERRY, GIRL OF 1,000 GIMMICKS!
YOUR PLANES'LL BE A LOT LESS TROUBLE--
--WITH THEIR ENGINES ALL GUMMED UP!
THANKS. I'LL HANDLE THESE ROBOTS!

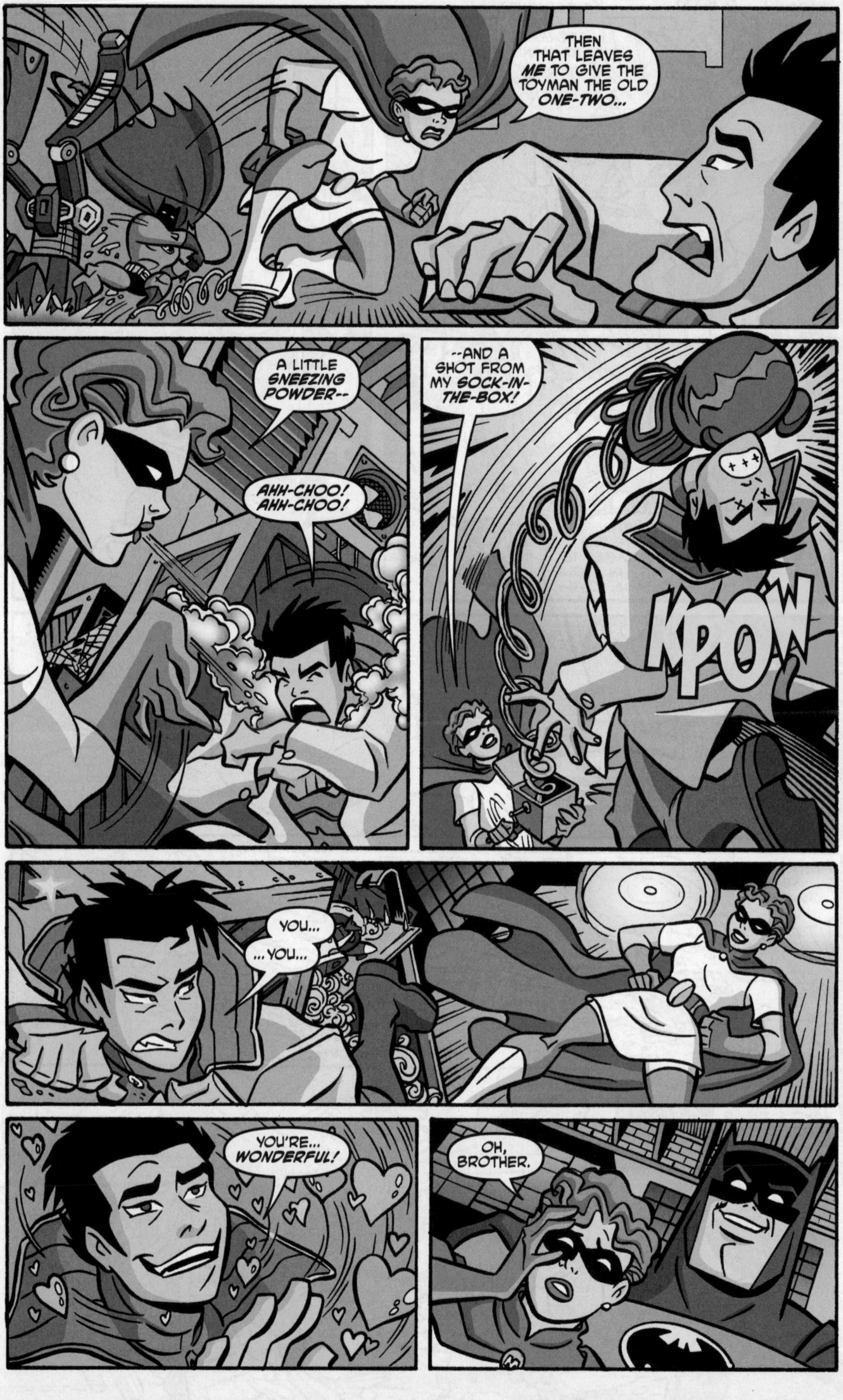
THEN THAT LEAVES ME TO GIVE THE TOYMAN THE OLD ONE-TWO...
A LITTLE SNEEZING POWDER--
AHH-CHOO! AHH-CHOO!
--AND A SHOT FROM MY SOCK-IN-THE-BOX!
KPOW
YOU...
...YOU...
YOU'RE... WONDERFUL!
OH, BROTHER.

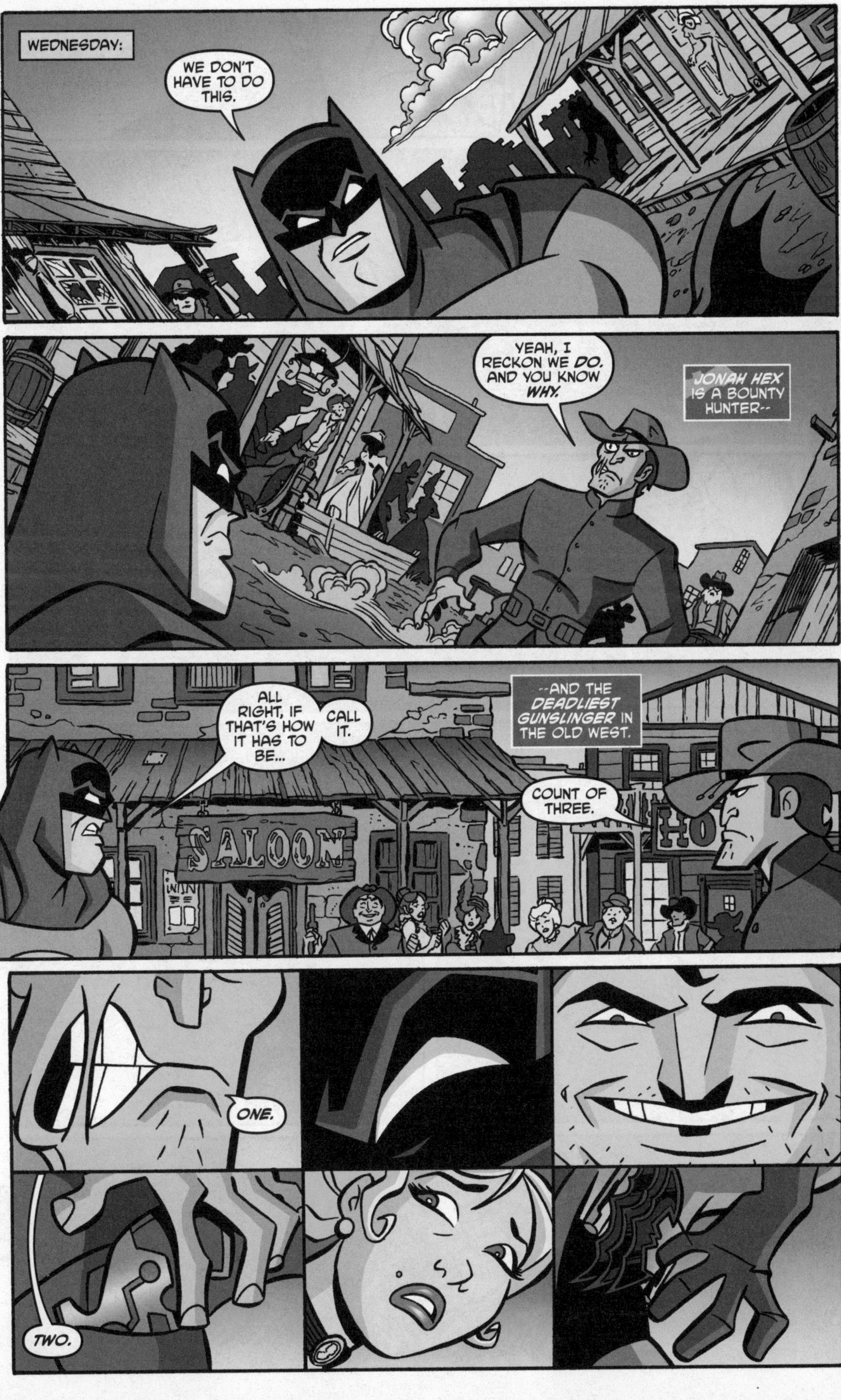
WEDNESDAY:
WE DON'T HAVE TO DO THIS.
YEAH, I RECKON WE *DO.* AND YOU KNOW *WHY.*
JONAH HEX IS A BOUNTY HUNTER--
--AND THE *DEADLIEST GUNSLINGER* IN THE OLD WEST.
ALL RIGHT, IF THAT'S HOW IT HAS TO BE...
CALL IT.
COUNT OF THREE.
SALOON
ONE.
TWO.

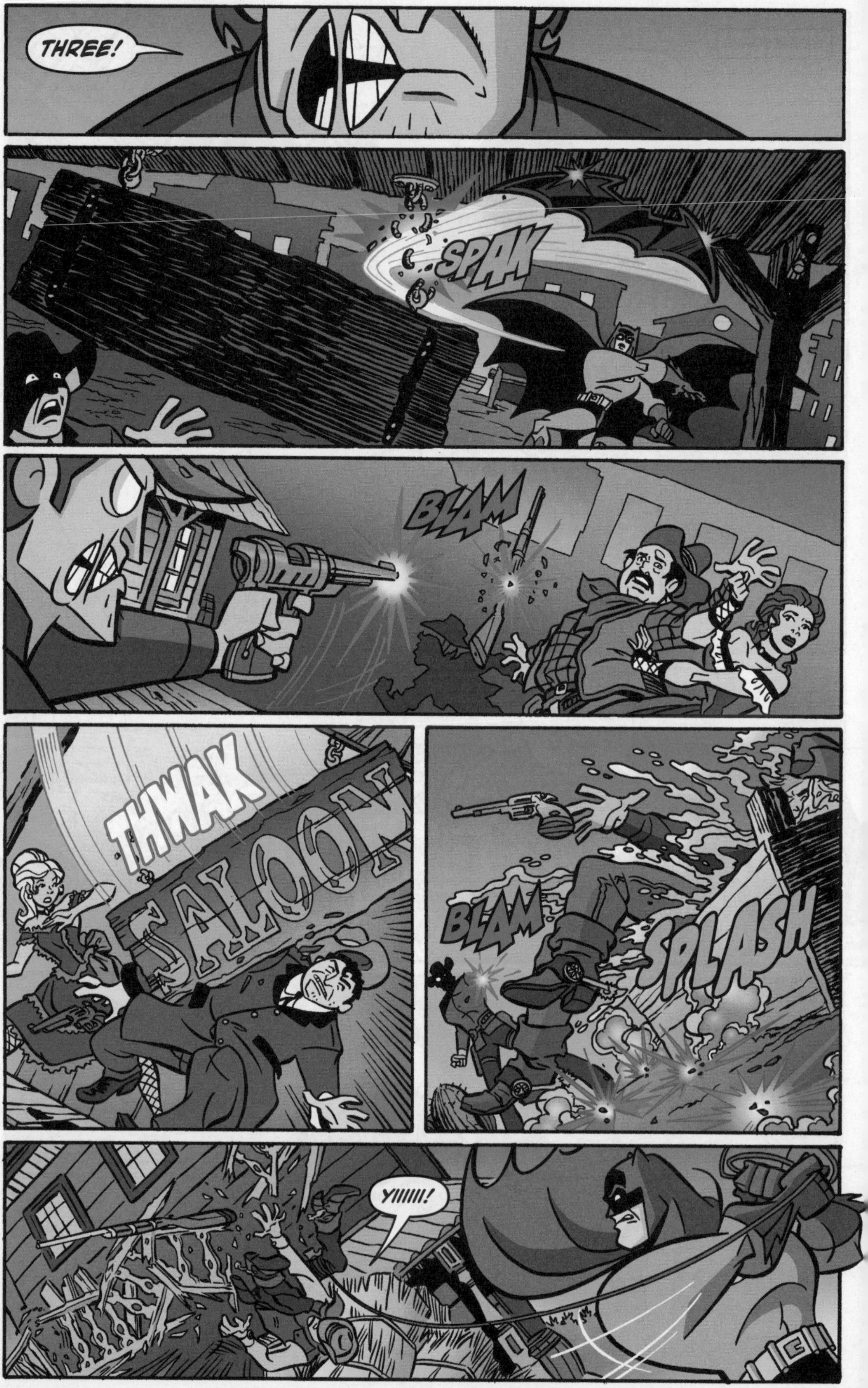
THREE!
SPAK
BLAM
THWAK
SALOON
BLAM
SPLASH
YIIIIII!

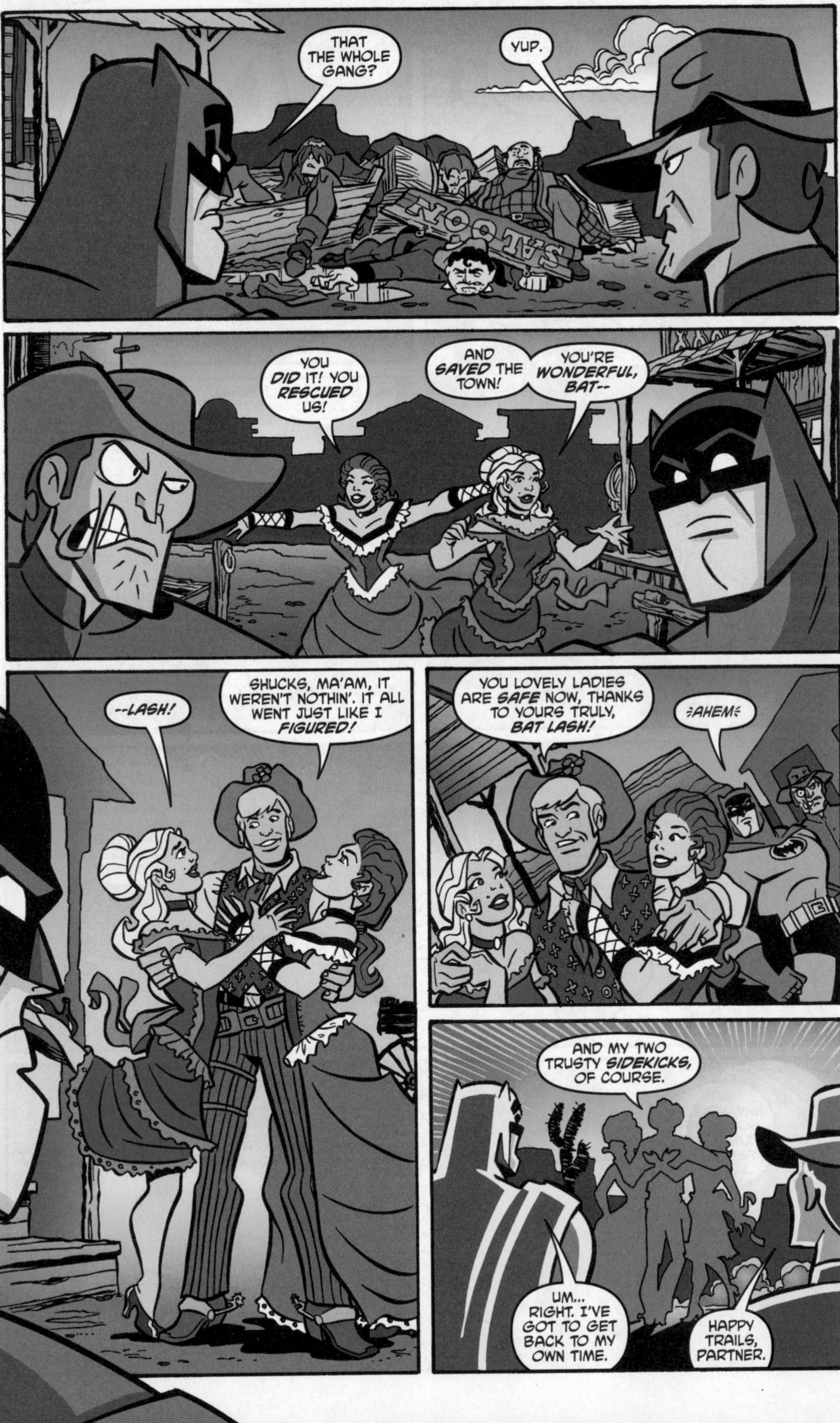
THAT THE WHOLE GANG?
YUP.
SALOON
YOU DID IT! YOU RESCUED US!
AND SAVED THE TOWN!
YOU'RE WONDERFUL, BAT--
--LASH!
SHUCKS, MA'AM, IT WEREN'T NOTHIN'. IT ALL WENT JUST LIKE I FIGURED!
YOU LOVELY LADIES ARE SAFE NOW, THANKS TO YOURS TRULY, BAT LASH!
AHEM
AND MY TWO TRUSTY SIDEKICKS, OF COURSE.
UM... RIGHT. I'VE GOT TO GET BACK TO MY OWN TIME.
HAPPY TRAILS, PARTNER.

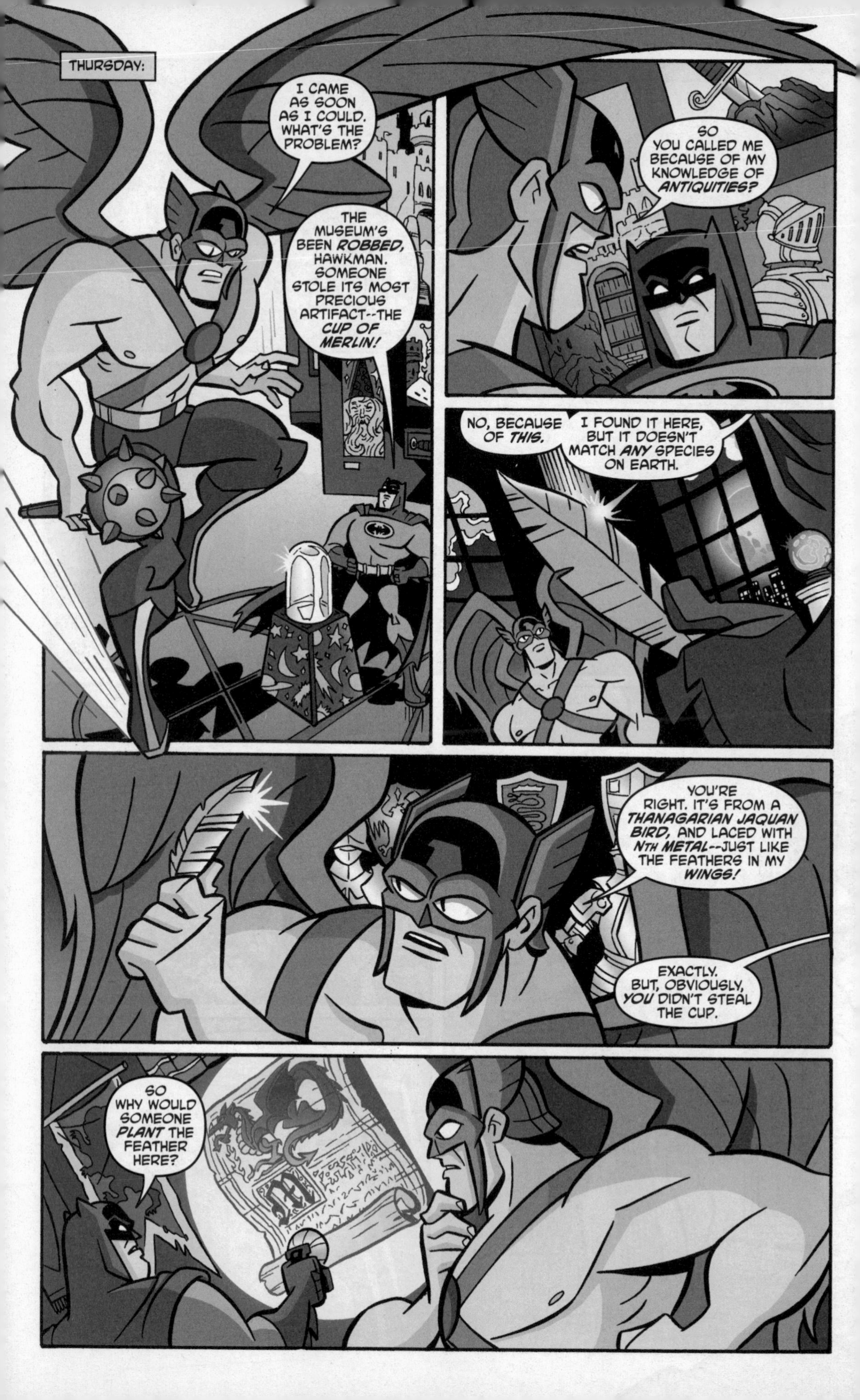
THURSDAY:
I CAME AS SOON AS I COULD. WHAT'S THE PROBLEM?
THE MUSEUM'S BEEN *ROBBED,* HAWKMAN. SOMEONE STOLE ITS MOST PRECIOUS ARTIFACT--THE *CUP OF MERLIN!*
SO YOU CALLED ME BECAUSE OF MY KNOWLEDGE OF *ANTIQUITIES?*
NO, BECAUSE OF *THIS.*
I FOUND IT HERE, BUT IT DOESN'T MATCH *ANY* SPECIES ON EARTH.
YOU'RE RIGHT. IT'S FROM A *THANAGARIAN JAQUAN BIRD,* AND LACED WITH *NTH METAL*--JUST LIKE THE FEATHERS IN MY *WINGS!*
EXACTLY. BUT, OBVIOUSLY, *YOU* DIDN'T STEAL THE CUP.
SO WHY WOULD SOMEONE *PLANT* THE FEATHER HERE?

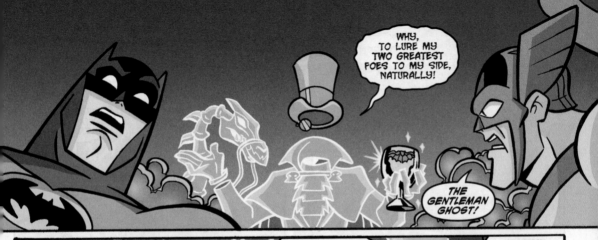

WHY, TO LURE MY TWO GREATEST FOES TO MY SIDE, NATURALLY!

THE GENTLEMAN GHOST!

AH-AH-AH! THAT MAGICAL BARRIER SHOULD RESTRAIN YOU.

NOW THAT I HOLD THE MYSTIC POWER OF MERLIN'S CUP IN MY GRASP, I NEED THE TWO OF YOU HERE--

--SO THAT I CAN TRADE YOUR SPIRITS TO A DEMON--

--AND WIN MY CHANCE TO LIVE AGAIN!

WE HAVE TO GET OUT OF HERE!

ENJOY YOUR LAST MOMENTS OF LIFE, AS I RECITE THE ANCIENT INCANTATION THAT WILL SUMMON MY DEMONIC CONSORT...

FREE THE MIGHT FROM FLESHY MIRE, BOIL THE BLOOD IN HEART OF FIRE!

GONE, GONE THE FORM OF MAN!

HEH.

WHAT?

RISE THE DEMON--

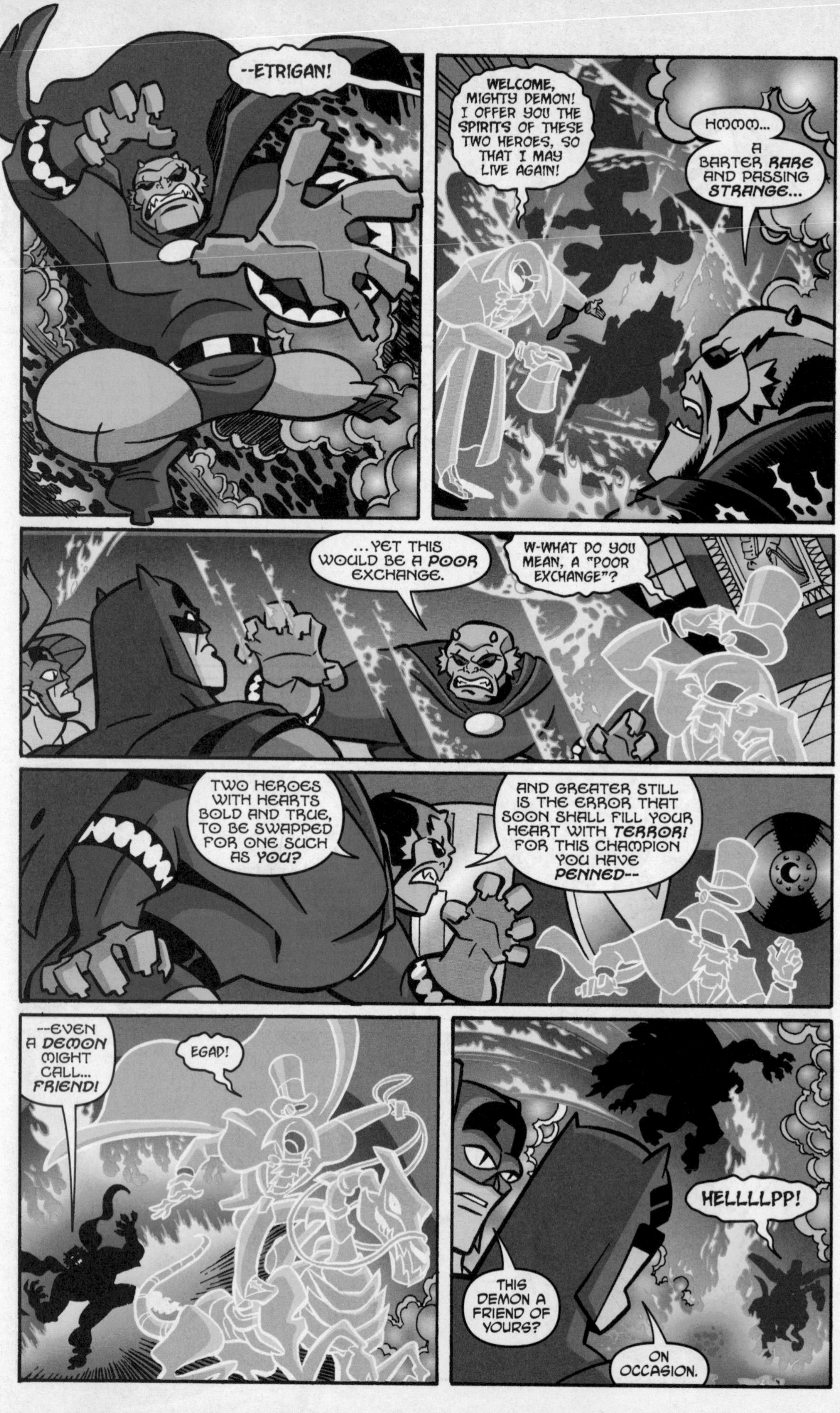
--ETRIGAN!
WELCOME, MIGHTY DEMON! I OFFER YOU THE SPIRITS OF THESE TWO HEROES, SO THAT I MAY LIVE AGAIN!
HMMM...
A BARTER RARE AND PASSING STRANGE...
...YET THIS WOULD BE A POOR EXCHANGE.
W-WHAT DO YOU MEAN, A "POOR EXCHANGE"?
TWO HEROES WITH HEARTS BOLD AND TRUE, TO BE SWAPPED FOR ONE SUCH AS YOU?
AND GREATER STILL IS THE ERROR THAT SOON SHALL FILL YOUR HEART WITH TERROR! FOR THIS CHAMPION YOU HAVE PENNED--
--EVEN A DEMON MIGHT CALL... FRIEND!
EGAD!
HELLLLPP!
THIS DEMON A FRIEND OF YOURS?
ON OCCASION.

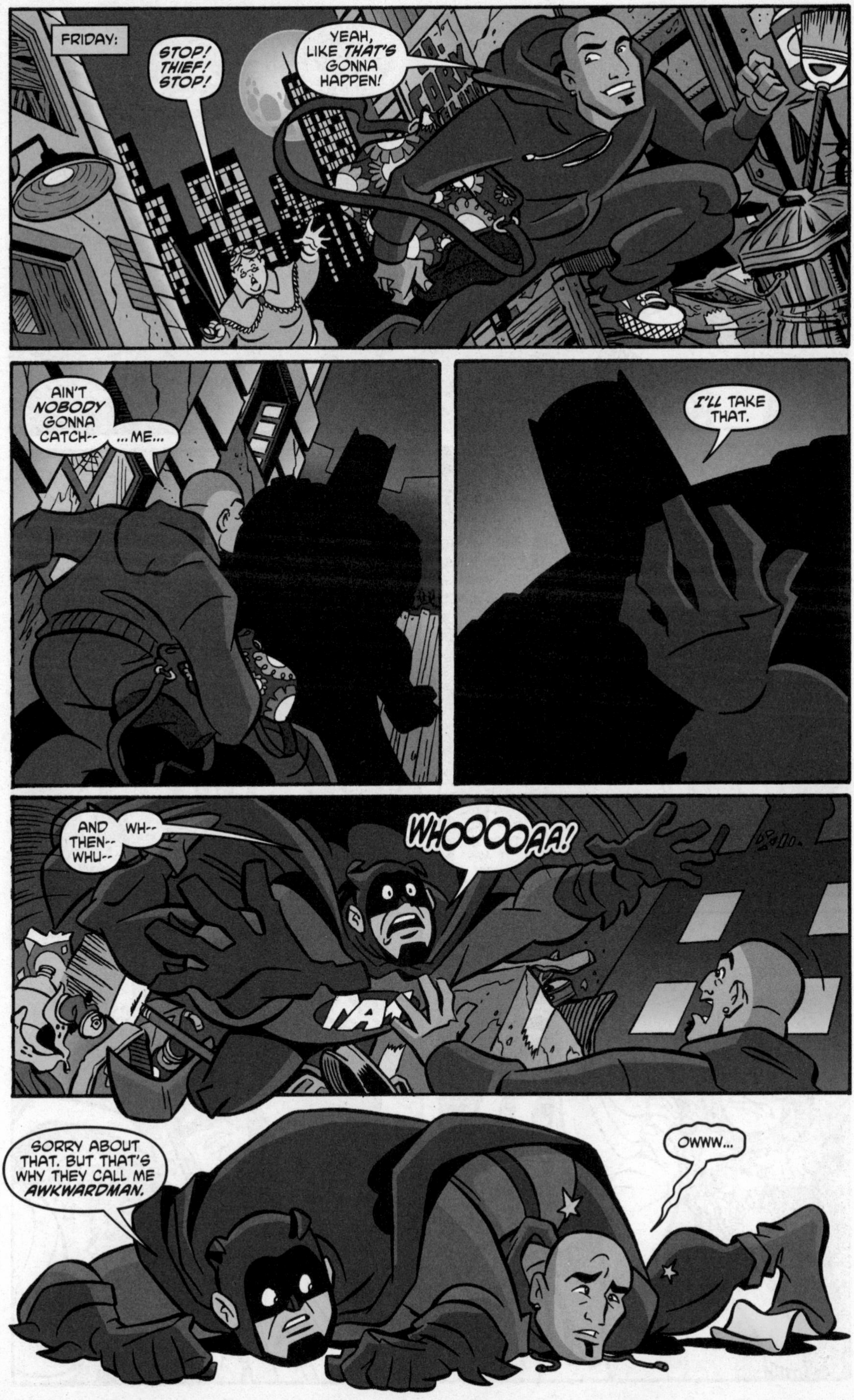
FRIDAY:
STOP! THIEF! STOP!
YEAH, LIKE THAT'S GONNA HAPPEN!
AIN'T NOBODY GONNA CATCH--
...ME...
I'LL TAKE THAT.
AND THEN-- WHU--
WH--
WHOOOOAA!
SORRY ABOUT THAT. BUT THAT'S WHY THEY CALL ME AWKWARDMAN.
OWWW...

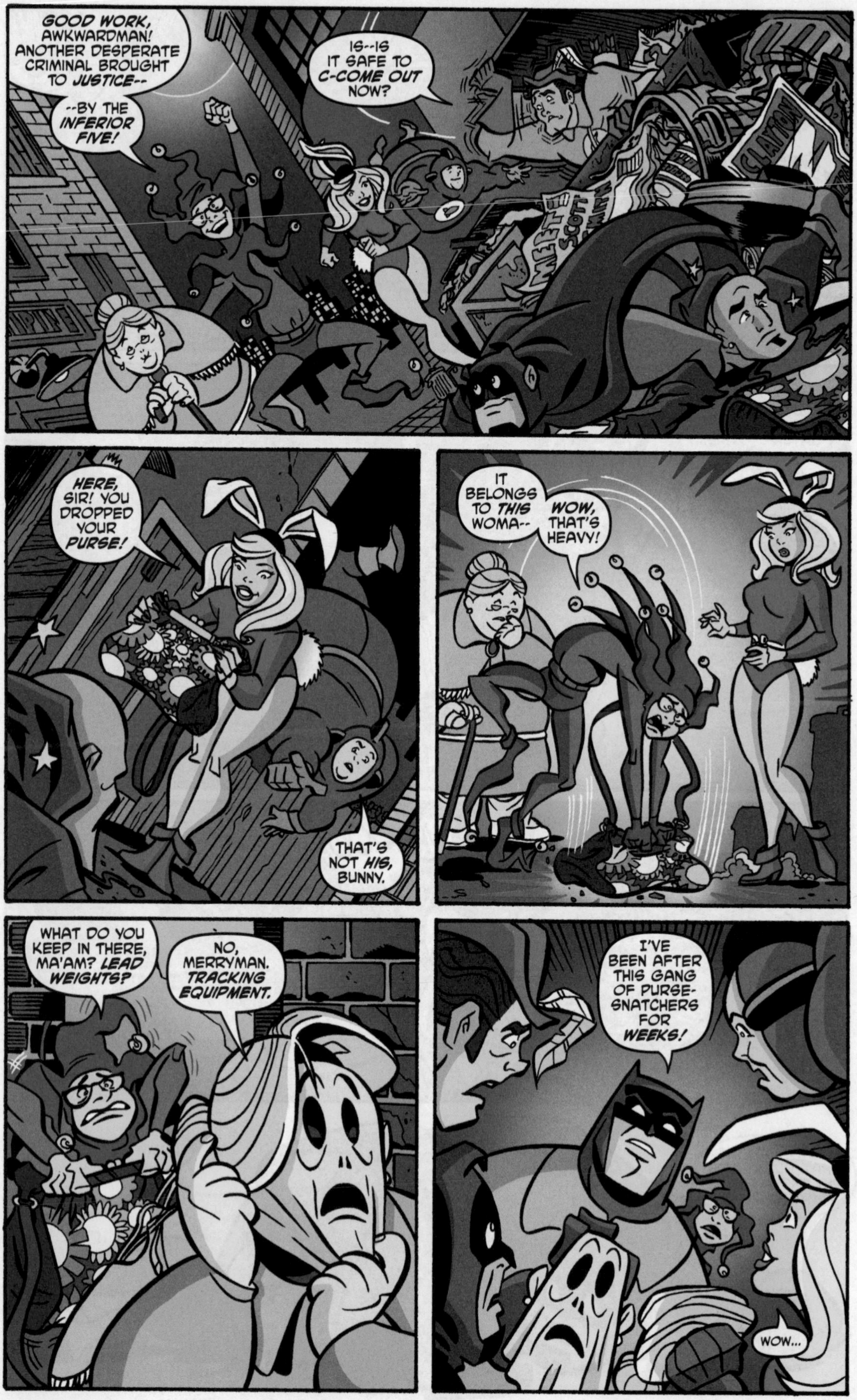
GOOD WORK, AWKWARDMAN! ANOTHER DESPERATE CRIMINAL BROUGHT TO JUSTICE--
--BY THE INFERIOR FIVE!
IS--IS IT SAFE TO C-COME OUT NOW?
HERE, SIR! YOU DROPPED YOUR PURSE!
THAT'S NOT HIS, BUNNY.
IT BELONGS TO THIS WOMA--
WOW, THAT'S HEAVY!
WHAT DO YOU KEEP IN THERE, MA'AM? LEAD WEIGHTS?
NO, MERRYMAN. TRACKING EQUIPMENT.
I'VE BEEN AFTER THIS GANG OF PURSE-SNATCHERS FOR WEEKS!
WOW...

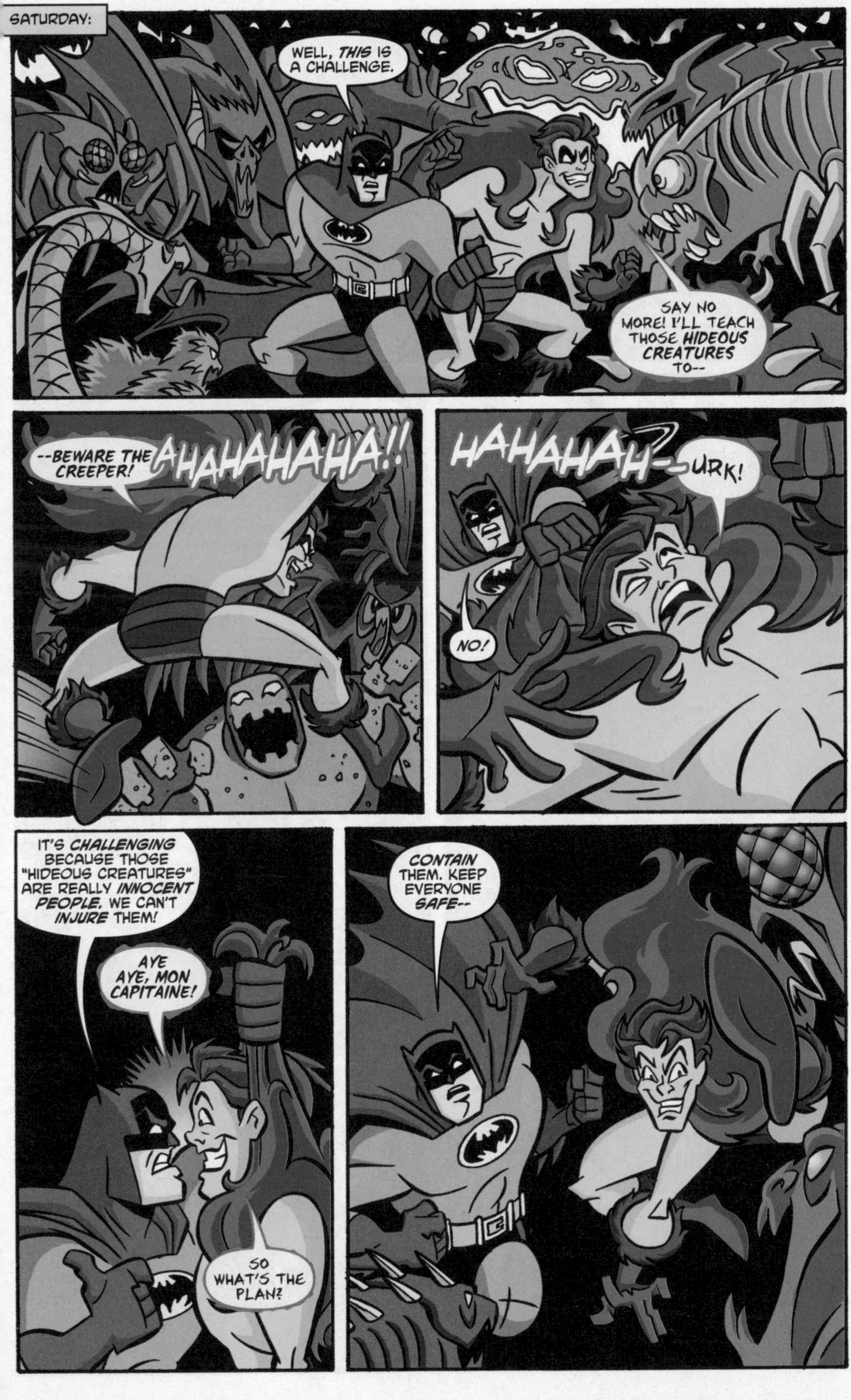
SATURDAY:
WELL, THIS IS A CHALLENGE.
SAY NO MORE! I'LL TEACH THOSE HIDEOUS CREATURES TO--
--BEWARE THE CREEPER!
AHAHAHAHAHA!!
HAHAHAH--URK!
NO!
IT'S CHALLENGING BECAUSE THOSE "HIDEOUS CREATURES" ARE REALLY INNOCENT PEOPLE. WE CAN'T INJURE THEM!
AYE AYE, MON CAPITAINE!
SO WHAT'S THE PLAN?
CONTAIN THEM. KEEP EVERYONE SAFE--

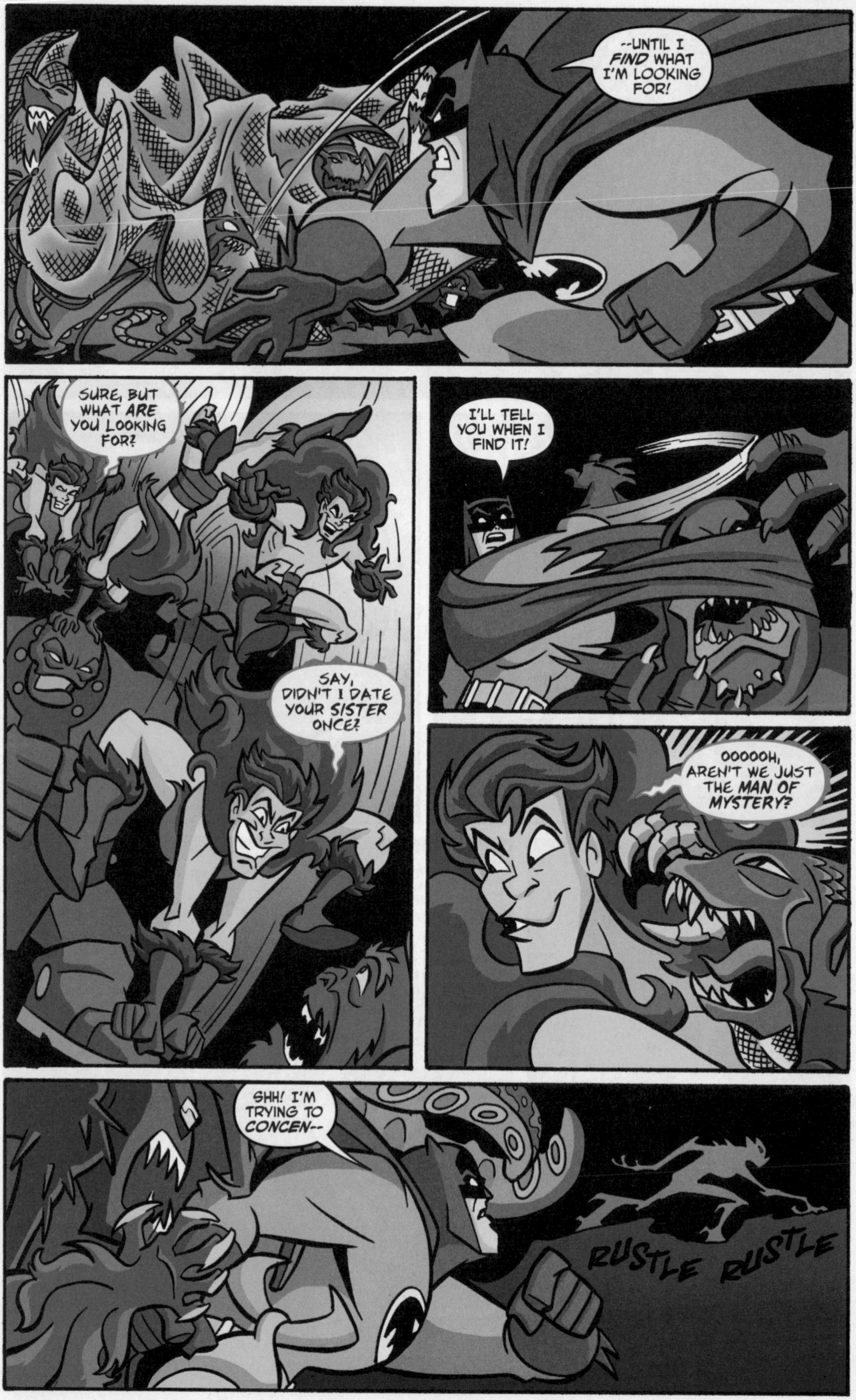
--UNTIL I FIND WHAT I'M LOOKING FOR!
SURE, BUT WHAT ARE YOU LOOKING FOR?
SAY, DIDN'T I DATE YOUR SISTER ONCE?
I'LL TELL YOU WHEN I FIND IT!
OOOOOH, AREN'T WE JUST THE MAN OF MYSTERY?
SHH! I'M TRYING TO CONCEN--
RUSTLE RUSTLE

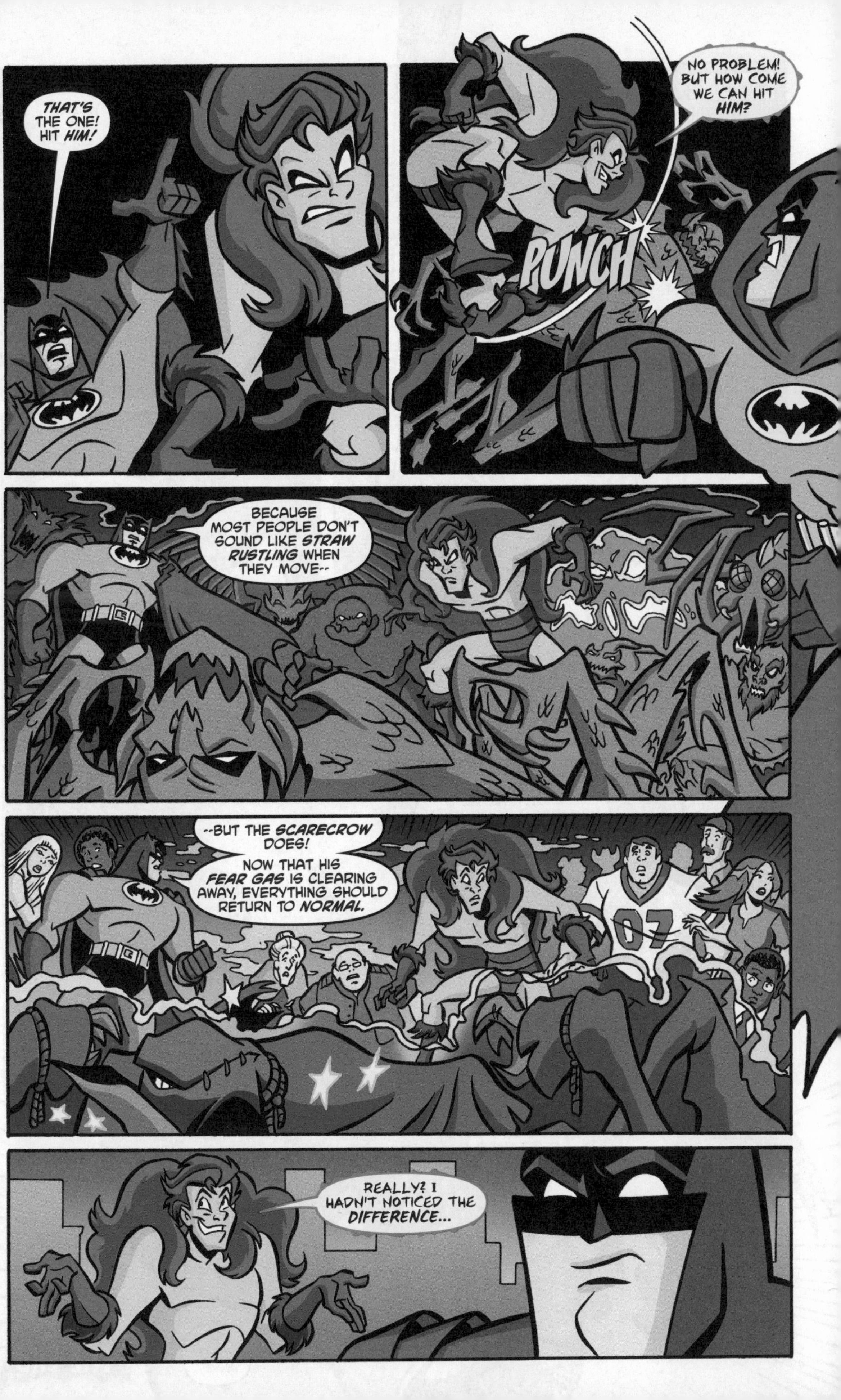
THAT'S THE ONE! HIT HIM!
NO PROBLEM! BUT HOW COME WE CAN HIT HIM?
PUNCH
BECAUSE MOST PEOPLE DON'T SOUND LIKE STRAW RUSTLING WHEN THEY MOVE--
--BUT THE SCARECROW DOES!
NOW THAT HIS FEAR GAS IS CLEARING AWAY, EVERYTHING SHOULD RETURN TO NORMAL.
07
REALLY? I HADN'T NOTICED THE DIFFERENCE...

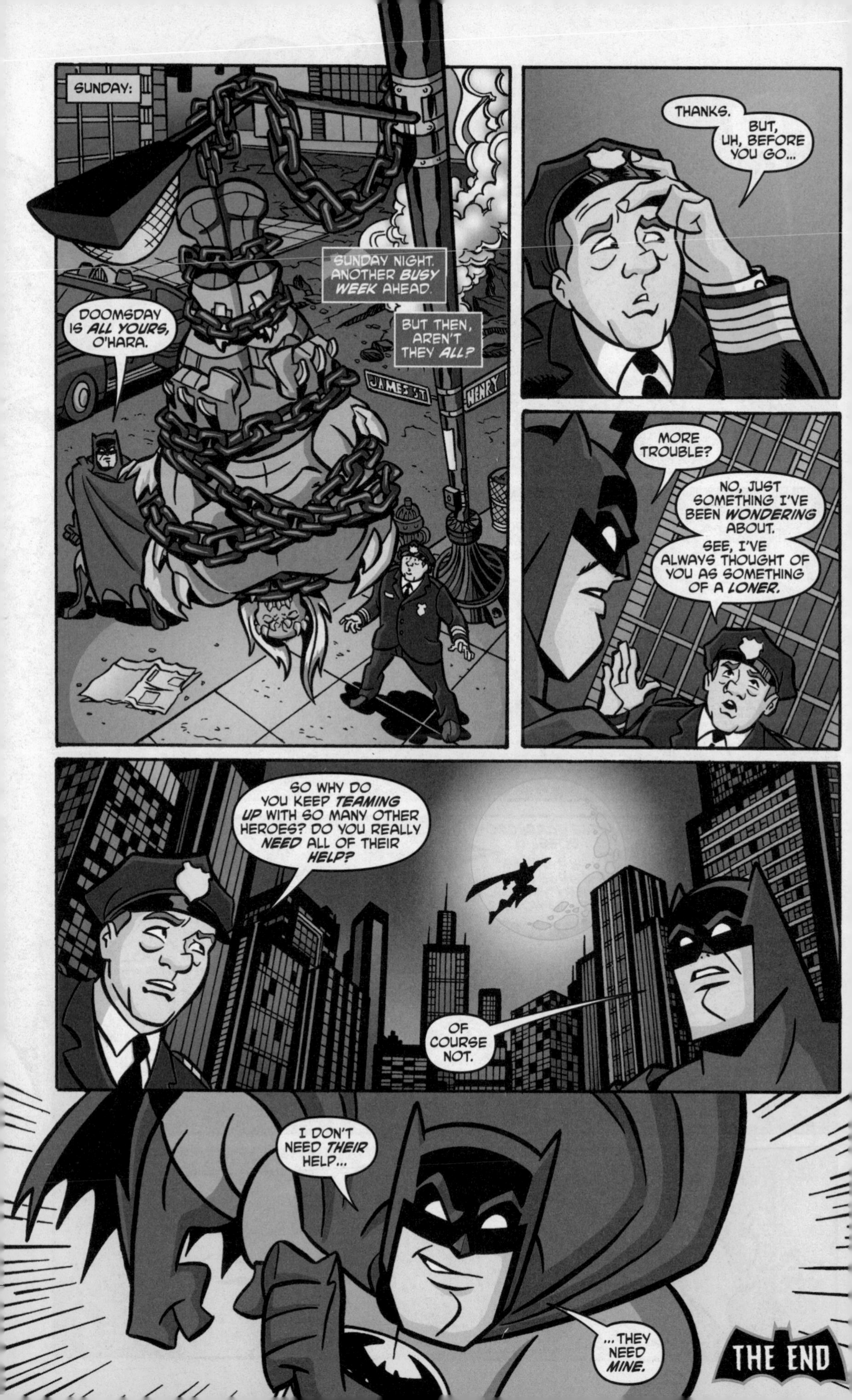
SUNDAY:
SUNDAY NIGHT. ANOTHER BUSY WEEK AHEAD.
BUT THEN, AREN'T THEY ALL?
DOOMSDAY IS ALL YOURS, O'HARA.
JAMES ST
HENRY
THANKS.
BUT, UH, BEFORE YOU GO...
MORE TROUBLE?
NO, JUST SOMETHING I'VE BEEN WONDERING ABOUT.
SEE, I'VE ALWAYS THOUGHT OF YOU AS SOMETHING OF A LONER.
SO WHY DO YOU KEEP TEAMING UP WITH SO MANY OTHER HEROES? DO YOU REALLY NEED ALL OF THEIR HELP?
OF COURSE NOT.
I DON'T NEED THEIR HELP...
...THEY NEED MINE.
THE END

THE ALL-NEW BATMAN: THE BRAVE AND THE BOLD #13

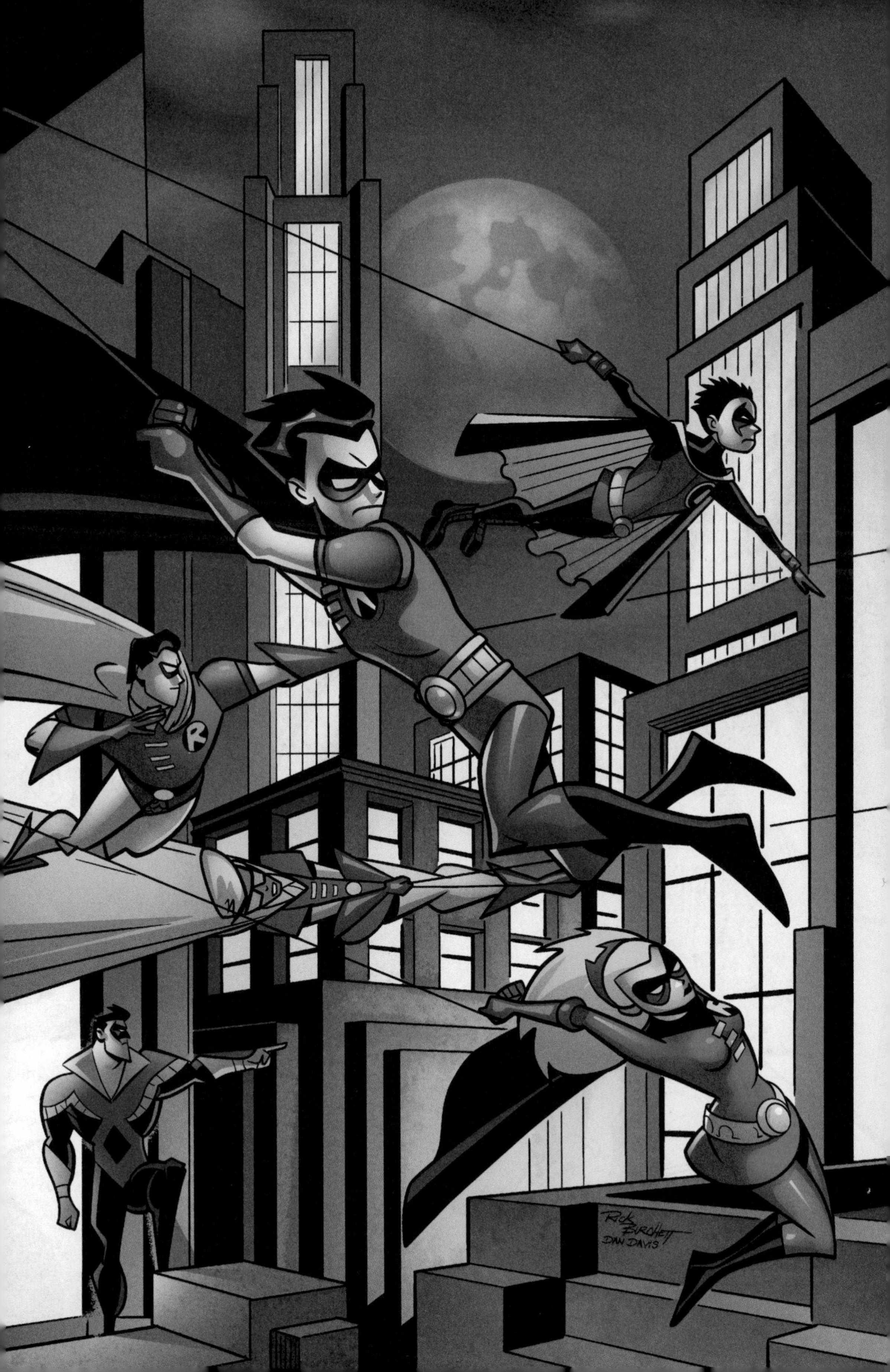
RICK BURCHETT
DAN DAVIS

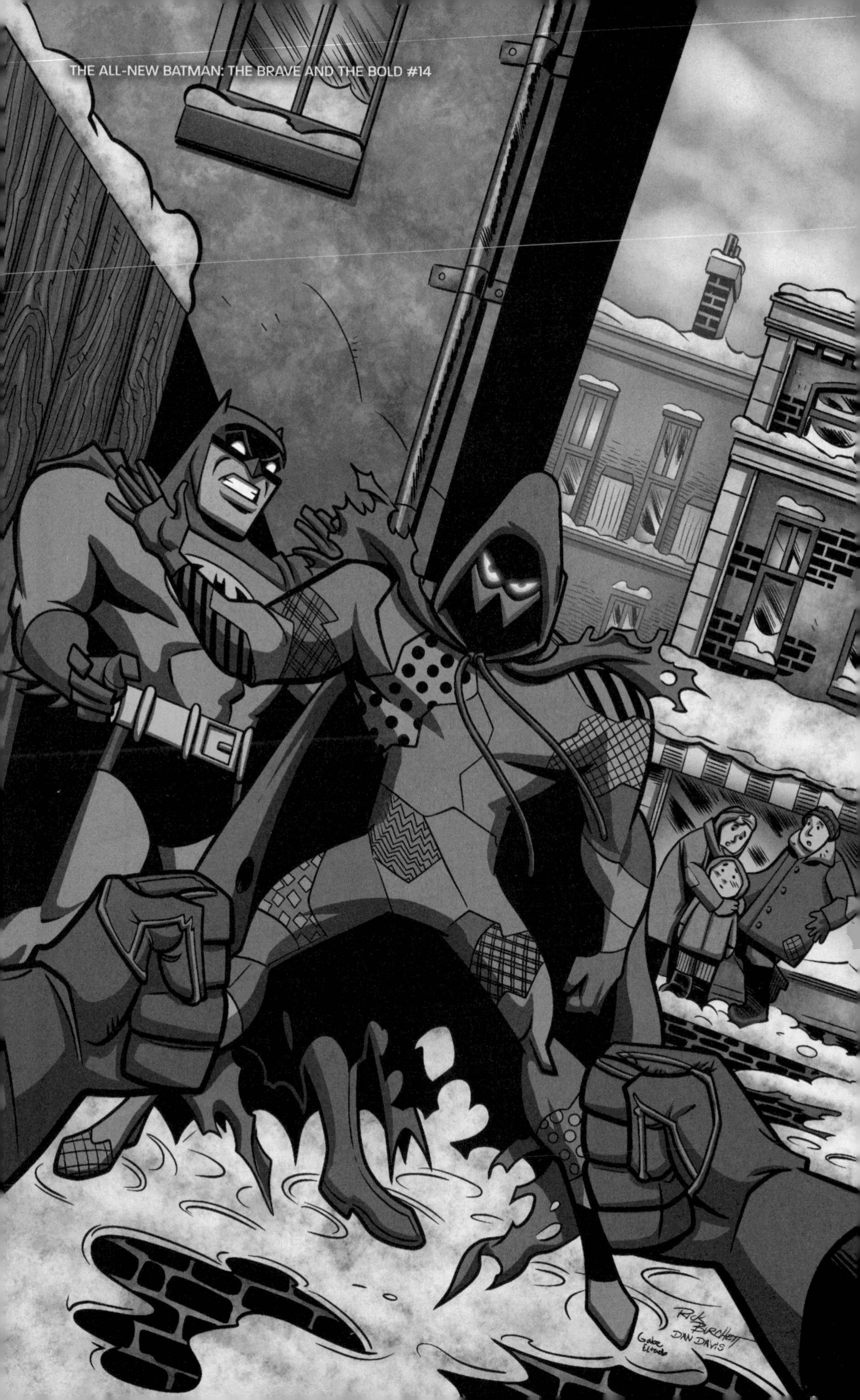
RICK BURCHETT
DAN DAVIS

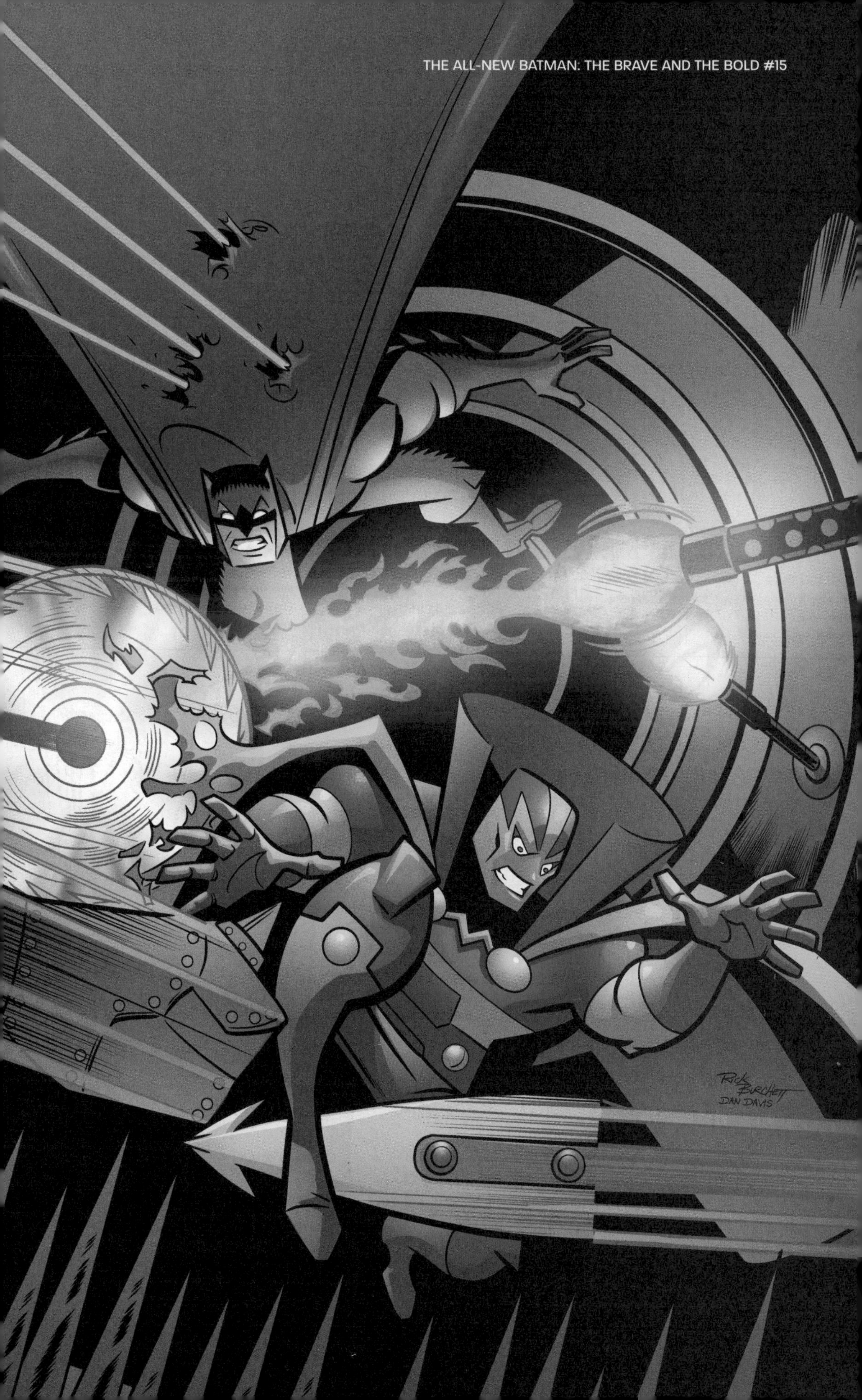
RICK BURCHETT
DAN DAVIS

THE ALL-NEW BATMAN: THE BRAVE AND THE BOLD #16

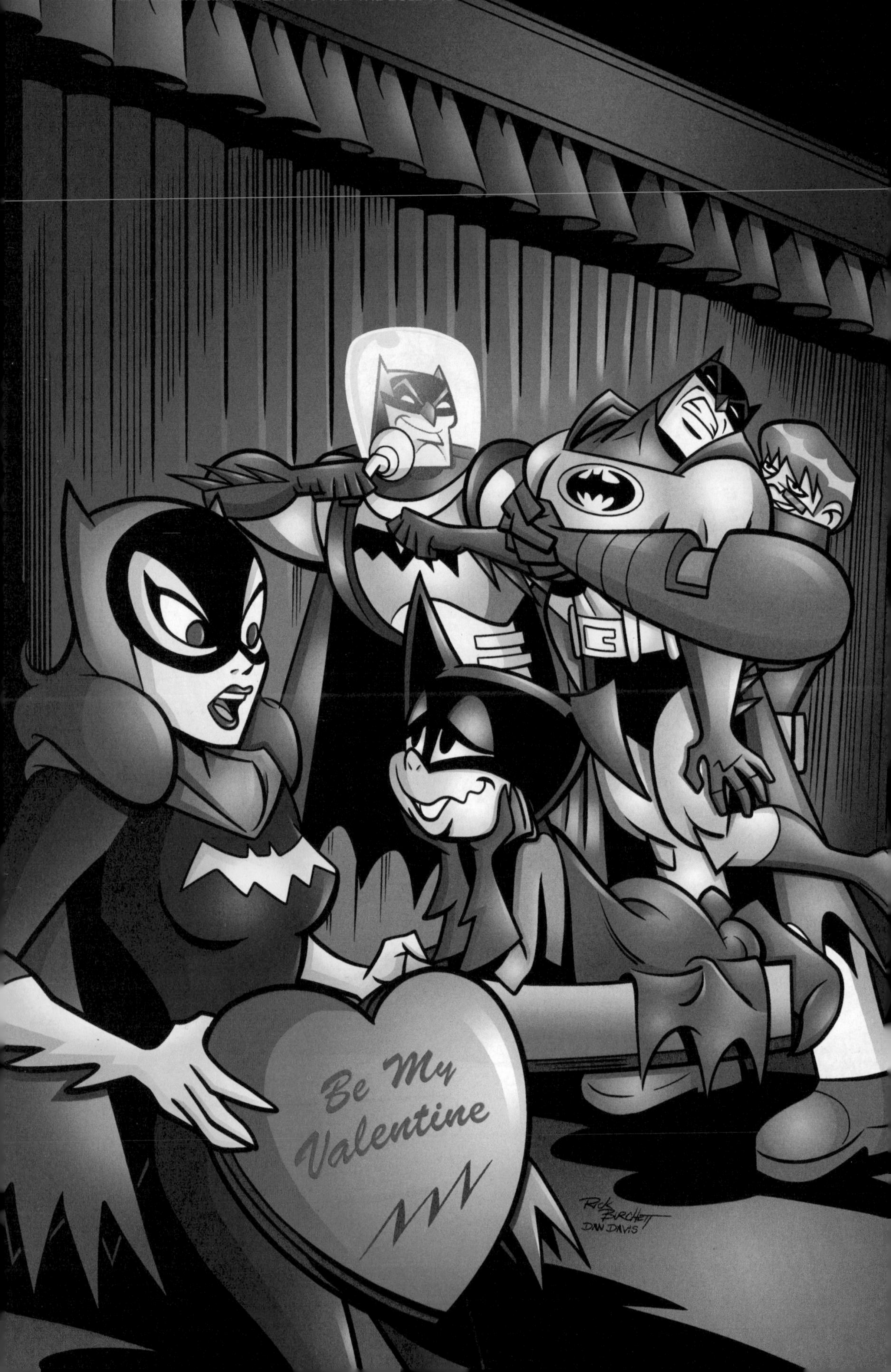
Be My Valentine
RICK BURCHETT
DAN DAVIS

BATMAN: THE BRAVE AND THE BOLD #15

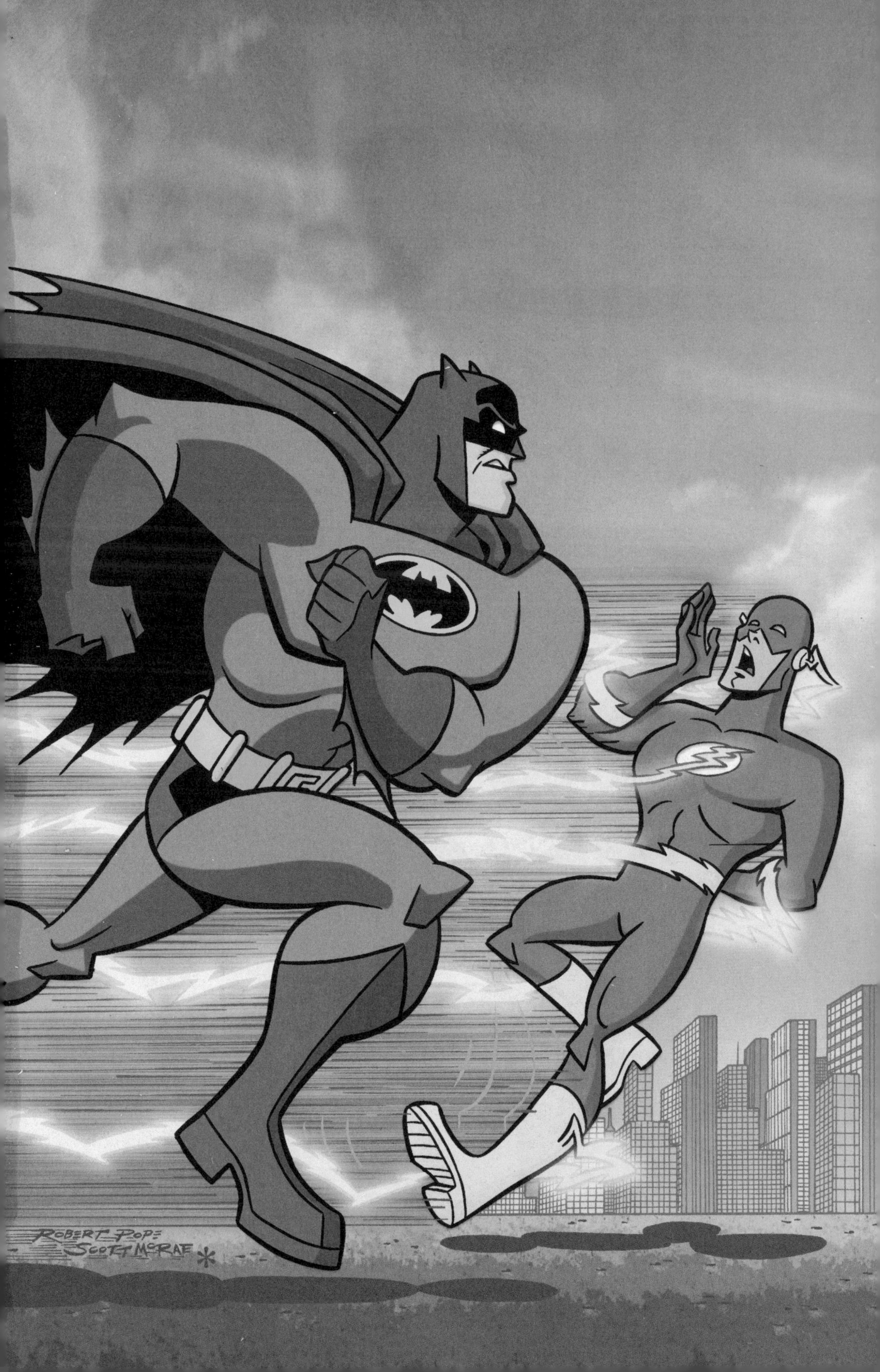
ROBERT POPE
SCOTT McRAE

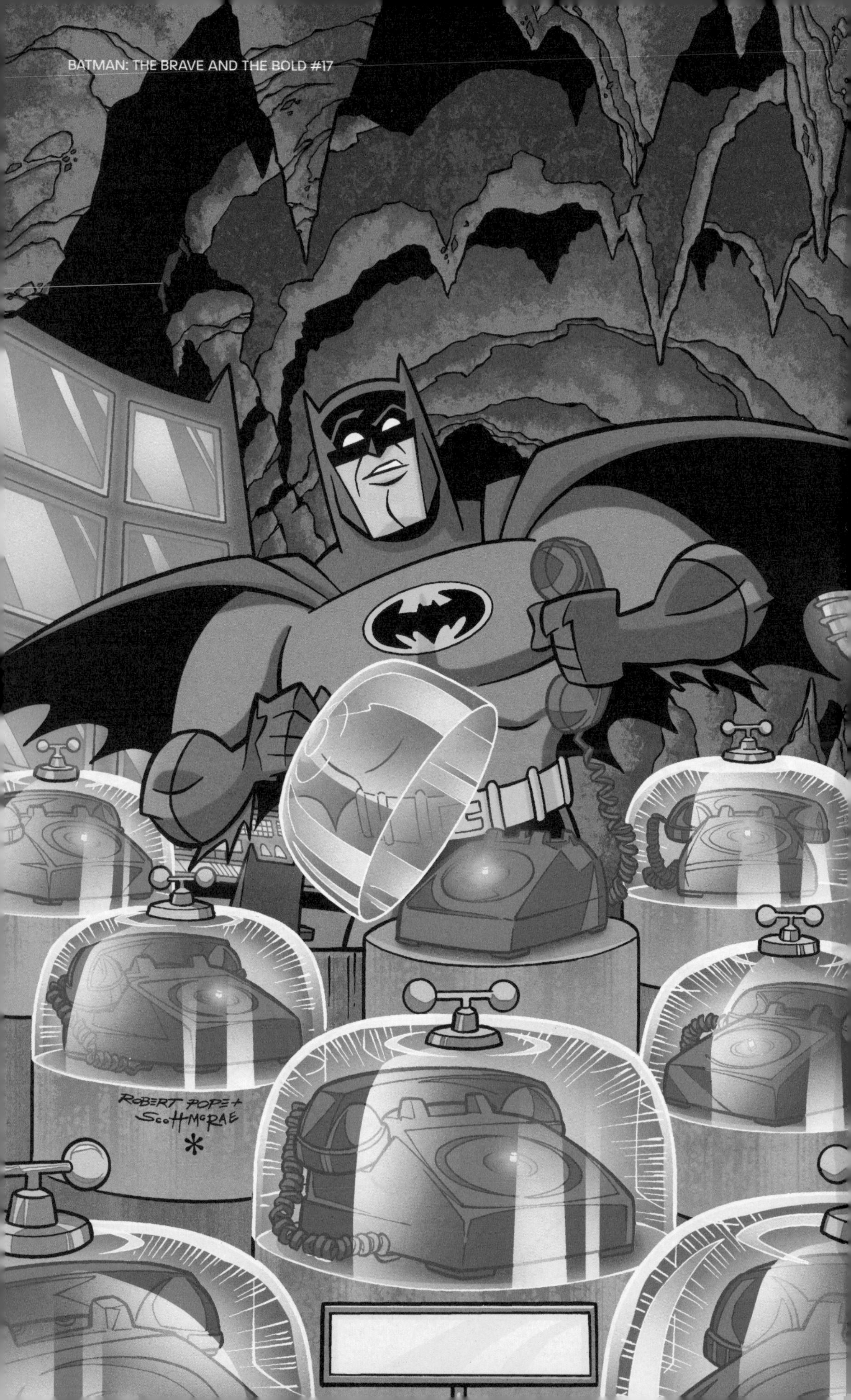
ROBERT POPE +
SCOTT McRAE